An
Affair
to
Dismember

An Affair to Dismember

THE MATCHMAKER SERIES

ELISE SAX

BALLANTINE BOOKS • NEW YORK

An Affair to Dismember is a work of fiction. Names, characters, places, and incidents are the products of the author's imagination or are used fictitiously. Any resemblance to actual events, locales, or persons, living or dead, is entirely coincidental.

Published in the United States by Ballantine Books, an imprint of The Random House Publishing Group, a division of Random House, Inc., New York.

BALLANTINE and colophon are trademarks of Random House, Inc.

This book contains an excerpt from the forthcoming book *Citizen Pain* by Elise Sax. This excerpt has been set for this edition only and may not reflect the final content of the forthcoming edition.

ISBN 978-1-62490-021-1

Cover design: Lynn Andreozzi
Cover photograph: © George Kerrigan

Printed in the United States of America

For all those who believed, especially my mother.

An
Affair
to
Dismember

Chapter 1

✦ ♥ ✦

When you first start out, you're going to ask people what they're looking for. This is a big mistake. Huge. They want the impossible. Every woman wants a Cary Grant with a thick wallet who doesn't mind if she's a few pounds overweight. Every man wants a floozy he can take home to Mom. See? Asking their opinions only leads to headaches you could die from. Take it from me, I've been doing this a lot of years. Nobody knows what they want. You have to size a person up and tell them what they want. It might take convincing, but you'll widen their horizons, and they'll thank you for it. Eventually. Remember, love can come from anywhere, usually where you least expect it. Tell them not to be afraid, even if it hits them on the head and hurts a lot at first. With enough time, any schlimazel can turn into a Cary Grant or a presentable floozy.

Lesson 22,
Matchmaking Advice from Your Grandma Zelda

THE MORNING I found out about Randy Terns' murder, I was happily oblivious. I was too busy to care, trying to make heads or tails of my grandma's matchmaking business. Nobody actually mentioned the word "murder" that morning. I sort of stumbled onto the idea later on.

That Thursday I sat in my grandma's makeshift office in the attic of her sprawling Victorian house, buried under mounds of yellowed index cards and black-and-white Polaroid pictures. It was all part of Zelda's Matchmaking Services, a business I now co-owned at my grandma's insistence as her only living relative and what she called "a natural matchmaker if ever I saw one."

"Gladie Burger," she had told me over the phone three months before, urging me to move in with her, "you come from a long line of Burger women. Burger women are matchmaker women."

I was a Burger woman, but I had strong doubts about the matchmaker part. Besides, I couldn't decipher the business. It was stuck in the dark ages with no computer, let alone Internet connection. Grandma fluctuated between staging workshops, running group meetings, hosting walk-ins, and just knowing when someone needed to be fixed up. "It's an intuitive thing," she explained.

I pushed aside a stack of cards, stirring up a black cloud of dust. I had been a matchmaker in training for three months, and I was no closer to matching any couples. To be truthful, I hadn't even tried. I wiped my dusty hands on my sweatpants and stared at the giant mound on her desk. "Grandma, I'm not a matchmaker," I said to her stapler. "I've never even had a successful relationship. I wouldn't know one if I saw one."

I had a sudden desire for fudge. I gave my stomach a squish and tugged at my elastic waistband. My grandmother was a notorious junk food addict, and I had slipped into her bad habits since I moved in with her. Hard to believe I was the same person who not even four months ago was a cashier in a trendy health food store in Los Angeles, the second-to-last job I had had in a more than ten-year string of jobs—which was probably why Grandma had twisted my arm to move to Cannes, California.

I decided against fudge and picked up an index card.

It read: *George Jackson, thirty-five years old.* Next to the note, in Grandma's handwriting, was scribbled *Not a day less than forty-three; breath like someone died in his mouth.* Halitosis George was looking for a stewardess, someone who looked like Jackie Kennedy and had a fondness for Studebakers. Whoa, Grandma kept some pretty old records. I needed to throw out 95 percent of the cards, but I didn't know which 5 percent to keep.

Putting down the card, I stared out the window, my favorite activity these days. What had I gotten myself into? I had no skills as a matchmaker. I was more of a temp agency kind of gal. Something where I wasn't in charge of other people's lives. My three-week stint as a wine cork inspector was more my speed.

A man and his German shepherd ran down the street. I checked my watch: 12:10 P.M. Right on time. I could always count on the habits of the neighbors. There was a regular stream of devoted dog walkers, joggers, and cyclists that passed the house on a daily basis. Not much changed here. The small mountain town was low on surprises. I tried to convince myself that was a good thing. Stability was good. Commitment was good.

With sudden resolve, I took George Jackson's card and threw it in the wastebasket. "Bye, George. I hope you found love and an Altoid."

I tried another card. *Sarah Johns. Nineteen years old.* She had gotten first prize at the county fair for her blueberry pie, and she was looking for an honest man who didn't drink too much. My grandma had seen something more in her. *Poor thing. Art school better than man,* she had written in the margins.

I tossed the card, letting it float onto George. Matchmaking was no easy task. It wasn't all speed dating and online chat rooms. Lives were on the line. One false move and futures could be ruined.

The house across the street caught my attention. It

had seen better days. A bunch of shingles were missing, leaving a big hole in the roof. I watched as the mailman stopped at the mailbox. He would arrive at Grandma's in twelve minutes. I could set my watch by him.

Across the street, the front door opened. An elderly woman stepped out and picked up her mail. She glanced at the letters and then stood staring at her front yard. Something was not quite right about the picture. I didn't have time to dwell on it, though. I had promised Grandma I would pick up lunch for us in town.

I grabbed my keys and hopped down the stairs. Outside, it was a typical Cannes, California, August day: blue sky, sunshine, and warm. Normally it didn't turn cool until October, or so I was told. My experience with the town was limited to summers visiting my grandmother when I was growing up.

"Yoo-hoo! Gladie!" Grandma's high-pitched cry cut through the country quiet. She stood in the front yard, hovering over the gardener as he cut roses. The front yard was about half an acre of lawn and meticulously groomed plants, flowers, and trees. It was her pride and joy, and Grandma supervised the gardening with an obsession usually reserved for Johnny Depp or chocolate. I doubted she had ever picked up a spade in her life. "Yoo-hoo! Gladie!" she repeated, flapping her arm in the air, her crisp red Chanel knockoff suit bulging at the seams and the glittering array of diamonds on her fingers, wrists, and neck blinding me in the afternoon sun.

"I'm right here, Grandma." I jiggled the car keys to remind her of my lunch run.

"Jose, leave a few white ones for good luck and be careful with the shears," she told the gardener. "You don't want to lop off a finger." Jose shot her a panicked look and crossed himself.

Grandma walked as quickly as she could across the large lawn to the driveway. She had a grin plastered across her face and, no doubt, some juicy bit of news bursting to pop out of her mouth. Her smile dimmed only slightly when she got a good look at my state. I pulled up my baggy sweatpants. As usual, she was immaculately coiffed and made up, whereas my brown hair was standing up in all directions in a frantic frizz, and my eyelashes hadn't seen mascara in months. I didn't see much reason to dress up because I rarely left the attic, but standing next to Grandma, I was a little self-conscious about my attire. As a rule, her clothes were nicely tailored. I listened to the soft *swish-swish* of her pantyhose-covered thighs rubbing together as she approached. I wondered vaguely if the friction of her nylon stockings could cause them to burst into flames. I took a cowardly step backward, just in case.

"I'm so glad I caught you before you left," she said, a little out of breath from either her run or the excitement over the piece of gossip she was about to blurt out. While Grandma never left her property, she somehow knew everything going on in town.

"I didn't get much done," I said. "I can't figure out what to keep and what to toss. Should I throw out everything older than ten years?"

"Fine. Fine. Listen. Randy Terns is dead. They found him yesterday morning, deader than a doornail."

I racked my brain. Who was Randy Terns? Was he the new secretary of state? Really, I had to read a newspaper once in a while. What kind of responsible citizen was I?

"That's terrible," I muttered, a noncommittal edge to my voice in case Randy Terns was a war criminal or something.

"Yes, yes. Terrible. Terrible." Grandma waved her hands as if everything was terrible. The sky, the trees, my car—all terrible. She grabbed my arm in a viselike grip and pulled herself close to make sure that I heard every word. "I'm on Betty like white on rice to sell that old run-down excuse for a house. I'd love to get in some people who will fix it up. Look at me! I'm drooling over the thought of waking up, going out to get the paper, and not having to see that dreadful lawn across from my prize-winning roses." She made air quotes with her fingers when she said "lawn."

She turned to face the house across the street. "I bet you will be thrilled not to have to stare at that falling-down roof every day!"

Falling-down roof. My brain kicked into gear, and I recalled the woman standing by her mailbox. Randy and Betty Terns were the neighbors across the street. I'd never had much interaction with them. And now Randy was dead. Found yesterday morning, deader than a doornail.

I hate death. I'm scared it's contagious. At funerals, I feel my arteries start to harden. Medical shows on TV send me into neurotic fits. McDreamy or McSteamy, it doesn't matter—I only see my slow, agonizing death from a terrible disease. Like Ebola or flesh-eating bacteria. Or a drug-resistant superbug yeast infection. If I found out that poor Randy Terns died of a heart attack, it would only take five minutes or so for my chest pains to start.

"Betty said she would think about it," Grandma said with disgust. "Said she has a funeral to organize and a houseful of kids. Kids. Huh. The youngest is thirty-seven. Three of them still live at home. It's time to push those birdies out of the nest, I say."

She harrumphed loudly and kicked the cobblestoned driveway with her left Jimmy Choo. Gold-tipped. Very fancy.

"Five children. Why do people take things to extremes?" she continued. "Anyway, they come and go like they own the place, moving in and out whenever they want. They're holding on for dear life. A bunch of losers, the lot of them. I didn't make an index card for any of them." She looked at me expectantly, and I nodded vigorously in agreement, even though the most I saw of the "bunch of losers" these days were some faceless figures going to and from various cars.

Grandma patted a stray hair in place on her head and continued. " 'Betty,' I told her, 'you could buy yourself a condo on the beach for cash and have enough left over to last your whole life if you sell now.' But she didn't have time for me. You know, Gladie, that house is one of the biggest on this street. And it's got a pool."

Grandma let out a big why-are-people-so-stupid sigh. Then she slapped her forehead. "I almost forgot! I have news about the house next to ours, too."

Geez. I really didn't want to hear that another neighbor had died. I would need therapy.

"Don't look at me like that, Gladie. It's good news. Jean the real estate lady told me there's been a bite on the house next door." She nodded to the house on my left. "A big bite. A whale bite. A . . . a . . . what's bigger than a whale? Whatever it is, it's one of those bites. Anyway, I can't talk about it yet. Might jinx it. Won't you be happy to have that house filled?"

I was only dimly aware that the house next door was empty and for sale, but my real estate ignorance would be sacrilegious to Grandma. The town was her business, and it was supposed to be mine now, too. A couple of speed-walkers made their way past us, distracting us from talk of houses and death.

"Daisy Scroggins," Grandma called out, flapping her arm at one of the speed-walkers. "You are the sweetest thing. How could I resist homemade chocolate chip cookies right out of the oven?"

The speed-walker, who I assumed was Daisy, stumbled in surprise. "How did you know I baked—" she started, but stopped herself midsentence. "I'll be back in fifteen minutes with a plateful, Zelda. It's the least I could do."

Grandma leaned into me. "Her daughter's wedding is next month," she whispered. "That was a tricky one, but in the end I convinced her to go for the plumber with one leg. She's never been happier, of course."

I had a familiar feeling of dread. Grandma's shoes were hard ones to fill. When the moment came, would I know to fix up someone with a one-legged plumber?

Jose let out a bloodcurdling scream. He jumped up from the rosebushes, clutching his hand. It grew redder by the second and started to drip.

"What did I tell you?" Grandma shook her head and clucked her tongue at him.

"I cut off my finger," he yelled, his eyes wide with terror.

"No, you didn't," Grandma insisted. "It's just a scratch. Good thing I told you to be careful. Let's go in, and I'll wash it." Jose followed Grandma into the house, holding out his hand in front of him as if it was a snake. I took that as my cue to hop in my car.

I drove a block before I realized I didn't know whether to go to Burger Boy or Chik'n Lik'n. I could have gone to Bernie's Rib Shack, my grandmother's favorite, but it was in a strip mall next to Weight Wonders, and I didn't want to face any dieters while getting an order of baby backs. I decided on Burger Boy because it was the closest and had the quickest drive-through.

My grandma's house was one of the oldest in town and located right in the center of the historic district on Cannes Boulevard near Main Street. The houses were a mishmash, most built in the haste of newfound money during the gold rush in the nineteenth century. The gold had run out pretty quickly, but people stayed on to enjoy the mountain views. The town had never grown to much of anything, topping out at around four thousand people.

I drove south out of the historic district toward Orchard Road, where just beyond, hundreds of acres of apple and pear trees stood as a beacon to all those who came up the mountain for the town's famous pies.

Burger Boy was at the corner of Elm and Park, a few blocks before the orchard and across the street from Cannes Center Park. The park had been established about 150 years before in a wise attempt by the town's founders to preserve and protect the natural beauty of this little corner of Southern California paradise. It was a huge expanse of rolling hills, sagebrush, and eucalyptus trees. It used to have a lovely gazebo in the center with park benches all around, where they held weekly concerts and regular picnics. Then, in the late fifties, a few bored and prudish housewives caught some couples kissing on the park benches, and they lobbied to have the benches removed. It was decreed that the park should be used for brisk exercise and that lounging on benches and in the gazebo would only lead to trouble and moral decay. The gazebo fell into disrepair. Gone were the kissing couples, and with them went the concerts and picnics. Today, brisk exercise was relegated to the historic district and the little park on Main Street. Cannes Center Park welcomed mostly skateboarders and teenagers searching for a little excitement in the bucolic small town.

Across the street from the park, Burger Boy had location, location, location and a killer dollar menu. It was a gold mine, a favorite of locals who did not particularly enjoy pie or tea.

An explosion rocked my car, jolting it forward a few feet before it slowed to normal. "Whoa, Nelly," I said, patting the dashboard. "No more car farts. I need you a while longer." I called them car farts. My mechanic called them a cataclysmic end to the catalytic converter. He had grumbled something to me about being one car fart away from total destruction and probable death, but I couldn't afford to fix it. Besides, it ran fine as far as I was concerned. It was a 1995 silver Cutlass Supreme, and I had gotten it for free when I worked at a used car lot for one month. I loved it, even though it had more rust than silver paint, and the interior was ripped, with foam poking out in tufts.

I rolled into the parking lot past a group of skateboarders hanging out in front, their skateboards leaning up against their legs as they packed away burgers, fries, and shakes. I followed the drive-through sign, winding through the parking lot toward the talking Burger Boy. I opened my window, and the smell of french fries hit me like nectar to the gods. Really, happiness was truly easy to acquire if you're honest with yourself. Maybe I could start eating right tomorrow.

Burger Boy's mouth was open in a big smile, and I yelled in its direction. "I would like two Burger Boy Big Burgers. No pickles. Extra cheese, please. Two large fries, and a Diet Coke."

There was a long silence, so I tried again. "I would like two Burger Boy Big Burgers, please!"

"Dude!" a voice shouted back at me.

"Yes, I would like two Burger Boy—"

"Dude! It doesn't work!"

I leaned out the car window and tried to look into Burger Boy's mouth. The voice sounded much clearer than usual, but I still didn't understand what it was saying.

"Hey, dude. Like, the drive-through doesn't work, man." A skateboarder rolled up to my car, a shake still in one hand.

"Didn't you hear me? I've been yelling at you for, like, forever."

His shorts hung down well past his knees, and he wore a T-shirt that announced the price of beer bongs. "Dude, I just thought of something," he went on. "If I didn't say anything, you would still be talking to the Burger Boy. So trippin'." He thought this was riotously funny and got so caught up in his own giggles that he didn't hear me when I said thank you and backed out of the drive-through lane.

I was disappointed about the drive-through, but I still had to get lunch. I was careful to lock up my car before I walked to the front door, passing the four skateboarders deep in conversation. Their attention was drawn to the sky.

"Dude, like, I think it's an eagle, man."

"No way, dude. It's an owl."

"I don't know, man. It's pretty big."

"Dude, it's been up there, like, you know, forever."

"Oh, man. It's been up there since last week at least. Maybe it thinks it's a tree or something."

"Cool."

I looked up. Sure enough, an owl was perched on top of a telephone pole. I don't normally notice wildlife, don't know much about it, but two years before, I had had a job typing up a doctoral thesis on the endangered Madagascar red owl, and now I was staring up at one on a telephone pole at Burger Boy.

"Check it out. An eagle is up there," one of the skateboarders said, pointing it out to me.

"Actually, it's an owl," I explained.

"Oh, dude. She so burned you. I told you it was an owl." This came from the beer bong skateboarder, who I figured had held on to a few more brain cells than his friends.

"It's an owl from Madagascar," I informed them.

"Cool."

"It's not supposed to be here," I said. "It's highly endangered, and it's nocturnal. I don't understand what it's doing here."

They looked at me with empty stares. I had the strongest urge to knock on their foreheads to see if anyone was home.

Two things were certain: the four great geniuses were not about to help the endangered owl, and if I didn't help it, I would be responsible for driving the Madagascar red owl that much closer to extinction.

I sighed and dialed information on my cellphone. A minute later I was on the line with animal control, which proceeded to pass me to seven different offices around the state before I got to wildlife management. They said they couldn't get someone out here due to budget cuts and would I be so kind as to shoo it off or get it down.

"Get it down?" I asked.

"Yes. If it's too weak, just go up, grab it, carry it down, and take it over to animal control. We'll handle the rest."

"What if it has rabies or something?"

"Ma'am, birds don't get rabies. Just throw a shoe up there or something. It will fly away. It probably is enjoying the view."

The wildlife person hung up, and I stood there a moment, looking at my phone. Our tax dollars at work. Sheesh.

"We have to shoo it down," I told the skateboarders.

"What? With our shoes, man?"

"You know, shoo. Like, shoo fly," I said. "But in this case, with our shoes. Throw your shoes up there to shoo it away. We have to make sure it's okay."

The beer bong guy was the first to take off his shoes, and the rest followed. I guessed he was kind of their leader. They threw their shoes up at the owl in unison, and I shielded myself from the onslaught of laceless, skull-embossed sneakers as they made their way back down to the ground. I looked up, and sure enough, the owl was still there. He hadn't even blinked, which made me think he was in distress of some kind. Possibly more distress than what I was feeling at being stuck with a bunch of pothead skateboarders having to save an endangered species because my government wouldn't fund its budget properly.

"Okay. Well, that didn't work," I said. "So one of you is going to have to go up there and get it down."

The guy who had thought the owl was an eagle looked at the telephone pole and whistled. "I don't know, dude. Can't you get electrocuted or something touching one of those poles?"

"No, no. This is a telephone pole. There's no danger with a telephone pole," I said. I was almost sure there was no danger with a telephone pole.

"I'm not much into climbing, man," said the beer bong guy. And that seemed to clinch it for all of them. Without saying goodbye, they put on their shoes and rolled off into the park.

I waited a moment to see if some nice passerby would pass by, and then I kicked off my flip-flops, grabbed the pole, and started climbing. I got about halfway up before I got stuck on a metal doohickey and started screaming.

I was surprised and impressed that it only took about seven minutes for the police to come. Cannes was a very small town, and I didn't know it had so many police. Two squad cars and an unmarked car with a flashing light on its roof drove into the parking lot. I was amazed I had garnered so much attention.

"What the hell do you think you are doing?" one of the policemen yelled up at me.

"I was trying to get the owl," I shouted down with as much dignity as I could muster.

"Get down immediately!"

"I can't. I'm stuck on the metal doohickey."

I was stuck. Stuck, and nothing was going to get me to move. I was sure any little movement would precipitate my plunge to earth. I sat on the metal ladder rungs, my legs wrapped around the pole in a death grip. My pants leg was punctured all the way through by the metal thing, my fear of heights had suddenly kicked in, and I was sweating so much that a nice slippery coat covered my body from head to toes.

I looked down at the policemen, who were deep in conversation. Four were in uniform, but one was dressed in plainclothes, an expensive suit.

A couple of minutes later I heard a siren and saw a giant hook and ladder fire truck come my way. Presto chango, they had a ladder against the pole, and a big fireman was climbing up to me.

"Don't worry, miss. I'll help you," he said.

"I was trying to get the owl for the wildlife management department. They have budget cuts," I told him.

"Happens all the time, miss. Come on. I got you."

He put his arms around me and gave a little tug, and the ripping sound from my sweatpants could be heard across state lines. I pulled back, trying to minimize the tear, and my elastic waistband gave way as I fell upside down, my pants pulled down to my knees, my pink Victoria's Secret special three-for-fifteen-dollars boy's-cut underpants out for everyone to see.

I heard snickering from the group below, which now included not just the police and the firemen but the entire staff of Burger Boy. In a moment of lunacy, I waved to them.

The fireman carried me over his shoulder down the ladder. Once on firm ground, I pulled up my pants.

"You have to get the owl. It's distressed and endangered," I told the fireman. He nodded and went back up to retrieve the bird.

The policeman in the suit approached me. He was tall. His thick, wavy dark brown hair was perfectly cut and combed, his chin was shaved down to the last whisker, and despite a manly Gerard Butler kind of face, he looked like he was not averse to using moisturizer and the occasional clay mask. He had largish dark blue eyes and thick eyebrows. He arched one of those eyebrows as if he had a question.

"Yes?" I prompted.

"Cinderella?" he asked, his mouth forming a smile, revealing white teeth.

"Excuse me?"

"I was thinking you must be Cinderella." He held up my flip-flops. "I found these. They're yours, right?"

I put my hand out, and he placed the flip-flops in it. "I guess that makes me Prince Charming," he said.

Ew. Who did he think he was? I had just had a near-death experience.

He stood with his hands on his hips. His suit jacket was pulled back a bit, and I could see his badge and gun.

"I was trying to save the owl. It wasn't my idea. Wildlife management told me to do it," I said.

He smiled and cocked his head to the side. "I don't usually come out for these kinds of things, but I heard the call come out about a woman up a telephone pole and had to see for myself. I'm not complaining, though, and neither is anybody else. Sergeant Brody over there says you have the finest rear end he's ever seen."

"Well, I'm sorry I wasn't up there longer to give everyone a better view."

"Don't worry about it. They all took photos with their cellphones," he said.

A deep heat crawled up my face, and my ears burned.

He studied me a second. "Hey, don't feel bad," he said, a smirk growing on his perfectly shaved face. "The town has cut back our overtime allowance, so the men have been pretty down. You just made everyone's day. I heard one guy say he hasn't felt this alive in twenty years."

One of the firemen approached us with the owl in his hands. "I got your owl," he said. He tapped it, making a hollow sound. "Plastic. It was put up there to scare away the pigeons so they wouldn't crap all over Burger Boy. I took it down so we don't have to go through this again. Although"—he winked at me—"I wouldn't mind the experience."

"But it looked so real," I moaned.

Prince Charming took the owl from the fireman. "Here," he said, presenting it to me. "You should have it."

"Thanks, but no thanks." I walked to my car and opened the door with a loud creak. Prince Charming was on my heels. He threw the owl behind me onto the backseat.

"Think of it as a souvenir."

I felt I needed to explain myself to him, and I hated myself for it. "I was just trying to be proactive."

"You were being a Good Samaritan," he said.

"I'm not like this normally."

He gave me another annoying little smirk. "I'm thinking there isn't much normally in your normally."

I gave him a sufficiently snotty look back and started the car. "I don't think you're Prince Charming at all," I said.

He smiled from ear to ear. "Nice car."

The Cutlass chose that moment to let rip its biggest car fart ever. I tried to retain my dignity, although I was guessing it was a little late for that. Besides, how dare he make fun of my only means of transportation? I was about to send back a zinger when he patted the roof and turned on his heel. "Bye, Pinkie," he called, waving as he walked.

I took a long, healing breath. The day had been a big lesson for me. I would never wear elastic-waist pants again.

Chapter 2

✦ ♥ ✦

First dates are a first step. And as the joke goes about the man who falls off the roof, that first step is a doozy. People have a lot of fear about first dates, and when people are scared, they do everything wrong. So you have to make sure they have that first date in a nice, relaxing place. Don't let them go to one of those fancy-shmancy French restaurants where the portions are so small you could die from hunger and the waiters are Genghis Khan on a bad day. Send them to someplace comforting, like a diner. Send them to the IHOP. Who gets scared in an IHOP? I'll tell you who—nobody. They get a table, they eat some pancakes, some eggs, and suddenly they're comfortable with who they're with. If the setting is relaxing and comforting, love will bloom.

Lesson 12,
Matchmaking Advice from Your Grandma Zelda

I DROVE toward home, and my stomach growled in protest. Damn, I didn't get a single fry. Grandma was going to be upset, but I wasn't about to attempt any more stops. There was some leftover chicken in the refrigerator and a bottle of mayonnaise. Grandma would have to be satisfied with a chicken salad sandwich.

I pulled into the driveway, careful not to hit Grandma, who stood waiting there, holding a plate piled high with chocolate chip cookies.

"Just the person I wanted to see," she gushed.

As I grabbed one of the cookies, she looked me up and down, and her eyes grew enormous. "*Bubeleh*, what has happened to you? You're a mess. Your pants are ripped to shreds. I can practically see to China."

I glanced down at myself while cramming the cookie into my mouth. She was right: I was a mess. What could I do? I took another cookie.

"An owl got me," I said, little bits of cookie flying out of my mouth as I spoke.

Grandma must have had experience with owls because this piece of information didn't seem to faze her.

"I have wonderful news, Gladie. Just wonderful. The whale took the bait, and the house is sold, sold, sold. I wanted to tell you earlier, but I waited until it was all done."

"What house?"

Grandma playfully punched me in the shoulder. "Oh, you. Always kidding around. The house next door, remember? Well, he bought it, and I really shouldn't be telling you this, but he bought it for cash. Cash. Can you imagine?"

I couldn't imagine. These days I wasn't buying anything for cash. I was planning on paying my credit card bills with more credit cards. Grandma had offered me a salary as a matchmaker, but I didn't want to take anything until I could contribute to the business with my own matches.

I grabbed another cookie and took a bite.

"That's great, Grandma," I said.

"That's not all. The man is thirty-three years old and gorgeous." She winked at me. "Never been married; no children, either." She winked at me again. "And no, he's not gay. I always know these things."

She looked at me expectantly. "So, what do you think?"

I was about to tell her that I wasn't looking to date, which was a big lie. I was going through a long dry spell. My hormones were oozing out of my skin, and I was just about ready to jump the next man who walked by.

"Don't you think he would be absolutely perfect for your first match? He would be an easy one." Grandma's eyes twinkled with the brilliance of her idea.

"I guess so," I said between mouthfuls. What I really wanted to say was: *What about me? What's wrong with me?* I was single, and I would have loved a thirty-three-year-old straight, single rich guy. I looked down at my torn sweatpants, T-shirt, and once-flat abs—flat until I had moved in with Grandma three months before. Obviously Grandma thought I was out of the running, and I wasn't sure I disagreed with her.

I took another cookie. Grandma stared over my shoulder, her attention riveted. I turned. Two cars drove up to the house across the street, the falling-down-roof house. A blonde jumped out of her sedan and stomped over to the man in the Porsche.

"You are an asshole! Ass! Hole!"

"Bitch!" he yelled back.

They screamed at each other while they walked up the path to the house.

"Not a one of them is worth their salt," Grandma muttered.

"Are those Randy Terns' kids?"

"Yep, the dead guy's kids. The rest of them landed this morning. They've been skulking around, like they expect to find money in the walls or something. I wouldn't be surprised if they rip out all the copper pipes to sell. And you want to hear the dumbest thing? They refuse to convince their mother to sell the house, when selling is clearly the best thing for her. They could sell that house in a heartbeat, and they would all be better off." Grandma's eyes glazed over, and I was sure she was picturing the Sold sign being hammered into their front yard and new neighbors moving in who would fix the roof and plant something prizeworthy.

Grandma went back in the house, but I stood for a while in the driveway until the Porsche guy came out of the Ternses' house and lit up a cigarette. He was dressed to the nines, and he looked impatient as he puffed on his cigarette. He reminded me of a hunter who had lost his prey. Something about him made me uncomfortable, like he was potentially dangerous to anyone within a relatively small radius.

He stomped out his cigarette and tipped his head toward me. He must have noticed me watching him. My day had been interesting enough, and I didn't want it to get any more interesting. I willed my legs to get me inside fast, but I was rooted to the ground. He took a step toward me, just as a green Volkswagen Bug came barreling down the street. It honked twice and turned sharply into our driveway, making me jump out of the way.

"Oh, thank goodness you're there. You can help me." Bridget Donovan climbed out of the Volkswagen and opened up the backseat. "A lot of pigs died for these ribs," she noted, gazing at me from behind her large hoot-owl glasses. "She got enough food for an army. Ribs, macaroni and cheese, sweet rolls. It's amazing your grandmother didn't drop dead years ago. Her arteries must be rock solid."

I took a couple of bags of food. "What is all this? I was supposed to pick up lunch," I said.

"Who knows? All I know is that Zelda called me three hours ago and told me to pick up her order at Bernie's at one-thirty. She said something about you and burgers and bad karma. You know your grandma."

Grandma had a way of knowing things that couldn't be known.

"Anyway, here I am." Bridget slammed the door shut with her hip and froze. "What happened to you? You look like you were attacked."

"An owl got me when I was trying to buy lunch," I said.

Bridget wasn't any more shocked than Grandma at this news. "You want to go with me tomorrow to a demonstration in front of the elementary school? It's time I gave them a piece of my mind."

Bridget loved to demonstrate. She would protest just about anything. She was my grandmother's accountant, and I had met her the first week after I moved in, when she was doing the books at the kitchen table. We had hit it off right away.

I told her about the new neighbor and my grandmother's suggestion. Bridget caught me pouting. The lack of romance in my life was a familiar discussion between us. The attic and the sweatpants didn't help matters.

"She didn't think you were setup material, huh?"

"She told me that the perfect man was moving in next door and I should fix him up," I said.

"That's crazy. You're the prettiest girl I know, Gladie."

I swallowed. "I am?"

"You're the only one who doesn't think so. The other day, Maggie at the butcher shop was talking about how pretty you are. She said she would pay good money to have your nose and that she had searched everywhere for contacts the color of your eyes, but she couldn't find that blue-green color."

"Maggie had fat from her butt injected into her face. I don't think we should go by her opinion."

"And your figure. You know how I feel about the objectification of women, but you have a great bod, Gladie."

"I've gained a few pounds," I pointed out. Bridget ignored me.

"Sure, your hair has a life of its own, but there's nothing wrong with frizz. When you talked with your grandma, were you wrapped in bandages from head to toe? Because it sounds like she thought you were the invisible woman or something."

"I was sort of wearing these torn pants," I mumbled.

"If I'm not mistaken, Gladie, this is the fourth time this kind of thing has happened to you in the past month."

"I think this makes five times."

"All right, I'll save the protest for another day. We need some inter-female support time. Let's have lunch tomorrow," she said. "Lucy is back in town. I'll invite her, too. Ladies' lunch at Saladz. Regular time."

We carried our Bernie's Rib Shack bags toward the house. "You know," she said, "your grandmother is right. You *should* be thinking of matching people. The new neighbor is a good start."

"Yeah," I said. "It's just that I don't know how."

"You have to dive in sooner or later."

I didn't want to dive in anywhere. In fact, I had a strong desire to run. Three months was the longest I had stayed in one place in years, but I wasn't going to let Grandma down. I felt invisible strings holding me in place, and she was the one holding them.

I spent the afternoon and much of the evening working in the attic with renewed purpose. I wouldn't let Grandma down. She was getting on in years, and she was counting on me to take over the business. I had promised to at least try. Maybe she was right and I was a born matchmaker. Perhaps I would bring love and happiness to the masses.

In the office, I filled three large trash bags with ancient index cards and Polaroids, but I was still buried in paper, and I didn't seem to be any closer to getting the business organized.

I stretched and looked up from my desk for the first time in a long while. Outside, across the street, the neighbors' lights were on, and a young man was pulling out the trash can. Damn. I had forgotten tomorrow was trash day. I hurried around the house emptying the wastebaskets, then rolled our large black trash can down the driveway.

The guy across the street stood by his trash can and lit up a cigarette. He wasn't the Porsche guy, but I assumed he was one of Betty Terns' many children. What was with this family? Hadn't they read the warning labels?

I tried to ignore him as I put the trash can in place on the curb, but he waved to me. In my head, Miss Manners badgered me to wave back.

It was a huge, huge mistake. It was a skorts, goatee, shoulder pads, Bay of Pigs kind of mistake. I've wondered many times since then how my life would have been different if I had only ignored Miss Manners, ignored the guy by the trash can, and returned to the attic to throw out more index cards.

But I waved, and he waved again, and he upped the ante with a smile. I saw his smile and raised him an "I'm sorry for your loss."

"What?" he called from across the street.

"Your loss. Your father. Sorry about your father."

"Oh, thanks," he said. He shuffled his feet and cocked his head to the side, studying me. "You're the Burger girl, right? I haven't seen you since you were, you know, little."

I didn't remember him at all. Grandma stayed clear of his family, and I couldn't remember ever setting foot in his house.

"You came and swam here. Your mom brought you,"

he said, as if he could read my mind. "Then your grandma got upset and took you back home."

The story sounded familiar. "You have a pool slide, right?" I asked. A scene came back to me in a wave of memory. In my mind's eye, I saw the pool and Grandma's burly arm pulling me away, her face angry and concerned.

"That's right," he said. "You wanna come in? We're all sitting around, having a drink."

"Oh, no thanks. I have to get back," I said, turning.

"Not even for a second? My mom would get a kick out of seeing you. Besides, don't you wanna see the scene of the crime?" he asked.

"Scene of the crime?"

"Yeah. It happened in the kitchen, you know." I must have looked a little horrified because he added, "Oh, I guess you didn't know that. My dad died in the kitchen. Come on in. I'll show you."

"Um . . ."

"My mom sure will be happy you said, you know, that you're sorry about my dad."

He stubbed out his cigarette and held his hand out to me. I didn't feel I could refuse, and I walked across the street to him and shook hands.

"My name's Rob, if you don't remember," he said.

"I'm Gladie."

"Yeah. Peter reminded me."

"Who's Peter?"

"My brother. He's the smart one in the family. You'll meet him. Come on in."

The doorknob hung broken at an angle. "Dad wasn't much for fixing things," Rob explained. "The door's been broken as long as I can remember. Easier that way. Don't need keys." He tapped the door, and it swung open for me. I stepped inside.

"Come on in and take a seat," he said, his voice tinged with uncertainty.

The house was crammed with furniture. How to pick a seat? And how to get to it? I tiptoed around a sofa wedged in the entranceway. Rob waved me into the living room. More furniture there. I counted at least four couches, plus a bunch of chairs and ottomans. There was a sea of knickknacks wherever I looked.

In one of the corners was a curio cabinet filled with little porcelain dolls. On the mantel was a collection of ceramic elephants. The rest of the room was stuffed with shelves and cabinets crammed with figurines. A creepy feeling went up my spine, and I shivered.

Rob looked around for a place to sit, but the furniture was too overwhelming, and it was doubtful there was a navigable path through it all. I was wondering if I was going to have to climb over the furniture to take a seat, when Rob looked at me and shrugged. He'd given up.

"Everybody is in the kitchen," he said, steering me away from the living room. The house was big, but not as big as my grandmother's. Hers was one of the first real homes in Cannes, built by a lucky gold miner who spared no expense. But Grandma was right about the Ternses' house. It was sizable and would bring a pretty penny.

I spied on the rooms as we walked the long way to the back of the house, where I assumed the kitchen was located. Clutter, clutter everywhere, but not a drop of dust. Either Rob's mother, Betty, was an obsessive-compulsive cleaner or she had a dynamite cleaning lady.

"It's just a couple hundred dollars, Mom. You act like I'm asking for the world."

I heard the kitchen before I saw it. Rather, I heard the voices. The first was a woman's, with the remnants of a teenage Southern California whine. The second was a woman who was fed up with everything, especially those close to her.

"Grow up, Christy. Jesus, you just got out of jail. Don't you think you should try to get a job? At the very least, you should kiss Mom's ass for getting you out of the slammer and not kicking you out of the house."

It was awkward, to put it mildly, and I was sure that Rob would stop and turn me around, but he acted as if nothing was out of the ordinary. Before I could fake some sort of ailment and bolt out of the house, I was face-to-face with Betty Terns' kitchen, a museum piece from the late 1960s in all its avocado-green glory. Wow, there was a lot of linoleum in that room.

At the table were Betty and two youngish women who I assumed were her daughters. One I recognized as the bitch from earlier. She was the one angry at Christy, who had just been released from jail. Rob didn't introduce me. In fact, he seemed to have forgotten about me altogether. His attention had shifted to the gleaming light in the small room beyond the kitchen. A big-screen TV was broadcasting a baseball game. He walked toward it as though in a trance. I watched in fascination and irritation as he took a seat in a recliner and leaned back, feet up. Obviously Rob was one of the Terns kids who wouldn't leave the nest.

I stood at the entrance to the kitchen, hoping that somehow the women hadn't seen me and I could turn around and go back home, but I wasn't so lucky. The three women were genuinely pleased I was there and gave me all their attention. Even though I had never taken any notice of them, they knew who I was.

"Oh, Miss Burger," Betty said. "I am thrilled you came by. This is so sweet of you, to give your condolences in person."

Betty Terns was small. The top of her head reached not far above the midsection on my five-foot-seven frame, and her hair was bleached blond. Very bleached. Clorox bleached. And she was clearly not averse to wearing as much pancake makeup as she thought she needed. I bit my lip, awash in shame. I was supposed to be giving my condolences, and all I could do was mentally critique the physical attributes of the poor widow in front of me. How would I feel if she could read my mind? Poor lady. She had just lost her husband, for goodness' sake. I looked at her with fresh eyes.

Geez! She was skinny. Really, really skinny. Clearly the woman hated food. I fantasized a moment about giving her a few of my extra pounds. I could give her five pounds for her rear alone, and then both she and I would look so much better.

"Honey? You went out on me for a moment there."

I blinked. Betty's big blue eyes were staring up into mine with concern.

"Sorry. I was just thinking of your husband." Good save but terrible lie. I was going to hell for sure.

"You are so sweet, Miss Burger. Won't you sit with us? We were just talking about my Randy, bless his soul." Well, well. It turned out that I wasn't the only liar in the group.

"Thank you, but please call me Gladie."

"And I'm Betty, and these are two of my daughters, Jane and Christy."

I shook their hands and sat down. Christy smiled from ear to ear, and I noticed she was missing more than a couple of teeth near the back of her mouth. Jane's smile was more circumspect and a lot more hygienic.

"I'm sorry for your loss," I said. I had heard the phrase on TV and didn't know what else to say.

"That's where he died. Right there," Christy announced.

"Excuse me?"

She pointed at me. "Where your arms are. His head

hit right at that spot on the table. It split his head open like a melon."

My arms flew off the table as if they had been electrocuted, and I backed up in my seat.

"His head didn't split open like a melon. It was dented, like it was bashed in," Jane the "bitch" added for good measure. "Besides, his head might have hit there, but he didn't die there. He died on the floor." She pulled out a cigarette from a pack on the table and popped it between her lips.

We were interrupted by banging from another part of the house.

"There he goes again," said Christy.

Betty turned to her. "Would you please tell your brother to stop that noise and come here? We have a guest, and he's being plain rude."

Christy sighed loudly and shuffled out of the kitchen.

"Peter thinks we might have termite trouble, and so he's been digging in some walls," Betty explained to me.

"Yeah, right," Jane mumbled.

Christy came back quickly with Peter, who turned out to be the Porsche guy, on her heels. He was more disheveled than before, and his suit was covered in a fine layer of white dust. I thought back to Grandma's comment about Betty's kids looking in the walls for gold.

"Hi," he said. He took a beer out of the refrigerator and sat next to Christy, the jailbird.

"I was just telling Gladie that Dad died right where she's sitting," Christy said. She was practically jumping up and down with excitement. Where had I landed? I felt that creepy feeling up my spine again, and I racked my brain trying to make an excuse to get out of there.

"Don't sweat it, Gladie," Peter said. "They didn't find any hair or blood or brain bits there, but his head was bashed in pretty good and there was a huge mess on the floor."

My eyes were drawn to the floor. It was clean as a whistle.

"Nope. No brain bits on the table. Makes you think," Peter said.

"Well, it makes *me* think," Jane added.

Makes them think about what? I had no idea, and I didn't want to find out.

"And the acrobatics," Jane started.

"The acrobatics?" I asked.

"He had a dent in the back of his head, but he fell forward," Peter said. "Like he was hit, not like he fell backward onto the table."

"Idiot coroner called it an accident," Jane added, taking a long drag on her cigarette. "Convinced the police, I guess, but they seemed interested at first."

Betty stood up suddenly and left the room. I figured all this talk about her husband's death had gotten to her, but she came back in holding a purse and wearing a scowl on her face. She was followed by what I assumed was another daughter, possibly older than Jane and Christy, her clothes unmatched, like discards from a thrift store circa 1972. "I love pennies," the daughter said, her voice high and singsongy.

"Don't you have enough pennies, Cindy honey?"

"I love pennies," Cindy insisted. She floated around the kitchen like a fairy, searching in nooks and crannies, obviously upsetting Betty's strict notions of order and cleanliness.

"Oh, Mom. Let her have my purse. It's perfectly all right with me," Jane said.

Betty reluctantly handed the purse back to Cindy, who plopped onto the ground and began rooting around in it.

"My sister got a brain injury when she was a kid. It was an accident at school on the playground," explained

Jane. "She's got a thing about pennies and looks for them everywhere, especially in purses. It's no big deal."

"It is a big deal," Betty corrected, her hackles up. "It took me three hours to find my keys yesterday. She takes things out, puts things in. It's a mess."

It was time to get out of there. I did a big theatrical yawn and stretch. Betty took the hint and walked me to the door.

"Thank you so much for coming, honey. It really did brighten my day," she said.

"It was the least I could do." It *was* the least I could do. I hadn't even bothered to bring flowers.

I needed another cookie, fast.

"You'll come to the memorial on Wednesday, won't you? It would mean so much to me."

"Of course, Betty. I wouldn't miss it," I said. This was guilt talking.

She hugged me, and I saw Peter over her shoulder.

"I'll see her home, Mom."

I didn't want Peter or any of the Terns family near me or my home. "Oh, no," I said. "I can walk home by myself. It's just across the street. I wouldn't want to put anybody out."

"You're not putting me out at all, Gladie," he said, and escorted me out the door.

We walked across the street. "Your mother is very kind," I said to fill the moment.

"You don't know the half of it. My mom suffered like a dog for years and years, and all with a smile on her face. You can't imagine what she had to put up with."

I had the strongest desire to stick my fingers in my ears and sing the national anthem—anything not to hear how Betty Terns had suffered through the years. If I heard how much she'd suffered, I would feel the need to help her, and I had enough problems. I was tired. I was supposed to be a matchmaker, but I had no idea how to go about it and would probably bankrupt my grandmother. I had gained ten pounds. Half of Cannes, and almost all of its police force and fire department, had seen my underpants. And most important, I had to shower in antiseptic as soon as possible because I had just spent an hour resting my arms on the table where poor Randy Terns had bashed his brains out.

Peter Terns didn't seem to sense my discomfort, couldn't tell that I had problems of my own. He planted his feet on the sidewalk in front of my house, halfheartedly dusted off his tie, and looked me in the eyes. "My mother was married for fifty-four years," he said.

"Th-that's wonderful," I stammered.

"Wonderful? It was hell. My father treated her like crap." A vein on his forehead popped out.

"Domestic abuse is a terrible thing," I said, taking a step back.

"It sure as hell is. You know what he did?" I took this as a rhetorical question. "Dad didn't like to share." He spit out the last word with a sneer that made me step back again. To my horror, he made up the difference, advancing toward me. "She should have left him long ago," he said. "But she stayed with him, and what did it get her? What did it get *me*?" He hit his chest for emphasis.

Peter took out a cigarette, the go-to drug for the Terns family. I jumped on the break in his little tirade to say goodbye and hightailed it up the driveway. Just as I reached my front door, I heard Peter grumble to himself, something like, ". . . if he slipped or not," and ". . . rat's ass if someone knocked his head, he deserved it."

I locked the door behind me and checked on Grandma. She was sleeping soundly in her canopy bed, probably dreaming about Cupid, not about bashed-out brains.

I grabbed a well-deserved cookie from the kitchen and went back up to the attic. After I'd spent fifteen minutes scouring through index cards, Peter's words came back to me with a jolt.

Share? What didn't Randy Terns want to share? Whatever it was, it sure made his son Peter angry. Angry enough to bust open the walls in his house, most likely.

Peter wasn't shedding any tears over his father's death. In fact, I hadn't noticed any tears in the Terns household. Instead, they were almost ghoulish in their curiosity about the exact cause of Randy Terns' demise. Supposedly he had slipped, cracked his head open on the corner of the table and died on the floor.

I was starting to understand what was so interesting about the kitchen table being clean. Something was definitely fishy about Randy Terns' death, and at least one of his children thought he deserved to be murdered.

Chapter 3

✦ ♥ ✦

If you're lucky, if you've done your job right, the couple has a twinkle after their first date. But you have to investigate this twinkle. Is it a good twinkle or a bad twinkle? Don't kid yourself. Bad twinkles exist. Tragedy has happened many times from bad twinkles. Romeo and Juliet, for example. That was a case of a bad twinkle. If they'd had a good twinkle, they could have done without the drama and poison and probably lived happily ever after. So you need to ask them about their twinkle. Investigate a little. Go ahead. Don't be shy. It's what you're supposed to do.

Lesson 30,
Matchmaking Advice from Your Grandma Zelda

I WALKED up a block to Main Street and took a left. It was a gorgeous day. There wasn't a cloud in the sky, the temperature was a dry seventy-eight degrees, and the breeze was blowing, sending me wafts of wild-flower scents. This part of Main was covered in cobble-stones with narrow sidewalks and quaint stores. If you were looking for antiques, silver jewelry, pies, and tea, you didn't have to look any farther than Main Street in the historic district of Cannes.

I wasn't after any of those things. I was on my way to Saladz restaurant to meet up with my friends Bridget and Lucy. In addition to salads, Saladz offered a wide selection of sandwiches, soups, homemade pies, and assorted tea. But its coffee was horrible, and I desperately needed a shot or two of caffeine. I decided to stop at Tea Time to grab a coffee to go.

Tea Time was housed in a former saloon. The bar was still there, and so were some well-placed bullet holes in two walls, but otherwise Tea Time was all lace tablecloths, yellow painted daisies, porcelain teapots on every table, classical music piped in at a respectable level, and a rack of crocheted tea cozies for sale at ludicrous prices.

The shop was owned and operated by Ruth Fletcher, an eighty-five-year-old woman who possessed more energy than I. She viciously hated coffee drinkers.

"I hate when you come in," she said.

"I'm sorry, Ruth." I placed my Visa card on the bar. She looked at it as if she was debating whether or not to take it.

After a few moments she took the card and sighed. "You venti, grande, caramel mochaccino, Starbucks generation people have no taste. The same?" she asked.

I nodded. She got busy with the espresso machine and in a couple of minutes handed me a cup to go. I took a sip.

"Ruth, you make the best lattes in the world."

"Like that's a compliment. You people are ruining this town. I have to make coffee now in order to stay in business. Coffee! What next? I'll have to put in Internet access. You make me sick." Ruth's coffee was great, but her customer service left a little to be desired.

"Gotta go," I said, and headed for the door.

"Tell your grandmother I finally caught her," she said as I reached the door. "She said it would rain today, and there's not a cloud in the sky. I even checked with NOAA. No rain expected all week. Ha! That woman thinks she knows everything. I finally got her."

Bridget and Lucy waited at Saladz at an outside table. They sipped raspberry iced tea and waved hello when I approached. They didn't look like they should be together. Where Bridget was no-nonsense in a starched shirt, slacks, and pulled-back hair with no makeup under giant round glasses, Lucy was Southern charm and elegance, waiflike and beautiful in a flowy chiffon number and long, wavy blond hair. I was somewhere between the two. I had ditched my sweatpants for linen slacks. On top, I wore a white pima cotton T-shirt. I'd had no luck in managing my frizzy hair, even though I had spent twenty minutes and used up most of a bottle of mousse struggling with it.

"They are selling Christmas ornaments at the grocery store," Bridget yelled as I sat. "Christmas ornaments in August! What is wrong with this world? Has the world gone completely cuckoo-doodle-doo? We are living in the dark ages. When will people stop living their lives according to outdated mythology and superstition? Oh, by the way, we ordered for you, Gladie."

Lucy rolled her eyes and gave me a pointed look.

"Speaking of the dark ages and outdated mythology and superstition," she said, her voice dripping a languid Southern drawl. "Nobody has asked about my trip to England."

"You're always going somewhere with your work," Bridget said, shrugging. She was right. Lucy was in marketing, whatever that was. She worked for some unknown company based far away but chose to live in our small mountain town. She and Bridget had been friends for years, and we became a tight circle when I moved to town.

Lucy was a marketer, Bridget was an accountant, and I was pretty much nothing. I was treated like I was heir to a great business, but I wondered what they would think if they knew I was ready to quit any second and leave town as an abject failure.

Lucy put on her crystal-laden sunglasses and crossed her arms in front of her. I thought I heard her harrumph but couldn't be sure.

Bridget turned to me. "Any update on the new neighbor? Did you find him a match?"

Lucy perked up. "What new neighbor? How is all that matchmaking coming along, anyway?"

Our lunches arrived, and I dug into my Cobb salad. "It's not coming along anywhere," I said, deciding on honesty. "I have no idea what I'm doing or how to get started."

"Isn't your grandmother helping?" Lucy asked. "Isn't she training you?"

"Sort of, but she just knows what to do. She doesn't have to think about it." Bridget and Lucy nodded.

"And what about the neighbor?" Lucy asked.

"Nothing exciting," I said.

"That's not true," Bridget interrupted. "Thirty-three years old, gorgeous, rich, single, and straight."

Lucy took off her sunglasses. "Oh, darlin', that is *the* definition of exciting."

"I haven't spoken to him yet."

"No surprise there. You don't talk to anybody."

I flinched. Was that true? Was I some kind of recluse? I was. I was a recluse with a paunch and no prospects for a successful career or an orgasm.

Lucy rubbed my arm. "Ouch. I'm sorry, darlin'. I didn't mean to hurt you."

I sniffed. "You didn't hurt me."

"It could be worse, darlin'. Look at Bridget. She doesn't even believe in men."

"I believe in men," Bridget screeched. "I see them. I know they exist."

"But you don't believe in intersecting with them."
Lucy crossed her hands to illustrate her point.

"My intersections are more like head-on collisions,"
Bridget said.

"At least you make contact," said Lucy. "Contact is
good, Gladie." She wagged her finger at me. Then her
head snapped to the side and her jaw dropped. Bridget
followed her gaze.

"I wouldn't mind making contact with that," Bridget
said in an unusually low voice.

I turned to see what all the hubbub was about.

"Oh, no," I moaned. I slid down in my chair and put
my hands over my face. "Pretend I'm not here," I whispered. "Don't draw any attention to me."

"Why not?" asked Bridget.

But it was too late. A heavy hand tapped me on the
shoulder.

"Pinkie, we've got to stop meeting like this." I felt his
breath on the back of my neck, and right there and then
I began to ovulate. I dropped my hands from my face
and turned around.

"You don't remember me? Prince Charming," he said.
He had a perfect, cultivated five o'clock shadow. His
eyes were bluer than I remembered. He was dressed in
yet another expensive suit, but this time it came with a
supermodel attached to his arm. She was blond, six feet
tall, and obviously in the midst of a protracted hunger
strike. She wore a peach-colored handkerchief-sized
swath of silk that almost covered her boobs and would
have almost covered her rear end if she'd had one.

How annoying.

"Not in a talkative mood today?" he asked. He nodded to Bridget and Lucy. "Good afternoon, ladies. I'm
Spencer Bolton."

"I know exactly who you are," Lucy drawled.

"The new police chief," supplied Bridget. She smiled

from ear to ear, pulled her hair out of its ponytail, and gave it a shake.

"Nine months new," he said.

"From Los Angeles," said Lucy. "How do you know our Gladie?"

"Well . . . ," he began.

"Go. Away," I hissed.

"Are we going to sit down or what? I'm hungry," the supermodel whined.

The attention at the table shifted to the supermodel. Bridget and Lucy looked like either it was the first time they had noticed her or they were genuinely surprised she could speak.

She could speak, but I was having a hard time. *Yes, go feed Barbie,* I wanted to say. *Can't you see she needs to eat? Hurry up before someone starts a telethon for her or something.* Instead, I didn't say a word. I scooted my chair away from him and dug my fork into my salad.

"Yes, we're going," he told the model. "Gladie, it was a pleasure, even if your pants were on this time."

I choked on my salad, coughing and sputtering until Lucy gave me a couple of whacks on my back. When I came up for air, Spencer Bolton and his date were gone.

"You've been holding out on us, darlin'," Lucy said.

"No, I haven't. It was a strange, humiliating chance encounter. Nothing happened. First him and then the dead guy. I've been having a very weird week."

Bridget perked up. "What dead guy?"

I explained about Randy Terns and his fatal fall. Then I filled them in on the crazy family. The family looked so normal, so all-American through the window of my attic office. But at the very least, Betty's daughter Christy had just been released from the "slammer" for whatever reason, Jane was an angry "bitch," Rob seemed aimless and hopeless, Cindy was brain-damaged and liked pennies, and Peter was a creepy Porsche owner who spent his evenings ripping holes in walls.

I put my fork down and cleared my throat. "I don't think Randy Terns slipped and hit his head on the table," I confided to Bridget and Lucy. "I think he was murdered. I think someone hit him over the head." I told them about the clean table, how he'd had a dent in the back of his head but had fallen forward away from the table, and how suspicious the kids were.

"Brain bits," Bridget added. "It would have been covered with brain bits and shards of skull. What? I saw it on the Learning Channel."

I nodded. "It would have at least had bloody goop all over it. But Betty Terns' son said Betty didn't even have to clean the table." I leaned forward. "Betty Terns, the OCD clean freak, didn't clean the table."

Lucy pointed at me. "Look at you. Look at you. You've got the bug like your grandma. But instead of love, you have the murder bug. You can't help yourself. You *know* things."

I wasn't like my grandma. I didn't *know* things. But Lucy was right. I couldn't help myself.

"Let's call back the police chief," Bridget urged, scanning the restaurant for Spencer Bolton.

"Randy Terns was older than dirt. Old people slip," I explained before she could call him over. "They say he slipped."

"It's that regional coroner's fault," Bridget said. "He comes around whenever it suits him, stuffs his face with pie and full-strength eggnog, and does nothing."

Lucy rolled her eyes. "Bridget, there hasn't been a murder in Cannes in at least one hundred years," she said.

"How do we know that?" Bridget said. "The coroner never rules a death as murder. For all we know, there's been a murder a day here. Besides, autopsies are performed on less than one percent of all deaths of people over sixty. What? I saw it on PBS."

"Murder is usually committed by the spouse," Lucy announced. Her eyes were shining with the excitement of a possible murder in quiet Cannes. "The skinny wife must have done it. Hungry people can get awfully mean."

"Lucy Smythe, I'm shocked that you would dare to say something so blatantly discriminatory and sexist!" Bridget sat up straight in her chair. Her face was bright red and she looked like she was ready to blow. I headed her off before she could start her rant.

"Randy and Betty were married for a million years," I said. "I don't think Betty was big enough to do anyone harm. Besides, he did the gardening and he took out the trash. I watched him through Grandma's attic window. How many wives would kill a husband who did that?"

Bridget and Lucy nodded.

"I think Peter did it," said Bridget. "It sounds like he had a real axe to grind with his father."

"Or it could have been Christy," said Lucy. "I mean, we don't know why she was in prison. Maybe she's a habitual criminal. Maybe she evolved from a sociopath to a psychopath. I saw that on *Dr. Phil*."

They went down the list of possible suspects, shouting "He did it!" or "She did it!" until they ran out of suspects.

"It could have been anybody," I said. "Even a five-year-old boy could have broken in. There's no lock on the door."

"You know," Lucy said, "the name Randy Terns is awfully familiar to me. I can't place him, but I'm sure I've heard of him somewhere. Give me time. I'm sure I'll remember who he is. Or was, I should say."

I got home just as the rain started. Big drops hit the dry pavement. It was odd to see rain in Cannes in August. I had a moment's sympathy for Ruth at Tea Time. She had looked forward to catching Grandma in a mistake.

It was bedlam at my grandmother's house. People milled about, moving chairs into the large front parlor. "The monthly Cannes Astronomy Club meeting," Grandma explained. She supervised, as usual, telling amateur astronomers where to sit. "We were supposed to meet in the back garden, of course. No one believed me about the rain, and now they are running around like chickens with their heads cut off. Instead of looking at the stars, we're just going to talk about them. It's got Gerald all turned around."

She pointed to a tall, thin man in a threadbare tweed suit, who I figured was Gerald. "He's president of the club, you know, and he takes these things very seriously. But his focus will shift after tonight's meeting. We have a new member coming: Sweetie. Sweetie and Gerald were made for each other!" Grandma clapped her hands and bounced on her toes.

"Do you want me to help?" I asked. "It's about time I get started matchmaking."

"You will! You will!" she said, patting my arm. "Tonight's the night for you. But not at the meeting. Just go back up to your attic and organize some more. It will come to you."

I sighed. I didn't have my grandmother's knack for things coming to me. If nothing had "come to me" after all the days I had spent in the attic, I doubted anything would come to me tonight.

"I'm having sex! I'm having sex! Zelda, I'm having sex!"

A middle-aged woman with long brown hair and a euphoric smile ran toward us. Startled, Grandma took a step back.

"Right this second?" Grandma asked.

"No," the woman explained. "This morning. Last night. Practically every day, thanks to you. You set me up with Daryl."

Grandma blinked several times. "Oh, right, right. Good. Good. Sex is lovely, isn't it? I remember it fondly. It's been a while, of course. Let's see, the last time for me was . . . hmm . . . I think it was a leap year."

We had entered the realm of too much information. I was dangerously close to picturing my little grandma in her control-top pantyhose getting her freak on. I snuck out of the parlor and crept up the back stairs to the attic.

I TOOK a break around dinnertime to raid the Cannes Astronomy Club's potluck offerings. There was a wide array of astronomy-themed foods. While the group was listening to Gerald describe the expanding universe, I grabbed three moon pies, a handful of starfish sticks, and some cosmic potato salad.

I stood in a corner and ate while Gerald wound down, finishing up with a prediction of our planet's eventual destruction. "That was lovely, Gerald," Grandma said as she stood and initiated applause. She gently nudged him toward a seat next to a platinum blonde in a tiny skirt. Surely that couldn't be Sweetie. She didn't look like Gerald's soul mate. She looked more like Lou the auto mechanic's soul mate. But who was I to question Grandma's tactics?

Grandma introduced the next speaker, the man who cleaned the lenses of the Palomar Observatory telescope near San Diego. I ate the last of my moon pies and returned upstairs.

At around ten that night, I finished cleaning the attic. On the desk were only a clean stack of blank index cards, an ancient Polaroid camera, a stapler, and some pens and pencils.

"Ready for business," I announced to the empty room.

Then the rain stopped.

The house was abruptly draped in complete silence. Grandma must have gone to sleep, and the amateur astronomers were long gone. It seemed like the whole town was tucked away safely in their beds.

I yawned. It was time for me to go to bed as well. I went to turn off the desk lamp when movement outside caught my eye. A shadow passed across the lawn in a blur. It was large. I stood and pressed my face against the window to get a better look. I stayed like that for a moment until the shadow moved into view again. I jumped back.

The shadow was a man. A man stood on my grandmother's front lawn. All the talk of murder and death had my mind reeling. I grabbed the stapler for protection but immediately felt ridiculous. "What am I going to do? Staple him to death?" I asked and set it back down.

I turned off the light and pressed closer to the window. The man was tall and wide, and it looked like he was inspecting Grandma's bushes. Then he turned, and his gaze locked onto mine, a story above. There was the unmistakable glint of metal in his hand.

Chapter 4

✦ ♥ ✦

Most people you want to help. If you're like me—and I know you are—everyone you want to help. But there are some you should stay far away from. Drive to Cincinnati to get away from them. Anything. Anywhere. Just stay away. You'll know the ones I'm talking about. Never-gonna-happen-matches. Like Neddie No Underpants, who used to beg on Main Street next to the post office. Yes, I tried to match Neddie No Underpants. What was I thinking? Underpants or not, he was a pain in the ass I wouldn't wish on my worst enemy. Stay away from the Neddie No Underpants of this world, pupik. *Let them find happiness on their own.*

Lesson 33,
Matchmaking Advice from Your Grandma Zelda

MY BREATH hitched. I forgot how to breathe. I waited for the inevitable shot to ring out in the night and hit me right between the eyes.

But there was no shot. The shadowy figure turned and rooted around in the bushes again.

I took a gulp of air and seethed with anger. It had been a rough couple of days. I had been humiliated and frustrated, but I was not about to be scared by anyone. I ran down the stairs and out the front door, stopping to grab a flashlight on the way.

The man was bigger up close, tall and muscled. I

shined my light on him and cleared my throat. "Just what do you think you're doing?" I asked.

He stood and faced me. He had dark blond hair and striking green eyes. He was wearing Levi's, a T-shirt, and work boots. Our eyes locked, and I moved my hand to my face to see if it had caught fire.

"Oh, hello," he said. He had a rich baritone voice that turned my spine soft. He was quite possibly the most handsome man I had ever seen. He lifted up a metal tape measure and brought the long metal tape back to its holder with a snap. "I was just measuring."

I wanted to ask something, but for the life of me, I couldn't figure out what it was. In fact, my tongue had swollen, and I wondered vaguely if I was going to swallow it and die right there in my grandmother's front lawn next to her prize-winning roses.

"The property line is marked incorrectly," he said. "I'm going to have to dig up part of your lawn."

"What?" My hormones were popping all over. My head was spinning, and my body was sweating. I had a sudden craving for a mango smoothie.

"Dig it up. Move my fence over," he said.

"What?" I snapped to attention. My hormones stopped popping. I didn't know what he was talking about, but the gist was clear: he was threatening Grandma's lawn. "You're going to dig up my grandmother's lawn? You can't do that," I said.

"Oh, this isn't your house? I just assumed."

"This is my house. I live here with my grandmother. This is her lawn. Those are her prize-winning roses." I pointed to the roses with the flashlight.

"They're very nice," he said. He smiled and put out his hand. "I'm Holden. Arthur Holden. I just moved in next door."

I gasped. "The single guy?"

Holden dropped his hand. He arched an eyebrow,

and his lips curved up in a small smile. "Yes, I'm single," he said softly. His baritone voice dripped out all velvety soft and yummy.

It's amazing how life plays tricks on a person. I was standing two feet away from Mr. Perfect, and I had to match him with someone else. I sighed. It was now or never. I owed it to Grandma. How could I let this guy get away?

"I know someone for you," I blurted out. It was almost the truth. Who wouldn't want him? Who wouldn't give their right arm to be near him?

Holden took a step toward me. "You do?"

"Uh . . ."

"Tell me, what does your husband think about me digging up the lawn and moving the fence?" he asked. His eyes twinkled bright enough to give any of Gerald's constellations a run for their money. They also sent a message my way. He didn't care a thing about what my husband thought about the garden, but he did care if I had a husband. I noticed him eyeing my ring-free left hand. I clutched it to my chest and stumbled backward. He shot forward and caught me, easily.

"Easy does it," he said. I pushed against him, trying not to feel his muscles and extremities. Too late. I felt all of them.

"Uh . . ." I stammered.

I ran back to the house and slammed the door shut behind me. I leaned against it and caught my breath. "Wimp," I said out loud. "Wimp. Wimp. Wimp."

"GLADIE, YOU don't look good."

"I know." I turned the coffeepot on and fell onto one of the kitchen chairs. "I didn't sleep well."

"That means you got unfinished business. Make a list. Finish it up, and you'll sleep like a baby." Grandma stood by the open refrigerator. She was drinking orange juice out of the carton. Her hair was rolled tight in big electric rollers, and she wore a blue and orange housedress with pink slippers that clacked when she walked. She looked well rested.

Two bagels popped out of the toaster. She grabbed them and brought them to the table with a tub of cream cheese. I flipped through the community paper, looking for potential clients. There was a photo of the mayor and his dog, a piece about a lice outbreak in the local high school, and a blurb about the upcoming city council ball, which would take place in the high school gym. I guessed the city council didn't care about lice.

"I had crazy dreams last night," I explained. "I was an ice skater, and my partner kept dropping me on my head, but I didn't mind because he promised me he would take off his shirt. How's that for weird?"

Grandma smeared cream cheese on a bagel and handed it to me.

"Then I was riding around town on a scooter with a police siren attached to my head. Dogs were chasing me down the street, and my siren was blaring, giving me a huge headache. Just when the dogs were about to get me, they turned into James Bond in a bathing suit with a spear gun. I pleaded with him to help, but he laughed and said he didn't help women who wore sweatpants."

Grandma nodded. "So, you met our neighbor last night? What did you think of him?" she asked.

"How did you know . . . ? Never mind. Yes, I met him." I squirmed in my chair and took a bite of my bagel. "I haven't found a match for him yet."

"You will. He'll be around for a while. You've got time. You've got the gift. I was just telling that to one of those no-good neighbors across the street."

"One of the Ternses?" I asked.

"Yes, they have strange notions, those no-goodniks.

The boy wants me to do them a favor. I told him I do love. I don't have time for their nonsense. And I told him you have the gift. You do love and maybe more."

"I'm not so sure," I said. I didn't do love, and I wasn't sure I did anything else.

"You'll see. It will grab you. You'll smell out those in need. Unfinished business. It will eat at you until it's done. You won't rest until you solve the problem. You and me, we like happy endings. We like justice. And we've got the gifts to make it happen. You understand, dolly?"

I didn't understand. I thought Grandma was way off base for once, but I nodded anyway, and she pinched my cheek.

"I want to get my hair done," I said. "I can't walk around like this anymore." I was filled with resolve to turn myself around. The next time Mr. Perfect jumped out of a bush, I would be ready with highlights and long layers.

Grandma patted my hand. "That's what I figured. I made an appointment for you with Bird in an hour. Don't take the car. Bad day for driving."

Bird Gonzalez owned the beauty shop up the street. Everybody who was anybody in Cannes went to her for their cut and color. There were three other hairdressers in her salon, but Bird was the star. She was crazy fast, able to shuffle clients around so that she worked on three heads at once. She had memorized the hair color of every local woman over the age of twenty-five and could mix up a batch of dye at a moment's notice without consulting notes.

It was Saturday morning, and Bird's place was packed. I didn't know how Grandma had managed to get me an appointment, but she and Bird went way back. Bird made regular house calls for Grandma on Mondays.

"Hi, Gladie. It's about time you came in." Bird waved

me over to her chair with a big smile. "Where have you been hiding? Oh, my." Bird studied my roots. From the expression on her face, they didn't look good.

"Just make me look natural," I told her. "Like a natural Angelina Jolie or something."

Bird snorted. "Angelina Jolie is out of the question, but with a few highlights you'll be a dark blond Kate Hudson with boobs."

While Bird gathered her foils, I scanned the room. There were at least three viable women for Arthur Holden, my new perfect neighbor. I could kill two birds with one stone. I would get my much-needed makeover and get contacts for Arthur's match. I slouched in the chair, proud of the new proactive me.

"Bird, is it weird that all of a sudden I'm noticing a lot of attractive men?" I asked.

"In this town? That *is* weird."

"I've got a new neighbor," I mumbled. "And there was this policeman . . ."

Bird clutched her chest. "Police Chief Spencer Bolton! Yum-*my*!"

The salon erupted in appreciative murmuring. The new police chief had gotten a lot of attention. "Get in line, honey," said one of the hairdressers. "He's gone through half the town already, and he's only been here a year."

"Nine months," corrected one of the clients. "I put in hair extensions and bought a new wardrobe the day he arrived."

"He's been a boon for business," said the other hairdresser. "There's been a lot of upgrading going on."

Bird tapped the end of a comb against her lips. "You say you only just noticed him? You must be going through a libido thaw."

"Uh," I said, "I'm not sure what that is."

"You were in a libido freeze for some reason. You

didn't care about men, good-looking or not. Usually a libido freeze is caused by divorce or death."

"Or commitment issues," said one of the hairdressers.

"That's a laugh. Zelda Burger's granddaughter with commitment issues," piped up one of the customers. The salon broke out in giggles.

"Anyway," Bird continued as she put the final foil wraps in my hair, "you're thawing out. You're probably emitting pheromones right now. It comes with the thaw. Men will be flocking to you and your pheromones. Soon you'll be losing weight, too."

I wondered if Bird smelled something on me that I didn't. Unless pheromones smelled like the drugstore's generic antiperspirant, I didn't think I was emitting them. As for men, I had no idea what I would do if they started flocking to me.

"I can't lose weight. My grandmother's house is junk food central," I said.

"There's only one good diet," Bird said. "The Spit It Out Diet. It's not bulimia. It's safe and effective."

She stepped back from my chair and did a dramatic turn. Her point was taken. She was slender and fit. She was a poster child for the Spit It Out Diet, whatever that was.

"You put it in your mouth for a taste, and if it's not worth the calories, you spit it out," she explained.

I tried to hold back a look of disgust.

"She does it all the time," said one of the hairdressers.

"Here, let me show you," Bird said. She took a bite of a doughnut and spit it out in the trash can. "Ta-da!" she shouted triumphantly.

I tried to hold back my gag reflex.

"Everyone is a skeptic," she said. "Try it. You'll see." Bird shampooed me and started on my trim. There was no jiggle in her upper arms as she wielded the scissors, and it made me think that maybe she had a point.

Maybe there was something to her Spit It Out Diet. If I was going to give myself a makeover, shouldn't I try her diet?

"Hey, don't you live next to that guy who was murdered?" Bird asked.

The back of my neck tingled, and I sat up straighter in the chair. "I live across the street from an old man who died after he slipped and hit his head on the kitchen table," I said.

"That's weird. I heard he was murdered. Hey, Joyce, wasn't that guy murdered?"

Joyce, the manicurist, nodded.

"Where did you hear he was murdered?" I asked.

"Here." Bird scanned the salon. "It wasn't my client. Whose client was it?"

Joyce shrugged.

"I think it was Sandy's client," said Bird. "I don't know her name. But Sandy isn't here today."

"She was the dead guy's daughter," said one of the hairdressers.

"Yes, the blond one," said Bird. "The blond daughter said her father was murdered. She said it matter-of-factly. You say it was an accident?"

"SO WHAT do you want me to do?"

"Talk me down. Talk me out of this. At least talk me out of the bushes."

"How did you get in the bushes in the first place?"

That was a complicated question. I had wandered home in a haze. I couldn't remember my haircut, the blow-dry, or paying Bird. My brain was working over-time, trying to recall which of Randy Terns' daughters was blond, and it had no room to think of anything else.

Walking down my street, I had seen movement in

front of the Ternses' house. I had ducked into the bushes in order to stake them out without being seen, just as Rob's car drove by and slammed into Peter's Porsche. Peter ran screaming out of the house toward his car. I waited for nearly an hour for the sisters to come out of the house, but there was no sign of them. Instead, the brothers continued to study the damage and yell at each other. I had no graceful way of exiting the bushes without revealing myself as the buttinsky spy that I was.

I sat with my cellphone glued to my face. Bridget had few words of wisdom.

"Gladie, why are you staking out the Ternses' house?" she asked.

"I don't know. I can't remember which daughter was blond. I want to find out. I want to know why she thinks her father was murdered. For some reason, Randy Terns' death has wormed its way into my psyche. I'm on the precipice of obsession. Help."

"Couldn't you just have knocked on their door to see if they needed anything? That way you could see who was blond," Bridget said in her usual logical manner.

"I don't want them to know I'm curious. I don't want to get involved."

Peter stood by his Porsche, taking a break from yelling at his brother. He focused his attention on my grandmother's house. He looked like he was deciding on something.

"I definitely don't want to get involved," I hissed into the cellphone. "I don't like death. I don't like dead people. They creep me out."

"Gladie, you used to work in a funeral home."

"Only as the receptionist. And I didn't actually make it to work. I passed out on the steps to the building. I saw a wreath of black flowers being delivered and lost consciousness. Does that sound like the kind of person who should get involved in a possible murder?"

"Well, Gladie, you know you don't actually have to get involved," she said reasonably.

I thought about that for a few moments.

"Oh, crap," said Bridget, breaking the silence. "Lucy was right. You're just like your grandma. You can't stop yourself. But instead of love, it's crime. Murder. You're a nosey parker. You're Curious George. Gladie, you're a yenta."

Rob returned to his car and drove off with Peter following in his Porsche.

"I'm taking your advice," I told Bridget. "I'm going in."

And I climbed out of the bushes, dusted the leaves off me, and headed across the street to the Ternses' house.

Chapter 5

✦ ♥ ✦

Women come to me, and they all say the same thing: there are no single guys out there. They have been looking for years, and they've come up with nothing. Bubkes. You may come across the same problem. It's slim pickings, dolly. So, where do you go to find single men to match your ladies with? The grocery store can supply only so many men and then you need to look in other places. You look at the park, the pharmacy, and the tire store. You even fake a toothache to try out the single dentist. Once, I'm ashamed to admit, I went so far as to call Jerry Schwimmer, the proctologist, for a sensitive, emergency house call, just because I heard he was recently divorced. You can make yourself crazy this way. It's hard not to get run-down, running down single men. Dolly, don't worry about it. It doesn't have to be this way. You are not alone. Don't knock your head against the floor; your friends can help you out. They can look, too. It's like networking or schmoozing. It's not what you know, it's who you know. It's like that commercial . . . Let someone teach you to sing in perfect harmony. Let someone buy you a Coke.

Lesson 17,

Matchmaking Advice from Your Grandma Zelda

THE DOOR opened before I had a chance to knock. Betty Terns, her slight body draped in tweed slacks and a burgundy sweater set despite the heat, went for the mail in her mailbox but stopped in surprise when she saw me.

"I came over to see how you were getting along and if you needed anything," I lied.

"Oh. Isn't that nice." Her eye twitched, and she pursed her lips. I suspected my presence wasn't nice at all. In fact, she looked put out. Nevertheless, she waved me in. "Come in. We were just about to sit down to some cake and coffee."

The kitchen was a swirl of cigarette smoke. There wasn't a window open. Any fresh air left in the house had been sucked out long before. I coughed into my sleeve and dabbed my watering eyes. I dimly made out Betty with a small plate in her hand. She motioned me to sit and handed me a piece of cake.

"Jane and Christy are around here somewhere. I don't know where the boys are." She lit a cigarette and fiddled with her bedazzled lighter. She motioned at my cake. "Eat. I made it myself. Everyone just loves my coconut cake. Randy used to beg me to make it every week."

The cake was white with two inches of white frosting. It was calling me to eat it, but I hesitated. It didn't fit in with my makeover program. I had the hair. Now I wanted my flat stomach back. On the other hand, Betty was the skinniest woman I had ever seen, and she made the cake every week. Surely one piece of cake wouldn't do me any harm. Maybe Betty's coconut cake was the secret to beauty and flat stomachs.

I dipped the side of my fork into the thick, oozy frosting just as all three of Betty's daughters tumbled into the kitchen.

"If you won't take me, I don't see why you won't lend me your car so I can drive myself," Christy whined. She came in behind Jane, screaming at the back of her head. Jane kept her cool. She sat across from me, lit up one of

Betty's cigarettes, and took a long drag. There was the teensiest of smirks on her face, the same expression a cat wore when it played with a mouse.

"I won't take you because I don't feel like it," Jane said, her voice even and calm. "I won't lend you my car because the judge suspended your license after you got a DUI while your baby was in the backseat without a seat belt. The baby you lost to social services."

Yikes. The Brady Bunch this was not.

Christy took notice of me for the first time and had the decency to blush. "What are you doing here?" she asked, none too charitably.

"Gladie just came by to see if we needed anything," said Betty, tapping out her cigarette in an ashtray.

"We could use some sanity," Jane suggested. Christy took a seat and lit up as well. The only ones in the kitchen who were not smoking were me and Cindy, who was dancing in and out of the kitchen in a purple caftan, happily rummaging in a purse as she spun around. I was pretty sure I felt tumors forming in my chest.

I didn't want to make chitchat. My enthusiasm had waned, less because I was sucking in the equivalent of two packs of smokes than because of the fact that—faced with all three daughters—I was no closer to discovering which one thought their father had been murdered. All three daughters, it turned out, were blond.

Just eat the cake and leave, I told myself. Why was I there in the first place? I didn't want to get involved with these people. Of course the old man had slipped and hit his head. Old men did those kinds of things. It happened all the time.

I took a bite of the cake. The oozy frosting settled on my tongue. My taste buds came to life, triggering my fight-or-flight response, and I nearly spit out the cake. It was awful. Worse than awful. Was Betty trying to poison me?

Emily Post would have swallowed the cake. She wouldn't have cared if it was gross or poison. But Bird Gonzalez would have spit that baby out halfway across the room. I weighed the advice of two sage women, and I came out on the side of my hairdresser.

It was not worth the calories. Or food poisoning, for that matter. I scooted the cake over to the side of my mouth between my cheek and gums and asked to use the restroom. I spit the cake into the toilet and flushed it. Bird was a wise woman. I felt invigorated and empowered.

It was time to get out of there. I had to reprioritize my priorities. I needed to match up my new neighbor and let Randy Terns rest in peace.

I opened the bathroom door and walked face-first into Jane, who must have been waiting for me to get out of the bathroom. She wasn't her usual smug self. Instead, concern etched every line in her face. She put her index finger up to her lips in the international shushing gesture. She moved in close to me until I felt her cigarette-laden breath on my face.

"I have to speak to you," she whispered. "Please, you have to help me." Sweat beaded on her forehead, and I smelled fear on her.

I nodded.

"I have to talk to you about something," she said. "I have to talk to you about murder."

"The blond daughter," I whispered in realization. My heart beat with a *thud thud thud,* surely loud enough to bring attention to our conversation from the rest of the house. I was rooted to the spot, unable to move. I was riveted, determined to hear what Jane had to say.

Then Peter, the Porsche driver, appeared in the hallway from nowhere. He was still wearing a very expensive suit, but it was wrinkled, and his tie was askew.

"Jane, are you bothering Gladie?" He was clearly irritated at her.

"Get lost," Jane told him. Gone was the worried Jane of a few moments ago; the hard-as-nails Jane was back. "Gladie and I were just talking. She wants to talk to me."

"Yeah, right," he said. "Nobody wants to talk to you, Jane." He grabbed my upper arm and gave me a strong tug, sending me flying past Jane. He walked me down the hall, my arm clutched in his hand in a viselike grip. I turned long enough to see Jane wave at me, her cat smile plastered on her face.

"Toodles," she called.

Outside, I found my voice. "Let go of me! I wanted to talk to Jane. You interrupted us."

He tightened his grip. "You don't want to talk to her. She's nuts. She has nothing to say." His eyes twirled around in their sockets. Crazy eyes. "You want to know about Jane's childhood love of cutting off the heads of her sisters' Barbies? Or maybe you want to hear about Jane's first and last babysitting job. Huh? You wanna know about that?" He shook me.

"Not particularly," I said.

"I have to talk to you," he continued. "I've learned something very disturbing about my family. I need you to solve the murder."

I gasped. Murder was the catchword of the day. Did everyone in the Terns household think Randy Terns was murdered?

"Why don't you go to the police?" I asked.

"You think I haven't? Of course I did. They don't believe me. The coroner ruled it an accident, and that's all they care about. Listen, I don't care if my father was killed, but it's not the end, Gladie. I might be next."

"You?" I breathed. "Did someone threaten you?"

"I know who you are. I know about your grandmother. She tells everyone that you're just like her, that you have the gift. And since she won't help me . . ."

"What do you want me to do?" I asked. He was scary and hurting my arm, but I wanted to know what the very disturbing thing about his family was and what it had to do with murder and why he might be next. The disturbing thing had to be worse than Barbie heads, babysitting horrors, and DUIs with babies in the backseat. Nothing could have stopped me from hearing what he had to say. I wished I had a stiff drink or at least some popcorn to eat while he spoke.

"Is there a problem?" Arthur Holden, my new neighbor and possible new client, seemingly materialized from thin air. He was dazzling in the daylight. He looked yummy. I thought about licking him: much tastier than Betty's coconut cake and well worth the calories.

"Piss off," said Peter. "Can't you see we're talking?"

"I see that you're manhandling this young lady, and I want you to stop." He'd called me young. I sucked in my stomach.

"Who the hell are you?" Peter demanded.

"I'm the one telling you that you better let go of her and go back in your house before I get in your face." Arthur Holden stood a good head taller than Peter. Some kind of silent man code passed between them. Peter had sized up the situation and decided on the wisest choice of action. He let go of my arm, scowled at me, and went back into the house.

"Are you okay?" Holden asked. He tenderly lifted up my arm for inspection. It was red and throbbing and would probably be black and blue for days. All I felt were the tiny pinpricks of sexy filtering through his fingertips.

"I got no information," I said, waking out of my haze. "You interrupted Peter before he could tell me anything.

Everybody talked about murder and they wanted to spill the beans to me, but I didn't get any information. I had to spit out cake!"

"This sounds like an issue for the police," he said. I couldn't argue with his reasoning, but I was obsessed, and I was still annoyed at him for blocking me from getting at the truth.

"Look, the man was shaking you." He touched my arm gently. "Welts," he said with sympathy. Goose bumps rose all over my arms. I gasped. "Are your eyes blue or green?" he asked, leaning down.

I pulled my arm away and swayed in place. "Stay on your property," I mumbled. I ran halfway across the street when I remembered. "I'm finding you somebody. Your soul mate," I called to him.

"OH, GOOD. You're alive. I was about to call the cops. What'd you find out?" Bridget demanded over the phone. I had called her as soon as I got home.

The kitchen phone was plastered to my face, and I had a mouthful of chili cheese dog in my mouth. Grandma was busy in the parlor with the Cannes Ladies' Craft Show board, discussing the importance of chairs made of twigs. She had kindly left me a lunch of hot dogs and onion rings on the kitchen table.

"They're all crazy. I am never going over to that house again. I'm with my grandmother on this one. I wish Betty Terns would sell and they would all leave"—after they told me about Randy Terns' murder. Was that so much to ask?

I told Bridget all about crazy Jane and crazy Peter and Holden running interference.

"Sounds like Arthur Holden has a Superman complex," Bridget said. "Men are all alike. How dare he think he can save you? You're some kind of hopeless female, and you need his help? You can't take care of yourself like a grown-up? Tell me more about his chest."

We talked all about murder, the crazy Terns family, and Holden's body parts until I finished the hot dog and two orders of onion rings.

"You know, Gladie, you can't just let this Randy Terns death drop," Bridget said. "Those crazy people think you can help, and they might not leave you alone until you do. You might have to see this through just so they'll get off your back."

"I've got other things to worry about. I have to fix up Holden. I have to get my waistline back, and I just ate thirty-five hundred calories. I should have spit."

"It sounds like Holden is an easy one. Pick a match at random from your grandmother's index cards."

I jumped a foot off my chair as the kitchen door swung in and slammed into the wall with a loud crack. Lucy Smythe stood in the doorway in a sparkling blue and black Chanel cocktail dress and four-inch black Prada pumps with white silk bows. She had an air of achievement around her, as if she had just conquered Mount Everest or the Hermès twice-yearly sale.

She pointed at my phone with an imperious gesture. "Whoever that is you are talkin' to, darlin', tell them you will call them back later. You and me, we've got business to attend to."

"Who's that? Who's that?" asked Bridget on the phone. I hung up. She would figure it out eventually. There weren't too many Southern belles in Cannes.

"You can't go like that," Lucy said, eyeing me.

"Can't go where?"

"You are going to die when you hear what I've got to tell you. Let's get you changed. Come on, get up. I'm not going with you dressed like that."

A minute later, we stood in front of my closet. Lucy

shook her head. "I don't believe this. I know there's more."

"Are you going to tell me what this is about?"

"If you tell me where the real clothes are," she said, tapping her foot on the floor.

"These are the real clothes. These are my clothes, Lucy."

Lucy poked my chest with her manicured finger. "You are holding out on me, Gladys Burger. I'm convinced there is an inner tramp in there somewhere."

"I don't know what you're talking about, and don't call me Gladys."

"I know they're around here. I can smell fashion, you know."

Lucy walked slowly around my room, pointing at drawers and doors. "Duck, duck, duck, duck," she said, "and goose." She stopped at a narrow door in the corner. I ran and threw myself in front of it.

"It's nothing. It's the ironing board," I cried.

Lucy tried to push me away. We struggled. She was stronger than she looked. "This has to happen, darlin'. You have been a nun for too long."

She had a point. Besides, I had had enough physical violence for one day. I stood aside. Lucy opened the door. The closet was stuffed with garment bags from ritzy stores, and the floor was lined with shoeboxes.

"I knew it! I knew it! Don't worry, darlin'. This won't hurt a bit," she said, pulling out the garment bags and throwing them on my bed.

"I don't want to wear them until I lose weight," I explained.

"Hogwash. Don't you know that clothes are supposed to fit? They're not supposed to hang on you like potato sacks. I'm sure the police chief isn't fond of potato sacks. He didn't look like the potato sack kind of man. Or your sexy neighbor, either."

I pawed the ground. "Can I know what's going on now?" I asked.

"Okay." Lucy sat on my bed and flipped her hair. "Randy Terns was no ordinary man. Randy Terns was a bank robber."

"A what?"

"A bank robber. A criminal. A thug. A murdered ex-con. Gladie, the plot thickens."

My mind raced. Did Randy Terns' family know of his criminal past? Maybe Peter was actually looking for gold in the walls, like my grandmother said. Didn't bank robbers hide their loot in walls and floors? Maybe the family was in danger, and that's why they needed my help.

"I recognized his name when you mentioned it yesterday at lunch," she said. "Already a murder in our sleepy town got my attention, but there was something about his name. I knew it was important. I couldn't remember where I had heard his name before. It bothered me all night. Randy Terns. Why did his name sound so familiar? Then, around two-thirty this morning it hit me like a ton of bricks. Of course, Randy Terns was a bank robber. A little-known bank robber, obviously, but a bank robber all the same. I had no idea he lived here. Gladie, this is really big."

Lucy pulled out a red dress from one of the garment bags.

"This will do nicely," she said.

"Where are we going?"

"We're going to Uncle Harry's house. He knew Randy Terns, and he's going to help us solve this case."

This case? Were we on a case? Was this an episode of *Law and Order*?

I unbuttoned my blouse.

"Years ago there was an idiot walking around dressed like a tree and robbing banks," Lucy said. "You're probably too young to remember. I'm a few years older than you, and I was just a child then, and it got national news. Uncle Harry mentioned it to me only recently. That's why it was fresh in my mind."

"A tree-dressing bank robber?"

"Randy Terns painted his face green and stuck branches and leaves to his body with duct tape. Then he went into a bank with a gun. He got a bunch of cash, but he had trouble running away. Trees don't move fast, you know."

I tried picturing Randy Terns dressed as a tree, robbing a bank. It wasn't something a person saw every day.

"What a rack," Lucy announced, eyeing my cleavage. The red dress was cut a little low with cap sleeves and flowed down to just above my knees.

"You think it's too much?" I asked.

"Are you kidding? You can rule the world in that dress. That's the original va-va-voom dress. But be careful. You don't want the va-va-voom to bust out altogether and take someone's eye out."

WE DROVE out of the historic district on Pear Lane and up farther into the mountains, where a gated community had taken root against the wishes of the Cannes Historical Preservation Society. Cannes citizens had an aversion to McMansions in their otherwise quaint town, but the McMansions fed the town with much-needed property taxes, and not everyone was against them.

We had gotten off to a slow start. Grandma was right about it being a bad day for driving. Lucy's Mercedes had a flat about a block away from my grandmother's, and the auto service ran into a fire hydrant on its way to help us. Luckily, Ruth Fletcher was walking by at the time and changed the tire for us, muttering something about how many worthless cappuccino drinkers it took to screw in a lightbulb. We made a promise to switch over to Earl Grey and visit her at Tea Time as soon as possible.

The mountains were beautiful in summer, filled with wildflowers and virtually untouched by civilization. It was hard to imagine that a bank robber would live in a town like Cannes, let alone that a murder had taken place here.

"You like dogs, right?" asked Lucy.

"I love dogs. I worked as a groomer in Long Beach for five days, and I was a dog walker in Pittsburgh for two weeks."

"Good. Uncle Harry has two dogs. The important thing is not to show fear. Pretend you're not scared." Lucy gripped the steering wheel, and her knuckles turned white.

"Should I be scared?"

"Yes," she said. "And today's his poker game, and having all those men around makes the dogs extra nervous. They're Rottweilers, the biggest Rottweilers I've ever seen. Every time Uncle Harry has a poker game, he has to have an ambulance standing by."

"Can't we just call him?"

"Uncle Harry is more of a face-to-face person."

LUCY ANNOUNCED us to the guard at the gate. He wrote something on his clipboard and opened the gate with a push of a button. I heard that the cheapest house in the neighborhood was $9 million. The homes were all large, sprawling affairs, stone-faced structures in earth tones. Lucy drove to the top of the hill. There was another gate with another guard. She gave him our names, but this time the guard checked the inside of the car, the trunk, and underneath.

"I didn't know you had family in the area, Lucy," I said while the guard shimmied on his back.

"Uncle Harry isn't technically family," she said.

The guard opened the hood and inspected the contents. "How did you meet Uncle Harry?" I asked.

"It was at the beginning of my career," she explained.

"He's in marketing, too?"

"Uh, something like that."

The guard gave us the thumbs-up and opened the gate. As Lucy drove up the driveway, we heard the dogs bark, growl, and snap their teeth.

"Maybe this isn't such a good idea," I said.

Lucy reapplied her lipstick. "Listen, Gladie. We are meant to get to the bottom of this. I'm sure that a murder took place across the street from your grandmother's house. You are involved, whether you like it or not. The murderer is still hanging around town, and the police are not looking for him because some stupid eggnog-addicted coroner says it was an accident. For all we know, a killer may be living across the street from you. Did you ever think of that? Doesn't that make you the least bit nervous?"

I did think of that, and it did make me nervous. It also occurred to me that Peter and Jane were playing a cat-and-mouse game with me. And I wasn't the cat.

"Let's go," I said. "Let's say hi to Uncle Harry."

Chapter 6

✦ ♥ ✦

A little boring goes a long way. Just ask anybody unlucky enough to be at a Cannes mayoral inauguration speech. You could die from that much boring. A little interesting goes a long way, too. A man doesn't need to be too interesting to be a good man. You know who was very interesting? Al Capone. There was an interesting man. Jack the Ripper, also interesting. So, my words of wisdom to women are, fall in love with a man who has a little boring and a little interesting in him. But no one listens to me, Gladie. They all want interesting and only interesting. The world revolves around interesting. You get sucked into interesting, and you won't be able to breathe from it. The Chinese—also interesting people—have a curse: May you live in interesting times. They knew what they were talking about.

Lesson 29,
Matchmaking Advice from Your Grandma Zelda

THE DOGS threw themselves against the closed, thick wooden door, making a terrible racket, like bears caught in a trap.

"Don't show fear, don't show fear, don't show fear," Lucy repeated over and over—to me or to herself, I wasn't quite sure. I was trying to recall the last time I'd had a tetanus booster when the door opened, and a bald man—the butler, I assumed, who resembled Lurch from

The Addams Family—greeted us with a nod. He motioned us to enter, but the Rottweilers were jumping and barking with drool spilling from their fangs, and I didn't know how we were expected to get past them alive.

Nevertheless, Lucy stepped over the threshold. I held my breath, waiting for her screams of pain, but the dogs didn't touch her. They didn't calm down, either. They continued their growling and barking. I closed my eyes and followed her in. I prepared myself to be mauled any second, and I was considerably surprised when we made it all the way past the living room, down the hall, and into the card room without a puncture wound.

"You can shut up now."

I turned toward the speaker, a man who was at least three inches shorter than my five foot seven. He wore gray slacks and a button-front striped shirt with the sleeves rolled haphazardly to his elbows. His hair, what was left of it, was shoe polish black, and his eyes were small but expressive. His most notable physical trait was a complete lack of a neck, which suited him somehow. Despite his looks, charm oozed out of him, and he had an unmistakable charisma that had an instant effect on Lucy.

"I said, shut up," he repeated to the dogs. They ignored him and continued growling. "They'll calm down eventually. Hey, sexy, how's tricks?" He embraced Lucy and gave her a juicy kiss on the lips.

Lucy lit up with a toothy smile. "Hello, Uncle Harry. Thank you for inviting us. This is Gladie. The one I spoke to you about on the phone."

"Yeah, sure, sure. Gladys Burger, how you doin'?"

I took his hand, and he gave me a firm shake.

"You can call me Gladie," I said.

"Correction, Legs," he said, eyeing my lower half, on display in my dress. "I can call you whatever I want."

He winked and turned back to the table to gather his chips.

He was right. The dogs did calm down. They found a place in the corner on a red velvet couch, and they went right to sleep. There was a lot of red in the room. Red couches lined the walls, which were draped in erotic tapestries. The center of the room was taken up by a large poker table, covered in red velvet and surrounded by thronelike red chairs. High ceilings were crisscrossed with dark wood beams. We were not alone. The entire cast of *The Godfather* was there. Not really, but the men who were there could have been their first cousins.

Uncle Harry's four poker buddies and a professional dealer were at the table. The game was winding down when we entered, and the players were busy cashing in their chips. They stood up when they saw us.

"Come, sit," Uncle Harry said to Lucy and me. "My friends were just leaving. We'll have some privacy." He poured whiskey into a tumbler and took a seat in one of the red thrones. Lucy and I sat at the table and watched Uncle Harry say goodbye to his friends. They cleared out, and a silence descended on the room, making it very serene, even in its bordello-like way.

"You play poker, Legs?" Uncle Harry asked me.

"I've never played."

"I bet you'd be good at it. Maybe I'll invite you to join us one day."

Me and the guys anteing up, raising stakes, going all in, and reminiscing about how *Sopranos* got it all wrong? Maybe not. Instead, I said, "Thank you. That sounds wonderful, especially if you're playing for matchsticks."

Uncle Harry roared with laughter. "Matchsticks. Ha, that's a funny one. Lucy, I like this kid. Thanks for bringing her around." He cleared his throat and took a swig of his drink.

"Down to business. I hear you got a problem with Randy Terns," he said.

"I don't have a problem," I said. "He's the one with the problem. He's dead."

Lucy piped up. "Dead, Uncle Harry. Gladie thinks he was murdered."

"She does, does she?" This came from the other side of the room. I jumped in surprise. I hadn't seen him sitting there, but there he was, wedged between two erotic tapestries, dressed in his shirtsleeves and Armani trousers. Spencer Bolton, the irritating cop, was even more attractive than I remembered, perhaps because his hair was slightly tousled and he had a look of surprise on his face that softened his Mr. Smooth image just enough to make him human.

"What are you doing here?" I asked.

"You know each other?" asked Uncle Harry. "We allow Spencer to play with us on occasion. Even though he's a cop, we like him 'cause he's young and energetic. We've decided to hold off killing him for the time being."

"I appreciate it, Harry," Spencer said.

"Coincidence of coincidences, Spencer has been asking questions about Randy Terns as well." Uncle Harry finished off his drink and poured a new one. "It was ruled an accident, you know, Legs. Old man slipped, but Spencer has some doubts. I don't know if Randy Terns was murdered, but if he was, he deserved it."

"Uncle Harry, Gladie didn't know about Terns being the tree bank robber," Lucy said.

"Oh, that. Yep. The idiot tried to rob a bank while he was dressed as a tree. And not even a good disguise, just some leaves taped to him. What an idiot. It didn't work, of course. He was caught, and he served major time. But that wasn't the only bank robbery."

"He used the tree disguise a lot?" I asked.

"You're not asking the right questions, Legs," he said. "Nobody cares about the tree thing. Listen, Randy Terns was in the business a long time. Randy was a wingman, and not a very good one at that. If somebody needed an extra hand, they would call him. But the guy had no luck. He was part of so many cockamamie schemes. He was with this one group that called ahead for the robbery. They actually called the bank and asked to have the money ready in bags ahead of time for when they got there, just like Chinese takeout. I'll tell you, if idiots were dollars, there'd be a whole lot of money lying around. All those guys went to San Quentin for that one.

"Then there was the time he tried to stick up a miniature golf course. Miniature golf! So Randy's standing there at the putter rental counter, and he's got his gun in the face of this pimply-faced teenager at the cash register, and it's hot outside, and 'cause Randy is sweating and all, his gun slips out of his hand—splat!—onto the pavement and falls apart into a million pieces. Randy dropped to the ground to put it back together, but by then the teenager had run eight blocks to the local police station. Randy didn't serve no time for that one. He got away before the cops showed up, but you get what I'm trying to say? You understand who Randy Terns was?"

I nodded. "He wasn't Einstein," I said.

Uncle Harry smiled and patted my shoulder. "He wasn't Einstein. Hell, he never even heard of Einstein."

"Are you saying Randy Terns never successfully pulled off a job?" Spencer asked.

"See, Legs? Spencer asks the right questions." Uncle Harry stretched his legs under the table and patted his hair in place. "All right. It's 1972. Randy's fed up. He's got a couple kids and more on the way. He's tired of all the penny ante stuff. So he puts together a gang. I might have helped him meet a couple guys. I'm not saying I did, and I'm not saying I didn't. But there were two guys with him, and they did pretty well together, a couple small jobs here and there that kept them flush enough to make it to happy hour every night. They broke up in 1977, the year the John Travolta movie came out."

"*Saturday Night Fever,*" I supplied. "So, where does murder come in? Did Randy's gang break up amicably?"

"There's not a lot of amicably in the bank robbery line of work, Legs. I heard this rumor about Randy, and it goes something like this: Randy had one big score. He knocked over a bank solo and cut his two colleagues out of the proceeds. According to the rumor, Randy made it into the safe of the Lichtenstein Bank out in Los Angeles. A really big score. They never proved a thing, and no one ever saw the money. In fact, the Lichtenstein Bank never reported the robbery, for whatever reason. So, who knows? But it's hard to explain how a guy could raise a big family and live all these years in the historic district of Cannes without *doing a job*. His day job as stockroom supervisor at the Mart-N-Save didn't pay great. You know what I mean?"

I did know what he meant. I also knew that his two colleagues would have been pretty angry about being cut out of so much money. "He hid the money from the other gang members?" I asked.

"That's what I heard," he said. "Before you ask, I don't know where the other gang members are," he said. "Jimmy the Fink and Chuck Costas. For you, Legs, I'll ask around and get back to you."

UNCLE HARRY dismissed us quickly after that in order to attend to his business. My mind was reeling. The little old man who lived across the street from my grandma had been a bank robber, and he might have been murdered by his former gang members because he hid bank robbery money from them. I wondered how much Peter knew. Obviously he wasn't looking for termites in the walls, but did he know that his father had hidden a big score from his partners? Did he know that his father's partners might be looking for the money, too, and may have killed his father because of it?

Lucy unlocked my car door. "This is fabulous," she said, her face beaming. "We just have to find the partners, and we can solve a murder! This is much better than the stupid book club Bridget forced me to join. Like I give a hoot about the cultural impact of feminist literature. But murder! I feel alive just thinking about it. I feel like Monk. No, that's not right. I feel like a sexy, female Monk. Who would that be? Hercule Poirot! No, that's not right, either. Anyway, I've got your back, and you've got mine, darlin'. It will be fabulous. Best-buddies detectives, out to fight crime, like Abbott and Costello. No, that's not right. Like Rodgers and Hammerstein. No, that's not right, either."

Lucy walked around the car to the driver's door, talking to herself about the joys of murder. I wasn't beaming as much as my Southern friend, but I couldn't help forming a plan in my mind to find Jimmy the Fink and Chuck Costas.

"Lucy, maybe we should go to the library first to see if we can find something on the partners."

"Great idea, Gladie," she said, pointing the keys at me.

"Not so fast." Police Chief Spencer Bolton tapped me on the shoulder. Gone was his usual cocky, arrogant expression. He was dead serious, and his eyes bored right through me. "What do you think you are doing?"

"I'm getting in the car."

"No, you're not," he said. He stood six inches away.

He smelled of cologne and Uncle Harry's cigars. Suddenly the day felt warmer.

"I'm not?"

"No. You and Scarlett O'Hara are going to poke your upscale noses in something that doesn't concern you, and I can't let you do that. This is police business."

"Police business?" I asked. "So it *is* murder and not an accident. I knew it."

Spencer turned a light shade of puce. "It is not police business. I mean, it wasn't murder. The coroner ruled it an accident. There's no reason to suspect murder."

"But *you* suspect murder," I said, poking him in the chest. "You guys jumped to a conclusion about an old guy slipping and hitting his head, but his family is not so sure, and Randy Terns has a shady past, and now you have your doubts, like Uncle Harry said." I was pretty proud of myself. I was some kind of detective genius.

Spencer wasn't thrilled by my powers of deduction. He looked like his head was going to blow up.

"Listen, this is not safe." He waved his arms in the direction of Uncle Harry's mansion and guard shack.

"Uncle Harry? Oh, please."

Spencer ran his fingers through his hair, making it stand up. "All right, then. You're coming with me."

"What?" I asked. "I'm not going anywhere with you. I'm going with Lucy."

Spencer turned to Lucy, who stood watching our conversation over the car, her hand on her chest, her eyelashes fluttering at an alarming rate.

"Is this vehicle insured?" he asked her.

"My Mercedes SLR? Does Elvis eat pork chops on Sunday? Of course it's insured."

"Good," he said, and walked to the back of the car, where he kicked in the taillight with the heel of his shoe.

"Oh, my," exclaimed Lucy, sounding more like a satisfied lover than a recent victim of vandalism.

Spencer grabbed me by the wrist. "You're under arrest. You're coming with me."

"On what charge?"

"Broken taillight."

"It's not my car," I yelled, stumbling in my high heels as he pulled me away from the Mercedes.

"Prove it," he said.

"Lucy," I called. "Show him your registration."

Spencer stopped and turned toward Lucy. "Don't do it, Lucy, or I will impound your vehicle for the next two months."

"Oh, darlin', I need my Mercedes. I have an important meeting in L.A. tomorrow."

"Lucy!" I yelled. "What happened to 'I've got your back and you've got mine'? What happened to Abbott and Costello?"

"Well—" she began.

"Don't do it, Lucy," Spencer said. "I'll have her back by dinnertime. Promise."

Lucy shrugged. "You two have a good time! Don't do anything I wouldn't do, which for your information, you devilishly handsome Mr. Police Chief, is not much."

"Attica! Attica!" I shouted.

Spencer opened the passenger side of his Buick. "Get in," he ordered, gently pushing me forward. I ducked down, but not enough, and banged my head on the door frame.

"Ow!"

"Why did you hit your head? You did that like it's the first time you sat in a car," he said.

I rubbed the side of my head, where a bump was already forming. "You were supposed to do the head thing. You were supposed to protect my head with your hand and say, 'Watch your head.'"

I got out of the car and punched him square in the solar plexus. It was like punching a wall. "What's the matter with you? Haven't you ever seen *Cops?*" I demanded. "They always protect the heads of murdering, shirtless crackheads when they arrest them. You couldn't have done the head thing for me, an innocent bystander? You put a woman in a cop car, you do the head thing. Didn't you learn the head thing?"

"I learned the head thing," he said. "We do the head thing for criminals in handcuffs when we put them in the back of a squad car. You're not in handcuffs. You are just getting in a normal car like a normal person. Normal person, hmph. I should have known."

I leaned close to him, giving him a good view of my bump. "Is there blood? I feel blood."

"There's no blood. C'mon, get in the car."

He walked me back over to the car and put his hand on my head. "Watch your head," he said.

We drove ten minutes in silence. Then his cellphone rang. "Hey, baby," he said. He smiled and glanced at himself in the rearview mirror. "Sure, baby. I'll pick you up at eight-thirty. . . . Whatever you want. You can wear nothing as far as I'm concerned. In fact, that's a good idea. Wear nothing." Spencer chuckled and turned off his phone.

I opened the glove compartment.

"What are you doing?" he asked.

"I'm looking for a barf bag." I stuck my finger in my mouth and made a dramatic gagging sound. Spencer leaned over and slammed the glove compartment shut.

"You obviously have plans, and you'll have to get ready," I said. "What do you metrosexuals do to prepare for hot dates? Don't you need to wax something or prune something? Before you get your nails buffed, you can drop me off at my grandmother's."

"You're coming to the station, where I can keep an eye on you."

"Only until your date. Then I can do what I want. You might as well get rid of me now."

"I'm the chief of police. I have people who can watch you when I'm out."

"You promised Lucy you would have me back by dinnertime."

"I lied."

"What if I promise not to look into Randy Terns' death?"

"Now you're lying."

I crossed my arms in front of me. He had me there. I was a big fat liar with my pants on fire.

We drove the rest of the way in silence. The police station was located on Park between Lake Indian Springs and Cannes Center Park. It was a two-story building made of stone and glass. I recalled hearing something about a new police station, and it definitely looked new.

Spencer parked in the lot in the back. He got out and opened my door for me. "Watch your head," he said with a smirk, his sense of humor having returned—probably because he had won and I was officially in custody. I got out, and he stepped closer to me. He bent down, grazing my face with his lips as he spoke low in my ear.

"Pinkie," he said, "make no mistake. I don't wax, prune, or buff. I'm more the come-as-I-am kind of man. I come natural."

A tiny droplet of spittle dripped from my mouth. Okay, I wasn't immune to his charms. But the man was responsible for my false arrest, a bump on my head, and the derailment of my investigation into my neighbor's death. Besides, Spencer Bolton had a well-known scorched-earth policy when it came to women. He was pure poison to anyone in a dress. He was the Al Qaeda of penises, and I was determined to never see him naked.

It was a matter of national security.

We passed two giant bronze, stainless steel, and glass fountains shaped like magnifying glasses on our way to the back door of the police station. The inside was smaller than the one in *The Closer* but larger than I had imagined. It was shiny, too. The main room consisted of six desks with computers and phones. On the side, I counted three offices, one that looked like a lunchroom.

Spencer garnered a lot of attention. He was clearly in charge and was approached immediately by two policemen in uniform with questions. He answered them quickly. "Is Brody here?" he asked one of the cops.

"No, he's out. Lytton is on desk."

Spencer walked me to the corner office—his, I assumed. Plaques, awards, and photos scattered across the walls and his desk drew my attention. I sashayed over to a photo of him and the mayor of Los Angeles.

"No, Pinkie. Over here. Sit." He pulled out a chair, and I took it. He sat on the edge of his desk and took a deep breath.

"I can't actually arrest you," he said.

"Now you tell me."

"Let's say you're my guest. I need you here for a few hours. Don't look at me like that. I'm trying to keep you safe. It's just until I can get some things worked out. You'll be treated with the utmost respect. I promise."

"You wanted to see me, Chief?" A tall, lanky, red-haired policeman poked his head in the door. He saw me, and a flash of recognition passed over his smiling freckled face. "Hey, it's Underwear Girl! Hi, Underwear Girl. I'm Fred. Sergeant Lytton, I mean."

Spencer's jaw dropped, mirroring my own. Birds could have nested in our mouths. He put his hands in his lap in a defensive gesture. "This is Gladie Burger, Fred," he said. "We're not going to call her Underwear Girl."

"Oh, okay," Fred said. "Nice to meet you."

"Fred, why don't you take Gladie with you?" He turned to me. "Fred's doing a tour of our new facilities for a VIP group. You'll enjoy it." Spencer grabbed my hand, tugged me up with a jolt, and steered me out of his office with gentle pressure on my lower back.

I jogged to keep up with Fred's long legs. It would have been very easy to sneak out. I could have simply said that Underwear Girl needed some fresh air, and I would have been free. But it occurred to me that not only wasn't I under arrest, I was now a VIP with special access, and where better to find information on bank robbers such as Jimmy the Fink and Chuck Costas than at a police station?

"You're in for a real treat, Miss Burger. This new station is sweet. Back home we only had three metal chairs and a desk from the local junior high."

We walked through the main room toward the front lobby, which was decked out in green marble and a birch front desk with overstuffed chairs for visitors. Sweet, indeed.

"Where are you from, Fred?"

"Me? Utah. Not anywhere you ever heard of. I found out about the job here and moved six months ago."

"Have you been a policeman long?" Except for his height, he didn't look old enough to have a driver's license, let alone carry a gun.

"A year and a half. Well, here we are."

Fred motioned to the lobby with more than a little pride. Three other VIPs were there, ready to take the tour. Two men and a woman, all older and pillars of society. I recognized them from my grandmother's house, from one committee or another, and said hello.

"Welcome, everybody," Fred began. "As you know, we are in the five-point-four-million-dollar facility built to bring Cannes' law enforcement abilities into the twenty-first century. This building houses the field operations bureau, the criminal investigation division, the communications center, animal control, and the public information center."

"How many cops you got here, son?" asked a gentleman in shorts and flip-flops.

"Good question, Mr. Smith. Currently we have the chief, three sergeants including me, eight patrol officers, and a school resource officer. The chief is looking to get us two full-time detectives, and we're going to have our very own 911 call center. I'll show you that in a moment. If you call 911 at the present time, you get the neighboring town. It can cause some confusion. If you'll come with me, I'll take you to processing."

We walked through a doorway on the right. "Here's where we bring in suspects and process them," Fred said. "If you want, I'll give you your very own mug shot and fingerprint card to take home. It's not like the movies. We've gone digital here. Come take a look at our cutting-edge technology."

But nobody moved toward the fingerprint scanner or the mug shot camera. Instead, we all stood paralyzed in place, our eyes glued to a spot on the wall where an almost life-sized photo hung of a woman's rear end, covered in pink Victoria's Secret boy-cut underpants, her upper body hanging down and her face in profile in the midst of a scream.

Me.

The VIPs seemed to recognize the subject of the photo at the same time, and they turned their heads toward me, slowly and in unison.

"Uh . . . ," I said.

"Oh, you noticed Underwear Girl," said Fred, perceiving what held our attention. "I mean Miss Burger. I'll tell you, that picture sure calms down the collars. They come in here and they're like, 'Wha? Huh?' A lot of us guys like to have our coffee in here, too."

I gasped and clenched my fists. Fred flinched.

"We can hold off on the mug shots till later," he said, his eyes sliding toward me. "Let's go see that 911 call center now."

We meandered through the call center and the interview rooms. I spotted an empty office with a computer, perfect for my purposes. I planned on feigning a trip to the bathroom so that I could get into their files.

Fred brought us into a large room. "You'll love this. For sure, you've never seen anything like this before."

"It's a box," said Mr. Smith.

"It's a clear box, a glass box," said the woman.

"It's the newest in cell technology. It's for our really big criminals," Fred explained. "It's the era of terrorism, ladies and gentlemen, but don't you fear, because we have this to contain the most dangerous individuals before we send them off to Gitmo or whatever."

"What is it?" I asked. It was a large glass box set in the middle of the room. I didn't see any doors, any way in. Actually, it wouldn't have looked out of place in a modern art gallery.

"I'll show you," Fred said. "This baby cost eight hundred fifty thousand dollars. It opens with an eye scan at the entrance to the room." Fred scanned his eye in a gizmo, and the glass box opened up with a whoosh, revealing the hidden door.

"Well, would you look at that," said Mr. Smith.

"I didn't even notice the door. I thought it was just a box," said the woman.

"Show us how it works," said the other VIP. A tingle went up my spine, a sense of foreboding that I couldn't shake. I wanted to shout out, "No! Stop!" but I didn't want to appear ridiculous in front of Grandma's friends and clients.

"Yeah, get in," said the man in shorts.

Fred smiled, no doubt thrilled that the glass box cell was such a hit on his tour. He entered the box, and the VIP shut the door tight behind him. "No!" shouted Fred, his voice muffled by the thick glass. He pounded on the door but to no avail.

"How does he breathe in there?" asked the woman.

"I think he's wondering the same thing himself," I said.

Fred pounded on the glass, spinning like a top, trying to find a weak spot in his high-tech, Gitmo-in-a-box wonder cell. His eyes were enormous. The kind of eyes cows have when they know they are about to have their heads bashed in.

The woman halfheartedly searched for the opening in the door, but the box was sealed up pretty tight. The men went to the scanner and stuck their eyeballs in, but that didn't work, either.

"Maybe we should call someone," I said.

Fred was really freaking out by then, pulling at his clothes and his hair, his eyes darting back and forth.

"That boy's going to blow," said the VIP in shorts.

"Maybe we should stand back," said the other man.

It was good advice because just then, Fred pulled out his gun and shook it like a maraca.

"Smith and Wesson," explained the woman. "My husband had one just like it. It can blow a pretty good-sized hole in a person."

I let that bit of information soak in just as Fred fired off a round. The sound was enormous, even from outside the box. We ducked in terror, but the box held true to Fred's boast. It was bulletproof.

"Not even a dent," noted one of the VIPs.

But that didn't help poor Fred, who was now threatened by a ricocheting bullet hell-bent on killing him.

"That boy is going to get killed six hundred times over," said the woman, as we watched with fascination usually reserved for pinball games the bullet's untiring trajectory, bouncing off one wall to the other.

"Maybe we should get somebody," I said, my eyes never leaving the action in front of me.

I didn't need to bother. We soon heard the pounding of standard-issue police boots on the marble flooring coming our way at a pretty good clip. Fred couldn't hear them from inside the box, and his panic increased, sure that he was stuck forever in a claustrophobic nightmare.

The entire Cannes police force stormed into the room and froze when faced with the spectacle of Fred in the box, the ricocheting bullet seconds away from killing him.

Only one cop continued to move. Spencer tackled me from the side, knocking the air out of me. He picked me up in a bear hug and shoved me out of the room. "Get the civilians out!" he shouted.

When we were out of the line of fire, he scanned his eye, and the box opened and the bullet flew out, landing in one of the walls. Free at last, Fred fell in a dead faint on the floor.

"Is he okay? I can't see a blasted thing," said Mr. Smith.

"I think he just fainted," said the other VIP. "They're slapping him around pretty good now."

"I can't wait to tell my canasta group about this," said the woman.

Mr. Smith whistled. "I wish I had a bet on this. The odds against his surviving had to be astronomical."

Fred regained consciousness and was being read the

riot act by Spencer. With everyone's attention on Fred, I decided it was the perfect time to slip out.

I made it right through the police station to Spencer's office. The place was deserted, and I was reasonably confident that I would hear them coming back in enough time to get out of the office without being caught.

Spencer's computer was on, but I was distracted by the paper files on his desk. There were files on Peter, Jane, and Christy Terns. I opened Peter's file. The words "sexual assault" jumped out at me just as my cellphone rang.

"Legs, it's Uncle Harry. I found Jimmy the Fink for you. You got a pen? He's in town near the park."

I jotted down the address. It was what I wanted, what I had been looking for, and it was being handed to me on a silver platter. But it posed obvious problems. Spencer didn't want me to have the address. He didn't want me to look up Jimmy the Fink. In fact, Spencer would do everything he could to prevent me from talking to Jimmy the Fink. So, sharing new information with Spencer was out of the question. I reasoned it was best to keep it to myself and get out as quickly as I could before Spencer found me.

I debated with myself whether to take the files and Spencer's car keys. I decided against stealing state's evidence, but I had fewer qualms over grand theft auto. I don't know. Maybe Uncle Harry was rubbing off on me. Maybe it was divine retribution for Spencer kidnapping me. Maybe I was just pissed and that's why I jacked Spencer's ride.

Chapter 7

✦ ♥ ✦

I cannot tell a lie, dolly. I have gotten in over my head more than once in this business. I bite off more than I can chew. I think I've got it all taken care of and then—boom! zing!—it all changes on me. What do you do in times like these when you're drowning? Tread water and call for help, of course. Maybe the lifeguard will be a cutie pie and you can match him up with the mayor's daughter. Silver lining, Gladie, silver lining.

Lesson 41,
Matchmaking Advice from Your Grandma Zelda

I ADJUSTED the seat and the mirrors and turned off the police scanner. Spencer's car was nice. It had leather interior, a navigation system, and a gun rack, complete with an adjustable-objective rifle-scope-outfitted shotgun. I opened the windows and headed out toward Jimmy the Fink's.

The ride was smooth, and the fresh air blowing through my hair was intoxicating. I didn't know what Grandma was talking about. It was a great day for driving, as far as I was concerned.

Jimmy lived in a decrepit motel turned condo complex. It was blue with white trim, one of those places where you park right in front of your room. It was two stories, and Jimmy was on the second floor, apartment 213 at the end.

I dabbed on some lipstick, ran my fingers through my hair, and adjusted my boobs in my bra to make them pooch out a little more. I didn't look half bad in my red dress and wanted to make the most out of it. I wasn't totally clear on what I was going to ask Jimmy the Fink, but I had a hunch it would come to me when I met him. Though he was old enough that I wasn't frightened for my safety, I tucked Spencer's can of Mace into my purse, just in case.

I walked down the long balcony to Jimmy's place. I knocked on his door for a while, but there was no answer. The curtains were drawn, making it impossible to peek inside. I had stolen a cop car to speak to a known criminal about a murder, and the guy wasn't even home? *Hmph.* The guy wasn't home. Since I had already spied on confidential papers in the chief of police's office, I didn't see the harm in spying on an average citizen. A man below was sweeping the parking lot and whistling "Camptown Races." It was the super. Perfect timing.

"Yoo-hoo!" I called, imitating Lucy. "Aren't you a sight for sore eyes? My, oh my." I ran down to him.

"What do you want?" he said, clearly unimpressed by my beauty and charm. He smelled like he hadn't bathed in a long time, and his clothes looked like they had been slept in.

"My uncle Jimmy," I said, changing tactics from flirty to no nonsense. "I need to get in to give him his medication, but his door's locked, and I forgot my key."

"Oh, why didn't you say so? Here." He handed me the key, making me promise to return it later.

I strutted back up the stairs. I was starting to sympathize with Randy Terns and his cronies. A life of crime was easy to get into. You just sort of slipped from one thing to another.

"Do you realize how much trouble you're in?"

I jumped three feet in the air. Police Chief Spencer Bolton stood in front of Jimmy the Fink's door. His five o'clock shadow was growing in nicely.

"What are you doing here?" I demanded.

"My job. Harry called me with Jimmy the Fink's address." Spencer blinked. "What am *I* doing here? What are *you* doing here?"

"How's Fred?" I asked.

"Never mind Fred. You stole a police vehicle."

"No, that's not correct. You said it was just a normal car. I just stole a normal car." I tucked Jimmy's key behind my back.

"You can get a lot of years in prison for stealing just a normal car, woman."

"Yeah? And how about kidnapping? How many years do you get for kidnapping? I wouldn't have needed a normal car if you hadn't kidnapped me. I could have taken my own car," I pointed out.

"For what? To knock on the door of a dangerous criminal in your little dress and high heels and ask him if he happened to have murdered Randy Terns?" It was a good guess. That was exactly what I had planned to do.

"I don't care for your tone," I said.

"My tone? How about my gun? You like my gun?" He pulled back his jacket to show me his sidearm.

"Big bad policeman." I pulled out the Mace.

"Is that my Mace?" Veins popped out on his neck, and his nostrils flared.

"Maybe."

"You stole my car and my Mace?"

"I borrowed them. Don't be so dramatic. I would have taken the shotgun, but it was locked." I was baiting him, but he deserved it. He was stomping on my territory.

"You are impeding a police investigation," he said.

"What investigation? I thought Randy Terns' death was an accident. Besides, nobody's home."

"I know that. I'm waiting for a warrant."

"Well, while you wait, I'll go in to take a look around." I waved the key under his nose. "The super gave it to me. So, it's not technically breaking and entering."

"I don't know what Harry was thinking, dragging you into this. Your legs aren't that great."

"I'll ignore that, but I might Mace you later."

Spencer followed me in. The apartment was stuffy. A game show played low on the television, and there were take-out containers scattered around. It was a one-room deal. There was a bed, a table, and two chairs, but what really got our attention was the body lying on the floor in a heap. It was a man, and he wasn't breathing.

I swayed and saw stars.

"Stay with me," Spencer said, catching me. Once I was steady on my feet, he pulled me behind him and took out his gun. "Stay here," he said. He checked under the bed, then took the man's pulse.

"Is that Jimmy the Fink?" I asked.

"Well, I didn't know him personally, but I would say it's a good bet this was Jimmy. He's dead."

I shivered. "I don't feel so well." And then everything went black.

I woke, sitting in a chair at the table. Spencer was on his knees, holding my hands and blowing gently in my face. "There you are," he said. "You went out for a while. I'd get you some water, but I don't want to destroy evidence."

"Oh." A wave of nausea hit me. Spencer caressed the fleshy spot between my thumb and forefinger and spoke softly.

"You're just fine, Gladie. Your reaction is completely normal. Breathe deeply. You'll feel stronger in a moment. Don't look over there. Look at me. That's right. That's it."

Spencer's eyes were big, filled with concern for me. The Al Qaeda of penises had a sensitive streak after all. I had the strongest desire to nestle my head in the crook of his shoulder and let him pet all of me. "I'm fine," I said.

I dared a peek at the corpse. "He doesn't smell," I noted. "I thought they're supposed to smell."

"I figure he's only been dead a few hours. I have to call this in. Don't touch anything."

I focused away from Jimmy the Fink's body while Spencer called the coroner's office. I couldn't help but notice the stack of mail on the table. Jimmy wasn't talking anymore, and he probably wasn't Randy Terns' murderer, since he had been murdered himself. Perhaps my only chance of gleaning insight into the murders and the whereabouts of Chuck Costas was in Jimmy's mail. The envelopes were open, so, it wouldn't technically be a federal crime if I borrowed them. Besides, Jimmy the Fink didn't need his mail anymore. I was really doing a service for the cleanup crew, I figured. I slipped them into my purse a second before Spencer whipped around to face me.

"Did you touch something?"

"No," I lied. I coughed and sputtered and sweat rolled down the side of my face. I stood up. "Look, I have to go home and work. I've taken off way too much time today. Love calls, you know."

He put his hand on my shoulder. "You're not going anywhere, Pinkie, until my men arrive and we get this wrapped up. Sit down."

"Hands up, punk!"

The super crashed through the open door, the biggest gun I had ever seen in his trembling hands, his finger on the trigger. Spencer didn't lose his cool.

"Whoa, buddy," he said, calmly. "Take it easy."

"I will not take it easy. Get your hands off the girl before I blow a hole through your middle so big they'll be able to drive trucks through it."

Spencer removed his hand from my shoulder. "It's not what it looks like. I'm a cop. Let me show you my badge."

But the super wasn't listening. Instead, he was looking down at Jimmy the Fink's corpse. "What'd you do to Jimmy? Jesus Christ, you got a gun!" Spencer had reached for his badge but in doing so, had revealed his sidearm.

"Sir, I'm a cop. I'm the chief of police. Let me show you my badge."

"Is that true?" The question was directed to me.

"Well . . . ," I said, shrugging.

This seemed to be the answer the super was looking for.

"Freeze! Don't move a muscle," he shouted at Spencer.

"May I go now? I'm not feeling very well," I said. And just like that, I left the room, the super's gun pointed at Spencer's head, Jimmy the Fink dead on the floor, and Jimmy's mail stuffed in my purse. In a few minutes the police would arrive and everything would be settled. In the meantime, was my presence really necessary?

I hopped in Spencer's car and drove home.

I PARKED Spencer's car down the block from my grandmother's house and walked the rest of the way. Despite the heat of the afternoon, I was chilly and exhausted. The reality of seeing my first dead body hit me hard. In the adrenaline-filled moment of investigating a murder, I had forgotten about the humanity of the lifeless form on the floor of that room. Now it was rushing back at me, and I felt light-headed and weak.

Grandma's parlor was quiet for a change. She met me at the door, taking my hands in hers. "There, there," she said. "You've had quite a day. There's fried chicken, mashed potatoes, and macaroni and cheese for dinner with peach pie à la mode for dessert. That will pick you up."

"Thank you, Grandma," I said. My eyes welled up and a few tears rolled down my cheeks.

"And we have company," she added. "He's such a nice young man. I think you've met." We walked into the kitchen, and the man rose from his seat at the table to greet us.

"Yes, I have had the pleasure of meeting your grand-daughter. Gladie, how nice to see you again."

Holden was dressed in a button-front shirt, worn Levi's, and work boots. He was tall and took up a lot of space in my grandma's kitchen, but he looked like he belonged there, like the house was built around him. The evening light shined through the windows, high-lighting him like a saintly figure in a cathedral. An image of Holden dressed as Sir Galahad flashed through my mind. Only a few hours before he had saved me from Peter Terns. My very own Sir Galahad, and I hadn't thanked him.

Here he was now in my grandmother's kitchen, per-haps to save me from the rest of my day. His eyes fo-cused on me with caring, concern, and something else. Attraction. Or maybe hunger. I was hungry, too. The fried chicken smell was awfully strong. But I didn't think it was the aroma that had Holden's appetite up. His eyes flicked to my cleavage, and his eyes grew dark. My breath hitched.

"Thank you," I told Grandma. What better to go

with all my favorite comfort foods than a man I wanted to melt into and forget my troubles?

"Holden brought the food," Grandma said. "Wasn't that kind? A man who brings mashed potatoes is a keeper." She smiled big and gently slapped Holden's cheek. He gave me a crooked smile.

"We were talking outside earlier, and your grandmother mentioned you might need a good meal," he explained.

We ate dinner together. Me in my red dress, Holden in his rugged Levi's, and Grandma in her pink faux Galliano off-the-shoulder gown and blue-feathered hat with black lace veil. We didn't discuss the police, dead people, or even matchmaking but stuck to cozy subjects like Paul Newman movies, old roller coasters versus new roller coasters, and Grandma's roses. It was comfortable, easy, with an undercurrent coming from Holden that made me warm all over.

After dinner I walked Holden to the door, and he took my hand. "Thanks for a beautiful evening," he said.

"My grandmother likes you."

Holden chuckled. "After I promised not to dig up her roses, she positively loves me. Do you think we can do this again?"

"Dinner with my grandma?"

"Dinner with you, just you and me. Maybe you could wear this dress again." He slipped a finger under my shoulder strap and ran it over my shoulder. My body went warm. My throat constricted.

There was a reason we weren't supposed to be standing so close, but I couldn't think of what it could be. There was a reason I shouldn't allow him to kiss me, but I couldn't think of what that could be, either. Too late. He bent down, an unmistakable look in his eyes, his lips centimeters from mine. I closed my eyes and felt the electricity between us as he grew closer.

"Leftovers!" Grandma's voice sang out. She skipped into the parlor, carrying a large package. "I'm so glad I caught you. Boy, you take a long time to say goodbye. Oh, Gladie, you look flushed. Maybe you should go upstairs and lie down." She handed the package to Holden. "There you go. Perfect for your lunch tomorrow."

Holden left with a handshake and his package of leftovers.

"Grandma, you're bad for my sex life," I said.

"That's the first time anybody has ever said that to me, dolly." She was wide-eyed innocence with a devilish grin.

I should have thanked her. It wouldn't do to kiss my first client. Besides, I was completely exhausted. I took a quick shower, put on my comfiest sweats, and fell asleep as soon as my head hit the pillow.

The good thing about having two sexy men enter your life is the dreams they provoke. That night I had a stellar dream about Spencer and Holden. They were naked, and I was eating ice cream. They pleaded with me to choose one of them. I pointed and did the eenie-meenie-miney-moe routine, even though I knew which one I would pick.

"Don't scream."

His voice was calm and quiet, but gravelly. The images of my dream disappeared, leaving me half awake, cuddled under the covers of my bed, lying on my side in a fetal position. I squirmed, trying to get back to sleep. That's when I realized I wasn't alone.

"No, don't scream."

My eyes fluttered open. Lying next to me on his side was Spencer. Our noses nearly touched. His sleepy eyes watched me with great interest.

"I'm going to scream," I said.

"Don't scream."

"The scream is bubbling up in the back of my throat."

"Hold it back. Swallow it."

"It's too big. I can't stop it. Here it comes."

"Gladie, do not scream," Spencer said in his best cop voice.

"Hey, this is my bed. You're in my bed," I said, stating the obvious.

"It's nice," he said. "The mattress is a little soft for my taste, though."

"Spencer, get out of my bed."

"Not just yet. We have unfinished business."

"Yep, I really think I'm going to scream."

"If you scream, you'll wake up your grandma."

"What time is it?"

"Four-thirty."

I had a sudden realization about my morning breath and put the blanket over my mouth. "What are you doing here?" I asked.

"Well, for starters, you stole my car."

"I parked it down the street."

"With the keys in it. Very thoughtful. It was a miracle it was still there. Grand theft auto aside, you almost got me shot. The super had his gun to my head for twenty minutes. I should throw your little behind in jail."

As much as I was thrilled he thought my behind was little, I was tired of our early morning chat.

"This is breaking and entering," I pointed out.

He pulled the blanket down away from my face. "You want to call the cops?" he asked. "Seriously, you need to listen to me. Stay away from this case. Randy Terns' gang members are serious business."

"It's down to one gang member," I reminded him.

"All the more reason to stay away. Whoever's out there is impatient and making things move fast. If you get in his way, he may not like it."

I chewed the side of my cheek. Spencer knocked gently on my head.

"Am I getting through to you? Are you going to back off? Curiosity killed the cat, you know. Aren't you supposed to be fixing up people? Doesn't that keep you busy enough?"

"Business is slow."

He arched an eyebrow, and his lips curved up in his signature smirk. "You didn't answer me, Gladie. Are you going to back off?"

"Uh . . ."

"Look, as far as you're concerned, this case is over. So, say goodbye, adios, au revoir, ciao, sayonara, baby."

"How did we get on the It's a Small World ride?"

Spencer rolled his eyes. "I promise you'll be the first to know when I find out anything." He kicked his shoes off the bed and turned onto his stomach. "I'm beat. I was up all night processing the scene. If I play my cards right, I can get three hours in before I have to go back to work."

"You're not sleeping here in bed with me."

"Fine, you can go. I need some sleep."

Spencer's breathing grew deep. I gave him a shove. "Spencer, how was Jimmy the Fink killed?" I asked.

"Undetermined. Waiting on a tox report. Go to sleep. And don't snore."

"You have to go. I'm serious." Spencer yawned and punched his pillow.

"Is that what you normally wear to bed?" he asked. I pulled the blanket closer to me.

"Did you look under the covers?"

"Just a peek," he muttered.

I gave him another shove, but he was dead to the world. I closed my eyes, but sleep was hard in coming. Something Spencer said would not leave my brain. Randy's gang meant business. Tomorrow was Sunday, and I knew what I had to do.

Chapter 8

✦ ♥ ✦

I'm going to tell you a little story. Once upon a time, I was a little girl, and I wanted a candy bar real bad. In those days a candy bar only cost five cents, if you can imagine. But needless to say, I didn't have five cents, and my mother didn't have nickels to throw away on my sweet tooth. So. I got a feeling that Mr. Smith at the corner drugstore would be in a really good mood if I went to visit him with my mom's friend Mavis Brady and see if he had any extra candy bars lying around. I don't know where the feeling came from, but I decided to listen to that feeling. I snuck out of the house, dragged Mavis from her ironing job, schlepped us down to the store, and wouldn't you know it but Mr. Smith's face lit up when he saw me. "Little girl," he said, "this is your lucky day." And he gave me thirteen candy bars to eat while he asked Mavis all about life as an ironing lady. Dolly, it was a good thing I listened to that feeling. Some say it's listening to your gut or your heart. You're asking now, "Grandma, what does this have to do with matchmaking?" Well, Mr. Smith had had a secret crush on Mavis but never worked up the nerve to talk to her. She became Mrs. Smith, they had four children, and she never ironed again. What I tell you is to just listen to your feeling. It comes in handy. But don't do like I did. I ate all thirteen candy bars at once and was sick for two days. Blech. I still can't look at chocolate the same way.

Lesson 8,
Matchmaking Advice from Your Grandma Zelda

* * *

I WOKE up before Spencer. We lay glued together, my head on his shoulder, his arm wrapped around me, my left leg draped over his hard belly. I was horrified and clueless on how to extricate myself from the embarrassing position when he woke. His eyes popped open, and he took stock of his place on my bed. He stretched and removed my leg like he was removing lint from his shirt and this sort of thing happened to him all the time.

"Morning," he said. Rubbing his eyes, he swung his legs over the side of the bed and put on his shoes. "Thanks for the bed. I got to go to the office for a few hours."

"You want some breakfast?" I asked, and hated myself for my good manners.

"Thanks, Pinkie, but I need to finish up some reports before the baseball game. I don't want my Sunday to be a total wash."

I had forgotten it was Sunday. What a crazy week I'd had. The death toll was rising, and I wasn't any closer to figuring out who had murdered Randy Terns or matching my neighbor. I walked Spencer to the door. He stopped at the threshold. Smirking, he patted my hair.

"Do your worst, Spencer," I said. "Go ahead. Give me your wisecracks. I can take it. I know what my hair looks like in the morning." It usually stood straight out in spiky curls about a foot from my head. Spencer's hair was perfect, just slightly mussed, but still thick and wavy, a wet dream of hair.

"I kind of like it," he said, his fingers weaving through my hair. "I like the unwashed look on women. You look like we did something other than sleep in your bed."

I was distracted by movement in the corner of my eye. Holden walked over my grandmother's lawn, his attention on the scene in our doorway. I couldn't read his facial expression. Whether distressed, angry, or jealous, it didn't matter. It wasn't good. I held back an almost compulsive desire to run to him and stick my tongue down his throat and explain that no matter what it looked like, I didn't have sex with Spencer.

After staring at Holden a few seconds, I allowed my eyes to wander back to Spencer. He smiled right at me, as if he could read my dirty thoughts. I blushed beet red and looked at the floor.

"I see," Spencer said. "Fair enough." He removed his fingers from my hair and nodded to Holden. "Just remember what I said, Gladie. Stick to matchmaking and your friend over there. Stay out of my business. We got a deal?"

"Fair enough," I said. I was getting good at lying to Spencer. It was almost fun.

Spencer walked down the front steps to the walkway, but Holden blocked his path. I could feel the testosterone build, a macho force field between them. They couldn't be more different. One was light while the other was dark, one was borderline metrosexual while the other would be more at home at a lumberjack convention. But they were evenly matched, Holden a couple of inches taller, Spencer about ten more pounds of muscle. Spencer said something to him, and Holden's face relaxed, but he didn't move. Spencer walked around Holden, giving him a wide berth, and walked toward his car.

"What did he say to you?" I called out to Holden across the distance. He arched an eyebrow and walked quickly toward me, a determined look in his eye. He made up the distance between us, pushing me against the doorjamb, his body leaning into mine.

"I like trouble," he said, his voice brushing against

my lips. My knees buckled, and I held on to him for support.

"He said that?"

"No, I did," said Holden. He pulled me hard against him and captured my mouth with his. The kiss was long and deep. My head spun, and I saw rainbow-colored shapes behind my closed eyelids. It was like a Grateful Dead concert, but instead of music, my body was humming rather loudly.

"HE SAID that?"

"Yes, he said he liked trouble and then kissed me."

I sat at the desk in the attic and shuffled blank index cards while I was on the phone with Bridget. I had called her immediately after Holden left.

"Then what happened?" she asked.

"Then he asked me out to dinner tonight, and he went home."

"What did you say?"

"About what?"

"About dinner."

"I think I said yes."

"You're not sure?"

"I think I had a little stroke."

"Was the kiss that good?" asked Bridget.

"Yes."

Bridget whistled. "You've got it bad."

"I know. Grandma is going to be so disappointed in me. My first client."

"That's not important now. How tall is he?"

"About six foot four."

"Good-looking?"

"Bridget, I had a stroke, remember?"

"Okay, he's good-looking. Well, I think you should jump him," Bridget said matter-of-factly. "You shouldn't be penned in by Judeo-Christian ethics that were made up by misogynistic men millennia ago."

"He's a perfect stranger," I said. "I don't know why he kissed me. I told him I had someone perfect for him. I guess he doesn't think I'm a good matchmaker."

"Yes, that must be it," said Bridget, her patience wearing thin. "Wait till Lucy hears this. We need to set up an emergency lunch, but she's out of town today. She tried reaching you all evening yesterday, by the way."

"I was busy. And my cellphone died, and Grandma decided to store all the plugs, wires, and chargers in the bread box. She says it's safer that way. What a nightmare. Wires everywhere. It took me an hour to find the plug to the coffeemaker last week, but on the plus side, I did find the remote control to the VCR. Grandma's behind on technology."

"Gladie, you're drifting," Bridget said. She didn't know the half of it. I had drifted far out. I was a polar bear on a sliver of ice.

"I know," I said. "What did Lucy want?"

"She wanted to know what happened with the hunky police chief. Oh, crap. Gladie, what happened with the hunky police chief?"

"Nothing. Well . . ."

Bridget's breathing grew ragged. "Well, what? Well, what?"

"We might have found a dead body." And we slept together. I didn't want to get into that, let alone Jimmy the Fink and Randy Terns' gang. My head was swimming.

"No way!" Bridget screeched. "You're the mysterious woman!"

"I'm the what?"

"The mysterious woman. It was on the news. A mysterious woman fled a murder scene."

I gasped and choked on my spit. "Did they say it was murder?"

"I don't remember. There was a dead body. But listen, they described you, hair and all."

An icy feeling of dread crept up my body.

"You know what that means, Gladie? It means the killer knows who you are."

"I need coffee," I said.

"All right."

"I need coffee," I said, louder, my voice an octave higher than normal.

"All right. Get some coffee, and then meet me at Saint Andrew's. You can volunteer with me today. It will get your mind off things, and you can tell me about the dead body and the live bodies."

I put the phone down and gathered the blank index cards that I had scattered over the desk in my nervousness. Since I'd effectively gotten rid of my first client by dating him myself, I didn't need the cards for matchmaking. Instead, I found myself jotting down a name on each card. By the time I finished, I had a card for every member of Randy Terns' family and his gang. Any of them could have murdered Randy and Jimmy, except for maybe Jimmy, who was dead.

I wrote down what I knew about them. Peter, Jane, and Christy all had prison records. Peter seemed the most violent, with sexual assault. I had gotten a taste of his temper, and I had the bruises on my arm to prove it. Christy was a drug addict. It was completely possible for her to commit a criminal act while under the influence. Jane was a mystery—she seemed odd and bitter, but harmless enough if you didn't count maiming Barbies. And what about Betty? Wasn't it usually the spouse who did it? It was a stretch to imagine skinny little Betty taking on her husband, let alone Jimmy the Fink, but stranger things were known to happen.

Speaking of Jimmy the Fink, the gang angle was the most obvious. If Randy had hidden away money from his former partners, that would be a strong motive for murder. But why had they waited so long after the bank robbery to come looking for Randy?

By the time I finished, I had index cards spread out over the desk, but I was no closer to solving the murders. "What am I playing at? I'm no detective, and now I've made a mess," I said out loud. I gathered the cards together into a file folder I marked "Terns" and slipped it in Grandma's file cabinet between Sadie Symons and Joseph Thomas. Poor Sadie Symons. She was one of Grandma's failures, dumped by the seemingly perfect Dr. Marchi with a Dear John letter, written in iambic pentameter.

I shut the file cabinet, and my brain cells fired all at once. How stupid was I? How could I have forgotten? I had Jimmy the Fink's mail in my purse. I rifled through it quickly and found what I was looking for.

"THE BIGGEST cappuccino you've ever made." I slapped my Visa card down on Ruth's bar.

"You promised you were going Earl Grey," she said with a scowl. "How much patience do you think I have? I don't have long to live, you know."

"Please, Ruth," I said. "I need coffee. I've been going through a very rough patch."

"Look at these people," Ruth said with a sweep of her hand toward her store. Tea Time was packed with *New York Times*–reading patrons, sitting leisurely at her antique tables. "Half of them are drinking lattes. Lattes. Don't you people know that coffee kills? A cup of tea soothes. When you were sick, what did your momma give you? Did she give you a cappuccino? No. She gave you a nice cup of tea."

"My mother?" I said. "When I was sick, she told me to think happy thoughts and run down to the store to get her a pack of smokes. Please, Ruth, the coffee."

Ruth grunted and moaned, but she relented and gave me the world's biggest cappuccino in a to-go cup. It was heaven. Almost as good as Holden's kiss, but with fewer repercussions.

I was about to leave when there was a thunderous crash at a nearby table. A slight young woman, no bigger than a ten-year-old boy, had dropped a teapot, breaking four china cups and sending three customers scattering, probably with third-degree burns.

"That girl," Ruth muttered.

"Is she a new waitress?" I asked.

"My grandniece, Julie. Nice enough, but skittish as all get-out. She can't even go into the supply closet. Claustrophobia, you see."

I gave Julie a good look. She was petite like a Kewpie doll, with striking blue eyes and long red hair pulled back in a knot. I heard a *ding ding ding* sound in my head. Suddenly I had a feeling. I knew who would make Julie happy. It happened just like that. I had graduated. I was going to make my first match.

I ached to stay behind and speak with her, but I had promised Bridget I would meet her for lunch. Besides, I had things to take care of, and Julie looked like she would be single for a while longer.

I drove the couple of miles to Saint Andrew's Shelter just north of the historic district, near the old mine on Farmer Way. The shelter for battered women was set back at the end of a narrow dirt road that wound through the forest, providing much-needed privacy for the women, who came from all over the Southwest to escape their abusive relationships. It was one of Bridget's many causes.

The shelter was a compound of several buildings, all

one-story and painted white and cheery. The center of the compound was open, with a playground for the children and tables and chairs for the women to meet and have their meals when the weather was good.

Today was gorgeous, and it seemed that all the residents of the shelter were outside enjoying the day. I had been there before, and Sister Cyril, the den mother, recognized me and welcomed me with a bear hug.

"Thrilled you're here," she said. "Just in time for lunch. If Bridget ever takes a breath."

Bridget was speaking to a group of around twenty women who were fingering their boxed lunches longingly as they politely listened to her diatribe.

"The inequalities of the sexes. You're living proof of its existence," she yelled. "You must turn to yourselves for help, not the patriarchal church that runs this place."

Sister Cyril patted my arm. "Come and have a seat," she said. "I'd love for you to meet Sarah. She's new, and I think you two will get along real well."

Sarah was in her forties. She had a cute bobbed haircut—and a huge shiner on her left eye. I took a seat next to her.

"I'm Gladie," I said.

"I know. Sister Cyril told me all about you. All about your grandmother, in any case. She's on some kind of committee with her. I've never met her."

"She doesn't get out of her house much," I explained.

"I was like that," said Sarah. "My husband never let me leave the house." She shrugged and touched her black eye.

Bridget's voice reached a crescendo. She shook her fist at the sky. "Rules! They talk about rules! Do we live in Abu Ghraib or something?"

Sister Cyril leaned over and whispered in my ear. "We all love Bridget. She's one of our best volunteers, but she's been going on for an hour and a half. It's egg salad sandwiches for lunch today. I'm afraid they're going to turn and I'm going to wind up with a group of battered women suffering from food poisoning. We need to get on to lunch." She fixed me with a pleading look I couldn't resist.

I got up and shuffled over to Bridget, carefully avoiding her swinging arms, which she used to punctuate her speech on the everyday abuses of women in society.

"Psst, Bridget," I said. "I'm here. I need to talk to you about the body."

I startled her, and it took a moment for her to recognize me, but once her eyes focused, she smiled. "Oh, good," she said. "I've been waiting for you. Hey, you look great. Lucy told me she found your stash of nice clothes. Nice dress."

I looked down. I was wearing a black and white wrap dress. I had forgotten to go back to my normal clothes.

We sat down with Sarah to eat our egg salad sandwiches. With her there, Bridget and I had to hold off on discussing Jimmy the Fink. "Where are you from, Sarah?" I asked.

"She's not allowed to say," said Bridget. "It's all top secret here to protect the women."

"Oh, sorry."

Sarah wiped her face with her napkin. "Don't worry about it. I forget the rules, too. I'm just happy to be here, away from Don."

"Was that your husband?" I asked.

"Yes. We were married for twenty years. You're wondering why I stayed with him all those years." She was right. That was exactly what I was wondering. "I didn't have a choice."

"But you did leave," said Sister Cyril, taking a seat at our table.

"Yes. If I had stayed, he would have killed me for

sure." Sarah's eyes darted toward the nun, and her cheeks flamed red. Sister Cyril patted her hand.

"It's okay, Sarah. You have nothing to be ashamed of. You did the right thing."

"I had an affair," Sarah blurted out. "No one had been nice to me in so many years, and Jeff was so kind to me."

Sister Cyril supplied the rest of the story. "Don found out about you and Jeff, and now you're here."

Sarah sniffed, and a tear rolled down her cheek. "Excuse me," she said. She jumped up and scooted away. Sister Cyril was fast on her heels. I heard her give Sarah some words of comfort as they retreated back into the main building.

"Don killed Jeff," Bridget said.

"What?"

"Sarah's husband killed her lover. He found out about it and beat him to death with a hammer."

I gasped and choked on my egg salad. "That's horrible."

"He had locked her up all those years, and she wound up falling in love with the exterminator. They had a monthly service, you see. Her husband didn't want her betraying him by having a life outside the house, and when she managed to have a life without him, all the while locked up in the house, well, he went crazier than he already was."

"Geez, what's wrong with the world? Everybody is killing everybody else all of a sudden."

"I'm pretty sure murder has been around for a while, Gladie. As long as men have been around. Tell me about your dead body."

I told her about Uncle Harry, stealing Spencer's car, and discovering the body. I skipped the part where Spencer and I slept together. I didn't think that was need-to-know information for the moment.

"How dare he tell you not to get involved," Bridget said. "Who does he think is?"

"The police chief," I reasoned.

"No, he thinks he's a man, and he doesn't want a helpless female sticking her hysterical nose in. But this is public information, Gladie. You have just as much right as anyone else to look into these murders. You're only doing it for the welfare of our town."

"I am?"

"Yes, you are. Spencer Bolton may be the hottest thing to walk on two legs, but he's not worth his salt. I heard all about him from Bird Gonzalez when I got my hair done yesterday. Did you know he is so shallow he weighs his girlfriends every morning?"

As much as I loved the image of him weighing his girlfriends, I thought Bird had exaggerated Spencer's shallowness just a tad.

"I'm not going to quit looking into Randy Terns' gang," I told Bridget, "but not because Spencer is a sexist. I have more information, and I'm in this thing too deep. If the killer knows who I am, I can't afford to wait for the Cannes police department to get around to catching him. Hell, they haven't even ruled it a murder yet."

Bridget nodded.

"I need your help," I said, pulling out Jimmy's mail from my purse. "I need you to hang on to this for me for a while. I'm not ready for the police to see it yet."

Bridget opened up the bank statements and skimmed them.

"Jimmy the Fink was depositing a tidy sum every month in addition to his Social Security check," I told her. "Bridget, I think he was blackmailing Randy Terns."

"This is big," Bridget said. "Jimmy was blackmailing Randy? You've got motive right here. But for who?

Jimmy killed Randy because why? Because he wouldn't pay anymore? Then who killed Jimmy?"

"I don't know. Maybe the other one, Chuck Costas. I have to talk to Uncle Harry again. Spencer said something to me. He said the gang meant business. It got me to thinking. Uncle Harry is all business, and I'm sure he would make it his business to know more about Randy and his gang than he let on."

THIRTY MINUTES later, Uncle Harry's door opened, this time by Uncle Harry himself instead of his butler. I threw a handful of dog biscuits inside to calm his dogs.

"How you doin', Legs?" He greeted me with a kiss on my cheek and let me into his living room.

"I forgot something," I told him.

"Yeah? What was that?" Spencer came into view, his arms folded in front of him with an expression on his face that said I had been a naughty girl. Was he following me or something? The man was constantly stomping on my territory.

"Do you have a room here or what?" I asked, annoyed.

Spencer scowled. "Never mind that. What did you forget? A lipstick? A book? What?"

"Uncle Harry," I said, making a point to ignore Spencer. "I forgot to ask you something. Did Randy Terns speak to you recently, before he died? Did he tell you he was scared?"

Chapter 9

✦ ♥ ✦

In the words of Lady Gaga, "I don't wanna be friends." We're not matching friends. If you want friendship, join a bridge group. We're making romance. There's no friendship in romance. Sure, later on, when they're discussing mortgages, college funds, and where to go to dinner, then a little friendship goes a long way. But that comes later. Now, it's romance. Don't know what romance is? Just like porn, you'll know it when you see it.

Lesson 14,
Matchmaking Advice from Your Grandma Zelda

UNCLE HARRY poured himself a drink and took a seat on his extra-deep, extra-plush white couch.

"Did Randy Terns tell you he was scared?" I repeated. "Perhaps he was being blackmailed?"

"She's better than you, Spencer," Uncle Harry said. "Spencer didn't guess about the blackmailing."

I exhaled. It was a wonderful feeling, being right. I was vindicated somehow, like I was finally good at something. I helped myself to Uncle Harry's bar, popped off the top of a Corona, and took a long swig. I felt Spencer's eyes on me, trying to read me, trying to figure out how I had guessed blackmail.

"Randy Terns was a scared man in general," Uncle Harry said. "I think he was scared about a lot of things, but honestly, I don't know what they were."

"But he was being blackmailed?" Spencer asked.

"Yes. Randy was being blackmailed, and he wanted to find his gang."

We let that information settle for a minute. Randy had been after his old gang. But Randy had never found Jimmy, or if he had, he'd left Jimmy alive and well.

"But you didn't help Randy," I said. "You didn't tell him where Jimmy was."

Uncle Harry downed the last of his drink. "I did one better. I pretended to help him, pretended I was looking for his old gang. But I would never have told Randy where to find Jimmy the Fink or Chuck Costas. I didn't trust that Randy just wanted to talk, and contrary to popular belief, I don't condone murder. Even if they were blackmailing Randy, I didn't think Jimmy and Chuck needed to die over a few bucks, a few bucks that they had earned, really."

"Did you think Randy Terns was capable of murder?" I asked.

"I don't know, but anybody who dresses as a tree to rob a bank is erratic at best, if you know what I mean. He could have done anything."

"How long did you keep pretending?"

"Not long. Randy was dead a week after he came to me."

I gasped. Randy had been noisy about finding his former colleagues. Maybe they had found him before he found them. Maybe they had objected to the change in plan regarding the blackmail. Perhaps I had stumbled on the motive for Randy's murder. "Do you think Chuck Costas, the third gang member, killed him?" I asked.

"It's a possibility."

"Are you really looking for Chuck Costas or are you pretending?"

"You'll have to wait and see, Legs."

* * *

"IT WOULD be safer if you just offered yourself to Harry's Rottweilers for lunch."

Spencer had followed me out to my car. I put my key in the lock and opened the door with a loud creak.

"I'll think about it," I said.

Spencer scowled. I could see him debating with himself whether to arrest me again.

"It's not like I'm going after the third gang member," I said. *At least not until Uncle Harry tells me where he is.* "Besides, I've got work to do. I've figured out a match, and I need to handle it."

Spencer's face relaxed. "Good. Just put this whole thing out of your mind."

"That's what I plan on doing. I'm going to work, try to start drinking tea, and go to the memorial on Wednesday."

He put his hand out, palm toward me. "Wait, don't do that. You should stay clear of the Terns family. Randy wasn't the only one who was a little loopy. His kids all have a screw or two loose."

"I'll be careful. They seem pretty harmless, though," I said.

"That may very well be, but people have been dropping dead, and I would prefer you weren't one of them."

"You said that with a straight face."

Spencer shrugged and smirked.

"You beginning to like me, Spencer?"

"Let's just say I hate paperwork."

I slipped into my Cutlass Supreme and turned on the motor. "Do me a favor," I called out over the roar of my V-8. "Let me know how Jimmy the Fink died, when you find out."

"I could do that."

* * *

I WAS lying about putting the murders out of mind. And I was lying about trying to love tea. But I was telling the truth about getting to work. I was on my way back to Tea Time to sign up my first matchmaking client. Grandma was right. It had come to me in a flash that morning, and I knew for sure just how to match Ruth's niece, Julie.

The day was heating up. I rolled down Main Street, looking for a parking spot, and almost crashed when I spotted Betty Terns coming out of the drugstore. It was the first time I had seen her away from her house, and it startled me. I had somehow assumed she was like my grandmother, forever close to home.

Betty wore a forty-year-old pink suit in perfect condition—it wouldn't have looked out of place on Mamie Eisenhower. She clutched her purse like it was going to fly away.

I parallel-parked perfectly in a space three inches too short for my car and bolted down the sidewalk after her.

"Betty!" I called. She continued walking, even picking up the pace. I ran after her in my heels on the cobblestone walk, praying I wouldn't break a bone.

"Betty!" I called again, finally reaching her and tapping her on the shoulder. She turned around slowly. Her eyes squinted at me, her mouth turned down in frustration. No, not frustration. Anger. But then in an instant, her face brightened into the most welcoming smile.

"Gladie," she gushed, "what a wonderful surprise."

"I'm so glad I caught you. Would you like to get some iced tea with me? My treat."

Betty looked around, as if waiting for another person to appear with a better offer, but she nodded. "Sure. I would love to. It's warm today."

Tea Time had calmed down since the morning. Only two other customers were in the place; they were sitting at a table, pouring black tea from light blue miniature teapots.

"Again? And you expect me to serve you here?" Ruth sidled up to our table carrying a rag, which she had been using to wipe down the bar.

"Two peach iced teas. Extra ice," I ordered, cutting off her rant.

Ruth stumbled backward. "Tea? Are you sure? Did I hear you correctly?"

It was the closest to vulnerable I'd ever seen her.

"Yes," I said. "I've been dreaming about your peach iced tea all day."

"I'll bring you some scones, too. On the house."

Ruth practically skipped back to the bar. Betty studied her surroundings. She picked up the lace doilies off the plates and put them back down. She fingered the silver napkin holders with nothing short of wonder.

"Have you been to Tea Time before?" I asked.

"Oh, no. Randy and I were homebodies. He liked my cooking better than the restaurants, and we didn't like the movies on account of the language. Why do they have to use such words to get their point across?"

Shit if I know, was what I was thinking, but I said, "They don't make them like they used to."

Ruth arrived with the iced tea and scones. She beamed, her mouth curled up in a smile that made her unrecognizable and a little scary.

"Taste that and tell me it's not the best thing that's ever passed your lips," she ordered. We took sips and gave her the accolades she sought.

"Where's your grandniece?" I asked Ruth.

"Getting stitches."

"Stitches?"

"That damned girl. Her arm can be fixed, but not my

antique blue willow china. Service for sixteen. What are the odds on breaking the whole lot at one time?"

"Astronomical, I would think," I said.

"My sister made me take on that girl. 'All she needs is a chance,' she said. I'm going to be chanced right out of business by that tsunami on legs." Ruth pointed her finger at my nose. "I'll give you some words of wisdom free of charge. Family sucks. Don't let anybody tell you different."

"She's usually much nicer," I told Betty after Ruth left.

"She's wrong, you know," Betty said.

"Don't I know it. Coffee is much better than tea."

"I meant her comment about family. Family is wonderful. My family is wonderful. They've brought me only joy in my life."

Either Betty was mixing up her family with someone else's or Ruth had put something extra in her iced tea.

"Is that so? That's so nice," I said. "I've had the pleasure of speaking to a couple of your children. They seem very devoted."

She looked past me, as if seeing a scene play out in the empty room.

"They are devoted, each in their own way," she said.

I took a big breath. "They mentioned that maybe Randy's death might not have been an accident."

Betty snapped to attention. "Suicide? Oh, no. No. Randy was very happy. Not a care in the world."

"Well, they didn't mention suicide, actually."

"What else could it be?" Betty took my hand in hers. "You have been very kind to me. You've been such a source of comfort in my grief."

Suddenly it was hard to swallow. I had a big lump of guilt blocking my throat. I tried to speak, but I squeaked instead, and tears welled up in my eyes.

"You are such a sweet girl, feeling that way for me

and my poor Randy," she said, mistaking my guilt for heartfelt emotion. "You're so pretty. I didn't see it at first, but you are. Real pretty. I used to be pretty."

"You're still pretty."

Betty pounded the table with a swipe of her fist. "I have stayed the same weight for the past forty-five years, except for the times I was pregnant. How many women can say that?"

"Certainly not me. That's admirable."

"I shrugged off the baby weight within a month. Each time. How many women can say that?"

"Certainly not me." I giggled, but Betty was all seriousness.

"Randy wasn't concerned about my weight. He thought I was just fine and told me I didn't need to watch my figure as much, but I did. I did it for him. I took my wifely duties very seriously, Gladie. I believed in my vows. They were given in front of God, after all."

I touched her hand. "Of course you believed in your vows. You were a wonderful wife. You were a lovely couple." It was a stretch, but I thought she could use some cheering up.

"Thank you. Well, I've got to go." She stood up, our conversation seemingly forgotten. She patted her purse. "Just came from the pharmacy. The doctors have me on so many pills. I have to take one and go to sleep." It was a curt dismissal, and it threw me, considering the emotional conversation we were having.

"Oh, okay." I stood and shook her hand.

"Perhaps we can do this again sometime. Maybe lunch."

"My treat," I said. What was I saying? I had no money, and Betty hadn't gone out to eat in forty years. She was probably sleeping on half a million dollars under her mattress.

Fifteen minutes alone with Betty, and I had made no

headway into her husband's possible murder. I hadn't wanted to upset her any further, and my empathy made the experience a thorough waste of time. Betty hadn't even eaten her scone. What a crime that was. I grabbed it from her plate and took a bite. Delicious and well worth the calories. Besides, how many calories could a scone have?

I finished eating and dusted the crumbs off my chest. Tea Time was abandoned except for me. I found Ruth in the back, counting tea balls.

"How many calories in a scone, Ruth? One hundred? A hundred and fifty?"

"The kind I gave you? Around five hundred."

I gasped. "Five hundred calories? Five hundred *American* calories?"

"Look at me," she said. "Do I look like I speak Hungarian calories or something? Five hundred American calories."

"For a chocolate chip scone?" I asked.

"Did I give you a chocolate chip scone? Oh, for heaven's sake. Sorry. The chocolate chip ones are five hundred and fifty calories."

"I ate two!" I touched my stomach to see if it had grown.

"Stop whining," Ruth said. "There isn't an ounce of fat anywhere on you. Besides, you eat worse than that every day with your grandmother. I swear, that woman's a human garbage disposal." She had a point. The scones weren't any worse than chili cheese dogs. I took a couple of deep breaths and tried to focus.

"Has Julie come back?" I asked.

"You're awfully curious about my grandniece."

"She's new in town, and I thought I would be neighborly."

Ruth grunted and started on the doily count. "Wear a helmet and protective clothing while you're doing it.

Julie is a one-woman walking natural disaster. I'll tell her you're looking for her."

With my future client more elusive than I planned, I decided to go the other route and seek out her match-to-be. I had gotten halfway to my car when my cellphone rang.

"Gladie, I'm hurt."

"Grandma? Is that you?" She sounded weak and frightened, two things my grandmother never was.

"Yes, dolly. I'm hurt. Someone hurt me."

"I'll be right there." I ran to my car while I dialed 911 and then I remembered that Cannes didn't have a call center yet. My car roared to life, and I peeled out of my parking spot. I was a menace on the road, driving fifty in a twenty-five-mph zone, swerving around old ladies and poodle-walking middle-aged men. I was also illegally on my cellphone, calling information to get a number. When Spencer answered, I screamed incoherently into the phone.

"Come to my grandma's house! Hurry!" And I hung up.

I screeched into the driveway, clipping a hydrangea bush and sending pink flowers flying over my windshield. I ran into the house and found my grandmother in the kitchen, sitting at the table, eating her way through a box of Pop-Tarts. I stood for a while and took stock of the situation. She was breathing. She wasn't bleeding or lying in a coma.

"Look closer," she told me.

I sat down next to her. Sure enough, her left eye was swelling up, and a bruise was forming. "I was attacked," she said.

"Who did this to you?" I choked. Tears rolled down my cheeks, and I wiped my eyes with the hem of my dress.

"I don't know."

"You didn't see the attacker?" The question came from behind me. I whipped around. Spencer stood in the kitchen. His face was all police seriousness, even though he was wearing baggy basketball shorts, flip-flops, and a neon multi-colored baseball jersey.

"Oh, you must be Chief Bolton," said Grandma. "No, handsome, I did see the attacker. I was surprised, and I was surprised that I was surprised. Gladie, you know I'm rarely surprised."

"Grandma's never surprised," I said, sniffling.

Spencer sat at the table. "Tell us what happened."

"I was at the sink, getting myself a glass of water. The window was open, and I recall thinking how glad I was it was open on account of the lovely breeze blowing in at that moment. Then, all of a sudden, *boom!* I was smacked right in my face. Somebody threw this in and hit me right in my face. Hang on, I'll get it."

Grandma pulled a brown round blob about the size of a deck of cards out of the sink.

"It looks like—" I started.

"A knish," Grandma provided.

"You were injured by a knish?"

"A frozen knish. Potato-filled."

"What's a knish?" Spencer asked. "No, scratch that. I don't want to know. Maybe it was thrown in by accident, or a kid was playing outside."

"It was no accident," Grandma said. "I saw the top of a head right before the attack. A blond head. I think it was a woman because I smelled Shalimar. It was thrown with intent to harm."

"A blond head?" I asked.

Spencer sat up straighter. "Why? You have somebody in mind? Does that ring a bell to you?"

It rang a lot of bells. There were six blond heads across the street, capable of all kinds of weird behavior, even assault with a frozen knish.

"A lot of people are blond," I said.

Spencer's eyes narrowed.

"Why are you looking at me like that?" I pushed back my chair, putting some space between us.

He worked his jaw but stayed silent. I think my grandmother had a quieting effect on him. I tucked my arm under hers and rested my head on her shoulder. She patted my head lovingly.

"Don't worry, Gladie. The attacker was sending a message, but she won't come back," she said.

"A message?" asked Spencer. "What kind of message? A knish message? How do you know she won't be back?"

"I think the knish wasn't important. A wonton or twice-baked potato would have served the same purpose. They were trying to scare me off or scare off a loved one through me. Maybe I was an easier target."

The room fell silent. The attention was on me and with it a lot of unspoken questions. And accusations. But I didn't know who'd thrown a knish at my grandmother, and I didn't know what the message was or whether it was intended for me.

The blond head could have easily be one of the Terns heads, but both Jane and Peter had talked to me about the murder, even asking me to look into it. Perhaps they had changed their minds, or perhaps it was one of the other Terns family members. It could be that Rob wasn't as clueless as he let on. And just maybe it wasn't one of them. It was also possible that the third gang member, Chuck Costas, was blond. Grandma could have been wrong about the Shalimar, or maybe Chuck liked to smell like flowers with amber, woody accents.

Someone knew I was the mysterious woman who fled the scene of a crime, the scene of Jimmy the Fink's murder. Someone thought I knew more than I did, and whoever it was wanted to scare me through my grandmother. I shivered.

"I'm so glad you're here, Gladie dear," Grandma said, breaking the awkward silence. "Meryl is coming over to spend time with me after the incident, so I need someone to replace her."

"Replace her for what?" I asked. Meryl was the town's blue-haired librarian. She personally brought Grandma a selection of library books every Tuesday so that Grandma didn't have to venture out. But today was Sunday, and the library was closed.

"Meryl was going to do a little spying for me today," Grandma said. "I finally got Shep Smothers matched, and he's going to surprise his girl with a proposal this evening right at sunset on the rocks at the beach in San Diego. Oh, it's going to be so lovely. I need a report and photos."

"Grandma, San Diego is over an hour away."

"And you'll just make it if you leave now." The screen door slammed, and we heard someone shuffle through the house. "There's Meryl now. You'll go with Gladie, Chief Bolton. You'll come in handy."

"Uh—" Spencer began, but it was too late. Grandma had set her face. She would brook no discussion. She handed me a picnic basket from the counter.

"I prepared a picnic for you two to share during the drive," she said, and scooted us out of the house.

"You don't have to go with me," I said once we were outside.

"Get in the car."

"This is not my fault."

"Get in the car." He opened the passenger door of his car. "Watch your head," he muttered.

"It's not my fault."

He drove out of Cannes in silence. It was a beautiful drive. Grandma had thoughtfully pinned the directions to the outside of the picnic basket. Inside was an old Instamatic camera, two Reuben sandwiches from the deli, a bag of barbecue potato chips, two cans of root beer, and an apple.

"Wow, an apple," I said. "I wonder who that's for."

Spencer wasn't hungry, and neither was I. I took off my seat belt and turned around to put the basket in the back. I narrowly missed knocking Spencer in the head, and I had to do a bit of gymnastics to get it done. When I turned back around, I realized my dress had hitched up pretty high, and I caught Spencer ogling my backside. I sat back down with a thud.

"What was that?" I asked.

"What was what?"

"That. You looked up my dress."

"I did not."

"You did. I caught you looking."

"Fine. I looked."

Spencer kept his eyes forward, his mouth set in a wide smile. His dark hair was slightly mussed where he had run his fingers through it in exasperation earlier. Now, his hands were locked on the wheel at the ten-and-two position. They were large hands, made to work. Since his baseball jersey was short-sleeved, I got a good look at his forearms and a good chunk of his biceps. I wondered how much working out it took to get so muscular. I cracked my window to let in some fresh air.

"Why did you look?" I asked.

"What do you mean? I'm a man. I looked."

"Hmm . . ."

"You don't believe me? You want me to say you're my type."

"Oh, please. I am so not your type." I giggled like a little girl and flipped my hair back, hating myself instantly.

"You think you got me pegged, don't you? Heard

some things around town, have you? How do you know what my type is? You think you're like your grandmother? You know my type right off the bat? Maybe you're exactly my type. Maybe I lie awake at night thinking about you."

I had known him for seventy-two hours, and during one of those nights he had slept with me. I didn't think he spent much time lying awake thinking about anyone. Spencer stopped for a red light, turned, and stared into my eyes. He was all earnestness, unblinking, the picture of honesty. I snorted.

"Yeah, right. You're full of it," I said.

"You're right," he said after a moment. "You're not my type."

"What's your type? No, let me guess. Skinny . . . that's a given. Long legs, big fake boobs, and hair extensions."

"Commitment issues," he said.

"Excuse me?"

"Women with commitment issues, women who don't like commitment. They're my type."

I blinked. Spencer was the quintessential player. "That's disgusting."

Spencer shrugged. "You asked. Enough about me, let's talk about you. Tell me about the blond head who attacked your grandmother."

"I have no idea." It wasn't a total lie. I didn't know which blonde, but I was pretty sure I could narrow it down to a few suspects.

"You jumped on the whole blond idea in your grandmother's kitchen."

"I like blonds," I said. "Blonds are my type."

THE BEACH was crowded, but Spencer found a prime parking place in sight of the rocks where Shep

Smothers was going to propose to his girlfriend. The sun was about to set. This part of the beach, with its outcropping of large rocks, turned into a series of small tide pools when the tide was out.

"How romantic," I said. "It's the perfect place."

Spencer didn't say anything. He grabbed the basket from the backseat and tore into a Reuben. "You want one?"

I took one and opened a root beer. Spencer ate quickly and drank his root beer in three gulps. "There he is. Oh, shit. What is he wearing?" he asked.

Shep Smothers was wearing a suit. I didn't know whose suit it was, but it couldn't have been his because it was six inches too short. His legs stuck out like matchsticks covered in white tube socks with a blue stripe. His arms protruded from the jacket. In one hand he clutched something—the ring, I thought. In the other hand, he held his girlfriend's hand. She was cute. She had short red hair, freckles, and sixty additional pounds gathered around her lower body. I felt protective of the both of them. They had found each other against almost insurmountable odds. It made a person believe in the power of love.

"You ready?" Spencer handed the camera to me, and I took a couple of shots. "I can't believe what I'm seeing," he said. "Take a photo for me so I can prove it to the guys."

Spencer had a way of getting my hackles up.

"Hey, have you seen yourself, lately?" I shrieked. "Nice choice of shirts, pal. Why are you wearing that? You want aliens to spot you from space?"

Spencer looked honestly insulted. He was usually Dapper Dan, and I had caught him in a weak moment. "I was watching the game on TV when you called. I didn't have time to change. Anyway, this is a limited edition Padres Luau Celebration Collector's Jersey."

"Aren't the Padres the San Diego team?"

"Yes."

"I thought you were from L.A."

"What of it? Don't judge. Take your photos."

Shep Smothers was down on one knee, presenting the ring to his girlfriend. I took a picture just as she said yes, a big smile on her face, but before Shep could get the ring on her finger, an enormous wave came toward them. In a heartbeat, the wave hit the rock and receded, taking Shep's almost-fiancée into the ocean in a languid sweep reminiscent of water ballet.

"That wave hit just right," Spencer mumbled, obviously thinking out loud. He was right. It defied the laws of physics how waiflike Shep could have stayed on the rock, and his corpulent love was swept out to sea.

Spencer grabbed the police radio and called in the accident. He didn't need to bother. A whole army of lifeguards jumped into the water to rescue her. Spencer and I—along with a large group of tourists—ran onto the rock to see the action. Shep looked out over the water, calling to her. It was a relief to see her alive, flailing her arms, punching out lifeguard after lifeguard as they tried to save her.

"That's a common sight," Spencer said. "Drowning victims panic. She'll get tired after a while, and they'll get hold of her."

He was right. Her right hook didn't last much longer, and they managed to swim her to the beach.

"Do you have enough pictures? I have to get home," Spencer said.

"Sure."

Spencer started the car. "Was that romantic enough for you?" he asked.

* * *

SPENCER DROPPED me off at the curb in front of my grandmother's house.

"Looks like there's a party going on," he said. The lights were on in the front parlor. Undoubtedly she had summoned over the neighborhood watch group to bring their attention to the knish bandit.

"Thank you for your help today," I said.

"Are you sure you want to go in? The way we're going, I figure it's only a matter of an hour or two before we see each other again. Maybe we should tie ourselves together and call it a day."

"I'll take my chances," I said, but he had a point. It had been nonstop Spencer for two straight days. We had gone from murder to almost death so many times, I had whiplash. "No offense, but I need a break. I need quiet time."

"That's what I want to hear. Stay at home and rest. Give yourself a facial or something. Nothing exciting."

I stuck three fingers up. "Girl Scout's honor."

I watched Spencer drive away. He wasn't such a bad guy for a male chauvinist. I yawned. My bath and bed were calling to me. What a day! No murders, but emotional nonetheless. I couldn't shake the feeling that I had forgotten something, but it didn't matter now. I was too exhausted to care. I had just turned to walk up the driveway when Peter Terns' Porsche careened down the street and skidded to a halt next to me, one of his tires bumping up onto the sidewalk. The passenger's window rolled down.

"Get in," Peter said.

"I'm just about to go up to bed. How about we talk tomorrow?"

"Get in," he repeated. He leaned forward, the outline of a gun pushing against his blazer. "Or else."

Chapter 10

✦ ♥ ✦

Keep current. Don't be old-fashioned. If you don't have the skinny on the haps, you're just a fugly TC without a clue. Word.

You understand, bubeleh? Don't rely on old information. People get old. People change. One day a man has a winning smile and a butt you can crack walnuts on, and the next day, he's drinking his steak through a straw and his butt is . . . well, you don't want to know. How are you going to match that old man you think is still Mr. Robert Redford when you don't know he's turned into the Hunchback of Notre Dame? You're asking for trouble if you're not on top of things.

You can't match the unknown. Keep current.

Lesson 25,
Matchmaking Advice from Your Grandma Zelda

PETER'S VOICE crackled with the familiar sound of craziness I had come to expect from him, but now it was tinged with menace that made the hair on the back of my neck stand up. He patted his breast pocket, a promise of what was hidden inside.

Gone was my desire to hear his story, and in its place was blind, white fear.

"I really have to go in the house, Peter."

"You think I'm joking around, Gladie? Get in the car before you're sorry."

What had I learned from every after-school special and Lifetime movie I had ever watched? Don't get in the car. Don't ever get in the car. Once you're in the car, it's just a matter of minutes before you're locked in a home-made cell deep underground, waiting to be tortured, while slowly starving to death.

My eyes never left the bulge under Peter's blazer. It was shaped like a gun. Peter's hand was poised over it. I opened the car door and got in. As soon as the door clicked closed, he drove off.

The inside of the Porsche was the level of clean usually reserved for operating rooms. Peter must have gotten his OCD streak from his mother. Even in the dark, the dashboard gleamed.

Peter was twitchy. He moved his hands over the steering wheel, changing positions every few seconds.

I was worried. My stomach was making scary, apocalyptic sounds. I developed a strategy to jump out of the car if he ever slowed down.

"I've been dying to talk to you," he said. "Nobody will listen to me, and Jane is giving us all the evil eye. You don't know how scary that bitch is. I'm the only sane one in the family, you know."

I sighed. My stomach was rumbling and squeaking. We were heading farther up into the mountains. It was pitch-black outside, and he was driving too fast on a narrow dirt road.

"You told me about Jane and the Barbies," I said.

"And the babysitting? Did I tell you about the baby-sitting?"

"Uh . . ."

"She's such a freak. Always going on about what Mom wants, worrying if Mom is upset. I wish Jane would grow up. She's such a pathetic Goody Two-Shoes with Mom. Skulking off together for girl talk. What a kiss-ass brownnoser."

"Sibling rivalry sucks," I said.

"The police don't want to hear from me," he continued, forgetting the train of conversation. "I want you to help me. I know about you and your grandmother, how she knows things."

"That's my grandmother. She knows things. I don't know anything."

"That's not what she said. Besides, I've been watching you. I can tell how smart you are. You're going to help me or else."

Another "or else." My stomach rolled, and I belched.

"I can't sleep. I can't focus on anything else," he said, turning the car sharply as the road curved around the mountain. "I think my father was murdered, Gladie. I knew my family was a bunch of crazies who didn't give a damn about each other, but I've learned something that has blown my mind. Totally off the charts. I found this in the back of my dad's sock drawer."

Peter turned on the interior light, leaned across me, and opened the glove compartment without slowing the car down. He pulled out a press clipping and handed it to me. It was an article about the Randy Terns' bank robbery. There was nothing written there I didn't know, but what struck me was the photo: Randy Terns in police custody, dressed like a tree, his face painted green and four branches stuck to his body with tape. The reality was funnier than what my imagination had conjured. My shoulders heaved as I held back a wave of giggles.

"Did you read the last paragraph?" Peter asked. "It says he was a person of interest in a previous robbery."

I knew about the previous robbery, and I knew Randy had hidden money and was blackmailed by his gang members, but I kept my mouth shut. I didn't want to complicate matters. I wanted to get this over with as soon as possible. I hoped that Peter would get talked out and drive me home.

"You know what I am, Gladie?" he asked. The question was so loaded, I didn't know what to say.

"No, what, Peter?"

"I'm an entrepreneur."

"Been that for long, or is that a second profession for you?" Like hit man. Or serial killer. Or kidnapper. He seemed to have a talent for kidnapping.

"Let's just say I've always been an enterprising sort of guy," he said. Talking about himself relaxed Peter. His driving slowed, and he adjusted his position in his seat.

"I imagine," I said.

He slipped his arm around the back of my seat.

"Are you trying to flirt with me, Gladie?" That stumped me. His voice was low, husky, and wholly unappealing.

"I'm too hungry to flirt," I said, even though I was still digesting the Reuben sandwich.

"I would stop somewhere to get you something to eat, but I'm really pressed for time."

With that bit of information, he stopped the car. We had arrived at a large open area, riddled with old, abandoned mining equipment and metal barrels. The only illumination came from the car and the stars.

"Get out," Peter ordered.

"Here?"

"Get out!"

"I know. I know. Or else, right?"

I got out and followed Peter to the front of the car.

"Look around," he said. "This was my future. I was going to be a very rich man."

"You were a miner?"

"No. My brother, Rob, and I were going to develop the whole area."

We were in the middle of nowhere. There was no sign

of life, and the entire area was littered with rusty machinery and junk.

"You're not seeing it the right way," he said, reading my mind. "We were going to build hotels, restaurants, a strip mall. We were so close, but the EPA butted in, insisted we clean it up to their standards. Do you know what kind of money that takes? I'll tell you. Shitloads. Our father wouldn't give us the money. He said he didn't have it, but he lied. I know he lied because he must have been rich from robbing banks and had money to burn."

"Maybe he wanted to spend his money on something else," I said.

"Like what? My mom and dad never went anywhere, never bought anything worth anything. Just junk. Have you seen their house? Their car? They never spent a dime. My father ruined us. Rob and I sank all our money into buying this land, and we can't do a thing with it." He kicked a metal barrel. The sound echoed loudly in the quiet that surrounded us. "Rob wasn't always like he is now, sitting around and drinking beer all day. He used to be smart, quick. He used to have goals. He's almost catatonic now, and that's my father's fault. He destroyed Rob. But we're not finished. My father had more money than I thought. Bank robbery money, and that money is somewhere."

"And you want to find that money," I said.

"Damn right I want to find it."

"And you want me to help you find it?"

Peter waved his hands from side to side, clearly frustrated with me. "No, I can find it on my own. I want you to look into the murder, grab the murderer before he kills again. My father was murdered for the money. It's so clear, now. Don't you see?"

I nodded. "You think one of his old gang members killed him." It was my running theory.

"Gang members? What are you talking about? No! Don't you see? It was Rob. Rob went around the bend because of this failed land deal. La-la land. Crazier than a bedbug. He must have found out about the bank robbery, just like me. Only he decided to kill Dad. Rob isn't all there, you know."

"You would rather believe your brother killed your father than believe your father simply slipped in the middle of the night and hit his head on the table?"

Peter blinked a few times and cocked his head to the side. "I thought we went over that. There was no blood on the table. He was hit from behind and fell face-first. Nobody believes he hit his head on the table. Somebody must have conked him on the head. Even Mom thinks he was murdered."

That was news to me. Betty had told me over peach iced tea that her husband's death was an accident.

"Did she tell you that? Did she say she thought your father was murdered?" I asked.

"She didn't have to. She never washed the table. Trust me, if she thought anybody's head even touched her precious kitchen table, she would have cleaned it with Clorox."

A coyote howled, and the crickets chirped. The night had gotten louder. I tried to register what Peter was telling me. Betty Terns, the cleanest woman alive, hadn't cleaned the table where her husband supposedly suffered a lethal blow. Obviously, Betty didn't think he slipped in the middle of the night. So, who was she protecting? Someone in the family? Randy's reputation? Perhaps she was scared.

"Are you going to help me or not?" Peter whined.

"Peter, I don't think your family wants me involved in investigating your father's death." Like the knish-eating members, for instance.

"I just want you to help me with Rob. If you can prove

he killed my father, he will be out of my way. The guy's a nut job. He's not going to stop until he gets rid of everybody standing between him and the money. I'm probably next. Hell, you might be next," Peter said. "I have a plan. You distract him while I look for the money. Wear something nice. That outfit you wore yesterday would be perfect. I bet you can get him to spill the beans. It'll be easy. I'll call you when it's set up. Are you in?"

There were so many ways I wasn't in. At least four hundred ways I wasn't in. "I'm in," I said. "Can I go home now?"

"Are you sure you're in?"

"I'm in all the way, Peter. Can we go home, now?"

"Yeah, sure."

We got in the Porsche. Peter made a U-turn, careful to navigate the junk in the dark.

"You know what? This isn't going to work," he said.

"What? About Rob? That's fine. You can handle Rob on your own." What a relief. And what a lunatic. My first ride in a Porsche was a total bust.

"I mean driving you back. I've got a real important meeting, and I'm already late. We're going in opposite directions. So . . ."

Peter leaned over me and opened my car door.

"So what?" I slammed the door shut.

"Gladie, there's a path to the left. It will cut three miles off your trip."

"You can't be serious. You can't expect me to walk back to town. I don't know where I am. We're on a mountain in the middle of nowhere. It's pitch-black outside. There's coyotes!"

"I was going to give you a flashlight. Don't be so dramatic," he said, growing impatient.

"Peter, drive me home."

He leaned over and opened the door again. I went to

close it, but he took advantage of the moment to shove me out of the car. I landed in the dirt, scraping my elbows. I was still clutching the door handle, and my legs were still in the Porsche. Peter grabbed hold of them and tried to push them out. I kicked back. "C'mon, Gladie. I'm in a hurry."

"Peter, please. You cannot leave me here alone. It's dangerous. I could get hurt. Oof!"

Peter managed to throw my legs out of the car, making me land with a thud on my rear. I gripped the car door with renewed strength and tried to get my footing. He inched the car forward, forcing me to scoot on my knees.

"Let go, Gladie. You don't want me to drag you. It will hurt."

I tried to maneuver my body to get on my feet, but I couldn't find my balance. The car moved forward a little faster, and I fell flat, dragged on my belly. In a wise move of self-preservation, I let go of the door handle. A flashlight flew out of the car past my head.

"Don't forget. I'll call you when I need you to distract Rob," Peter called out. He pulled closed the passenger door and drove away.

I rolled over on the ground and stared at the stars for a moment. I didn't dare take stock of my situation or I would cry or have a panic attack. Instead, I sat up and found the flashlight. I shined it in the direction Peter had mentioned and found the path at once. It fell sharply down the mountain. Not the best for high heels, but still. I tried my cellphone, but there was no reception. No surprise there.

I watched Peter's taillights recede down the hill. *Stiff upper lip, Gladie,* I told myself. *Just put one foot in front of the other, and you will be home in no time.* I aimed the light in front of me and walked toward the path. I would have to be careful. The trail was rocky, and one false move would send me careening down. I plotted the course and took a step just as the path started to dim. I shook the flashlight, but instead of getting brighter, the light went out altogether. I smacked it against my hand, but nothing happened. Dark.

Somebody whimpered. I think it was me. I stood paralyzed on the spot, unable to move an inch. I looked up and tried to take solace in the starlight. No use. I was in trouble with a capital T. It took me a moment to recognize a noise. It was getting louder and coming closer. A car. Peter must have changed his mind. It was hard to believe, but he had come to his senses. The lights approached, illuminating the area. I relaxed, realizing that I had been holding my breath. I weighed my desires to alternately kiss Peter and to knock him unconscious with the flashlight, steal his car, and leave him to the coyotes. The flashlight scenario was winning by a landslide.

But something was wrong. The lights were big and too high up. After a minute, it became clear it wasn't Peter's Porsche driving up the mountain. It was a truck, and it was coming right at me.

I turned and ran, but my heel caught on a rock, and I went flying, scraping my hands and knees. I jumped up and ran again. The truck skidded to a halt and the door opened.

"Gladie! Gladie, it's me, Holden. I'm here to help."

I squinted, not daring to believe my eyes, but it was him. Gorgeous and strong and real. I hobbled to him, and he made up the distance, circling me with his arms when he reached me, letting me lean into him. He was warm and solid, and he took my weight easily. "I'm sorry I took so long," he said. "I tried to stop him on the way out, but he was driving too fast, and I didn't want to lose you."

"How did you know?" I croaked.

"You missed our date. I saw you get taken by that creep, and I followed. I got turned around on the dirt road and went a couple of miles in the wrong direction. By the time I got my bearings, he was driving the other way down the mountain. He had the light on in the car, and I saw you weren't in it. I put two and two together. Did he hurt you?"

"Not really. I made a lot of contact with the ground."

"I saw. Here. Let me help."

He lifted me in his arms like I was no heavier than a child and deposited me gently in the front seat of his truck. It was nice inside. Satellite radio and a moon roof.

We drove in silence. I must have dozed off because the next thing I knew he was lifting me out of the truck.

"I can walk," I said. But my injuries said otherwise. I was scraped up pretty badly. Holden carried me to the door. Grandma had left it unlocked, and the house was dark. It was later than I thought. *Time sure flies when you're kidnapped,* I thought.

"Where's the hooch?" Holden asked.

"The parlor."

He laid me down on a chaise longue and turned on a light. I pointed to a cabinet in the corner. Inside were bottles and crystal glasses.

"Two fingers of Dewar's on the rocks," he said.

"Four fingers and straight up," I corrected.

Holden arched an eyebrow.

"My kind of woman," he said. He poured us both drinks and sat down next to me, laying my legs on his lap. "Take a sip and tell me what happened."

I told him everything. I told him about the Terns family, about Uncle Harry, about Randy as a bank robber and the money he'd probably hidden away. I told him about the gang members, two now dead and one somewhere nobody knew. I told him about the blondes who wanted me to help solve the murder and the knish blonde who didn't; Spencer, who wanted me to stay out of it altogether; and Rob, who I was supposed to distract with my red dress while Peter searched for his ill-gotten inheritance.

After I finished, I took a long gulp of my drink and let it relax my insides, warming as it slid down my throat. Holden inspected my legs. They were scraped and bloody and bruises were forming. He took off my shoes and gently rubbed my feet. His expression had turned sad. My pain had made him sad.

"I'm sorry I forgot our date. Things have been so crazy," I said. My eyes filled and spilled over, and my nose ran. Long wrenching sobs tore at my body, and I was helpless to stop them. Holden pulled me onto his lap and held me until my crying jag ran its course. He handed me the box of tissues from the coffee table, and I blew my nose.

"The last thing you should worry about right now is our date. We'll have many more dates in our future," he said.

"We will?"

"Yes. Now, about this murder investigation you've found yourself in . . ."

"I know. I know. Stay out of it. It's much too dangerous."

"On the contrary," he said. "I don't think you have a choice. The sooner this is resolved, the better. It doesn't look like the police are taking it too seriously. So I don't think you can extricate yourself from the investigation of the deaths or murders, if that's what they turn out to be. But from now on, you take me with you. If you're looking for Chuck Costas, you take me. If you're distracting Rob, you take me. If you visit Uncle Harry, you take me." Holden pursed his lips. "Or you can take the cop, but I prefer you take me. Do we have a deal?"

We had more than a deal. I was ready to have his baby as well. Why couldn't he have made that part of the deal?

"It sounds like you've done this before," I said.

"Escorting Miss Marple as she investigates a murder?"

"Helping a damsel in distress," I corrected.

Holden's face dropped. "You do remind me of someone I once knew. I tried to be there for her, but it was a difficult situation." I tucked that information away for later. I didn't want to hear about anybody else at that moment.

"Why are you doing this?" I asked. "You barely know me."

Holden's mouth turned up into a smile. He was really handsome, like an advertisement for fresh air, muscles, and sex appeal. "I know you, Gladie," he said, his voice thick and low. "I knew you the first moment I saw you."

"I guess that makes me transparent and one-dimensional."

"That makes you the Ferrari in a Toyota car lot, the Faulkner in a stack of Grisham novels."

"The triple-layer chocolate cake in a bagel shop," I continued.

"Triple-layer chocolate cake with chocolate mousse filling," he said. "I'm a sucker for chocolate mousse filling."

My mouth had fallen open, and I snapped it closed.

"I don't like to see you hurt and in danger," he explained. "I sort of rescued you once. I might need to do it again. Would you humor me?"

"I could do that," I said. My body had grown warm and heavy, comfortable in the support and compassion he was offering. I yawned, and my eyes drooped.

"Let's get you cleaned up," Holden said.

He carried me up the stairs.

"Shower or bath?" he asked. "The shower you could do on your own. I would love to give you a bath, but you might want to hold off on that activity until our second date."

I took a short, hot shower. I had reached the end of my stamina. I was scraped over much of my body, but none of it was life-threatening. I threw away my clothes, which were in tatters, and dressed in a terrycloth robe.

Holden waited outside the bathroom door. He walked me to my bed and tucked me in.

"Thank you for everything. You're my knight in shining armor," I said.

Holden took a seat in the chair next to the bed and held my hand.

"I'm sticking around until morning, just in case Peter happens by or you get any more visitors bearing frozen food," he said.

"You don't have to do that," I said. But I was already halfway asleep. "I should have stuck with matchmaking. There's no death in matchmaking." I held his hand in both of mine. It was dry and warm and made me hungry for the rest of him. If only I wasn't so tired.

"You'll get back on the matchmaking wagon tomorrow. Now rest and dream something nice."

"I'll dream about you," I mumbled. "Handsome Holden with his wavy blond locks."

Chapter 11

✦ ♥ ✦

Like an itch you can't scratch (like that time with the mosquito bite under my bra strap—do you remember that, dolly?), once you get a feeling about a match, it will drive you crazy until you match them. You got the girl. You got the boy. And you push and you pull and you squeeze, but the stars are taking their own sweet time to get the two together. Oy. It will drive you crazy. Some say to have patience, that's what's meant to happen will happen. Don't listen to those stupid people, bubeleh. *Listen to me. I say push some more! Pull some more! Squeeze some more! Get those two together like your life depends on it. Pretend someone's got a gun to your head. If someone's got a gun to your head, do you move slow? I hope not. Keep at it. This is not a puzzle you're putting together. You don't need the pieces to fit just so. You can cheat a little. Don't tell anyone I told you that, by the way. That's just between us professionals.*

Lesson 11,
Matchmaking Advice from Your Grandma Zelda

WHEN I woke, the sunlight was streaming through my window, the birds were chirping merrily, and Holden was slumped in my armchair, his gorgeous, perfect face slack, and his long legs stretched out in front of him. He didn't snore. His Levi's were worn, and I let my eyes travel up from his boots to his waistband.

I sighed. Holden stirred and opened his eyes.

"No," I said. "Go back to sleep. I like watching you sleep."

"That's fair. I watched you a few hours last night, too." He stretched, standing up. He eyed me. "How do you feel this morning?"

"Great." But then I moved. "Not so great," I amended. I struggled to my feet. My muscles rebelled, tightening in protest. Every bruise and scrape was screaming at me.

"Easy," Holden said, helping me to my feet. "You don't have to run a marathon today. You can rest, take a day off from being Wonder Woman."

"Aspirin," I moaned.

"Where?"

"Downstairs."

"Stay here. I'll run down and get it."

"No, I'll go, too. I want a bagel to go with it."

Holden tucked an errant curl behind my ear, letting his fingers flutter against my cheek. He burned holes through me with his eyes. I was warm all over. It was like having my body slathered in Bengay but with a much better smell.

"Oh," I said.

"You know, I thought it would take me a lot longer to make it up to your bedroom."

"You've found me out. Getting dragged by a car was my little strategy to lure you up here."

"Clever girl," he said, his voice soft and deep. He leaned down and kissed my lips with a feather-light touch. He cupped my face in his hands and drew me closer. Our tongues met, and I took a step forward. I realized with a start that my body hurt a lot less. Even stranger, I had been transformed into a morning person.

* * *

WE MADE it downstairs to the kitchen a few minutes later. Grandma, Bird Gonzalez, and her pedicurist filled the room.

"Look what the cat dragged in."

I was conspicuous. I was still wearing my terrycloth robe. I had slept on wet hair, which meant that one side was plastered to my head and the other side was sticking up in angry spikes. I'm sure my cheeks were rosy— I had been trying to get my blood pressure down for the last ten minutes.

And those were the reasons for the gasps from the ladies-filled kitchen, or perhaps it was because of the man who followed me in, the man who was as rumpled as I but in a sexy Brad-Pitt-doesn't-even-come-close kind of way.

There was a quieter gasp from Holden behind me, more genteel and circumspect, which was admirable, considering. I would have bet it was the first time Holden had ever seen an elderly woman getting a perm and a pedicure in her kitchen with cries of "Get the bunions, will you?" coming from her at regular intervals.

Bird was spending the morning on Grandma. Her salon was closed on Mondays, but that didn't stop her from bringing it to Grandma's kitchen. "Your grandmother knows the importance of grooming," Bird had explained to me one day. "Age doesn't mean a thing. Neither does the fact that she never leaves her property. Your grandmother doesn't believe in gray roots."

So Bird came every Monday morning. The kitchen table was covered in Pop-Tarts, coffee cups, cheese Danish, rollers, brushes, and a callus grater.

"Yum, cheese Danish. Is there any more coffee?" I asked.

But no one was listening to mc. They had stopped what they were doing and were staring at Holden like he was the prize bull at the Cannes Springfest. All except for Grandma, who had seen him before, of course. She was pointing at her toes, telling the pedicurist to watch out for ingrown toenails.

"Everybody, this is Arthur Holden, our new neighbor," I said.

"You can call me Holden," he said, just as Bridget entered through the other door, a Danish sticking out of her mouth and a pile of papers in her hands. She noticed him, and the papers slid from her hands, falling to the floor in a tangled mess that undoubtedly would take her hours to set straight.

"Holden, this is my dear friend Bridget," I said.

"Nice to meet you." He put his hand out, but she stood dumbly, the Danish still in her mouth. I related to her. Holden had the same effect on me.

"Maybe you should go," I told him. At this rate, I would never get my Danish.

"Anybody home?" Lucy called from the entranceway. The screen door creaked closed. "Zelda? Gladie? Anybody here?"

Lucy pranced into the kitchen, a picture of Southern grace, elegance, and peach chiffon.

"Are we having a party?" she asked, looking around at the crowded kitchen. "Oh, my," she said, fanning herself once she had gotten a good look at Holden.

"Who do we have here? If you're the plumber, I would love for you to look at my pipes." She put her hand out for him to kiss. Holden took it and gave it a firm shake.

"Breathe deep and take a step back, Scarlett," I said. "This is Holden. The new neighbor."

"The sexy new neighbor. Yes, indeed. I can't tell you how pleased I am to finally meet you. Tell me, Mr. Holden, what is it that you do?"

"Whatever I can get away with, miss," he said.

"Did you hear that? He called me miss."

There was general giggling from the women in the kitchen. I had a terrible fear they would rush him at any moment.

"Bird, are you planning on frying my hair?" Grandma asked. "I pride myself on my thick head of hair, but one more minute in this solution and I'm going to be bald as a billiard ball."

Bird squealed and went to work on the rollers. "So sorry, Zelda. I don't know what came over me. I'll get you rinsed pronto."

"Maybe you should go," I told Holden again.

He nodded and pulled me out of the kitchen.

"Remember our deal," he said.

"Girl Scout's honor."

"I'll look into Chuck Costas. Maybe I can find something."

"You will?" I asked.

"Yes. And you'll rest, right?"

"Right."

Holden made his way to the front door, and I took a seat at the table.

"Holy crap. Did you see his ass?"

Bird washed Grandma's hair in the sink. I poured myself a cup of coffee, took a Danish, and sat at the table.

"Well? Did you see his ass or what?" Bird repeated.

"I thought it was a rhetorical question," I said. "I haven't gotten under the jeans, no. I just met the guy. Bird, watch your language. My grandmother is right here."

"She's right, dolly," Grandma said from under the tap. "Holden's got a great ass."

Bridget rifled through her papers, making little piles on the table. "Talk about winning the genetic lottery," she commented.

"I asked around," Lucy told me. "Your sexy neighbor used to be in the CIA."

I choked on my Danish. "CIA?"

"I heard he was the Navy SEAL who shot Osama bin Laden in the face," the pedicurist piped in.

"That's not true," Bird said. "I heard from a reliable source Holden is a drug runner."

Bridget snorted. "A drug runner in Cannes? Oh, please. Besides, I was at the grocery store, and the entire checkout lane said he was a stuntman and Brad Pitt's stand-in. Or a butt model."

"Holden is not a drug runner," Grandma said from under one of Bird's towels.

Our heads turned to Grandma. "Well, Zelda, what does Holden do?" Bird demanded.

"He never told me," she said.

Eyebrows raised all over the kitchen. "What does that have to do with anything?" Bird asked. "What does he do?"

"I sense strength from him," said Grandma. "And travel. And a nice ass." It was uncharacteristically vague for Grandma, and the disappointment in the room was palpable.

"I still think he shot Osama bin Laden," said the pedicurist.

"An international man of mystery," Lucy said. "Well, well. Cannes is getting so interesting."

Holden didn't seem like an international man of mystery to me. He wore jeans and work boots. Mystery men wore black turtlenecks and fatigues, and they lived in Monaco, Malibu, or at least Minneapolis. Holden was probably an architect or a writer, or maybe he was an importer/exporter. Although, it wasn't such a stretch to imagine him as Brad Pitt's stand-in or a butt model.

All the speculation about Holden was a fun exercise but made me realize I didn't know anything about him.

All I knew was that he was perfect, he wanted to save me, and he thought I was as tasty as chocolate cake with chocolate mousse filling.

Bird wrapped a towel around Grandma's shoulders. "Well, I was right. Those pheromones sure are working for you, Gladie."

Bird had a point. I was attracting top-tier men. And without makeup, Spanx, or even a brush through my hair.

"You've got some mighty fine flies buzzing around you, Gladie," said Lucy. "What are you going to do about it?"

What was I going to do about it? I hadn't given it a thought. My thoughts were elsewhere. Focus on murder, find love. Was there a lesson there?

"I'm going to fix up Ruth's grandniece, Julie," I said.

Grandma slapped her thigh. "Excellent. A man might act as a buffer, make her less dangerous. Find a man with a bulletproof vest."

"That was exactly my idea," I said. "Who wants to go with me today to work on the match?"

"I'll be here for a while getting your grandmother's papers organized," Bridget said. "And I have a protest later."

"I have a couple of hours," said Lucy. "I would love to go with you. Will we see Mr. Holden again?"

"I don't know," I said honestly. "I have a little work to do in the attic first."

Lucy jumped up from her chair. "Great. I'll spy on the Ternses' house and keep an eye out for any suspicious behavior."

That won't be hard, I thought.

"Those are weird people," Bird declared.

"I already told Gladie all about them," Grandma said. "Fools won't sell their house. Have you ever heard such a thing?"

Bird clucked her tongue. "That woman has never gotten her hair done. She does it herself." Do-it-yourself beauty was anathema to Bird. There was no greater sin. "Maybe she goes to a different salon," I suggested.

"Gladie, I'm a professional, and I know everybody in this town. That woman has been setting and coloring her own hair since the beginning of time. I don't make mistakes about those sorts of things."

I popped four aspirin, slipped on jeans and a long-sleeved T-shirt, and met Lucy in the attic. I made an index card for Julie and one for Sergeant Fred. Obviously the money would have to come from him, although it was possible Ruth would splurge to have her grandniece off her hands. I had seen my grandmother extract a matchmaking fee from the unlikeliest sources, and I thought I had the sales pitch down, but I practiced anyway while Lucy spied out the window.

"The part about jumping on the back of happiness when it gallops by is pure genius," Lucy said about my pitch.

"Really? You like it? I added the horse references. Fred's from Utah."

"Very nice. Gladie, don't you wonder where Randy Terns hid the money? They don't have a basement, and you said Peter broke through the walls."

"Maybe Peter found it and is lying," I said. I updated Lucy on my discussion with Peter, but I left out the part about him kidnapping me and abandoning me in the middle of nowhere. I had wonderful friends who would become overbearing and suffocating if they knew I had been dragged and threatened.

"I think it's that Jane woman," she said. "She seems like the type who would throw knishes and murder her own father."

"It's possible Jane threw the knish," I said. "But I think Chuck Costas is the murderer. I think Randy

Terns made waves about the blackmail, and Costas killed them both. Maybe he has all the money now."

I went to the window. Betty stood on her front porch with Cindy, her penny collector daughter. "That poor woman," I said. "Betty's never had her hair done. She's worn the same clothes for the past forty years. She told me that she and Randy didn't like to go out, but I think he didn't let her go out."

"He imprisoned her?"

"Not imprisoned, exactly. I mean, the front door doesn't even close properly. I don't know, but something wasn't kosher in that marriage."

LUCY DROVE me to the police station. Fred was conveniently at the front desk. I hoped to get in and get out in record time.

"Hey! Hi, Underwear Girl." Fred greeted me with a big smile. I was a little surprised to see him at work. The last time I had seen him, he almost shot up the precinct. I kind of figured he would be on vacation in a padded room somewhere.

"Hi, Fred," I said.

"I'm doing just fine," he offered. "Not a scratch on me. Can you believe it? That was one hairy pickle I was in."

"It was a hairy pickle," I repeated.

Lucy turned to me. "Underwear Girl?"

"I'm glad you're all right," I said, ignoring Lucy. "But I'm here because I want to talk to you about feeling even better than all right—about feeling great. Fred, I want to talk to you about love. True love. Soul mate love."

"Gee, Miss Burger, that sounds great." Fred smiled from ear to ear.

"Fred, when you find the someone to make you happy,

to love you like you've always wanted to be loved, well, life is so much better."

"I think you're awfully pretty, Miss Burger," he said.

"Uh-oh," said Lucy.

"Thank you, Fred," I said. "Are you with me? Are you ready to fall in love and live a life filled with love?"

"Yes, ma'am! I am!"

Fred jumped over the desk. I stumbled back, but he was fast, catching me and taking me into his arms. I tried to push him away.

"What are you doing? Get off me." He had me in a bear hug. I was having trouble breathing. Just as I was about to lose consciousness, I noticed he smelled like onion rings.

"Honey, you are bulging out her eyes," Lucy observed. "Loosen up. Let her go. She can't go very far very fast. You have all the weapons, remember? I promise you can Taser her if she bolts." Lucy was such a wise woman. Nobody could argue against her. Fred eased up, and I took a deep breath.

"What's going on? What's going on?" Spencer charged into the reception area. He wore a formfitting black suit with a black tie. He looked like the best man in a wedding, but he was madder than a spitfire.

"Get off her." With one move, Spencer dislodged Fred. "Are you okay?" he asked me. When I nodded, he went after Fred.

"Are you completely insane, or did that bullet find you and damage that tiny brain of yours?"

"Sorry, Chief. I was just giving my girl a hug." Fred looked pleased as punch. I had a strong desire to leave town and get my job back as receptionist at Porky's Pig Farm in Fresno. I deserved nothing better. How could I have messed up something so simple?

Spencer gave me his full attention, but his head was cocked to the side, his left eye closed, as if he had lost all power of movement on that side of his face. Then he turned back to Fred.

"Your girl?" he asked. "Gladie is your girl?"

"Uh . . . ," I began.

Lucy interrupted. "If you'll allow me, Officers. I'm afraid there's been the teensiest of misunderstandings. Gladie was just trying to initiate Sergeant Fred in the ways of love." She paused and looked up at the ceiling. "No, that didn't come out right."

"You came down here to pick up my desk sergeant?" Spencer asked me. "Wait a second. Let me get this straight. You came down here to pick up my desk sergeant?" He enunciated every word like he was reading my rights.

I took a step backward. "Of course not. I'm sorry, Fred. I was talking about another soul mate. You're a wonderful man. I just know that together with me you will find love. No. Hold on, that's not what I meant."

"She's shy," Fred explained to Spencer.

"Come with me." Spencer grabbed my elbow, and I yelped in pain. I had precious little skin left on either of my elbows. "What's wrong?" he asked. He pulled up my sleeves and studied my arms. I was scratched and scraped all the way down. He noticed my hands, too, which had been torn up from the dirt road.

Lucy gasped.

"What happened to you?" Spencer asked.

I debated with myself how much to tell, but he read something in my face and grew serious.

"Follow me," he ordered. I followed him to his office, and Lucy trailed along. Spencer closed his door and motioned for us to sit in the chairs in front of his desk.

"Tell me what happened to you," he said.

"I fell down."

"Who was there when you fell down?"

I tried to think of a story. I wasn't exactly protecting

Peter. I just felt that ratting him out would add to my troubles.

Spencer turned to Lucy. "Who was with Gladie when she fell?"

"Darlin', I didn't know she fell. She didn't tell me a thing."

I shrugged and smiled.

"However," Lucy continued, "she did tell me she had a protracted conversation with Peter Terns last night. That's Randy Terns' oldest son. I'm sorry, Gladie, but I won't be quiet if he is responsible for hurting you."

"Nothing's broken," I said.

"Did he hit you?" Spencer's voice was just above a whisper and stone cold.

"No."

"Did he push you?"

"Just out of his car. It wasn't going that fast," I added. "Just above a crawl, really, but I didn't want to get out."

"You didn't want to get out," said Spencer, calmly.

"We were in the middle of nowhere. I was scared. It was dark, and I didn't know how to get back."

"I see."

"And then he dragged me."

"He dragged you," Spencer repeated, rolling the words around his mouth, as if he was deciding what to do with them.

"Not for long," I explained. "I couldn't hold on for very long."

Spencer's blue eyes grew dark.

"You didn't think to report him? The man who dragged you with his car?" Spencer asked.

"I thought it would get complicated. I know with kidnappings you have to call in the FBI. And Spencer, I know you told me to stay away from that family, but it wasn't my fault. I was just minding my own business and up he drove and told me to get in. I didn't have a choice. There was a bulge in his pocket."

"Kidnapping?" he asked. "He kidnapped you?"

"Well . . . that." I gestured like it wasn't a big deal. "It sounds a lot more serious than it was."

"Darlin'," said Lucy, "the man kidnapped you, dragged you with his car, and left you for dead in the middle of nowhere."

"Well, when you put it like that, it sounds serious, but Holden found me and brought me home. No harm, no foul," I said.

"That tall friend of yours? He found you?" Spencer asked.

I REFUSED to make a statement and file charges, which infuriated Spencer no end. He insisted on going to the Ternses' house to put the fear of God into Peter to make sure he left me alone. He also insisted that I go with him in order to stay out of trouble.

Lucy, Spencer, and I left the police station together, just in time to bump into Bridget, who was picketing in front of the building. She wore a sandwich board on which was written: "Money for guns? How about books? What's wrong with books?" She attacked Spencer almost at once with a verbal onslaught.

"Nice building. You spent all of the town's money on this monument to tyranny. How about money for public services? How about that?" she demanded.

"Law enforcement is a public service, lady," he said, trying to walk around her, but she blocked him with her sandwich-boarded body.

"Arrest me! Arrest me! I dare you! Arrest me!" she yelled.

"Is this your friend?" Spencer asked me.

"Never mind that," spit out Bridget. "Arrest me, you . . . pig!"

"My life has gotten so interesting since I met you," he told me. I couldn't argue. I had definitely made an impact on him.

"Bridget, honey," Lucy said, always the voice of reason, "Gladie has been attacked. She was kidnapped last night by Peter Terns and dragged through the streets behind his car. The chief is going to see to her safety, and he is going beat the shit out of Mr. Terns until that low-life bottom-feeder begs for mercy."

"You were attacked?" Bridget asked. She hobbled over to me, the sandwich board swaying from side to side. She tried to hug me but couldn't get close enough.

"I'm fine," I managed. My voice wobbled—Bridget's concern had put me over the edge. "It really wasn't that bad."

"Waterboard him," Bridget instructed Spencer. "Waterboard him, and if that doesn't work, shoot him in the kneecaps. Make him pay."

With Bridget's concern for human rights thrown out the window, we left Lucy and Bridget, and Spencer drove me to the historic district. He parked in front of the Ternses' house.

"Tell me honestly. Are you all right?" he asked.

"Just some scrapes and bruises. I'm fine, Spencer."

"Listen, I got the initial report back from the ME. Jimmy the Fink died of a stroke. Natural causes," Spencer said.

"Stroke? What kind of stroke?" I asked. "A provoked stroke? Like something was slipped into his morning beer and gave him a stroke? That kind of stroke?"

"A stroke. Like if you don't eat right, don't take your blood pressure meds, and smoke like a chimney stroke. That kind of stroke. Natural causes. No murder. And no murder for Randy Terns, either. What we have here,

Gladie, are two old guys who kicked the bucket. Two unsuspicious deaths."

"Two mongo-sized coincidences," I said.

"I don't disagree, but we're not talking murder. So you're making enemies of the Terns family for no reason. They're crazy and not the nicest of people. They are not good enemies to have. We've got to calm this situation down before it escalates out of control. You got me?"

"How are we going to calm this situation down?" I asked.

"You are going to mind your own business, and I am going to suggest to Peter and his siblings that they leave town, that there is no bank heist money. I'm going to show them my pretty, shiny badge."

"Sounds like you've got everything under control," I said.

"Babe, I always have everything under control. You don't know me, but I'm very good at my job."

That's when we heard the bloodcurdling scream come from the Ternses' house.

Chapter 12

✦ ♥ ✦

This matchmaking business takes a lot of common sense and intuition. You want to peg the client's personality immediately. Easier said than done. Sometimes it takes a little shaking to get to the real person. You got to loosen them up, Gladie. Don't slap them around, but a little shaking never hurt anybody. Except for babies. Don't shake a baby. If the shaking doesn't work, be patient. They'll loosen up eventually and their true self will shine through.

Lesson 4,
Matchmaking Advice from Your Grandma Zelda

THE SCREAMS were unnatural, worse than cats, worse than someone being murdered. The screams kept coming in waves, like an air raid siren.

"Stay here," Spencer told me, and jumped out of the car, his gun drawn. He announced his presence at the Ternses' door and walked right in.

After a minute the screams were accompanied by yelling in a basso profundo. That was Spencer, I guessed. *He must have everything under control,* I thought. I got out of the car and walked toward the house.

The screams were a lot louder from the front porch with the door open. I had no idea how vocal cords could withstand such loud, prolonged screaming. Spencer was saying "Police" over and over, but the screams continued unabated.

I walked in and followed the noise down the hall toward the bedrooms. Spencer stood just inside the door of the master bedroom, where Christy the drug addict was having a complete breakdown, screaming, opening Betty's drawers, and throwing the contents everywhere. Christy had shaved her head and wore nothing but men's boxers, a wifebeater with no bra, and tube socks. Spencer tried to calm her, but she was obviously stuck in her own drug-induced world and didn't seem to be aware of him.

I jumped five feet in the air when Rob, Peter's brother, the one I was supposed to distract, appeared behind me. "She is tweaking balls," he murmured against the back of my neck. "She's up to her armpits in crank. She'll never get her kid back now."

I wasn't exactly sure what crank was, but I guessed it wasn't organic wheatgrass. The bit of information that she was tweaking balls didn't seem to bother Rob. He was stating it merely as fact. I couldn't keep my eyes off Christy, who was literally bouncing off the walls. She was a sight—a wild banshee. Next to her, Spencer seemed small and defenseless.

"Is she dangerous?" I asked Rob.

"Yep," he said.

Spencer took a few tentative steps deeper into the room, and Christy stopped screaming. She noticed Spencer for the first time and studied him like a lion studies a gazelle. Or like a crazy drug addict studies a cop who walks within arm-swinging distance.

"I called for help," he told her calmly. "Help is coming. They'll make you feel better. You'll come down, gently. I promise."

This was the wrong thing to say. I don't think Christy wanted to come down, gently or not.

"No! No! No!" she screamed. She bent down, scooped up an armful of clothes, and threw them at him. She ran around in circles, sidestepped Spencer, and ran out of the room past Rob and me and into another room, where she continued opening drawers. Spencer knocked the clothes off his head and ran after her. It was too late. Christy had found something in one of the drawers and pointed it at Spencer.

"Say hello to my little friend," she announced in her best Al Pacino *Scarface* voice. She held up a long black rod in a threatening manner. The rod was making a familiar whirring noise.

"What the hell is that?" asked Spencer derisively.

I knew what it was, but I had never seen it used offensively before.

"She looks like she means business," I said.

"Lady, whatever that is, you better put it down," he said.

She hit a switch, and the whirring noise intensified. She had locked it in for maximum sensation. She raised it above her head in a threatening manner, as if she was going to stab Spencer with it.

"Lady, I will take great pleasure in shooting you," he said. "Put. It. Down."

"Take pleasure in this," she screeched, and leapt onto him, her legs wrapping around his waist. She pummeled the weapon against his chest, trying to stab him, I imagined. Spencer wrestled it away from her with his left hand. I could tell the moment he figured out exactly what it was. It registered on his face. Disgust. Shock. He subdued and handcuffed Christy with his right hand, holding his left hand out in the air like it had been infected by the world's biggest case of cooties.

"Was that—?" he asked me.

"A vibrator," I said.

"She stabbed me with a vibrator?"

Just then the house was invaded by police and firefighters. Right behind them was Peter, who was fighting mad. He was also black and blue with a swollen eye and a cast on his left arm.

"What are you doing to my sister?" he spit at Spencer, standing way too close and thumping him on his chest with his good hand.

"Cool your jets," Spencer said. He removed Peter's finger and twisted his hand back with some kind of martial arts move. "Your sister took a little too much meth. We're treating her. She's going to be fine. If you calm down, I'll give you your finger back."

"She would never have done that. She's clean. She just got out of rehab," Peter yelled. "Rob, you son of a bitch, you set her up. Rob!" He grew even more agitated when Rob didn't answer. The sound of a ballgame came from another room.

"I think he went to watch TV," I said. Hard to imagine he could find something better to watch than his siblings attacking Spencer, but men act strange during baseball season.

"Shut up! What do you know?" Peter shouted. Spencer twisted Peter's arm, making him buckle down to his knees. It didn't stop Peter from taking a swipe at Spencer with his leg.

"That's assaulting an officer, pal," Spencer said, handcuffing him as well, careful to bind him around his cast. "I would have rather busted him for kidnapping, but this will do," Spencer remarked in my direction.

The firefighters gave Christy medical treatment. I gave her privacy and went out on the porch for some fresh air. Betty drove up and spoke to the authorities before joining me.

A policeman I vaguely recognized came out with a bag of pills. "Mrs. Terns, can you identify these pills as yours? Otherwise we'll need to take them in as evidence."

"That one is for my fibromyalgia. The others are for

sleeping, anxiety, and some personal hygiene concerns," she said.

He handed her the bag and went back inside. Betty looked downtrodden, and I held her hand.

"I take a lot of medicine," she said. "Jane calls me the zombie. I sleep most of the time. At night it would take a bomb to wake me."

I gave her hand a small squeeze. "I'm sorry."

Betty lit up a cigarette and took a long drag. "Randy was so proud of me," she said. "Giving him all those kids. Each time he would marvel how I carried them, birthed them, and reared them without stopping what I was doing. I never let a speck of dust fall anywhere in the house. No matter what."

"That's commendable," I said. Across the street, my grandmother was making a poor show of sweeping the driveway. It might have been the first time she had ever picked up a broom. She shook it with one hand, barely grazing a square inch of pavement. It was clear her attention was elsewhere—on us, to be exact.

"It didn't matter. None of it mattered," Betty continued. "I gave him children, kept the house clean, made him his favorite cake every week, kept my figure. What did it matter?"

"I'm sure it mattered to him, Betty. I'm sure he loved you very much."

"You're such a sweet girl," she said. "I feel like I can confide in you."

"You don't have to." And I meant it. I felt indescribably sad at Betty's life with her horrible children. Even though she was surrounded by her family, she was truly alone.

"I want to," she said. "I need to get it off my chest. Especially now when everything is falling apart. My marriage with Randy was a beautiful marriage, don't get me wrong. But there was this indiscretion. A woman. A terrible, terrible woman."

Betty took a deep breath, as if it took extra oxygen to divulge her secret. I gave her hand another little squeeze.

"He had always been faithful before that," she said. "Devoted. That's how everyone described him. I don't know what you heard, but not all his friends were devoted family men like my Randy. Randy wasn't like them. Family was important to him. He might not have coached Little League, but he showed it in other ways.

"It was after Cindy's accident that I noticed a difference. He wasn't staying home at night to watch TV. He went out of town on business more than usual. And he acted different. Like he was better than me. Like I didn't deserve him."

"That's horrible. I'm sorry you went through that. But remember, Betty, you got through it. Your marriage survived," I said.

"No, you don't understand. The woman," she started, but was cut off by Holden's appearance. He had showered and was wearing slacks and a button-front shirt. He cast a long shadow over us. He nodded to Betty and took my hand, helping me up.

"You didn't call me. I would have come. Are you all right?" Holden asked me.

"Yes. I'm sorry I didn't call. I know we had a deal."

"What deal was that?" Spencer walked out of the house with a gaggle of cops behind him. "You come save her when it's convenient for you, and you don't bother reporting her kidnapping to the police? That kind of deal?"

"Holden was looking out for me," I said. "He wanted to make sure I stay safe."

"Maybe he should pick a new hobby. He sucks at this one. She was with me this time. She was safe," Spencer said.

"You want me to arrest him?" asked one of the cops.

"We were just leaving," I said. "Holden was going to buy me lunch."

I took his hand and tugged, but he resisted. The field of testosterone built up around Spencer and Holden again. I could almost see the hormone swirling in the air. The porch was getting smaller as the men's chests puffed out.

"I'm really hungry, Holden," I said, tugging a little harder.

"She's hungry," Holden said to Spencer.

I heard Spencer's molars grind together and his blood pressure rise.

Holden was calm, but his attention shifted when another police officer brought out Peter in handcuffs. A glimmer of recognition passed between them. Peter flinched and took a step back before the officer pushed him forward again. Holden raised an eyebrow and smiled. A terrible thought flashed through my head, but I discarded it quickly.

Just when I thought the porch couldn't get any more crowded, Sergeant Fred bounded up the stairs in his uniform, carrying a clipboard. He saw me and broke out into a wide smile. "Hi, Gladie. You look nice."

"You saw me thirty minutes ago, Fred. I haven't changed."

"You still look nice to me. You wanna meet up later? I have a half day today." Fred was a little thick, but I thought that could work to my advantage.

"Sure, Fred. I'd love to," I said. "Let's meet at Tea Time at two. How does that sound?"

"That sounds great." He bounced up and down a couple of times, wrote something down on his clipboard, scooted around the group of cops, and went in the house.

Spencer turned to me. "You're killing me," he said.

Holden held my hand as we walked across the street. Grandma stood waiting for us in the driveway, her broom forgotten, tossed to the side.

"I told you those people were no good," she said as I approached.

"They arrested Peter and Christy," I said.

"Losers, the lot of them. If you're going out to lunch, bring me back hamburgers. No, scratch that. Tacos. It's a taco day."

"Tacos mean—" I began.

"I know, but I have a hankering. At least two are gone now," she said, looking at the Ternses' house. "Four more to go. The sooner the better. I don't know how this is going to turn out, Gladie. Best to stay away from them. All of them. No good, the lot of them."

"TACOS," I muttered as Holden drove us down the street in his truck.

"Do you mind if we stop someplace before lunch? Are you very hungry?" he asked.

"For tacos? No. What did you have in mind?"

"I have a surprise for you." Holden downshifted and turned sharply onto Farmer Way in the direction of the old mine.

"Holden, my tolerance for surprise is waning. I've had a lot of surprises lately."

"Okay, you've dragged it out of me. I found the third gang member. I found Chuck Costas."

Stuck in the midst of the craziness of the Terns family, I had forgotten about the gang and Chuck Costas. I had been distracted by blondes and knishes, and I had gotten thrown off the most obvious path.

Spencer could have been right and the deaths were natural and not murder, but I wasn't a huge believer in coincidences. Two dead gang members within a week of each other was too much for me to swallow. I was sure Chuck Costas was the key to the mysteries of their death and the missing bank robbery money. And with the mysteries solved, perhaps the drama with the Terns family would die down.

"So soon? How did you find him?" I asked.

"I was motivated. I didn't want you to cancel any more dates with me on account of kidnapping. So, I looked around, did some research. And I found him."

"That's better than the police. You amaze me."

"Amazement. Well, that's a start."

"So where are we going?" I asked.

"We're going to see him."

"Just like that?"

"I made an appointment. We're expected in twenty minutes."

"Wow, an appointment. Should we call Spencer? Get backup?"

Holden shifted in his seat. "I'll protect you," he said.

"Speaking of protecting me," I began, "you wouldn't know anything about Peter Terns' black eye and broken arm, would you?"

"It looked like it hurt," he said.

"Yes, it did. He was in perfect shape last night."

"When he was kidnapping you."

"When he was kidnapping me," I agreed.

"He must have slipped," Holden said. He gave me a pointed look. "I don't like to see you hurt, Gladie."

I didn't know what I thought about that.

"You don't look any worse for wear," I said. "Hey, I know this is a silly question, but you didn't shoot Osama bin Laden, did you?"

"What?"

* * *

WE DROVE past the old mine through a vast area of sagebrush until I saw a familiar sign. "Why are we here?" I asked.

"This is where our appointment is. You know this place?"

I knew it. My father was buried there. I hadn't visited since his funeral years before, when my life changed.

"The Cannes Serenity Cemetery," I said. "I know it. Kind of creepy meeting place."

Holden patted my leg. "It's going to be fine."

We wound around the cemetery. It was as old as the mine with its first residents victims of various mining accidents and bar fights. The cemetery was almost as big as the town, housing so many generations of Cannes citizens.

"Here we are," Holden announced.

He parked and guided me up a hill, his large hand on the small of my back. I felt safe with Holden. He had a calming effect on me. He walked with complete confidence, sure of himself without a hint of arrogance.

"What do you do again?" I asked, suddenly.

"What?"

"Your profession."

Holden stopped walking. "This and that."

"Your profession is this and that?"

"Does this matter to you, Gladie?"

Did it? He was more or less a stranger to me, although he had sort of saved my life, and we did kiss a couple of times, and the kisses nearly made my head explode. But strangers we were, and perhaps I didn't have the right to ask personal questions. On the other hand, why was he being secretive? Was he hiding something or being private?

"Anyway," he said with a smile, "here we are."

"Where?"

"Here." He pointed to the tombstone at our feet. It

was a small tombstone, set flush with the ground. CHUCK COSTAS, 1925–1979.

"Oh, no." It was literally a dead end. Chuck Costas couldn't be the killer because he had died more than thirty years before. My gang theory was completely wrong. I felt like a fool.

"Here comes the man I wanted you to meet," said Holden.

A priest walked up the hill toward us. He wore a collar and short sleeves. He was around Lucy's age, with salt-and-pepper hair.

"So pleased to meet you," he said, shaking first Holden's hand and then mine.

"Father Lawrence kindly agreed to meet with us to discuss Chuck Costas," Holden explained.

"Nice to meet you, Father. Did you know Mr. Costas?" I asked.

"No, I never had that pleasure. But I knew about him through his priest, Father Patrick. Mr. Costas returned to the fold through Father Patrick. He'd mended his ways, you could say."

"He went on the up-and-up?" I asked.

"Yes. It's no secret he had been a criminal at one time, but he turned to the church and a more sedate and honest life."

I guess I'm a suspicious person by nature because all I could think about was the missing bank robbery money and how a criminal could lead a sedate and honest life with that money in his back pocket.

"Was he well-to-do?" I asked.

"Mr. Costas? No, a very humble man. He was active in charity works in his later life." Father Lawrence removed his glasses and cleaned them with the hem of his shirt. "Are you a friend of the family?"

"A friend of a former colleague who recently passed away," said Holden.

"Is that right? Anyone I know?"

"Randy Terns," I said. "They used to work together."

"Did they? And how did you come to know him?"

Holden and I exchanged glances.

"He was my neighbor," I said.

"And why did you wish to reach Mr. Costas?" he asked.

"Randy Terns left something for him." It just slipped from my mouth. I had no idea why I decided to lie to a man of the cloth. Once I started, though, it was easy to keep going. "It's a shame, really. Randy wanted him to have it," I said.

Father Lawrence shifted on his feet. "Perhaps I can help with that, get it to his family. It's the least I can do, since you've gone to so much trouble trying to find Mr. Costas. Is this something he left large? Sentimental? Valuable?"

"I feel uncomfortable talking about it," I said. Of course I was uncomfortable talking about it. I was so going to hell.

"How about we call you later and make arrangements?" Holden asked.

"I have time today," Father Lawrence said. "I can come pick it up. Or maybe you have it here." The priest looked over at Holden's parked truck and took a couple of steps toward it.

Holden touched the priest's shoulder. "We don't have it here," he said softly. "But I'll arrange it with you later. Okay?"

"Yes. Yes. That would be fine."

"Thank you for meeting with us. It was nice of you to take time from your day," I said.

"No trouble at all." He shook our hands and gave Holden his card.

We stood a moment and watched Father Lawrence's back as he scattered down the hill. He got to the bottom, looked both ways, and crossed the street toward the cemetery's greeting hall.

"That was interesting," Holden said.

"I don't have a lot of experience with priests," I said.

"He was more eager to help than I expected. And inquisitive."

"He did ask a lot of questions. Do you think he knew about the bank robbery money?"

"It doesn't matter now. It appears, Sherlock, that we have run into a dead end."

"The deadest."

"Taco time?"

A woman and her daughter placed flowers on a grave near us. The mother wrapped her arm around the little girl, and they spoke quietly to each other.

"Would you mind if I wandered off and met you back at the truck in fifteen minutes?" I asked.

"Take your time. I'll wait at the truck."

It didn't take long to find my father's grave. The memory of his funeral rushed back at me with the scent of sagebrush on the wind. His grave was one hill over from Chuck Costas, and his tombstone was bigger than most around him. Grandma had made sure it was bigger. My father was her only child, cut down in the prime of his life, with so much promise cut down, as well. My grandmother had told me about the injustice of it all more times than I could count.

He was a poet. He owned words, Grandma liked to say. He transformed words into magic. Although Grandma was eager to point out to me as a five-year-old that the Tooth Fairy was not real and Santa Claus was for less intelligent children, she was insistent that magic was real when it flowed from my father's pen.

He died on a "blind day," according to Grandma, when her third eye was sleeping. But years later Ruth Fletcher told me the truth, about how Grandma had

warned my father about the motorcycle, how she'd told
him never to drive it, how she'd refused to let him park
it near the house, about how she couldn't look at it
without crying.

But he drove it on a Wednesday while I was in ballet
class with my mother when we were visiting Grandma
for the summer. Either the bike malfunctioned in some
way or he got distracted and swerved. We couldn't see
the body after. His injuries were too great.

He left three small published works of poetry and no
life insurance.

Grandma didn't allow friends or extended family at
the funeral. It was just us three—my grandma, my
mom, and me. There was no ceremony. Grandma read
Dad's poetry instead. I recalled one poem about a
curly-haired girl. I hadn't opened his books since.

Today the tombstone was dirty but otherwise the
same.

JONATHAN BURGER
1964–1992
Beloved son, father, and husband
"And this, our life, exempt from public haunt,
finds tongues in trees, books in the running brooks,
sermons in stones, and good in everything."

"I never went back to the ballet class," I said to the
stone. "I think Mom forgot about it."

Then I started crying. The tears came as a great
shock, and when I couldn't find a Kleenex in my purse,
I ran down the hill to the greeting hall to search out a
bathroom. The back door was wedged open with an
orange cone, most likely by a staff member out on a
smoking break. A sign on the door said "Absolutely No
Entrance" but I went in anyway and was rewarded with

a bathroom a few steps into a hallway with cinder-block walls.

I blew my nose and wiped my eyes. "What's wrong with you?" I asked myself in the bathroom mirror. "He died a long time ago. You barely knew him."

That made me feel worse. I started blubbering again. I was terrible at cheering myself up. Finally my tears dried and my snot was under control. I hoped Holden hadn't seen my episode. I hardly wanted to talk to him about my dead father before our first real date.

I had run into the greeting hall through the back door, but Holden was parked closer to the front. This part of the building was obviously off-limits to visitors, but if I exited from the back door, I would have to wind all the way around the building to get to Holden's truck. It would be much faster to cut through the building and exit from the front door, I reasoned.

I left the bathroom and found myself back in the long hallway. At one end was the door I had walked through, but now the door was closed. In the other direction, the hallway snaked around to an unknown destination.

I followed it until I got to two doors. One was marked "Personnel" and the other "Embalming." *Blech.* I envisioned tubes and foul fluids. I saw stars, and the world spun around me. *Keep it together,* I told myself. If I passed out, it would take days to find me, or worse, they might mistake me for a wayward embalming victim and finish the job. I sobered up immediately and opened the Personnel door.

The door led to a little alcove with lockers, most likely for the cemetery staff. In the crook of the alcove was a small flight of stairs with an Exit sign above. Perfect. I had just taken a step down when I heard voices. At first I panicked, but then I realized I only had to explain that I had gotten lost, which was more or less true. Then I heard a familiar voice.

"I don't know if they believed me. I heard that woman is too nosy for her own good, but Chuck wanted me to play it this way, and that's what I did."

The voices got closer. I spun around, looking for a hiding place. Two of the lockers had no locks on their doors. I opened one and stepped in sideways, but my butt got caught. I pushed, pulled, and sucked in my stomach. I cursed my weakness where junk food was concerned. "Why didn't I spit?" I muttered. Finally I squeezed in and closed the door just as two men entered the alcove. As I suspected, one of them was Father Lawrence.

"What did Randy Terns leave for Chuck?" asked the other man.

"I don't know. I couldn't get it out of her. But Holden is going to arrange it with me later."

"Did you talk to Chuck?"

"I'm going there now. He'll be at confession late this afternoon before dinner," Father Lawrence said.

"This is not a joke. If Holden doesn't come through for you, you're going to need to take more serious, permanent action. Chuck is not going to be happy. There are big things at stake here."

"No one knows that better than I."

The other man unlocked the locker next to mine. By the sound of it, he changed his clothes. After about fifteen minutes, they both left. I waited another five minutes to make sure they were really gone and then I opened the locker. It was harder to get out than it was to get in. I wasn't sure why; perhaps my butt had swelled. One thing I knew: Chuck Costas—the third gang member—was alive. I didn't want to think about who was buried in his grave.

Chapter 13

Over here! Over here! Over here! Okay, that was my little joke. What I wanted to say was: Focus. Minimize distractions. Not for you. Matchmakers are the original multitaskers. I mean, minimize distractions for your matches. Love needs focus in order to blossom. Here's what I tell my clients when they get distracted: "Keep your eye on the prize. You think something better is over there? No! You never found love before when you were looking all over the place. I got something right in front of your face. You may not recognize it, but it's called love. *So focus. Focus on what you're after. Remind yourself, in case you forgot." Gladie, the shortest distance between two points is a straight line. Now, unless you want to take the longest route, go straight. Go straight until you get what you want.*

Lesson 43,
Matchmaking Advice from Your Grandma Zelda

I STOOD in the alcove, unsure which direction to go. In one direction was the lying, suspicious Father Lawrence and his mysterious friend. In the other direction was Holden. Holden, who was supposed to come through for them. I felt sick at the thought that Holden was in cahoots with them, and possibly worse. I wasn't an idiot. I realized Holden was blond, too, like the knish thrower.

I walked down the stairs toward the exit at the front

of the building. I stood outside for a moment, searching for Holden's truck, but it wasn't parked where he'd left it. I was about to call Bridget to pick me up when Holden drove by.

"I put some gas in the truck," he explained. "I hope you haven't been waiting long."

"Not long," I said.

I stared at the truck for a while, weighing my options, and then allowed my eyes to travel to Holden's face. I studied him for a hint of liar, criminal, or worse. There was nothing there. Just Holden. Calm, compassionate, protective Holden. I got in. Holden made a U-turn and drove out of the cemetery.

"You okay?" he asked. "You're awfully quiet. Did everything go all right back there?"

"Yes. Maybe we should get my grandmother her tacos."

I hated suspecting Holden. I liked him. He had saved me. He was sensitive to my needs. He was hotter than Krakatoa.

"How did you find Chuck Costas?" I asked.

"Huh? I know a guy who finds people."

"And Father Lawrence? How did you find him?"

"When I called the cemetery about Costas, they took my contact information. The next thing I knew, Father Lawrence was calling me and setting up the appointment."

"Oh. So he set up the appointment."

Holden shot me a look, making me blush. "What's the matter?" he asked.

"I heard something back at the cemetery."

"Something about me?"

I looked at my nails and played with the door handle. Holden pulled the truck over to the side of the road and turned off the motor.

"Something about me?" he asked again.

"Holden, how do you know Father Lawrence?"

"I just told you how."

"Why does he think you're arranging to get something from Randy Terns?" I asked.

"Because I told him at the cemetery right in front of you, remember? You're the one who decided to make up that little story."

"Oh." Could it be that simple?

"Chuck Costas is still alive," I said.

Holden blinked. "What?"

"Chuck Costas is alive. I heard Father Lawrence tell another guy. He said Chuck Costas is still alive. I'm too nosy for my own good, and if you don't come through for them, they're going to have to do something serious and permanent. Oh, yeah, and Chuck is angry."

"None of this makes sense. We saw the grave," he said.

"Chuck is going to be at the church for confession this afternoon, right before dinner. I have to meet Officer Fred at Tea Time at two first. I'm going to match him," I said.

"There's only one Catholic church in town. So that simplifies things." Holden looked at his watch. "If we rush, we can get your grandmother her tacos, meet Fred at Tea Time, and make it to church on time." He smiled. "Get me to the church on time. That has a nice ring to it."

I melted in a heap on my seat. Holden had a way of making my hormones swarm like killer bees.

GRANDMA'S FAVORITE tacos were sold off the back of a truck in the little park on Main Street in the historic district. Holden hopped out of the car, but I stayed in my seat.

"You're not coming?" he asked through the open window.

"I'll wait for you."

"How many do you want?"

"Me? None!"

"If the tacos are so bad, why don't we go somewhere else?" he asked.

"They're not bad," I said. "They're the most delicious tacos ever made. Grandma only eats tacos from here."

Holden raised an eyebrow and went off to buy the tacos. After a couple of minutes he came back with a bag that was bursting at the seams. He shuddered and started the motor.

"I didn't notice at first," Holden said. "Then he took my money, and I got an eyeful. Does the CDC know about this place?"

"Grandma says he makes the best tacos, and she doesn't care if she catches smallpox or leprosy eating them."

Holden looked at the bag of tacos longingly. They smelled out of this world. "Maybe they're worth a small case of dysentery. If I eat one, will you ever kiss me again?" he asked seriously.

"It will never be the same," I said.

"Fair enough. I guess I'll never know what the best tacos taste like."

AFTER WE dropped off the tacos at Grandma's, we headed to Tea Time. As agreed, Holden and I split up once we entered. He chose a table in the corner next to the tea cozies. I made a beeline for Fred, who was the only other customer in the restaurant. He sat at the table in the center of the room. He was smoothing his hair with the palm of his hand when he saw me. His face turned up in a wide grin, and he stood up to greet me, upending the table and sending the china teapot and service for two crashing to the ground.

"Damn that girl!" Ruth hollered from the back.

"It wasn't me!" The voice came from behind the bar. It was an unnatural squeak, like the rats of NIMH had escaped. Julie's head popped up. I didn't know if she had been hiding or taking a nap. Some of her hair had escaped her ponytail, and she pulled it back behind her ear.

I checked out Fred to see if he had noticed Julie and if sparks had flown, but he was too preoccupied with the disaster he had wrought.

"Oh, gee," he said. He lifted the table over his head out of the way of the mess and searched for a place to put it down amid the shards of porcelain that littered the floor.

Ruth stormed out front and stomped her foot. "Don't just stand there, girl. Grab a broom and clean it up."

"It wasn't me," Julie squeaked.

"Clean it up before the man freezes like that," Ruth grunted, and rolled her eyes.

Fred's arms had started to wobble with the strain of the weight of the table. To his credit, he didn't yell obscenities at Julie as she hemmed and hawed and whined before getting the broom. But once she did, she was efficient, sweeping up the mess in a matter of seconds, maybe because of all the practice she got from her own mishaps. Anyway, a couple of minutes later, Fred and I were sitting at the table. Julie reset it with china on top of lace doilies. Fred clutched my hand in his, pinning his love-struck doe eyes on my face and sighing loudly.

"How lovely you set the table," I told Julie. "Doesn't Julie have a knack with tables, Fred?"

Julie swatted the hair from her face. She stared at me as if noticing me for the first time.

"Hi, Julie," I said. "I'm Gladie, and this is Fred. I'm a

friend of your great-aunt. She's said marvelous things about you." *Like you're Friday the thirteenth with legs.* "I love how you mismatched the china, putting different patterns together. It's very modern," I continued.

"Oh," Julie said. "Darn. I goofed, again. Don't tell Auntie. I'll go get the other pattern." She picked up my teacup and saucer and passed Ruth as she wandered away into the back.

Ruth beamed at me. "Couldn't stay away from my peach iced tea? I'm so glad you finally came to your senses."

"Actually, I could really go for a latte. Triple shot," I said.

I flinched, expecting her to throw something at me or at least pull my hair, but Ruth kept her cool. She sniffed. "I should have known. And what do you want, Red? Are you with her? You want coffee?" She drew out the word "coffee" in a long, threatening manner, but Fred was too distracted to notice.

"Sure. I like those iced coffee drinks. You got caramel sauce to go on top?"

"Caramel sauce?" she asked.

I put a protective arm out in front of Fred.

"He didn't mean that," I said. "You can skip the caramel sauce."

Ruth turned on her heel, muttering, "Caramel sauce." She stopped off at Holden's table. "You want some kind of coffee drink, too?" she asked him. "You expecting caramel sauce, too? Chocolate? What?"

Holden tilted his head to the side, the picture of magnanimous patience. "Lapsang souchong tea. Steeped for three minutes. No milk, sugar, or honey, please."

I couldn't help but notice the small smile of victory Holden threw at me.

"A man who knows tea," said Ruth. "A man who

knows tea," she repeated louder in case we hadn't heard. "I'll brew it myself."

I doubted my latte was going to arrive anytime soon, if at all, and Fred's chances of an iced coffee were worse than hitting the $100,000 jackpot on the nickel slots.

"Julie sure is cute," I said. I pulled my hand out of his grip. "Don't you think she's cute, Fred?"

"Who?"

"Julie, our waitress."

"Yeah, sure. You look great. I like you in jeans. You look pretty in dresses, too."

"Julie's wearing jeans," I said. "She has such a cute little figure. Pretty, too."

"I guess so. I've got tickets to the monster truck rally next week. You want to come with me?"

A drop of sweat rolled down my face. How had I gotten things so screwed up? I'd sucked face with my first potential match, and now my second potential match wanted to take me to the monster truck rally, which I assumed was the last step before he proposed. I didn't want to fail with Fred's match. I had had a strong feeling down in my gut the moment I saw Julie. It was like a blaze of light, a lightning strike, and I knew absolutely that Julie and Fred should be together. Was that the feeling my grandmother spoke about? Was she right about me being like her? I searched for the feeling again, and sure enough, it was right there in the pit of my stomach where I left it. I knew Fred and Julie were meant for each other. I knew they would fall in love and live happily ever after.

"Next week? I don't think I can make the monster truck rally, Fred. Besides, I hate monster truck rallies," I said.

Fred flinched.

I moved my chair next to him. "Julie likes monster truck rallies," I whispered in his ear. "Pretty Julie with her cute figure in her jeans sitting next to you, watching the big trucks."

As if on cue, Julie brought me a new cup to match the other setting. She exhaled, sending a lock of red hair flying off her face to reveal her button nose and blue eyes.

"Ask her," I whispered.

"You like monster truck rallies?" he asked.

"Um, I guess so. If it's outside. I don't like to be shut up inside with a lot of people," Julie answered.

Click click click. I heard the cogs of Fred's brain settling into place.

"I don't like to be shut up inside small places," he said.

Julie shuddered. "Me neither. I got locked in the closet here. I thought I was going to die."

"I almost died in a small glass box," he said.

Fred's love-struck doe eyes were now fully focused on Julie.

Julie's focus was elsewhere. She stared toward the back of the store. "That's nice," she said absentmindedly, and walked away. Fred popped up and ran after her, loudly regaling her with the wonders of monster truck rallies as he went.

Success. It was a wonderful thing. The tune to "Boogie Fever" played in my head, and I whistled it as I strutted to Holden's table.

"That looked successful," he said.

"*Cha-ching.* I'll get a check from him when things settle down," I said.

"You made it look easy."

I twirled around. " 'Boogie fever, I think it's going around,' " I sang. "I'm in a really good mood. I don't think I've been in this good a mood in months. You know what? I think everything has turned around for me. I've got a handle on matchmaking. Now we're going to find Chuck Costas and have the police throw his butt in jail. I should probably play the lottery, too. I can't lose!

"Ruth, bring me out my latte," I called. "I feel a party coming on."

Ruth brought Holden a gold teapot and put it on the table with a proud flourish. "I steeped it in my best china," she said. "I don't usually use this for customers, but I can tell you're different. Don't let the girl near it. If she breaks it, I'll lose years off my life."

"Don't worry." Holden's deep voice dripped charm. "The moment I'm done, I'll return it to you personally. It's the most beautiful teapot I've ever seen."

Ruth's eyes shined with pride. She sure liked tea.

"Where's my latte?" I asked.

She waved in my direction. "Shh. He's about to taste it. You'll get your travel cup when I'm good and ready."

Holden poured the black tea into his cup and took a sip. He closed his eyes and, after a moment of obvious appreciation, swallowed. He opened his eyes and smiled.

"The best Lapsang souchong I've ever tasted, Miss Fletcher. Really."

Ruth slapped her hands together and gushed, "I've got little tea sandwiches that will go perfectly with it. On the house. I'll be right back." She leaned down and looked me in the eye. "Sandwiches for one. They don't go at all well with lattes."

"That's okay. I'm not hungry," I said, but I was starving. I hadn't eaten lunch, and my stomach growled in protest. I could have eaten at least a dozen tea sandwiches.

Holden stood and took my hand. "Actually, we're strapped for time. Please allow me to pick up the check for both of us, and then we really must be going."

Ruth's face fell like the *Hindenburg,* in flames and in

slow motion, like the greatest achievement of our generation had failed miserably, bringing her great and irreparable disappointment.

Holden tossed a twenty on the table. "I'll come back as soon as I'm able, Miss Fletcher," he said. "How could I stay away from such marvelous tea?"

The tiniest of twinkles returned to Ruth's eyes. "The moment I saw you, I said to myself, 'There's a tea drinker. A real one,'" she said.

I gave Holden a good hard look. He was not what I would have described as a tea type. He was lumberjack material, someone who drank his coffee thick as mud with a shot of whiskey mixed in. Nevertheless, before we left, after minimal additional begging, Ruth made me a latte.

Holden unlocked the passenger door of his truck.

"Holden, you're not really a tea drinker, are you?" I asked.

"I like tea."

"Oh."

"I like tea and coffee and bourbon and brandy. I don't like wine. Never have. Don't know why."

As he spoke, he took a couple of steps forward, pushing my body against the truck. His heat made me warm all over. My fingers curled into his shirt, and my breathing stopped.

"Fred was right. You look good in jeans," he said. He trailed languid kisses down the side of my neck. My latte fell and hit the ground with a loud splat. I stumbled, and he held me up, pulling me into a tight embrace. I felt my pores dilate and my hair grow. All my senses were heightened, and I moaned.

"We're on Main Street in a small town," I said, either out loud or in my head. In any case, Holden wasn't listening, and he wasn't slowing down. He didn't care what the neighbors thought. He moved from my neck to my lips, parting them and taking my mouth with a strong urgency. My arms encircled his waist and traveled up under his shirt. His body was hard as nails and mine, mine, mine. My head swam in a sea of hormones, and I was wondering if it was possible to get pregnant like that, fully clothed, standing on Main Street, when Holden broke the kiss.

"Tastier than Lapsang souchong," he said. "Definitely much tastier."

I rested my forehead on his chest as I tried to catch my breath.

"I might need a defibrillator," I said.

"That's for when your heart stops. Did your heart stop?"

"No, it's going at a pretty good clip."

"Then you're fine."

"CHUCK COSTAS did it, did it, did it," I sang. Holden parked the truck in front of the Catholic church.

"Maybe just 'did it, did it.' There were only two deaths," Holden observed.

"How about you? You think he did it? I think he did it. Faking his own death? The priest lying for him? He did it. This is classic Hitchcock. This is classic PBS *Mystery*."

Holden turned off the motor. "Murder has got your color up. You're flushed."

"Solving two murders has got my color up. Getting the crazy Terns family off my back has got my color up. C'mon, let's go get Chuck Costas," I said.

I reined in my gung ho attitude after I walked into the church. Whereas from the outside the church was a nondescript little wooden building, not out of place in any Western town, the inside of the church was resplendent. It stopped me in my tracks, calmed me down, and put me in a spiritual frame of mind, which I guessed was the architect's intention.

The church dated from the eighteen hundreds like the town itself. It had high ceilings supported by white-washed wooden beams. The pews were covered in red velvet. The sides were decorated with stone sculptures of various saints, and behind the nave were rows of lit red candles and another set of doors.

Holden pointed back toward the candles. "The confessional is back there."

It looked like a large wooden closet, and the door was closed.

"Maybe he's in there right now," said Holden, reading my thoughts.

"What should we do?" It was probably a question I should have thought over before I walked into the church. What exactly was I going to do when I caught up with Chuck Costas? Point at him, tell him he's been a bad boy, and order him to follow me to the police station?

If Chuck Costas was the killer, then he might be after me, too. I could be his next victim, and here I was handing myself over to him on a silver platter without any means of defense. I looked over at Holden. He was definitely fit, but how would he do against a two-time murderer, a former gang member, and most likely a knish thrower? I could have kicked myself for not bringing along Spencer. Spencer had a gun and backup. But he also had an attitude, and he would never have allowed me to walk into the church to confront a fake dead murderer. He would have sent me home or arrested me or not have believed me about Chuck Costas in the first place.

Holden raised an eyebrow. "What should we do? We could wait until the door opens and see if it's him. He's an old guy, right?"

"Yes."

"I think we should play it by ear."

We stood at the front pew and watched the closed confessional for a sign of life. The church was empty and quiet, and I was just wondering if the Catholic community in Cannes had gone the way of the gold miners when the confessional door opened. I was greeted by a familiar face—so familiar I almost fainted in shock.

Chapter 14

✦ ♥ ✦

Sometimes love dies. It croaks. It bites the dust, buys the farm, kicks the bucket. Dead. Deader than a doornail. Are you getting the picture, bubeleh*? First you think he walks on water and then you're not sure he can even walk up-right. Falling out of love doesn't just happen to old married couples. It can happen to young matches who are dating. Things change. You start going left, and suddenly you switch right. So, as a matchmaker, you need something waiting in the wings. An understudy. A part two. A sequel with a better star in the leading role.*
Lesson 37,
Matchmaking Advice from Your Grandma Zelda

I PUT my arm out for Holden to steady me. I couldn't believe my eyes.

"What? Huh? You?" I sputtered.

"It's not what you think! Well, it is, but hear me out." Bridget, my atheistic, religion-hating, establishment-hating friend, pushed her glasses up her nose. She had broken out into a flop sweat and everything was slipping off her.

"Are you protesting the confessional?" I asked.

"Not exactly."

"The church?"

"Not really."

"Religion?"

"Well . . ."

"The Vatican?"

Bridget's glasses slipped from her nose and fell to the floor with a small crunch. Her body sweated and shook with equal force. I was close to calling the paramedics. Finally she erupted.

"I'm a Catholic!" Her voice echoed against the rafters like thunder. "I can't hide it any longer. I'm a Catholic. I go to mass every day, and I have to go in disguise so no one notices me."

"You go to mass *every day*?" I asked.

"I'll just be over there by the candles, looking around," said Holden. I had forgotten he was there. I nodded and watched him walk to the back of the church.

"Do you mind if I sit?" I asked Bridget. I sat in the first pew. It felt good to be off my feet. The pew was more comfortable than it looked. Bridget bent down and picked up the remains of her glasses. She was practically blind without them, and I had to guide her hand to find them.

"Darn," she said, fingering the broken lenses. "These were brand-new." She squinted at me. I patted the seat next to me and she sat, the glasses still clutched in her hand. "I can't see a blessed thing," she said, peering closely at my face. "You look an awful lot like George Bush now."

"Your speech is much cleaner in a church. No swearing."

Bridged turned red. "You know, Gladie, I come from a real religious family. And old habits die hard. I tried to turn my back on the Church, but I couldn't. Can you understand?"

"Of course I can. You don't have to apologize for your beliefs. You haven't done anything wrong."

"But I gave you the impression—"

"Of being a strident, militant, religion-hating atheist?" I asked.

"Yes."

"I love you for who you are. You don't have to hide anything from me."

Bridget sniffed. I took a Kleenex from my purse and handed it to her.

"I want to be a strident, militant, religion-hating atheist," she said. "I am one, really, but I can't let go of the Church."

"Traditions are great. I haven't had a lot of them. My parents didn't pass on many traditions to me. Mom liked after-Christmas sales. That was about it."

Bridget nodded and blew her nose. "The after-Christmas sale is kind of a universal religion, don't you think? Everyone can get behind it. It builds revenue, and it alleviates economic pressures on at-risk families. Although, you know I'm opposed to the cheap labor being used for today's products."

I wrapped my arm around Bridget's shoulder. "You're still the same Bridget," I said.

"What are you doing here with the hunk?" she asked.

"We've tracked down Randy Terns' remaining gang member, Chuck Costas. He's supposed to show up here for confession. I got the information from a lying priest."

"A lying priest?"

"It's a long story, but the important thing is that I'll finally have this whole mess wrapped up," I said. "Chuck Costas killed Randy Terns and Jimmy the Fink for the bank robbery money. I know he did it, the thieving, murdering bastard."

Bridget gasped and crossed herself three times.

"I'm sorry. I forgot where I was," I said.

The confessional door creaked open, and the priest's head emerged. I thought for sure I was in for a good knuckle-slapping.

"She didn't it mean it, Father," said Bridget. "It's her first time in a church."

This information didn't seem to mollify the old priest. He scowled at me, clearly angry at my outburst. He looked around, then stepped out of the confessional. That's when I saw the gun in his hand, pointed directly at me.

I stood up, ready to bolt or scream or throw my purse at him.

Bridget stood as well, a dopey smile plastered on her face. "How inconsiderate of me. Father Seymour, this is my dear friend Gladie Burger. Gladie, this is my spiritual advisor, Father Seymour."

Bridget squinted, blindly making her way toward the armed priest, not seeing the gun in his hand.

"Get back, Bridget, or I'll shoot," the priest said with an icy calmness in his voice that made me believe every word.

"Very funny, Father." Bridget giggled, still unaware of the situation.

"Bridget, he's got a gun," I hissed.

"What?"

"A gun. The priest has got a gun."

"What?"

"I've got a gun, Bridget. I've got a gun, and I'm going to shoot both of you unless you let me go."

"I'm all for letting you go," I said. "I'll let you go anywhere you want."

"What's going on?" asked Bridget, squinting harder.

"Why couldn't you let well enough alone?" He waved the gun at me. "I had changed my ways, turned over a new leaf. Then you started snooping around and bodies started piling up."

"Chuck Costas?" I asked. *Ding ding ding.* I'd hit the jackpot. Chuck Costas was now a priest. With a gun. The world is a strange place.

"I even had a tombstone made so nobody would come looking. It cost me two thousand bucks. That was a lot of money in the seventies. Everything was fine until you showed up."

I thought it was a little uncharitable to blame me since he was the murderer, but I didn't think it was a good time to remind him.

"The cops will be looking for you now. You should probably give yourself up," I said.

"Why would the cops be looking for me?"

"They frown on killing two people," I pointed out.

"Oh, my God. Oh, my God. My priest has a gun on me. My priest is a killer," Bridget said, finally taking stock of the situation.

"I didn't kill anybody," he said. "I'm the one running. I don't want to be number three. There's a crazy person out there. Haven't you figured that out yet?"

"My priest has a gun!" shouted Bridget. She flung her hands out, a little reminiscent of Jesus on the cross, and punched me square in the jaw, sending me flying to the side. Before I could right myself, a shot rang out. I searched my body for unwanted holes, but it was Father Seymour who fell to the ground in a bloody heap, half of his head blown apart into little pieces, some decorating my cotton shirt and jeans.

"Like broken eggs," I mumbled, and then everything went black.

I WOKE to music, Aerosmith's "Dream On." Then a man's voice.

"Chief Bolton here. No, I dealt with Holden. That's right. We'll follow up with Ms. Donovan at another time. Her statement is fine for now."

I opened my eyes. I was in a hospital room. Spencer was pacing, his cellphone against his ear.

"Did I get shot?" My voice came out gravelly. Spencer clicked off his phone and sat at the edge of my bed.

"Hey there. Are you up for good, or are you going to go away again?"

"Huh?"

"You've been slipping in and out for a few hours. Concussion," he said, pointing to my head.

"Was I shot?"

"No. As far we can make out, you fainted and hit your head on a pew."

"The priest—"

"Was Chuck Costas. Yeah, your friend Bridget filled us in. Do you want to talk about this now, or do you want to rest?"

"Do I have to rest? Am I dying? You're being awfully nice to me."

Spencer raised an eyebrow.

"I'm not usually nice to you? Scratch that. We don't need to argue in your condition."

"My condition?" I asked.

"A slight concussion. Some residual shock. You don't do well with blood."

A flash memory of the priest's head exploding made me shudder. I pulled the covers up to my neck.

"Is Bridget okay?" I asked.

"A little shaken up. She didn't see much since her glasses were broken. She's at home with your other friend Lucy. Your grandmother called me ten times. I was clearing up the mess with Peter and Christy Terns, but she insisted I go to the church. I was parking when the shot was fired."

"I was sure Chuck Costas was the murderer," I said. "But he told me he was running, hiding. He didn't want to be number three."

"Well, he was. A messy number three. But that doesn't mean Randy and Jimmy were murdered, too."

"Then who killed Chuck Costas?"

"No witnesses. And there's no guarantee the bullet was meant for him. It could have been meant for you. You were in the line of fire. Bridget explained how she accidentally pushed you. Maybe it was your head the shooter was aiming for."

"There's another priest. He lied to us. Father Lawrence," I said.

"Yeah, we talked to him. He said he was protecting Chuck Costas. He said that Chuck had become a priest and devoted his life to good works and required anonymity. When I pointed out that the good-works priest threatened to shoot you and Bridget, he said Chuck had a lapse of judgment due to stress. He doesn't like you. I think he meant you when he said 'stress.' He's also upset about the church. It's going to take days to clean."

"No witnesses?" I asked. "That's impossible." Even if Bridget was nearly blind, Holden had been there.

"Your friend Arthur Holden said he was investigating the vestibule in the back of the church when the shot was fired. He ran in immediately after but he didn't see anything."

A silence thick with suspicion and unspoken accusations filled my hospital room. It was entirely possible for my mysterious new neighbor to be the killer. Spencer waited for me to either indict Holden or defend him. I was reserving judgment. Besides, my head hurt. I had too much information to process.

"Peter and Christy are in jail?" I asked.

"Yes, for a while. They've got some strikes between them."

The gang members were gone. Two of the Terns children were gone. The suspects were dwindling as the bodies piled up.

"I guess you want my statement, but it sounds like Bridget told you the whole story," I said.

"Your statement can wait. They're keeping you here overnight."

"Thank you for visiting."

Spencer moved to the chair next to my bed.

"I'll stick around tonight. Don't have much else to do."

"No police work?"

"In this sleepy town? Not much crime here, if you don't count the five-foot radius around you. If something is going to happen, it's going to happen near you."

He had a point. I was a magnet for mayhem. I drifted to sleep and had dreams of gun-carrying priests flying overhead. They played a game where their goal was to throw their guns through a stained-glass window. The window was a huge picture of Bridget with enormous glasses that covered her face from forehead to chin. "Watch out, Bridget," I yelled in my dream, but they threw their guns anyway.

"You're dreaming." I fluttered my eyes open, tearing myself away from the Bridget picture window. Spencer caressed my face.

"I was dreaming about flying priests and Bridget's glasses," I said. "What time is it?"

"Eleven."

"You should leave. You don't need to babysit me."

The room was dim, but I could make out his face, the blink of his eyes. He was a very good-looking man. No wonder half the women in Cannes wanted him. Spencer was studying my face, too. His eyes wandered from my hair to my cheeks, my nose, my lips. Then our eyes locked.

I could hear the blood flow through my veins and Spencer's shallow breathing. I took his hand from my face and held it in my own. I found myself caressing his palm and stopped myself.

"Gladie," he began.

"I bet my hair is a mess," I said.

"I didn't notice."

"This isn't the part where we talk about the murders, is it?"

"No."

"I don't want to talk about anything else." I was Cowardly McCoward from Scaredy Cat Town. The quiet, brooding Spencer scared me to death. I would have rather faced crazy priests with guns than Spencer getting personal.

Spencer cleared his throat. "Fair enough."

"You should go home and get some sleep. I'll be all right."

He nodded. "I'll be back in the morning. Don't get any funny ideas and try to bust out and find Jimmy Hoffa or anything."

"Scout's honor," I said.

I was asleep before he left the room.

I WOKE with a start. The room was still dark, but there was a smell of stale cigarettes that wasn't there before.

"Spencer?" I asked, but I knew it wasn't him.

"Who's Spencer? Is that your boyfriend?" The woman's voice came from the corner, where it was too dark to see. I fumbled in the sheets for the button to call the nurse.

"You won't find it. I moved it. I wanted to speak to you alone. We're always getting interrupted, and I'm an impatient person."

"Jane," I said, recognizing her voice. The Terns sister with the penchant for cutting the heads off Barbies. Swell. *Why did I insist that Spencer leave?*

"What time is it?" I asked her.

"I don't know. Time doesn't matter to me. I don't sleep much at night."

"Sucks, doesn't it? Not sleeping, I mean," I said.

The irony was lost on Jane. She didn't care that she was waking me up in the middle of the night.

"Did you want to talk?" I asked. "Is this about Peter and Christy?" It was possible she blamed me for their arrest. After all, I had been there at the time.

"I don't care about Peter and Christy. I say let them rot in jail. Good riddance."

Jane came out of the shadows and approached my bed. She was taller than I remembered. Thin, like her mother. She wore khaki shorts and a cotton sweater and carried a small Prada handbag. She had nicer knees than I had. I hated my knees.

"To what do I owe the honor?" I asked.

"You're a hard woman to find. You move around a lot. Maybe I just wanted to say hi," she said.

"Hi."

"I heard you almost got shot."

"A priest got shot." I tiptoed my fingers around, still looking for the call button.

"I don't know much about priests. I'm a Lutheran. My mother used to be Mormon. Did you know that?" she asked.

"No," I said.

"She converted to be with my father, which was a joke because he wasn't what you'd call a religious or spiritual man." Jane laughed. It came out in one loud bark, like an explosion. I hoped the nurses heard and would be coming in soon to kick her out. Where were they, anyway? I had a concussion. They were supposed to wake me up every hour and ask me who the president was.

"Spiritual, that's a laugh," she said.

"Yeah, funny."

Jane came closer and studied my IV drip. "I thought you were going to help me," she said.

"Sure, what do you want?"

"The murder. Don't you remember?"

"Which murder?"

"My father's! Pay attention. Stay focused. I need your help. I thought you were going to look into it," she said.

"Huh?"

"Peter told me you were on top of it. He said you were just like your grandmother, but you seem pretty dense to me."

I was bone tired. I was in the hospital for rest, and I was getting anything but. The last thing I wanted was one more crazy person getting aggressive toward me. I had had enough.

"I've had enough," I said. "Peter told me Rob did it. There. That's help enough. Go wake up Rob. I need to get back to sleep."

Jane rummaged through her purse and took out a cigarette. Her eyes darted to the Oxygen and No Smoking signs. Without lighting it, she put the cigarette between her lips.

"Rob? Are you kidding me? You've been wasting everyone's time. Rob didn't do it. You haven't been listening. There's something about my father you don't know."

"I know."

"You know?"

"Yes."

"What do you know?"

"About his past."

"What about his past?"

"You don't know?"

"I know."

"What do you know? Wait. I'm getting dizzy," I said. "You're talking about the bank robberies?"

"My father? My father didn't have two brain cells to rub together. He couldn't rob a bank to save his life. I'm talking indiscretions. Infidelities."

"Oh."

"One infidelity."

I scooted up in bed. "Jane, your mother already mentioned this to me."

"You have to look into it right to the end. Do you understand? You have to get to the bottom of it. The truth." Jane squeezed her cigarette in her fist. "It's the key. Don't you understand? You have to look there. Follow the infidelity, and you'll solve the murder. I need you. I can't do this on my own. You have to do it. I'm scared, Gladie. I'm really scared."

"What are you scared of? You have to tell me more. If you know something . . ."

"I've always been a good girl. I'm the oldest, you know? People assume Peter is the oldest, but I am. I am the responsible one. A people pleaser, that's me. I could always be counted on."

A people pleaser? It occurred to me that Jane was having a psychotic break.

"I wish you understood. You're supposed to be like your grandmother." And then she was gone, walking out the door, lighting her cigarette on the way, inhaling like it was her first oxygen of the day.

I slid down in the bed, worming my way under the covers. I closed my eyes and flipped onto my side. I was exhausted. A lot of crazies had entered my life since I found out about Randy Terns' death on Thursday. Now it was the early hours of Tuesday, and I had been kidnapped, threatened, and nearly shot. I had been lied to by a priest, seen two dead bodies, had my clothes covered in brain bits, and had been sort of pursued by two men, one unwanted, one wanted. Three, if I counted Spencer. But Spencer was a question mark. It was a lot for a long weekend. On the bright side, I had made my first match.

Take that, Jane Terns. I might not be like my grandmother, but I had made my first match. Besides, Grandma would never have made it to the hospital. They would have treated her at home. And she would never have been in the church or kidnapped on a mountain. She would never have been anywhere, for that matter. Maybe that's why the Terns family had picked me, I thought. I might not have been as good as Grandma, but at least I was mobile.

I flipped onto my other side, but it was no use. I was wide awake. I found my phone and dialed Spencer. "If you don't come and get me, I'm busting out to find Jimmy Hoffa," I said.

"I'll be right there."

"Bring coffee."

IT TOOK longer than I expected to be released. True to his word, Spencer arrived thirty minutes later, at five in the morning, holding a large coffee from 7-Eleven. The nurses couldn't release me until the doctors signed off, and the doctors were nowhere to be found. Meanwhile, I was imprisoned in my room with Spencer tapping his foot on the floor, looking at his watch every five minutes and saying, "I don't have anything better to do with my time."

I thought about distracting him with the details of Jane's visit, but Spencer yelled at me whenever I had anything to do with the Terns family, and my head hurt enough already. He was clean-shaven and dressed to the nines, whereas I was dressed in scrubs because my clothes were considered evidence.

"How did you get cleaned and dressed so fast?" I asked.

"What do you mean? How long does it take for you to get dressed?"

"To get as pretty as you? A long time."

Spencer stopped tapping. "You think I look pretty?"

"I mean handsome."

"Handsome?" He cocked his head to the side and gave me his signature smirk.

"I didn't mean handsome or pretty," I said. "You know, dressed up. You're dressed up. You're much more dressed up than the average Cannes citizen."

"I bathe at night. This morning I shaved and slipped on some clothes. I have nice clothes. What of it? Don't hate me because I'm beautiful, Pinkie."

I groaned. "Ugh. You have a way of talking, Spencer. You're making my coffee back up on me."

"Nice."

Spencer took off his blazer and draped it on the back of his chair. He plopped down and stretched his legs out in front of him. He wore biker boots, a little out of line with his Dapper Dan persona.

"Fine, then," he said. "We've got a couple of hours before they get your paperwork done. What should we talk about? What's safe? I know. What do you like to do?"

"What do you mean, like to do?"

"Hobbies. What are your hobbies? C'mon, help me out here, Pinkie. I'm trying to make conversation."

"What's the matter? You sick or something? People really should get the flu shot."

"So, no hobbies, then?" he asked.

What were my hobbies? I didn't knit or collect stamps. I got a new job every couple of weeks. That was kind of my hobby, but I didn't want to tell Spencer that.

"I like to watch TV," I said.

"Gladie, everybody likes to watch TV."

I counted ceiling tiles and looked out the window. Nope, I couldn't think of a hobby.

"I like to butt into other people's lives," I said finally.

Spencer nodded. "That's what I figured."

* * *

WE DIDN'T get out of the hospital until nine-thirty. He was late for work, and I was desperate to take a shower and get to my bed. Besides, I wanted to see how Bridget was doing, and I wanted to follow up on my first match.

When we were a couple of blocks away from the hospital, however, Spencer got a call over the police radio. A man outside a store was holding a gun. All available police cars were racing to the scene. Spencer turned on the siren and the flashing lights, and we sped toward the scene of the new crime.

"If I see another gun pointed at me, I will throw up. I've had enough. Drop me off at the side of the road," I ordered.

"Too dangerous. You're going to stay in the car, and I'm locking it this time. No one is going to point a gun at you."

"It's all fun and games until someone gets hurt," I said.

"Trust me, you are not fun and games."

Spencer skidded to a halt behind two police cars. We were outside the historic district in front of an old brick building. The sign read Guns N Things in faded blue lettering. The window displayed enough weapons to make the Terminator question gun rights.

Two men in their sixties stood on the sidewalk in front of the store, being questioned by two officers. Spencer hopped out of the car and locked me in. I didn't fight him. I was tired of guns and violence. I slouched down, rested my head on the window, and closed my eyes. I was dozing when Spencer got back in the car.

He ran his fingers through his perfectly groomed hair, making it stand up. "I have inherited a swell group of guys. The chief before me loved to recruit idiots. I

thought I could train them, but I'm not so sure anymore."

Behind Spencer, four cops were whooping it up with
two armed old men. The men were talking, gesturing
wildly with the guns, and the cops thought this was riotously funny.

"What's going on?" I asked.

"Somebody called in a tip that a man had a gun,"
Spencer said. "Duh. It's the owner of the gun shop. He's
got a lot of guns. He's got more guns than the National
Guard. I'm going to wrap things up here, and I'm having two of the idiots drive you home. They should be
able to drive you two miles without incident."

The two idiots were Sergeant Brody and another guy
who turned out to be Officer James, who didn't look a
day over eighteen. They put me in the back of a patrol
car after reminding each other in a loud whisper not to
call me Underwear Girl.

"I heard you got brains splattered all over your
clothes. Some on your face, too. So cool. What was it
like?" Officer James turned around and looked at me
with his puppy-dog eyes, his fingers poking through the
mesh wire that separated us.

"It was cool," I said. "Brains are very cool."

That seemed to satisfy him.

"Man, I would have loved to see that. *Kapow! Splat!*"
He giggled, a low, warbling laugh. "You think I could
have your autograph later?"

"Because of the brains?" I asked.

"No, the picture. The underwear. I've brought in all
my friends to see it. I can't wait to tell them I finally met
you."

Sergeant Brody let out a slow, appreciative whistle.
"What do we have here? That's a beaut."

We were tailing a Lamborghini. It was red and shiny.

"Wow, you don't see one of those in Cannes every

day," I said. "It's like a movie star's car or a drug dealer's car. Oh, I know. I know. It's probably stolen. Don't
you think so?"

James and Brody looked at each other and sat up
straighter in their seats.

"I was just kidding," I said. "I'm sure it's not stolen."

"I'll bet five dollars it's hot," said Brody.

"I've always wanted to get behind the wheel of one of
those," I said. "Talk about a sexy car."

Brody ran the plates, and sure enough, the Lamborghini was stolen. The patrol car was filled with electricity. Even if Brody and James were idiots, they were
still good at their job. Within a couple of minutes, they
had pulled the Lamborghini over, handcuffed the
driver, and stuffed him in the backseat next to me. They
left me with him while they inspected the car outside
and filled out paperwork.

"Hi, I'm Paul," said the prisoner. He was about forty
years old, and he bore a distressing resemblance to my
elementary school principal, right down to the short-
sleeved button-front shirt, brown tie, and comb-over
that wound around his head like a turban. He adjusted
his position on the seat, trying to get more comfortable
with his hands cuffed behind him.

"Hi, Paul, I'm Gladie."

"Beautiful day, isn't it? Warm. I'm glad they kept the
windows open. Nice breeze," he said.

"Yes, beautiful. It's good to see you haven't let this get
you down."

"The arrest? All a big misunderstanding."

"You didn't steal the car?" I asked.

"Oh, I stole it. I got a good business going. I used to
be in encyclopedias, but nobody wants an encyclopedia
these days."

Didn't I know it. I tried selling encyclopedias door to
door for two days. What a waste of time.

"I make at least five grand on a Caddy or Mercedes," he explained. "A friend I know convinced me to take it up a notch, and I picked up this car for somebody else. Big mistake. Way too flashy. But it wasn't my idea. You see?"

I tried to see, but his reasoning was a little murky. "You're going to tell them it wasn't your idea, and they're going to let you go?" I asked.

"Yeah, exactly," he said, obviously thrilled that I had caught on. "Those cops sure like that car."

Brody and James had finished the paperwork and were checking out the Lamborghini, taking turns in the driver's seat.

"How fast you think this goes, Brody?" I heard James ask.

"As fast as you want," said Brody.

Paul shifted in his seat. "Uh-oh," he said. "I've seen this before."

"What?" I asked.

"While we wait for the tow, we could take it for a little ride," said James.

"What would it hurt?" asked Brody.

After a coin toss to see who would drive, they hopped in the Lamborghini and peeled out.

"That leaves just you and me," said Paul.

It was then that I noticed the door was locked and impossible to open from the inside.

I craned my head to see if the Lamborghini was on its way back, but it was gone. Then I heard the crash.

"The steering on that Lamborghini is a bitch," said Paul.

Chapter 15

◆ ♥ ◆

As you might have guessed, I do pretty well for myself. I pay my bills and have enough left over to buy at full retail. I don't advertise my prices. You could say they fluctuate. Anyway, when to ask for money? That's a very good question! I don't have an answer. I ask for it when I think the time is right. One of those right moments is when they first fall in love. You know, love makes a person feel very good. Like they're in the clouds, eating fudge, and it's making their skin tingly. That's a very good time to ask for money. Another time—and this is not going to sound nice, dolly, so forgive me—is when they come to me and they're desperate. Miserable. They think they're going to die without love. That's a really good time to ask for money. (Only if they can afford it, though. I'm a nice person, after all.)

Lesson 48,
Matchmaking Advice from Your Grandma Zelda

"WHAT DO you think that was?" I asked Paul.

"By the sounds of it, I would say the Lamborghini hit the brick retaining wall down the street, which means there's no more evidence to charge me."

"Do you think they're dead?" I asked.

"There's a good chance. Hey, don't look like that. I hate when women cry. Maybe they pulled through. They were young. Strong."

I pictured their young, strong bodies smashed against the wall.

"I have a cellphone!" I announced, remembering my purse. I pulled it out and called Spencer.

"Cops! Wall! Car!" I yelled into the phone. Sentences formed in my brain, but I couldn't get them to come out of my mouth. "Wall! Car! Cops!"

"Shit, I'll be right there," Spencer said.

"Would you look at that?" Paul said. "I would never have believed it."

Brody and James hobbled up the street. James held his left arm at a weird angle, Brody had a slight limp, and both were disheveled, with bits of their clothing burned away. Brody's sunglasses hung down one side of his face, still clinging to one ear, and neither had held on to his hat. But they were alive, mobile, and not much worse for wear. I was gobsmacked.

"It's like a miracle," said Paul. "I can't wait to tell everyone at church."

My door opened, and Spencer pulled me out.

"What happened?" Spencer asked. "Are you okay? Pinkie, what did you do?"

"It wasn't me. It wasn't me. I swear it wasn't me," I said.

"Who's that?" he asked, pointing at Paul.

"I'm Paul," Paul said.

"Who's Paul?" Spencer asked. "Why were you locked in the back with Paul? Wait. Don't tell me. I need to hear things in batches. I can't take it in all at once."

"Hey, Chief. Don't worry, we're fine."

Brody and James made it back to the patrol car and put on their best professional and authoritative faces in front of Spencer. Spencer eyeballed them, letting his eyes travel from their scuffed shoes to their singed hair.

"We caught a car thief," said Brody.

"Who you put in the back of the car with a civilian," supplied Spencer.

They looked at me. "Uh . . . ," said James.

"And then what?" Spencer asked. "Where's the stolen car? Will someone answer me? My mind is thinking up all kinds of crazy scenarios. What? Was it stolen again?"

"This is so good," Paul said from inside the patrol car.

Spencer pointed at Paul. "Do I need to ask him what happened?"

"It was an accident," James blurted out.

"We ran it into a wall."

"Ran what into a wall?" Spencer asked.

"It was such a sweet ride," said James.

"Hold on. You took a stolen vehicle on a joy ride?" Spencer was close to stroke level. His face was purple and his body shook slightly.

The tow truck and another patrol car arrived. It was a perfect time to get out of there.

I touched Spencer's arm. "Maybe we can let them handle it. You look like you could use a distraction and a good breakfast. You want to take me home?"

Spencer nodded. "Leave your guns and your badges with the desk sergeant," he told Brody and James. "And come in tomorrow so we can talk. If I talk to you today, I'll break your noses."

The ride to my grandmother's house was quiet. I sensed Spencer's blood pressure lowering the farther we got from the smashed Lamborghini.

There were at least a dozen cars parked in front of Grandma's.

"What day is it?" I asked Spencer.

"Tuesday."

"Oh, no. It's the Second Chancers singles meeting."

"Sounds bad."

"Not as bad as the Pregnant and Looking meeting. But still."

The parlor was packed. Instead of the normal, organized session with women sitting on the overstuffed furniture and my grandmother presiding with a kind but firm hand, it was bedlam. The women stood in small groups, talking to each other at different levels of panic. Grandma was nowhere to be seen. Spencer's entrance was first met with hushed appraisal, and then it was like I had thrown live meat into the tiger exhibit at the zoo.

"I've got to go. Not feeling well," Spencer told me, his eyes darting between the women who approached en masse, ever so slowly, like a scene from a zombie movie.

"What's the matter? Allergic to meaningful relationships?" I asked.

"Look," he said, showing me his arm. "Hives. I've got to get out of here."

I took him by the hand. "Mine," I announced to the ladies. "Mine, mine, mine." There was a general murmur of disappointment, which quickly turned to disbelief. They continued to advance. "Mine," I said a little louder. I heard a guffaw and a snort. They didn't think I could snag a good-looking police chief. I was insulted down to my disposable hospital panties under my unisex one-size-fits-all scrubs.

"My hair doesn't normally look like this," I said. "Mine."

"Hers," Spencer said, nodding my way.

He tugged my arm until my body bumped up against him, and he wrapped his arms around me, pulling me closer. His face was inches from mine, his breath sweet and warm. His eyes twinkled. *Take that, Second Chancers,* I thought. *You thought he was out of my league.* Spencer was playing a great game, fabulous for my ego. But then his eyes grew dark. He ran his hands up my back under my shirt, sending shock waves of sensation that caught my breath in my throat and melted my insides into estrogen-packed jelly. "Oh," I sighed.

The hospital didn't give out disposable bras. My breasts were pushed flat against him. He was hard everywhere, I noted to myself. My heart thumped against my chest so loudly I was sure everyone in the room could hear it. I had just enough time to register that playtime had ended when he captured my mouth.

Our lips touched, sliding across each other in greeting, getting to know the taste and feel of each other. I opened my mouth slightly, and he explored me with his tongue, the kiss deep and slow. I tried to remember where I was, that I was kissing and getting nakeder in front of a houseful of desperate women. But I didn't care. I cared only about Spencer's hands on my back, searing my flesh wherever they touched, and Spencer's mouth, fitted so perfectly on mine that I forgot where I began and he ended. I was on fire and burning up pretty quickly.

I raised my arms and wrapped them around his neck. I allowed my fingers to comb through his hair and rest there. Closer. Closer. I wriggled against him, and he groaned.

"Ahem." I heard it from a distance, like I was on a mountain somewhere, but the disgruntled onlookers were not standing two feet from me.

"Ahem!"

Spencer stopped. He slid his lips off mine and rested his head in the crook of my neck. "Whoa," he croaked. His breathing was ragged. I removed my hands from his head and dropped my arms. He released me, letting his hands travel slowly from my back to my waist and finally again at his sides.

His face was red, his lips swollen, and his hair was

standing up in every which way. Spencer looked good and used.

I inhaled a ragged breath and steadied myself.

"Any questions?" I asked the Second Chancers, my voice coming out deep and gravelly like Yosemite Sam. There were no questions. Sometimes showing is better than telling.

I turned back to Spencer. "We need to find Grandma. Something's wrong. She would never let a meeting go wild like this, normally."

Spencer nodded and gulped air like it was his first breath in quite some time.

"You know, maybe they need more convincing," he said, pointing at the women.

"They're plenty convinced," I said. "You did a great job."

"Oh, yeah?" He perked up. He straightened his shirt and smoothed out his hair. "Great job? You weren't half bad yourself. You might need a little more practice, though."

"Does that line normally work for you?" I asked. "Do women fall for that line? Is that how you hook super-models and cocktail waitresses? With that line?"

Spencer smirked. "I hook them with something else. Want to see it?"

"You are two years old," I said.

I FOUND Grandma in the kitchen with Bridget and Lucy. She still wore her housedress, and her hair was still up in rollers.

"What's going on?" I asked.

Lucy gripped me in a bear hug. "Oh, Gladie, thank goodness you're here. Your grandma is unwell. She's absolutely paralyzed with inaction."

"Grandma, what's the matter?" I asked.

Grandma sat at the table, her chin resting on her hands.

"It's a blind day, dolly. I can't see a thing. I don't know which way to go, and I don't know which way will go at me. I feel lost and helpless."

Grandma's blind days, when her third eye went dark, were few and far between. They only occurred maybe twice a year, but when they hit, they hit hard. Normally a strong force, Grandma turned into a terrified mush.

"I'll shoo out the Second Chancers, and then I'll call in Bird for an emergency brush-out," I said.

Grandma's hand shot forward. "No! Maybe today her car gets in an accident, or her brush misses and blinds me for good. I don't know. I don't know. Anything could happen today."

"Fine. I won't call Bird," I said.

"I'll brush your hair," Bridget said. "I'm already here, and I've never blinded someone with a brush before."

I kicked out the Second Chancers, and we got Grandma cleaned up and dressed for the day. It didn't take long before we were all sitting around the kitchen table, drinking coffee and eating bacon and eggs and toast.

Spencer ate five eggs and four slices of toast. I lost count on the bacon. Lucy and Bridget watched him eat every morsel with their tongues hanging out.

"I love a man with an appetite," said Lucy.

"Uh-huh," said Bridget, and broke out into giggles.

"How are you feeling, Bridget?" I asked.

"Wounded. Not physically but psychically. No offense, Zelda. How are you, Gladie? You actually saw what happened. I didn't see a thing."

"I was sort of unconscious, but it was gory."

Bridget pounded the table. "My priest. My spiritual advisor." Her voice cracked. "I told him all my deepest, darkest feelings, and he almost shot me. I'm having a crisis of faith."

"Darlin', I didn't know you ever had any faith to lose," Lucy said.

"It was my one weakness."

"It wasn't a weakness," Grandma said. It was the first we'd heard from her in an hour. "Everyone needs a foundation. Roots to hold them firm to the ground. Religion is good that way. Centers you. Focuses you. Makes you think outside of yourself and lets you see the beauty and grandeur around you. Wait. Scratch that. I shouldn't give any advice today. Pretend I didn't say anything."

Bridget sighed. "I have to rethink everything now. I need a good cause to settle into. I wish we had a Greenpeace office in town. Sucks that we're landlocked."

"Gladie, if it's not too difficult for you, tell us who you think murdered the old priest and why," Lucy said.

I took a sip of coffee. "He may have been an old priest, but he used to be a member of Randy Terns' gang. They robbed banks. He faked his death. I saw the tombstone, but I heard from another lying priest that he was really alive. I tracked him down to the confessional. Finding out he had become a priest threw me for a loop, though. I didn't expect that."

"Oh, lawd. Holy Charleston and Savannah! You can't write this stuff!" Lucy tossed back her hair. Her face was flushed. She tapped her cheek with her finger. "All the gang members are dead. Murdered." She put her hand up. "I know, Mr. Policeman, only one is murder for sure. But what are the odds? Three dead in such a short period of time? *Pow. Pow. Pow.* Cannes is buzzin' louder than bees by a honeypot. We have never seen the like here. Dead old men, piling up by the side of the road. It's like a war zone or something. Guns. Guns! And now we have no idea who the murderer or murderers are. It could be anyone. You can pick any of the crazies across the street. Any of them could've done it."

"But Peter and Christy were in the pokey," Bridget pointed out.

"That's right!" Lucy said. "Peter and Christy, the two craziest, have an alibi. Oh, Zelda, dear, you picked a bad time to be blind. Did you pick up anything about the Terns before today? Was your antenna twitchin' in any particular direction before?"

"I know love, not death," said Grandma. "If they had a crush on someone, I would have known. But they're losers, the lot of them. Not a good apple in that bunch."

"What about Father Lawrence, the lying priest who's still alive?" asked Bridget.

Spencer cleared his throat and gave me a warning look. He didn't appreciate all the talk about an active case, but I ignored him.

"Spencer spoke to Father Lawrence," I said. "He knew about Chuck Costas' past but thought he had turned over a new leaf, and he was trying to protect Costas' anonymity. He said Costas was scared. He had been approached by somebody. Threatened. He thought I was a troublemaker, stirring up things best left untouched."

"Smart man," Spencer muttered.

I kicked Spencer under the table, but he didn't flinch. He looked over at me and smirked.

"He was definitely freaked out," I said. "I can attest to that. I wonder who made him so scared? Who could scare a hardened criminal?"

Bridget gasped. "He could have just been trying to protect his secret, his past. It could have been a simple threat, like telling his flock he was a hardened criminal." Sometimes she could make a lot of sense.

Grandma decided to stay in the kitchen all day. Bridget decided to stay with her, and Lucy decided to stay with Bridget. I needed to rest, but Spencer was hovering, even though he swore that he never hovered and certainly wouldn't hover over me no matter how much hovering I needed. "Hovering over you with a baseball bat, a Taser, and a pack of wild dogs to try to control you, maybe," he said.

So Spencer mainly paced the house with his cellphone attached to his ear, chastising various members of his department, occasionally glancing my way to make sure I hadn't been the cause of any more death or havoc in his town.

My claustrophobia was overtaking my exhaustion. Since Grandma thought Ding-Dongs might hasten her recovery, I snuck out of the house when Spencer wasn't looking to go on a Ding-Dong run.

Once outside, I threw my car keys up in the air and caught them. Freedom. It had been a while since I'd spent any time alone, driving my own car with the wind in my hair. Suddenly I felt refreshed, ready to take on the world. Or at least to buy an unlimited supply of sugar and carbs.

I opened the car door with a loud creak and noticed Betty across the street. She stood on her front porch, smoking a cigarette. She was dressed in polyester pants and a rayon top. Her hair was extra bouffant. She studied me while she inhaled and blew out long columns of smoke. I hesitated. A little wave from me would be polite, I supposed, but just looking at the Ternses' house gave me an anxiety attack.

Betty crooked her finger at me.

"Come on over," she called. "It's quiet at the house. It's just me and Cindy. Rob is busy watching a game."

I tried to think of an excuse. What was I scared of? All the crazies were gone. Besides, I had a niggling little curiosity that wouldn't leave me alone. I shut the car door.

"It's good to see you, Gladie. I heard about what happened to you. Glad to see you're fine. Can you spare a minute? I'd like to talk to you."

I deflated like a balloon. "Sure," I said, following Betty into her kitchen, where she lit up, again. Soft television noises came from the other room.

"I was thinking about what I told you yesterday," she said.

"Don't worry about that. Consider it forgotten."

"I don't want to forget it. I want to explain myself. It's about time I talk to someone. I haven't been forthcoming in many years. Randy wouldn't let me, of course. I always bowed to Randy's desires."

There was a heaviness about her that reminded me of another woman I had met recently. If Betty had been forty years younger, wearing cotton clothes and with a black eye, she would have been Sarah from the battered women's shelter.

"Betty, was Randy cruel to you?" I asked.

"I didn't see it that way. I thought he was protecting me, keeping me in the house all the time, isolating me from the world. I thought he had my best interests at heart."

"But you've changed your mind?"

"No, never. Randy loved me, no matter what anybody has to say. That horrible woman was manipulative, capable of anything. A truly evil woman." She leaned forward. "Gladie, I think someone hurt Randy. I don't think he slipped," she whispered.

I sighed. Like her wardrobe, Betty was behind the times. She was spouting old news, and I couldn't muster any enthusiasm. I was tired of Randy Terns and his damaged head. Betty put out her cigarette and blew her nose.

I patted her arm and murmured something encouraging. "Betty, why do you think someone hurt Randy?" I asked.

"Weren't you listening?" she asked, slightly irritated. But she was interrupted by Cindy, who walked in, opened the refrigerator, and poured herself some apple juice.

"Pennies," she said, noticing me.

"Leave Gladie alone," Betty snapped. "Can't you see we're talking?"

"That's okay," I said. "Sure, Cindy. I must have some pennies in my purse, somewhere."

But I didn't, and Cindy wasn't interested in dimes or nickels.

"I have pennies," said Betty. "Gladie, would you be a dear and get me my purse? It's on my bed in the bedroom at the end of the hall."

I walked down the hall at a snail's pace. It was odd to experience such quiet in the Ternses' house. Every room was immaculate. No sign of a crazed drug addict on a rampage or group arrests. Betty had tidied the evidence. Peter's holes in the walls were gone, too. There was a sense of *all done* with the whole Terns drama.

But it was an illusion. The walls were patched up, not painted. In fact, the whole house needed to be painted and updated. It was clean but run-down. It seemed all done, but it wasn't. It was a sad house.

No wonder Betty was sad. She lived in a sad house, and her children brought her nothing but aggravation. It was a relief to have them gone. I hoped Betty could find peace and a sense of closure.

I brought Betty's purse back to her.

"Thanks," she said. "Cindy wandered off, again, though. I'll give her the pennies later."

I took my seat at the table.

"You know what?" she asked. "I know I invited you

in, but I forgot I have to run to the pharmacy. Would you pardon me?"

I stood. I was relieved from my head to my toes. I had unconsciously been clenching my jaw, and now I released it, leaving a residual headache. My purse wasn't where I left it in the kitchen.

"Cindy must have it," said Betty. She rushed off to find her.

Rob wandered in and went to the refrigerator. "Hi, Rob," I said. His head whipped around in surprise.

"Oh, hi there, Gladie. What's up?"

"I'm on my way out. Cindy's got my bag somewhere."

Rob nodded. "Yeah, Cindy does that. She's been a little out there ever since the accident when she was a little girl and she was home with Mom, and she fell out of the high chair. Hey, you know what? It was right about where you're standing."

I took a step to the right. I didn't have a lot of good luck in Betty's kitchen. Rob opened a bottle of beer and wandered back to his game without saying goodbye. A moment later, Betty returned, holding the purse out to me.

"Let me know if anything's missing," she said, and ushered me out of the door with a flourish.

Spencer was waiting beside my car.

"Are you kidding me?" he asked when I arrived at Grandma's driveway.

"She asked me to go in," I said.

"And you went in? Are you kidding me?" he repeated.

"How could I say no?"

"I think the word is the same in at least twenty languages. You could have shaken your head. You could have wagged your finger from side to side. You could have stuck your tongue out at her. She would have gotten the picture."

"Not everyone has your charm, Spencer."

"How is Mrs. Terns?" he asked.

"She thinks Randy was murdered."

"Oh, God."

"I didn't say much when she brought it up. Are you proud of me?"

"I'm having your trophy engraved this very second," he said.

I pointed to my car. "I have a Ding-Dong run to go on for my grandmother."

"You're not allowed to drive. You have a concussion and you lost consciousness. You are grounded until your checkup next week."

"I am perfectly fine. I can drive a few miles for medicinal Ding-Dongs." I rummaged in my purse for my keys.

"It's not my opinion. It's the law. You're not allowed to drive."

"What's this?" I pulled out a handful of letters and papers from my purse. "These aren't mine. Cindy must have put them in there."

Spencer took a paper from the top of the stack and read it aloud: " 'Randy, if you don't leave your wife, I'll kill you.' "

Chapter 16

✦ ♥ ✦

Sometimes a client will fall in love with you. It happens. Even with alter kockers *like me. You're important in their life, and they get attached. It's like baby geese to a blender, if it happens to be on making a smoothie or something when they're born. If you can get attached to a blender, you can get attached to a matchmaker. Nip it in the bud. It's unwelcome attention. Direct them to some other blender.*

Lesson 47,
Matchmaking Advice from Your Grandma Zelda

I FLIPPED through the papers. "There's at least a dozen letters here."

"This is evidence," Spencer said, reaching for the letters. "We have to get a warrant. We can't look at them."

I stepped back, out of his reach.

"Like hell I can't. I was given these letters by Cindy Terns, and if you're really nice to me, I'll let you look at them, too."

I hightailed it into the house and bolted up the stairs to my room. I kicked off my shoes and hopped on the bed, spreading the letters out. Spencer came in right after, and he threw himself on the bed next to me.

"Same envelopes. They must all be from the same person," I noted. "Let's organize them by postmark."

"Fine."

We shuffled the letters around. They were all post-marked in Cannes, but the dates went back decades. The first was from 1979.

Randy, how dare you do this to me? You told me you loved me. You told me you hated your wife. You said she didn't satisfy you. You made plans with me. I'll never give you up. I'll haunt you forever, you lying sack of shit. If you hurt me, I'll hurt you. If you won't answer the phone, I'll keep calling your wife. I call her every day, you know. I call her and hang up with-out saying anything, but I can tell her things, all about the dirty things we did together. This is only the beginning. You're going to wish you'd never met me. Love, Lulu

"Whoa, it starts out rough," I said.

" 'Love, Lulu'? She's a bit of a freak." Spencer kicked off his boots and sat back against the headboard. "Read the next one."

The next one was two years later. "I wonder if we have all the letters. That's quite a break she took," I said.

"Doesn't matter. Keep reading."

Dear Betty, I hope you don't mind if I call you Betty. I feel like I know you so well. You might as well for-get about Randy. He doesn't love you. He loves me. He told me he never loved you, and that I did things to him that no other woman would do. He told me he wants me back. Time for you to pack your bags.
   Sincerely, Lulu
   See, Randy? This is the letter I'll send to your "wife" anytime I want. You better not mess with me.

"I think I hate Lulu," I said.

"She's screwing with Randy's mind, threatening to target his wife. It's classic, but she wants to hurt Randy, not Betty," Spencer said. "We don't have all the letters. Maybe she was harassing him for years, and he stopped reacting so she had to pump up the volume."

"I'm surprised Randy didn't knock her off."

"I think we're missing something. When's the next one?"

"Two weeks later."

Dear Randy, Don't even think you can stop paying me. If I don't get the money every month like always, I'll tell Betty everything. How would you like that? You want me to break up your little home? Don't think I won't do it. I hate your ass, Randy Terns. I hate your ass.

"I've been following the wrong path," I whispered.

"What do you mean?"

"The blackmail. I just assumed Randy's gang members were blackmailing him."

"Well, Harry said—" Spencer began.

"Uncle Harry said Randy was being blackmailed and he wanted to find his gang. He didn't say the gang was blackmailing him."

Spencer groaned. "We've been following the wrong path."

I nodded. "Lulu was blackmailing Randy Terns, not Jimmy the Fink or Chuck Costa. Then something happened. Randy stopped paying. Maybe he didn't care if Lulu told Betty. Maybe Betty told Randy she already knew about the affair. Maybe Randy ran out of money. Whatever it was, Randy stopped paying, and Lulu got mad."

"Pinkie, you make sense."

The rest of the letters were pretty much the same, with varying degrees of vitriol. Then came the last letter, dated one week before Randy Terns died.

Randy, you think you have all the cards? You say you love me, and you think you can just dump me without any consequences? And now you don't want to pay me anymore. Well, you can count your days, Randy. I'm coming for you. Sincerely, Lulu

"Well," I said.

"Well."

"Find the Lulu, find the murderer. You know what? Betty warned me about Lulu, about the other woman. She said she was evil, capable of anything."

"Maybe she was right," Spencer said. "Tell me again where you got these letters."

"Cindy put them in my purse. She collects all kinds of things. She probably had a stash of Randy's stuff."

Spencer gathered the letters together. He swung his feet over the side of the bed and put his boots on. "I'll look into it," he said.

"Shouldn't Betty know?"

"Not yet. Give me a couple of days. I have to find Lulu. I'll have the paper analyzed for prints, DNA. It takes a while."

I put my hand on his arm. A little electric shock went through me, and I felt warm all over. "Spencer, I have faster methods for tracking down a mistress. Can we play it my way?"

Spencer took my hand in his. "You should be resting, you know. Haven't you had enough?"

"I'm just going to help you find Lulu. That's all. How bad can that be? Anyway, this way you can keep an eye on me. Make sure I don't drive. Make sure I don't get into trouble."

Spencer groaned.

"One day, Spencer. It's just for one day."

He groaned again and ran his hand over his face. "Get your shoes on. Where are we going first?"

"Where else? The kitchen."

Grandma was still in the doldrums, sitting at the table with a Coke and two Twinkies untouched in front of her. Bridget was recounting a study that had found that religion can be depressing.

Lucy was rolling her eyes. "I don't trust that study at all. I had a moment in the back of a church in Birmingham with a deacon that was anything but depressing, darlin'," Lucy said. "He told me I had the light of God in my eyes and proceeded to defile me in a most welcome manner. I recall feeling very spiritual, and I swear my body levitated. It was trying to get even closer to God, I imagine."

"I don't see how that has anything to do with religion," Bridget said.

"Hold on. I wasn't finished. Now compare that to an atheist I knew in Cleveland. We dated for two weeks, and one night at dinner, he says to me, 'Lucy, dear, I've thought about it, and I can't have sex with you because you're too smart.' Too smart! Well, I never. Lord knows, I'm too smart for my own good. At least, that's what my momma always said to me. But what an idiot he was. Like a smart woman can't be a good lover."

Lucy noticed me and took a breath. "Oh, Gladie. There you are. You and Mr. Handsome were gone so long, I was starting to wonder. Anyway, tell me. You're smart. Are you a good lover, or should I ask our police chief about that?"

I could feel Spencer smirk from behind me. "I don't think intelligence or religion has anything to do with it," Bridget said. "You've turned the path of our discussion all topsy-turvy."

"Maybe I was tired of the path, darlin'. I know you are in turmoil about your priest, but I think we need a new topic of conversation."

"I have a new topic of conversation," I interrupted, taking a seat. "Randy Terns had an affair with a crazy woman named Lulu. I need to find her. She's the new number one suspect in his murder."

I gave them the rundown on the letters. There were a lot of oohs and ahhs.

"I knew a Lulu in college," said Bridget. "Lulu Jones. She was a biology major, but she moved up to Alaska to study some kind of bug."

Lucy shrugged. "I don't know any Lulus."

"How about you, Grandma? Any ideas who Randy Terns had an affair with? Maybe she came to you to get fixed up," I said.

"My brain's all foggy today, *bubeleh*."

"I know. It's really important."

Grandma took a bite of Twinkie and washed it down with Coke. "You know, the name does sound familiar to me, but she was never a client of mine and was never on my radar."

She took another bite of Twinkie. "I could go for some ribs," she said to no one in particular. Then she popped up out of her chair and snapped her fingers.

"I got it," she announced. "Bird Gonzalez did a woman's hair out in the boonies somewhere. I don't think she does her anymore, but she would know. Lulu. Color and perm. Go to Bird and ask her."

I changed out of my scrubs into jeans and a T-shirt. It felt great to wear my own underwear again. I swiped my eyelashes with mascara and put a thick layer of Tango Fire lipstick on my lips. I ran my fingers through my hair and stepped back from the mirror. Not a bad look for hunting down a crazy murderer, but I wasn't ready to go to a ball or anything.

Downstairs, Spencer waited at the front door with Grandma. "I'm sorry you're not feeling well, Mrs. Burger," he told her as I reached the bottom of the stairs.

"I'll be better tomorrow. I always am. It's just a little disconcerting, not being my normal self. But I've already got my appetite back. That's a good sign. Lucy is going to get me ribs in a sec. I'll be back to my meddling ways in no time."

"Like grandmother, like granddaughter," said Spencer.

"Oh, I hope so. I've always wanted her to get into the family business. I think she's a natural, despite her past," Grandma said.

I cleared my throat in case they didn't know I was there and wanted to say something embarrassing.

"Her past? Gladie has a past?" Spencer asked.

"Oh, yes. Gladie has had a million jobs. She flitted from one thing to another for more than a decade. Never bothered graduating from high school, either. Commitment issues," Grandma explained with a whisper and a none-too-discreet gesture at my head. "But she'll commit to matchmaking. I'll change her. I'm the queen of commitment."

I shifted on my heels and studied the ceiling. I could feel Spencer's eyes boring through me. The room had altered, and he was seeing me in a different light.

"Blue skies again," Spencer said. He beeped his car, unlocking the doors. "Supposed to be foggy tonight, though. There's a weather alert in effect."

I was eternally grateful he had changed the subject. "There is?"

"Yep, very foggy."

Spencer's attention moved to the space behind me. I turned around. Holden was in his front yard, pushing a lawn mower.

"He's domestic," Spencer muttered.

I had tried to push Holden out of my mind. When I thought of him, I had that little kernel of suspicion that went with it. Where had he been when Chuck Costas was shot? Could he have been the shooter? If so, could he have been trying to protect me, or had he been aiming at me? That was a thought that kept rolling around in my brain, too.

If he wasn't the shooter, why hadn't he seen the shooter and why hadn't he stopped him? And most of all, why hadn't he visited me in the hospital or come by the house to see how I was? Or at the very least called?

"I told him to stay away from you until the investigation is over," Spencer said, reading my mind. "It took a lot of convincing. He finally promised to stay clear of you when I explained it would be better for you."

I turned back to Spencer. "Was he worried about me?"

"He seemed to be. He called me a piece of shit, said I wouldn't know what was good for you even if you came with a user's manual. He mentioned something about decking me, too. Does that make you feel better?"

"I don't know."

"Well, he'll still be there tomorrow. Maybe we can get this wrapped up today."

I hesitated. I wanted to ask Holden the questions that bothered me, but my doubt made me angry at him, and I didn't want to talk to him yet. "He'll still be there tomorrow," I said.

Spencer nodded. "Sure he will."

BIRD'S SALON was pandemonium. There wasn't a space available on the street, and women in orange smocks with tint in their hair milled about outside.

Spencer parked on the curb. There were advantages to being police chief.

Spencer turned on the radio to the sports station. "Go ahead and ask her. I'm not going in."

"Why not?"

"I have my reasons."

The ladies outside were sneaking looks into the car and whispering among themselves. "You've had sex with at least half of all the women in the salon, haven't you?" I said.

"That's a slight exaggeration."

"Man whore."

"I'm not a man whore. And man whore is not an insult to a man, by the way."

"Man whore. Guy slut. Penis hound dog," I said.

"Like I said, not insults." Spencer turned up the radio and leaned back in his seat.

I slammed the door and tried to walk with confidence through the crowd of women.

"Gladie Burger, is that you?" asked a woman in a smock and rollers.

"Yes."

"I'm your grandma's friend Sally. Were you with our new police chief?"

"Uh, yes."

"I told you!" Sally announced to the other women. "Gladie Burger bagged the cop."

"So why are we doing our hair if men don't care a thing about hair?" asked another woman, gesturing toward my head. My hand flew up to my hair, and I gave it a halfhearted combing through with my fingers.

"I'm only here to see Bird," I said, my voice just above a whisper. I tiptoed past them into the salon.

Hair was flying. The hairdressers were going full steam. Bird worked on three clients at once.

"Hey, Gladie," she called, her usual warm smile plastered on her face despite the chaos. "Do you have an appointment today? I don't have you written down."

"No, I just came in to ask you something."

"Oh, thank goodness. I don't think I can handle one more head today. How's your grandma? I heard it was a blind day. I just don't think it's safe in Cannes when she has a blind day. Anything can happen."

"What's happening here?" I asked. "I've never seen it so busy."

"Haven't you heard? It's the city council's summer ball this evening. But since there's a big fog warning for tonight, they changed the venue from the high school gym to the little historic district park down the street. Very romantic in the fog. Everyone's going. I think the city council is buttering up the town for November elections. Are you going?"

"I think I'm busy," I said. "But I wanted to ask you a question. I'm looking for a woman named Lulu. I don't have the last name. Grandma said you used to do a woman's hair out in the boonies."

Bird ran to wash the color out of a client's hair. I followed her and stood by the basin, where I played with the shampoo dispensers. "Lulu Finkelstein!" Bird announced, gesturing with the hose. "I haven't thought of her in years. She was troubled."

I should say so. Looney Tunes, in fact.

"How so?" I asked.

"She started off normal enough. She lived in town. She did some kind of art projects. Then something happened. I don't know what. She moved way up in the mountains, like the Unabomber or something. She used to call me out there every once in a while to do her roots. Then she stopped calling."

"Bird, do you remember her phone number?"

"No phone. She called from the pay phone at a nearby gas station."

"Do you remember her address?"

"You know I remember everything, Gladie. But it's not really an address. There's trees involved."

ACCORDING TO Spencer, stakeouts, mountains, and trees meant provisions. He gave me twenty bucks and stayed in the car while I went two doors down to the drugstore to stock up on Pop-Tarts and root beer.

"I'm never going to get rid of my paunch," I mumbled, knocking two boxes of strawberry Pop-Tarts into my basket.

"Gladie, if I didn't know better, I would say you were following me."

I jumped three feet in the air in surprise and threw the basket back over my head, shooting it clear out of my aisle. It landed somewhere on the cosmetics counter with a loud crash.

"Did I scare you?" Betty Terns put her hand up to her mouth and looked at me in wide-eyed wonder.

"No, not at all, Betty. I've been a little jumpy lately," I said.

"That's understandable."

"Who the hell threw the basket?" the manager yelled from the general vicinity of the cosmetics counter, then added a few obscenities.

"Maybe we should go outside," I said.

"I'll protect you. I'll be your alibi. I was with you the whole time, and you never had a basket." Betty winked.

"Thanks, Betty." I felt an instantaneous warmth and attachment to her. I wanted to protect and nurture her like a lost puppy. She had suffered through an abusive, cheating husband, five rotten kids, and a crazy stalker woman, and now she was stuck in a falling-down home and a polyester wardrobe. Betty looked at me with inquisitive eyes. Perhaps she saw a kindred spirit in me as well.

"What?" she asked, her smile gone.

"Excuse me?"

"What is it? You're looking at me funny," she said.

"Nothing, really. I was just thinking about Lulu."

Betty gasped. "You know her name? You found out somehow."

"Yes, Betty. I know. I know all about her. I am so sorry. You have been through so much."

"I tried to tell you about her. I told you she was evil. I don't think we should talk about this here." A perfect round tear rolled down her cheek.

"I'm sorry, Betty," I said. "I sort of stumbled on it. Did you always know?"

"A couple of years ago I intercepted a call. She screamed and threatened Randy. Called him unspeakable names. I had thought he was just a nervous man, but then it clicked. He had something to be nervous about."

"What did he say about it?"

"Oh, he never knew that I knew," Betty said. "I didn't talk to him. I didn't dare. If he wanted to talk to me about it, he would have. I didn't want to trouble him." I bit my tongue. Betty was a prime candidate for counseling or at least a subscription to *Ms.* magazine. As they say in Egypt, she was in de Nile.

"Randy didn't know you knew?"

"Not even after I spoke to her."

"You spoke to her?" I asked.

"She called me when he was away at a doctor's appointment, like she knew his schedule. She told me horrible things about them together." Betty's voice hitched, and her tears flowed in earnest. I patted her shoulder. I took a Kleenex box from the shelves, opened it, handed her a tissue, and took one for myself. I couldn't stand hearing people's problems. I shouldn't have said anything to Betty. I had sympathy pains down to my toes.

"I'm sorry, Betty. This is the worst thing I've ever heard."

"We all have our crosses to bear."

"I'll come by later. I'll bring Danish," I said.

Betty perked up. "That sounds great. Could you bring tacos, too? I knew you would be a great friend."

Betty picked up her prescriptions. I got a box of Pop-Tarts, two Slim Jims, and a six-pack of root beer. Grandma was rubbing off on me in the worst way.

I caught Spencer in the middle of a call to his officers, ordering them around. I put on my seat belt, and he clicked off his cellphone.

"A ball outside in the middle of the week with no advance notice whatsoever, and we have to arrange traffic and security. They couldn't leave the damned dance in the school gym where they'd planned it all along? Who cares about fog? Now I have to hand out overtime, and I'm screwed on budget. We have to make this quick," he grumbled.

We drove an hour up into the mountains. The road went from asphalt to gravel to dirt. "How many trees, Pinkie?"

"We should be near a gas station. Or we're lost, and in that case I get the Slim Jims," I said.

A couple of minutes later we found the gas station. It consisted of one pump and a little shack.

"Civilization," said Spencer. "I'll fill up the tank."

I got out and stretched my legs. It was a gorgeous day, a perfect day for a long hike and picnic. But I wasn't so sure I would ever want to live out in the middle of nowhere. We hadn't seen a house in the last twenty minutes. Besides the gas station, there was no sign of life.

I found the pay phone around the back of the shack. I touched it, trying to sense Lulu Finkelstein. She had come down here, put coins in the slot, and called the Terns to threaten them. If Betty was a case for counseling, Lulu was a case for the butterfly net.

Bird was amazing. Her directions past trees and around rocks brought us right to Lulu's cabin. It was about the same size as the gas station shack.

Spencer parked behind a tree a ways away from the cabin. He opened the car door. "Stay here, Pinkie." He slammed the door, walked two steps, and turned around. "I mean it, Pinkie. Stay here."

Spencer crept around the perimeter of the area. He sidestepped a few times as he approached the house. It took a good five minutes for him to reach the front door, and once there, he stood still. Listening, I figured.

The front of the cabin was peppered with all sizes of flowerpots and boxes, but there was no sign of actual flowers. Spencer eyed the pots, looked inside. Then he drew his gun but kept it at his side. He walked around the cabin, peering into the windows. I couldn't figure out why he didn't just knock on the door. Finally Spencer came back to the car.

"Pop open a root beer for me, would you? We're going to be here for a while."

He drank half a can. I handed him a Pop-Tart.

"She's one paranoid number, let me tell you," he said.

I opened a Slim Jim and took a bite. "Paranoid how?"

"She has booby traps all over her property. It's like Vietnam. I should bring my men out here to train in dismantling explosives. Meanwhile, there's no sign of her. The plants are all dead. No one is in the cabin, as far as I can tell, but there's furniture inside. We have no alternative. We have to wait for her."

"What would have happened if you'd tripped one of the booby traps?" I asked.

"I would have gone kaboom, and you would have inherited my share of the Slim Jims."

I looked longingly toward the woods. "Are the booby traps everywhere?"

"Why? You want to test them?"

"Yes."

Spencer raised an eyebrow.

"Why?"

"I have to pee."

"Pinkie, are you asking me to help you pee?"

"As much as I hate doing it, yes. I'm asking you to help me pee."

Chapter 17

✦ ♥ ✦

"*Someday my prince will come.*" *I love that song. It's from* Snow White. *She had it tough. A bad family situation. But her prince came and kissed her, and all was right in the world. People ask me all the time: "When will my prince come?" They also ask: "Is there a prince for me?" I say: "Yes, there is a prince for you! And he'll come when he comes." Actually, there's more than one prince out there for each and every person. There's probably a thousand Mr. or Miss Rights for every single one looking. What you do with your prince is a different story.*

Lesson 7,
Matchmaking Advice from Your Grandma Zelda

SPENCER TRACED a safe path to a grove of trees.

"Go away," I told Spencer. I was dancing the pee-pee dance. My bladder was ready to explode like one of Lulu's booby traps.

"I've got my back turned. Hurry up. I want to finish my Pop-Tart."

"Don't peek."

"I won't peek. I don't want to peek."

"What does that mean? You don't want to peek?"

"It means I'm not fourteen years old. I've seen women with their pants down before." Spencer had his back to me. He tapped his foot, making a small crunching noise as it hit the leaves on the forest floor.

"Don't peek," I said again.

"I'm not peeking. Hurry up."

I unbuttoned my jeans and unzipped them. Spencer broke out in stripper music. "Da, da, da, da, da!"

"Jerk! Stop that. I can't do this. You're going to have to go back to the car," I said.

"You could have peed three times by now."

"I can't pee with you there. It doesn't matter if you peek. I don't want you listening."

"I'm not leaving you alone. It's too dangerous. If you don't want to pee, you can hold it."

I was going to rupture something important if I held it in any longer. "Fine. Put your hands over your ears and sing the national anthem, loudly."

"Are you kidding me?"

"Start singing!"

Spencer put his hands over his ears and started singing. And I squatted.

BACK AT the car, I put my seat all the way back. Spencer took another bite of his Pop-Tart.

"Wow, that was loud," he said.

"You weren't supposed to listen."

Spencer smirked his annoying little smirk.

"And women like you?" I asked. "Maybe they mistake you for a human."

"Ouch. Okay. Let's play nice. I was just teasing. I didn't hear a thing. Not one drop."

"What kind of name is Spencer, anyway?" I demanded.

Spencer looked honestly shocked by my change of topic. "Excuse me?"

"It sounds like a made-up name," I said. "Like you're trying to be manly or macho."

"I am manly. I am macho. And it's not a made-up

name. My mother gave me this name, may her soul rest in peace."

"Oh."

"While we're on the subject, what kind of name is Gladie? Sounds like a third grader's name. *Gladie. Gladie.* Why don't you use your real name, Gladys? Gladys. Sounds like a schoolmarm. Horn-rimmed glasses, tweed skirt Gladys."

I put my hand up. "Fine. We won't talk about names."

Spencer smirked. "Ready to play nice?"

"Yes."

"It was a cheap shot about my name," he said.

"I know. I'm sorry. I've been on edge. People dying around me."

"I know. It can rub a person's nerves raw."

"You seem okay," I noted. "Not stressed at all."

"I've been in the business for a while."

"You came from L.A., right?" I asked.

Spencer raised an eyebrow. "You checked up on me, Pinkie? I like that."

"People talk. I can't help if people talk."

"Yes, I was in L.A."

"Big town. Lots of opportunities. A far cry from Cannes."

"You want to know why I came here."

I shrugged. "Only if you want to tell me."

"It all happened when a man pulled out his eye and ate it," he said.

I put my Pop-Tart down. "On second thought, I'm not sure I want to hear this story."

"I'll skip the worst part. That's the part where I arrested a man for killing his wife and their two very young children and ripping out their hearts."

"Thank you for skipping that part," I said. I had a big lump in my throat, and I was having a hard time swallowing.

"And the murderer is in jail because I put him in jail, and he's about to go to court, and he takes his own eye out and eats it."

"You're making this up, right?" I asked. "This is some kind of stakeout hazing you put people through, right?"

Spencer ignored me. He was into the story, more intent than I had ever seen him. "And the judge says he's incompetent to stand trial. The murderer goes to a cushy psych ward. Gladie, I found the dead woman and the dead babies, and I swore I would get them justice, and I couldn't do it."

"And Cannes has precious few murders," I supplied.

"Until recently," he said.

I scooted closer to him and leaned my head against his shoulder. He draped his arm around me and nestled his face in my hair.

"I like your hair," he said, his voice muffled. "It smells like you."

I let him hold me. He was strong and comforting, and I liked that he liked my hair. I nodded off and woke sometime later to Spencer on the phone with a federal agency, telling them to come clear away the explosives.

Our provisions were gone, and Lulu was nowhere to be seen.

"We might as well leave," said Spencer. "If she was around, we probably scared her off making so much noise."

"I don't pee loud!"

"I meant we spoke loudly," he said. "We drove up loudly. Besides, I think she's moved on. Let's ask at the gas station. They might know."

THE WORLD'S oldest man ran the gas station and the little post office that took up a corner in the shack.

His skin hung on him like it was trying to escape. He had few teeth and whistled when he spoke.

"Lulu Finkelstein. Sounds familiar," he said. He stared out into space, as if he was counting dust particles. It would take him a long time. The shack was filthy.

Spencer was patient. He talked about the weather and gas prices and bought a bag of chips. "She lives up the road," Spencer prompted. "Or maybe she's moved away. I don't know. I'd sure like to talk to her, though."

"Like her, do ya?" the man asked with a wink. "She was a pretty one. You know, come to think of it, she did move. She told me a few years back if any mail come for her to forward it."

"I don't suppose you still have the forwarding address?" asked Spencer.

"I think it's around here somewhere."

IT TOOK awhile, but he found the forwarding address under the cash register next to old lottery tickets. We hopped back in the car.

It turned out that Lulu Finkelstein had gone from backwoods Unabomber to senior citizen suburbanite, living in a tract home in a neighborhood reserved for over-fifties and rife with golf carts.

"This isn't half bad," I noted as we drove through the streets of her neighborhood. The houses were newish, one-story ranches with large yards. "I wouldn't mind living here. Pretty. Clean."

Spencer didn't agree. "A nightmare. Like Stepford Wives with jowls."

"Huh. That's funny. I figured you went for the Stepford Wives type."

"I thought we were playing nice, Gladys."

Lulu Finkelstein's house was beige with white trim.

The front yard was covered in different species of cactus. She had a double garage and a big Welcome sign on the front porch.

"What do you think?" I asked Spencer. "Any booby traps?"

"I think Lulu has wisely hidden in plain sight, in a big crowd. Smarter this way. And more comfortable. Shall we?"

Spencer slipped his hand to the small of my back, steering me down the walk toward Lulu's front door. "You do the talking. We'll get better results," he whispered in my ear, making the hair on my arms stand straight up.

He stopped dead in the middle of the walkway.

"What was that?" he asked.

"What?" I ducked, expecting an explosion or bullets to fly.

"Your eyes dilated."

I looked away. "No, they didn't."

"I touched you, and your eyes dilated. Dilate them again."

"I guess you'll have to wait until I'm dead."

Spencer smirked. "I have a feeling I won't have to wait that long." He studied my eyes, waiting for movement.

Despite all my attempts to remain calm and cool, my insides turned warm and mushy. "This is ridiculous," I stammered. Spencer held my gaze.

"Thank you," he said.

My hands flew to my face. "What? Did they do it again?"

"A man never makes a woman dilate and tells," Spencer said. Seemingly satisfied, he steered me toward the door.

"What will I say to her?" I asked.

"How about hello, for starters?" He rang the door-bell.

Two seconds later, the door opened. Lulu Finkelstein looked nothing like I imagined. Instead of a drooling lunatic with bug eyes, wearing a sequined tube top, pink hot pants, and neon purple pumps, she was a class act. Lulu had long, curly brown hair pulled back in ebony combs. She was tall, about two inches taller than me, and she was slim but not skinny. She wore no makeup and looked younger than the requisite age for her neighborhood. She was barefoot in jeans and a light blue cotton V-neck sweater. Small gold hoops adorned her ears, and silver Hopi rings covered most of her fingers.

She greeted us with a warm, welcoming smile, and there was intelligence behind her green eyes.

"Yes? May I help you? Are you here to see the vases?"

"Lulu Finkelstein?" I asked.

Lulu shrieked and slammed the door, but Spencer stuck his foot inside, blocking it. Lulu ran deeper into the house.

"Leave me alone! I'll call the police!" she screamed.

"I am the police, ma'am," Spencer called from the front door.

"I fell for that before. I wish they would leave me alone!"

Spencer and I exchanged looks. He was right about her being a paranoid number.

"I've got my badge out, ma'am. I'm Spencer Bolton, chief of the Cannes Police Department. We're here on a friendly visit. May we come in?"

I took a step toward the door, but Spencer blocked me with his arm. "Not yet," he whispered.

After a long moment Lulu came back to the door, but she held a Taser in her hand. "Show me your badge," she said. "Hand it over slowly." She studied the badge and nodded.

"Fine. You're chief of police. How did you find me?" she asked.

"May we come in?"

"I suppose so."

"Put down the Taser."

She did and opened the door wide. Spencer remained polite and laid on a thick coat of charm. "Your home is lovely," he said.

And he wasn't lying. Outside, the house looked like most of the others on the street, but the inside was completely unique. Southwestern furniture and rugs decorated the living room, and in the corner sat a large loom with a colorful tapestry half completed. The walls were covered with large photographs of scenes of the Southwest, and the coffee table was covered with the most exquisite glassware I had ever seen.

"You can touch it," Lulu said, sitting in a chair across from us. "I see you admiring the glass. Please, touch it. Enjoy. That's why I made it."

My hand went to a perfect hourglass. I turned it and watched the sand flow slowly from one side to another through the ice-blue glass.

"You have good taste," she said, clearly pleased by my choice. "I made that one for my own fancy. Not much call for an hourglass these days. It's a true hourglass, by the way. The sand takes exactly an hour to pass through."

I reluctantly put it back down on the table. "It's magnificent," I said.

"Why did you run?" Spencer asked Lulu.

"Because you used my old name. I changed it years ago. Safe people know I changed it. Those crazy people sent you, right? Why did I run? I've been running for years." Lulu's face turned grave, like her head had grown heavier.

"Which crazy people?" Spencer asked.

"You know which ones. Randy and Betty. They sent you, right? They have been stalking me for an eternity. I did everything to shake them. I thought I finally had. I guess I have to move again. Change my name again." Lulu's voice broke.

I was confused. I didn't know what to believe.

"We have letters from you to them," I started.

"They can't be from me," she said. "Believe me, I never contacted them. Well, sure, at the very beginning when this all started. The first week, I was upset that Randy broke it off, and I asked him to reconsider. A month later, after nonstop calls from Betty at all hours of the day and night, I called her and begged her to stop calling me and threatening me. But believe me, besides that, I never ever contacted them."

"But we have letters," I said. "Horrible letters where you threaten them." Spencer pulled one out of his breast pocket and showed her.

"This is not my handwriting. I didn't write this. I never wrote a word to them," she said. "Look, they are crazy. Especially Betty. Randy used to call me and threaten me if I didn't stop calling, even though I never called. Betty told him there was a strange woman calling and hanging up or calling and shouting obscenities at her. But I never called. I told him so, but he didn't believe me. Either she was lying to him or he was lying to me. I told him she was the crazy one. I told him I never called, but he didn't believe me.

"I stopped answering the phone. The calls to me were endless, though, mostly in the middle of the night. I hired a private detective to try to protect me and to contact them to ask them to stop. It made it worse. They sent blackmail letters. I didn't get a restraining order because they threatened to kill me if I did. Any attempt to ask them to cease and desist only made the harassment and stalking worse. I had to run and hide from them.

"Listen, I have letters from them. Actually, postcards. Hold on, I'll get them for you," she said.

After she left the room, I turned to Spencer. "What do you think?"

"I've heard stranger." Which one was the lying, crazy stalker woman, Betty or Lulu? Lulu was the one who rigged booby traps and was now in the other room with a Taser. My initial vote for the lunatic should have gone to Lulu. But I had a theory brewing in my mind that said otherwise.

Lulu came back and handed Spencer the postcards.

"There," she said. "Those are the ones I saved for evidence if I ever needed them. The rest I threw away because they upset me too much."

Spencer showed me the first one. "Sucks to be you" was scrawled on a postcard featuring a photo of the Cannes town hall. The next one said, "Die, whore."

"The handwriting is the same as on the letters to the Ternses," Spencer said.

"It's not my handwriting," said Lulu with a desperate edge to her voice.

The front door opened, and an older couple walked in. "Carol, we've brought fish!"

The couple wore shorts, matching Hawaiian print shirts, and Top-Siders. The man carried a large red cooler. They froze when they saw Spencer and me. "Everything all right?" asked the man.

"They were looking for Lulu," explained Lulu.

The man dropped the cooler and came toward us with a definite look of purpose on his face. Spencer jumped up and flashed his badge. "Hold on," he said.

"Everything is fine. You need to stay cool. Why don't you take a seat?"

The man stopped but didn't take a seat.

"When will those crazy people leave you alone?" asked the woman.

"We're here to clear up matters," Spencer said.

"Randy Terns is dead," I explained. Spencer shot me a look that said he wanted me dead, too.

"Thank God," said Lulu, and broke into tears. The woman hugged her, and they cried together.

"Finally," said the man. "Great news. I hope that means Carol is finally free now. I'm John Livingston, Carol's—I mean Lulu's—brother-in-law. That's Maisey, her sister." He shook Spencer's hand. "Beer for everybody," he announced. He went to the kitchen and came back with an armful of Heineken bottles. I took two.

"Not for me," Spencer told me.

"I wasn't offering you one. These are mine," I said.

The room toasted Randy Terns' death. After a moment, realization flashed on Lulu's face.

"Hold on," she said. "You're not here to notify me of his death. You're here because you suspect me."

All heads turned toward Spencer.

"Well, the thought did cross my mind," he said.

"We have a letter from you—or someone claiming to be you—a week before he was killed," I said. "You threatened him because he was going to stop sending you money to keep your mouth shut."

"My mouth shut about what?"

"The affair," I said.

"Is this some kind of joke?"

"My wife and sister-in-law inherited a great deal of money when they were young," explained John. "They don't need any money."

"And Lulu is an accomplished glassblower. She was an artist and started glassblowing a couple years before and became successful quickly. Any one of the vases on that table is worth fifteen thousand dollars," Maisey said.

"Maybe we can clear this up with examples of your handwriting. And your sister's," Spencer suggested.

Maisey rifled through her purse for a handwriting sample, and Lulu retrieved her shopping list. Neither was a match for the handwriting on the letters.

Spencer didn't look convinced.

"When did Randy die?" asked Lulu. "I'm out of town a lot."

And it turned out that she had been out of town when he died. She'd been in Venice, Italy, looking at glass for the past six weeks and had just returned the day before. She showed Spencer her passport. It cleared her not only of Randy's death but of Jimmy the Fink's and Chuck Costas' as well.

"Well, Lulu, I can answer one of your questions now," I said. "Your tormentor had to be Betty, not Randy. Randy thought you were blackmailing him. He was handing over money for years. Betty must have been forging the letters. She was blackmailing her own husband in your name."

"It doesn't surprise me. She's a nutcase. She told him I called when I didn't. So it's not that big a leap for her to write letters and blackmail him in my name," she said.

Randy had stopped paying the blackmail, and he'd gone to Uncle Harry to find his gang. Something had happened to make Randy stop paying and to make him switch his attention away from Lulu to his former partners in crime. I sighed.

It was disappointing that Lulu was not the homicidal maniac I'd thought she was. That meant there still was a killer on the loose, and I was possibly in danger.

"Ms. Finkelstein," Spencer said, "there's a matter of

explosives we need to discuss. We found deadly booby traps on your old property."

"I don't know what you're talking about," she said, and blushed a deep shade of red.

"I'm having it cleared out," he said. "I'll let it pass, considering what you've been through, but do me a huge favor and contact me if you hear anything from any member of the Terns family. I give you my word of honor, I will handle it, and you will have nothing left to fear in the future." He gave her his card, and she walked us to the door.

Lulu snapped her fingers as if she'd forgotten something. "Just a sec." She came back with the hourglass. "I want you to have it," she told me. "A present, since you admired it, and I want to thank you for giving me such good news. I feel freer than I've felt in years."

She hugged me, and John shook Spencer's hand.

"Wait a minute," Spencer said. "Aren't you . . . ?"

John nodded. "John Livingston. *The* John Livingston."

"The best shortstop in Padres baseball history," Spencer said, his voice all awe and boyish enthusiasm. "You made the greatest play in MLB history."

"Eighty-four World Series. Dick Williams, the manager, didn't want me to play that day. I had a pulled hamstring. Hurt like a son of a bitch. I told him nothing was going to stop me from playing in the Series. He didn't care what I had to say. Our owner had died a couple months before, and his widow heard that Dick was going to keep me out of the lineup. She came down to the locker room and told Dick I was playing, no matter what he had to say on the matter. And then I made the play."

Spencer supplied the rest, his voice reaching the rafters. "Lance Parrish, the Big Wheel, hit one made of thunder, and you made a miraculous catch, jumped ten feet in the air to catch it and triple play." He bounced on the balls of his feet.

"And I made the play. We won that game. The only game of any World Series the Padres ever won, I might add."

"Gee, Mr. Livingston—"

"Call me John, son. Call me John. And sure, I'll autograph whatever you got handy."

We carried our gifts back to the car.

"John Livingston." Spencer shook his head and smiled. "What are the odds?"

I leaned my head against the window. Grandma thought I was like her, but I had no third eye, no heightened sensitivity. I had let Betty Terns turn me all around with her lies about Lulu. I'd spent energy over her so-called plight, and even cried with her.

"That little visit we had," Spencer told me about fifteen minutes outside of Cannes, "didn't get us any closer to finding the murderer. And I want you to remember that two of the deaths are still considered natural and accidental."

I ground my teeth. "You're not even going to question Betty Terns?"

"Of course I am. Let me handle this investigation, will you? You've taken it as far as you can take it. Got it?"

I looked out the window and whittled my molars down further.

"Got it?" he asked again.

"I suppose you're right," I said.

"And I don't need to tell you to stay far away from Betty Terns. At the very best she's delusional. But she's probably closer to a sociopath or worse. And organized, too. It takes a lot of organization to stalk and harass a woman, all the while making her husband think it was the woman doing the stalking and the blackmailing."

I had a hard time picturing Betty as a criminal mastermind, but love makes people do crazy things. And Betty was a woman scorned, which was the scariest and most unpredictable of states.

We stopped at the police station on the way home. It was a madhouse. The ball, which had transformed into an outdoor event with the promise of a romantic fog bank, had taken over the town and put the police in the center of the frenzy. Roads had to be closed. Traffic had to be rerouted. Every cop, paramedic, and dogcatcher was on duty and waiting for orders. It was two o'clock, and the ball started at eight-thirty with the dark and the roll-in of the much anticipated fog.

"I'll be back in a bit to take you home," Spencer said. "If I get caught up in this mess, I'll have one of my men escort you. Pinkie, under no circumstances are you to leave without an escort. Do you hear me?"

I put three fingers up. "Scout's honor."

"Good girl."

I followed him into the police station. People came and went like ants in an anthill. The chairs were piled high with party favors, and I didn't have a place to sit. With all the commotion, I hadn't noticed Fred at the front desk. He stood, slumped over, his chin resting on his hands, a look of total defeat on his face.

"Hey, Fred, how goes it?" I asked. "A little overwhelmed by all the action?"

"Huh? Yeah, sure."

"Fred, it's me. Underwear Girl."

His eyes rolled in their sockets until he managed to focus on me. "Oh, hi," he said, his heart not really in it.

"Is something the matter, Fred? How's Julie?"

Fred inhaled a ragged breath and let out a loud sigh. "Julie."

"Is something the matter with Julie? Did she break

something important? Did she start a fire?" The possibilities were endless.

"Just the water heater at Tea Time. But she hates me, Gladie. She hates me." His head fell on the desk with a loud thud.

"She can't hate you. You're perfect together," I said.

"Gladie, she hates me, and I will never be happy again."

The world spun, and I gripped the desk for support. I was failing at everything: murder, love. I was good for nothing. I was letting down Grandma, and I would wind up back at one of my old jobs like Porky's Pig Farm for sure.

"I don't like pigs, Fred," I said.

"I like bacon," he said, his face against the desk's fake wood top.

"Bacon's fine, but pigs smell," I said. "Come on. Let's go." I yanked at his arm. "I'm going to fix your love life."

"How?"

"Fred Lytton, you are going to the ball."

"I am?"

"While we're on the subject, you can make the check out to me or Zelda's Matchmaking Services, whichever is more convenient for you."

"Do you take Visa?"

Chapter 18

✦ ♥ ✦

*F*ood. *You know I love food. But couples and food. Feh! There's a big lesson there, and a big headache, too. He only eats this. She doesn't eat that. It used to be we were just glad to eat! Now there's no gluten, no lactose, no meat. Vegan shmegan. Organic, my* tuchus. *You know what I mean? If they don't eat the same thing, it's a night-mare.* Unless. *Unless he can keep his mouth shut or she can keep her mouth shut and they can stop themselves from telling the other person they're stupid for saying cows are a plague on the planet. A man once told that to me, dolly. A plague! I sent him packing, I can tell you. Shut up about the food. Tell them to like it or lump it. Love waits for no diet.*

Lesson 36,
Matchmaking Advice from Your Grandma Zelda

"I'M SUPPOSED to watch the desk," Fred said.

"The chief told me I need an escort home. You'll be my escort."

Fred's eyes darted around, unsure where to turn. He was a goner. Lovesick.

"Don't worry. I'll get the chief to sign off on it." I pat-ted his back.

* * *

"FRED? ARE you kidding me?" Spencer was at his desk, drowning in paperwork. He barked orders intermittently. "Is this boyfriend thing for real?"

I shrugged and smiled. "I don't know. Something about Fred's red hair . . ."

Spencer followed me out of his office toward the reception area. "Are you *kidding* me? Seriously?"

I stopped suddenly and turned, making Spencer run into me. "I feel that you and I have shared a moment together," I said in my sultriest voice. "I feel we're closer."

Spencer raised an eyebrow and smirked. "Oh, yeah? I was feeling the same thing myself."

"Good. So when the time comes, you can walk me down the aisle," I said.

"You're killing me."

FRED REVIVED a little when we arrived at Grandma's. "Nice house. It's an oldie, isn't it?"

"Yes, over a hundred years old," I said. "Come on in. I'll introduce you."

Grandma was still in the kitchen with Bridget and Lucy, but now Sister Cyril was with them. At least six slabs of ribs in varying stages of being eaten were on the table, and Grandma had a telltale dab of sauce on her chin.

"Oh, Gladie, I'm glad you're back. Look who came to visit. Sister Cyril." Grandma had perked up considerably. Sister Cyril was one of her favorite people and had an inspiring influence over most. I caught Lucy's eye. I didn't think the nun was there by accident. Lucy had probably gotten tired of trying to lift the morale of both Grandma and Bridget. Lifting spirits and bringing back sinners to the fold were Sister Cyril's specialties.

"You look better," I noted.

"Still blind as a bat, but the ribs and the company helped considerably. You're back sooner than I expected. Who's that?"

Fred popped out from behind me.

"Fred Lytton, the man in the glass box," Sister Cyril declared. "Your story is legendary."

Fred smiled for the first time that day. "Really? That box was cunning. Had a devil of a time getting out."

"I heard it was hair-raising," said Sister Cyril, making the event sound heroic instead of what it really was.

"It was, ma'am. I think other men would have freaked out." If Fred had freaked out any more, he would have been picked up by a circus.

"Clearly," she agreed.

"I heard you almost became Swiss cheese," said Bridget.

"How are you holding up, Bridget?" I asked.

"I've passed self-loathing, but my psyche is scarred from being betrayed by a man of God. A so-called man of God."

"We're working on it," Sister Cyril said with an optimistic smile.

"Aren't you Julie's boy? How's that working out?" asked Grandma, pointing a rib bone at Fred.

Fred made a strange noise, like a chicken being strangled. His head slumped to his chest, and he let out a long sigh.

"That's what we're working on, Grandma," I said. "Lucy, can I borrow you after lunch? I have a project that I need help on."

Fred managed to eat a slab of ribs and a quart of potato salad. I didn't do too badly myself. At this rate, pretty soon I wouldn't be able to fit through the door.

Lucy, Fred, and I took the police cruiser to Fred's apartment, a small back room in Loretta Swine's house, way out in the southernmost tip of Cannes. Loretta owned the Christmas store in town. She sold Christmas all year round, and she took that holiday enthusiasm home with her. Her house was decked out from sidewalk to roof in lights and decorations.

"I'm blinded," Lucy said, stepping out of the car. "Somebody help me. I might be having a seizure." She closed her eyes tight and wandered around with her hands in front of her, Frankenstein-style. "Why would this woman have a hundred and fifty thousand Christmas lights turned on in the middle of the day in August?"

"Ms. Swine is very festive," Fred explained, his voice rising above the blaring Christmas music that played in a loop from loudspeakers over the front door.

"I heard about this house, but I never saw it in person. There's a lot of reindeer going on here," Lucy noted, letting her eyes open just a smidge. "I'm worried I'm going to get stampeded. What the hell is that over there? Is that baby Jesus playing with Santa?"

"Made of Legos. Yep," said Fred.

Lucy clutched her chest and took a step back. "Oh, lordy! I just now noticed the snowman collection on the roof. That's got to weigh two tons. Aren't you afraid the roof will cave in?"

Fred shook his head. "Loretta had the roof reinforced with steel beams. She has a life-sized nativity scene in the back totally in neon." He was plainly impressed.

"I've got to see that," said Lucy.

Fred had his own entrance at the back of the house. It was a lot quieter back there, away from the speakers. The entire structure was painted like a gingerbread house, and the door to Fred's apartment had a doorknob disguised as a green gumdrop.

"Do you mind if I take a couple of pictures?" Lucy asked when we stepped inside. Fred's bedroom was decorated in a winter wonderland theme. Giant tufts of cotton outlined his bed, making it look like he slept in a snowdrift. There were more lights. His mirror flashed green and red, and the floor was a replica of the Candyland game. Lucy took her phone out and snapped photos.

"This is so good," Lucy muttered.

"Fred, let's get you dressed," I said. "What do you have for a ball?"

Fred opened the candy-cane-striped closet. "I got a nice pair of pants from Sears. I had a good shirt, but my arms grew."

It was slim pickings. I didn't see anything that would bring Julie rushing toward Fred with love in her heart. "What do you think, Lucy?" I asked.

Lucy clucked her tongue. "Desperate times call for desperate measures. As General Robert E. Lee used to say, 'I can anticipate no greater calamity for the country.' Change of direction. Let's head over to my place."

LUCY'S HOUSE was just outside the historic district. It was a glorious Frank Lloyd Wright–style house all in white and glass. She had every luxury installed. My favorite was the eternity Jacuzzi on a large deck outside her bedroom. The power jets called out to me. If I hadn't had Fred to match, I would have jumped in.

Lucy led us through the house. "I'm sadly lacking in life-sized neon nativity scenes, Fred. I hope you do forgive me."

"Yes, ma'am." Fred's mouth had dropped open when we arrived, and he hadn't shut it since. I was worried that he had forgotten how.

"Let's go to my supplementary closets." Lucy guided us upstairs to a large room filled with men's clothes.

"You have an entire Men's Wearhouse in here," I said.

"More like the men's department of Neiman Marcus. A girl must be prepared for every eventuality."

"Marketing is an interesting profession," I said, running my hand over a stack of cashmere sweaters.

"Let's see. I would say you are a thirty-two long," Lucy said. "Thirty-two very long. Hmm . . . a ball outside in the fog on a warm August night. I have just the thing." Lucy was a swirl of activity, and when she was done, she had worked miracles.

"Why, Fred, you look almost dashing," she declared.

Fred stared at himself in the full-length mirror. "I feel like a movie star."

FRED HAD the siren on the whole way to Tea Time.

"Watch me work my magic," he said, and opened the door to the shop.

Tea Time was empty. In fact, most of Cannes was a ghost town, with its citizens busy primping for the big ball.

Julie sat at one of the tables, eating a burrito and drinking a Coke from a can. Fred sashayed up to her.

"Julie, my dearest, would you go to the ball with me?" he asked her.

"I told you I'm not interested in you," she said matter-of-factly.

Fred made the strangled chicken noise again and ran out the door. Lucy scampered after him while I stayed behind with Julie. I took a seat at her table.

"That burrito sure looks good. I had ribs for lunch, but I should have gotten one of those," I said.

"Do you want some tea or something? I'm kinda on my lunch break."

"Oh, no. No. I wanted to talk to you about Fred."

Julie's hair fell over her eye, and she left it there. "Who?"

"Fred. Sergeant Fred Lytton. He asked you to the ball."

"Oh, him. Yeah. No thanks."

"Really? I thought you were perfect for each other. Everybody thinks that. Don't you think he looked dashing just now? He's a snappy dancer, too." All of a sudden I sounded like I just walked out of a movie from the 1930s.

"Yeah. Not interested," she said.

Panic rose in my chest. I gasped for air. I grabbed Julie's burrito arm. "Look, Julie. You're going to the ball with Fred. You want to know why? I'll tell you why. Because I said so. And besides, you think you're just going to stay here all evening with Ruth, eating Oreos and watching reruns of *The Nanny*? Well, I have news for you. Ruth is going to the ball with Hank Frazier, who runs the fruit stand down the street. How's that going to look, your great-aunt cutting a rug and you just sitting home alone, trying not to set anything on fire? You might not think Fred is your dreamboat, but I have news for you, honey. Most dreamboats don't start out that way. So you're going to give him an ounce of respect and half a chance and tell him you'd love to go. Then you're going to put on a dress, pull your hair back, and swipe on some lipstick. You only live once, and there are precious few balls in this life. Don't miss out. You hear me?"

Julie dropped her burrito. "I guess so?" she squeaked.

"Stay here," I ordered.

I found Fred outside. Lucy was trying to tug him back to Tea Time. "Fred, you're on," I called.

"I can't go back in there, Gladie."

"Trust me, you can."

* * *

FRED DROPPED us off at Grandma's and went to buy a corsage to go with Julie's dress. Next door, a shirtless Holden was in his yard weeding a flower bed. I guessed it was gardening day.

"I'm going to head out and get ready for the ball," Lucy said.

"You too?"

"You'll never guess who I'm going with," she said. "Uncle Harry. I got a call out of the blue. He is so hot. He can charm me out of my Prada slingbacks anytime. Don't be fooled by his short stature and unorthodox hairstyle. He is a fabulous dancer."

I watched Lucy pull out, and I pretended to look at Grandma's roses while I spied on Holden. Wearing only jeans, he was beautiful with a capital "Oh, my." Still, I didn't know where I stood with him. He was a mystery man and possibly a murderer, although the possibility was slim—wasn't it?

"I see you looking at me," Holden called from his flower bed. "I'm not supposed to go near you."

"Oh."

"I want to go near you."

"Oh."

"I can't stop thinking about you. I didn't sleep a wink last night. I was worried. I called the hospital a dozen times and pretended I was a doctor to get updates on your health."

Oh. His voice was sweet and thick like molasses, rich and deep. It hit me in my nether regions with every syllable. I was supposed to be suspicious of him, but I couldn't drum up a negative feeling. I couldn't drum up an ounce of fear.

"Thank you," I said.

"I saw you out with that cop today. How'd that go?" he asked.

"All right."

"I can't say I like him, but I suppose I'm biased."

"Are you going to the ball tonight?" I asked. Where did that come from? I was letting my hormones lead the way.

"Only if you'll let me take you," he said.

"Uh," I said. "Well . . ."

And then he was there, in front of me. He smelled of fresh soil and sweat. He smelled good. He dusted his hands off on his jeans.

"How's your head?" he asked.

"Fine."

"You have a concussion."

"A slight concussion. I took a couple of Tylenols. I'm fine."

"You're not restricted in your activities?" He closed the gap between us and put his hands on my waist.

"I can't drive." My voice was hoarse and croaked when I spoke.

"But otherwise?"

"Otherwise, I guess so."

He nuzzled my neck, leaving a trail of heat as he traveled toward my mouth.

"Holden," I sighed. It was all the invitation he needed. He crushed his lips against mine. Feverish need pulsated through him, making me shiver with expectation.

"I think I like you," he said against my mouth.

I had been doing a lot of kissing lately. I really liked kissing, I decided. And I liked handsome men with broad chests and tight abs. But the gorgeous, attentive men who were kissing me had drawbacks. Spencer was an obnoxious womanizer, and Holden was mysterious, maybe a killer.

"I'll pick you up at eight-thirty?" he asked.

"Okay."

"I'm glad you're feeling better."

And then he was gone. Back next door, into his mystery house. I looked down to make sure my clothes were still on.

I was feeling good, but the day had left me tired. I had enough time to take a nap before I needed to get ready for the ball. I yawned. I wasn't much of a nap person, but I decided to give in and grab a couple of hours of sleep. Then I heard a "Yoo-hoo!"

Across the street, Betty Terns waved at me. My stomach clenched. She waved again and crooked her finger at me. I was a deer caught in the headlights.

"Gladie, be smart," I muttered to myself. I turned around and walked up my driveway and into the house. I closed the door behind me and leaned against it.

"Is that you, Gladie?" Grandma called from the kitchen.

"Yes."

Grandma's house slippers clacked into the entree. "There you are. I'm going to lie down. Everyone's gone. They're getting ready for the ball. Even Sister Cyril. Religion ain't what it used to be."

"By the way, Grandma, why did I have to be named Gladys?"

"Why? Were you teased again?"

"Yes."

"Oh, please. Be saddled with a name like Zelda for a day and see how you handle it."

The doorbell rang. I looked through the peephole. "Betty Terns," I mouthed to Grandma.

"I'm not here," she whispered, and tiptoed up the stairs.

"But you're always here," I whispered. "Where else would you be?"

The doorbell rang again. I took a deep breath and opened the door.

"Oh, Betty, what a nice surprise," I said.

"Didn't you hear me outside? I called you."

"No, I'm sorry."

"And I waved. Clear as day, I waved to you."

"I'm sorry. I must have been distracted. Is there something I can help you with?"

Betty eyed me. "Is that how you talk to me?"

"Excuse me?"

"Like *that*. You don't ask me to sit down. You don't offer me something to drink, to eat. How many times have I had you in my home? How many times have I opened my life to you? I've told you my darkest, most innermost thoughts and secrets. I told you about her, that woman who has harassed me and my family all these years."

"Hold it right there, sister," I said. "Don't give me that cock-and-bull story. I know the truth."

Betty's eyes closed to slits, and her forehead furrowed. "Which truth is that, Gladie?"

"You know what truth. Look, I'm tired. I know how you made up all those lies about Lulu."

"How dare you mention her name in front of me."

"Look, whatever. I get it. You were pissed that he cheated on you. But all the lies, the way you stalked that poor woman, how you punished your husband all those years, the fake letters, the fake phone calls, the blackmailing—you're cuckoo, lady, and I don't want anything more to do with you."

Betty's face went slack. She looked at me with dead eyes and poked my chest with her finger. "You think you know so much. You with your fancy house and your know-it-all grandmother and your big-city education. You don't know anything. You're nothing. I seen it the first time I laid eyes on you. I said to myself, 'There goes a big nothing.' You let your grandmother support you, and meanwhile you skulk around whoring with two men. I saw you kissing that half-naked good-for-nothing on the front lawn in the middle of the day.

Whore. You're just like that woman of Randy's. Maybe even worse. She thought she was better than anyone. With her art. An artist. What good is an artist? Nothing. Worse than nothing. She thought she was beyond punishment. No one could reach her. Well, someone could reach her. Someone knew how to punish her. You know what, Gladie? I thought we were friends, but you betrayed our friendship. Maybe you should be punished, too."

Betty made a guttural noise and spit at me, missing my face by inches. Before I could react, she was halfway across the street.

"You're wrong. I didn't have a fancy education," I called out to her. "I never even graduated from high school."

I bolted the door and took the stairs two at a time to the second floor. I was desperate to get in the shower and wash off my encounter with Betty. She was scary and mean, and some of what she said hit too close to home.

I let the hot water wash over me until it ran cold. Then I scrubbed with a loofah but still didn't feel clean. When I got out an hour later, I heard a pounding on the front door. Betty must be back again, I figured. I threw on a robe and ran down the stairs before she could wake up Grandma.

It wasn't Betty, though. It was Spencer, and he didn't look happy. He stormed in. "You got soda? I need something fizzy to settle my stomach."

He didn't wait for me to answer. He rushed past me into the kitchen and opened the fridge. "Perfect." He took out two cans and sat at the table.

"You're not going to be happy," he said.

"It's been a trying day. Not much happiness."

"Well, I'm here in a professional capacity."

I stomped my foot on the tile. "I hate those red light

cameras. They're not fair. If I start through the intersection when the light's yellow, how is it my fault it turns red before I get through? Is that fair?"

"I don't care about red light cameras, Pinkie. This is a serious complaint against you."

"Against me?"

"You want a drink? Like a real drink? Maybe you should have a drink." Spencer stood up, but I pulled him back down.

"What do you mean a complaint against me?" I asked.

"Betty Terns came in five minutes ago and filed a complaint, saying you have been harassing her, stalking her, threatening her."

"What?"

"And today you assaulted her. You hit her in the chest and you spit on her. She showed me the bruise. And the letter," he said.

"The letter?"

"In your handwriting, more or less. I pulled up your signature on your driver's license."

Steam came out of my ears. "Spencer—" I began.

"Hold on. I know your grandma has booze here somewhere."

Spencer followed me to the parlor. I pointed to the cabinet, and he poured me a stiff one.

"Take a big gulp," he instructed me. "Now, sit." I did as I was told. He sat next to me. He looked down at my robe, which had fallen open. He pulled it closed. "There. That was a distraction," he said. "Gladie, did you talk to Betty Terns this afternoon after I told you not to?"

"Yes, but—" I started.

"I told you not to!"

"It wasn't my fault!"

"What is with you, woman? Do you have brain trauma? Are you hard of hearing? Don't you have any common sense? I told you not to speak to her. Why did you speak to her?"

"She came to the house. She spoke to *me*. I didn't speak to her, not really."

"A neighbor heard you scream at her from across the street, something about high school."

I held my glass out. "Fill it up again," I said. I took a big gulp, then gave Spencer the whole story. I told him how Betty had come to the door, how she'd threatened me, spit at me, poked me. Spencer took notes.

"Do you believe me?" I asked. "Should I open my robe again?"

He smiled, but it wasn't the typical Spencer smirk. "You're always welcome to open your robe, Pinkie. This should do it for now." He closed his notebook and slipped his pen in his shirt.

I groaned. "For now?"

"She's persistent. As you know." Spencer leaned back on the couch. "What a day. What a week. And this headache tonight. Crazy town and its ball moved outside at the last minute."

I jumped up. "The ball! I have to get ready for the ball."

"You too?"

"Yes, I haven't done a thing." I tugged on Spencer's arm. "You have to go. I have to get ready. Shoo!"

I dragged him toward the door.

"If I didn't know better, I would say you're trying to get rid of me," he said. I waved goodbye and slammed the door behind him.

I DIDN'T look half bad. I had opted for Spanx and a push-up bra. It was a calculated risk. It meant I didn't want to get naked, but I wanted Holden to want me to get naked. I found a blue sheath dress and strappy sandals with impossibly high heels in my secret clothes closet. I slathered lotion wherever I could reach, and I put a smidge too much makeup on. I was still bruised and scraped from the escapade with Peter. The overall result was slightly less than Cinderella but much more than her ugly stepsisters.

Grandma was still asleep when Holden came to the door exactly at eight-thirty. He was breathtaking in a black suit. "You must be Bond, James Bond," I said.

"At your service, my lovely, lovely lady," he said with an uncanny Sean Connery impression. "It's a few blocks away. Can you make it in those heels? The entire town is there. I heard they moved the swing set and taco stand for this shindig. Shall we?"

He took my hand and kissed it. "This promises to be a memorable evening."

Chapter 19

✦ ♥ ✦

Life is not a romance novel. The mysterious, perfect man without a shirt doesn't live next door. The local cop isn't a grumpy, godlike creature who wants to bed you until you forget who you are. And a British mercenary is not going to kidnap you and stuff you in a burlap bag only to make you fall in love with him later. These scenarios are romance novels, those books you read while eating a pound of peanut M&Ms on the beach in summertime. Life is more complicated than a romance novel. Life has twists and turns that no one can predict, not even me. Prepare your matches for the twists and turns. They'll thank you later.

Lesson 50,
Matchmaking Advice from Your Grandma Zelda

THE CITY council had gone all out. The ball was a bash to end all bashes. The streets were blocked off. The taco stand was long gone, as were the swing set and slide. The little playground in the historic district was strung with white lights. A jazz band played on a raised platform. A large dance floor covered the entire area. On the side, elegant tables were set with champagne glasses and little finger foods.

The most magical aspect of the evening was the fog. It had come in just as predicted, covering the ground and giving the evening a romantic, Old World ambiance.

No wonder the whole town turned out for the affair dressed to the nines. I was glad Holden had asked me.

Holden put his arm around my waist, and I leaned into him. We found Lucy right away, standing with Uncle Harry.

"You clean up nice," I told Uncle Harry.

"You're not so bad yourself, Legs," he said. "Who's the pretty boy?"

Holden put his hand out. "Arthur Holden."

"Arthur Holden. Your face looks familiar. What line are you in?"

"This and that."

Uncle Harry furrowed his brow. "Is that right? Same here. And how do you know Legs?"

Holden's eyes cut to my legs. "She's the girl next door."

"Lucky you."

It wasn't clear which of us Harry was speaking to, or if "Lucky you" was a good thing or not. There was a definite protective energy emanating from Uncle Harry, and even though he only came up to the middle of Holden's chest and Holden was at least twenty years younger and vastly more fit, I thought Uncle Harry was going to jump him any second and give him a good pounding. Lucy picked up on the vibe, too. She took his arm.

"How long are you going to keep me off the dance floor, Uncle Harry? You promised me every dance," she said. She twisted her hips, making her dress fly up to reveal her perfect legs. Lucy winked at me and pulled Uncle Harry into a samba.

THE DANCE floor was packed. I spotted Bridget dancing with Terrence Lafferty, her on-again, off-again boyfriend. He was a CPA like Bridget, and they'd met at a conference. I had never actually heard him speak, but Bridget said he was almost perfect. She'd explained to me one day that she could never be serious with him because of his views on the Mideast peace process.

"Why don't we start with a glass of champagne?" Holden asked me.

"I can't think of a reason against it," I said.

"I'll be right back."

It was going to be a while. The champagne line was crowded, and a fight had broken out between the champagne lady and someone wanting three glasses at once.

The music was excellent. I swayed a bit in place to "The Way You Look Tonight."

There was a tap on my shoulder. "Gosh, you look awfully pretty."

Fred stood there, all alone. He stuffed his hands in his pockets.

"Where's Julie?"

"The heel popped off her shoe, and she fell into the punch bowl. Ruth took her home."

Somehow it didn't come as a surprise. "Is she coming back?"

"Her great-aunt said if she doesn't get eaten by a pack of wild dogs, she'll be back." I figured there was a fifty-fifty chance.

"How was it until her heel broke?" I asked.

"All right. She seemed more interested in the dessert selection than me."

"That's perfectly normal, Fred. Don't worry. I have a good feeling."

"You like this music?" he asked.

I nodded. "Oh, yes. It makes me want to move my feet."

"Well, I know how to dance."

"Are you asking me to dance, Fred?"

In answer, Fred swept me up in his arms and twirled me around the dance floor with polished expertise.

"Fred, you're a really good dancer," I said, breathless. Who would have thought clumsy Fred could trip the light fantastic?

"The only child of a dance teacher," he explained. "I was named after Fred Astaire."

The music changed to a slow number, and Fred pulled me close. "You smell better than anything. Better than bacon in the morning. Better than honeysuckle in June."

He nuzzled the top of my hair and sniffed.

"Uh . . . ," I began.

Suddenly Fred stopped dancing. Spencer was standing right there. "I can't watch this another minute. I'll be sick. Get off her or I'll drop you back to meters." He yanked Fred away and took his place.

"I thought you were joking about Fred," he said. "I might lose my lunch."

"I was joking, actually."

Spencer's face relaxed. He was a good dancer, too, but he concentrated more on body positions and less on fancy footwork.

"You're dancing awfully close, Spencer."

"Your point?"

"Shouldn't you be working?"

"I delegated." He dipped me slowly. His eyes flicked to my boobs, which threatened to pop out of my dress. "I'm glad to see you out and happy Betty Terns hasn't gotten to you. I'm sure we'll get that mess straightened out eventually."

I hoped he was right. "I'm surprised to see you out alone, Spencer. Where's your posse?"

He nuzzled my neck. "You like me being alone? You like that idea?"

I was just about to swallow my tongue when a shadow covered us. "I have your champagne."

I stumbled backward. "Holden. Thanks." I took a glass and downed its contents in one gulp.

"I thought we had an understanding," Spencer said. "You were going to stay away from Gladie."

"We thought otherwise."

"We," Spencer echoed. His eyes slid to me, and he raised an eyebrow questioningly.

I nodded.

"Fair enough," he said. "It's your funeral, so to speak. And perfect timing—there's my date."

A stunning, six-foot-tall supermodel wearing a mostly see-through gown glided toward us. "There you are, dahling," she said to Spencer in her Zsa Zsa Gabor accent. She wrapped her arms around his neck and gave him a long kiss, smearing red lipstick over his face. "I tink it is lovely, zis leetle party. Tank you for inviting me."

"Olga, allow me to introduce you to Gladie and her little friend."

"How do you do?" She thrust her hand in my direction. It remained limp as I shook it. *Yuck*. Spencer had terrible taste in women.

"How do you do," said Holden. "You look familiar to me."

"I am swimsuit model. I am cover of magazine *Sports Illustrated*," she said.

"That must be it," said Holden. Swell. I sucked in my stomach.

"How about some champagne, honey?" Spencer asked.

I cleared my throat. "Hold on, Mr. Chief of Police. Doesn't she have to wait ten years or so before she can legally drink champagne?" My voice came out catty and shrill.

Spencer shook his head. "No, not at all. It's just that

as you get older, Gladie, people look younger and younger to you."

I grabbed Holden's glass of champagne and downed that, too. "I need some fresh air," I told Holden.

"We're outside," he said.

"I need fresher air, away from the noise."

We found a bench half a block away. The fog swirled around us, and the music played in the background.

"This is nice," I said. I cuddled in close, and Holden caressed my arm.

"You wanted me to punch him, didn't you?" he asked.

"Just a little. A broken jaw or nose. I wanted to see blood."

"I didn't have to fight him because I've already won. I have the girl."

"You don't read *Sports Illustrated*, do you?"

"Me? Never. I just happened to see a copy at the doctor's office. Spencer must have imported her. I hear he gets around." His eyes twinkled, and he pulled me onto his lap. "So," he said. "Here we are. Alone in the fog, dressed up and smelling nice. But we didn't meet under the most romantic circumstances."

"I wasn't dressed very well."

"You weren't? I didn't notice. I noticed your eyes. And your lips. But then, our first date was in a cemetery."

"You're right. It was. I forgot," I said.

"It was eclipsed by what happened later in the day. Do you want to talk about that part?"

"No." I shut my eyes, trying to shut out the memory of the church and the priest murdered in front of me.

"But this is decidedly romantic, the fog, the music, the dancing," he said.

"And I'm dressed well."

"Yes, you are. I noticed that." His finger traced the top of my dress, gliding over the top of my cleavage. I gasped. I wondered how fast we could get back to the house, running in my heels. I thought of ways to get out of the Spanx without him noticing.

"There you are!" Ruth Fletcher from Tea Time plopped down on the bench next to us. "Can't see a damned thing through all this damned fog. What a night. I lost my date." She wagged her finger at us. "No funny comments about him running away. Hank couldn't run away to save his life. He's older than dirt and half his body parts are paid for by Medicare."

"You look nice," I said. Ruth wore a purple velvet shirt dress with four long strands of pearls and large gold hoop earrings.

"Thanks. Wasted on Hank, of course. He couldn't see a cow if it was flying directly at him." Ruth gave us a long look. "Something going on between you two? Huh. I had you pegged for the cop. Oh, well. What do I know? Anyway, you have to come along now, Gladie. You have to speak to my grandniece."

"Julie?"

"I caught on how you're trying to match her to that tall sip of water, Fred what's-his-name. Well, she's in crisis. You gotta come, now. You'll excuse her a minute, handsome?"

"Of course," said Holden, removing me from his lap. If Julie and Fred hadn't been my first match, I would have told Ruth to bug off so that I could get naked with Holden, but if I was going to prove myself and really give the matchmaking thing a go, duty called, and I had to heed it. Holden kissed the palm of my hand.

"I'll be waiting," he said.

Julie stood at the punch bowl—an unwise position, I thought, considering her past experience with it.

"How you feeling?" asked Ruth.

Julie blew a strand of hair away from her face. "Better, I guess. Fred went to get me some cake. I just wanted cake, you know."

"Sure you did," said Ruth. "The girl's got blood sugar issues," she said to me.

"He's not my dreamboat, though, Gladie. You were wrong."

"Have you danced with him yet? Once you dance with him, he'll be your dreamboat," I said, even though I was having some doubts.

Julie handed me a red envelope. "Here. You're supposed to read it in private. She said not to show it to anybody."

"She?"

"Yeah, an old blond lady. There he is. Finally, my cake."

I found a corner and opened the letter. The handwriting was familiar. It was the same as the blackmail letters.

I WAS supposed to come alone, the letter said, or else Grandma's life would be in danger. I had to hurry, but I searched for Spencer on the way out. In the fog and the crowd, I couldn't find him, but I stumbled on Uncle Harry.

"Tell me, Uncle Harry. Randy Terns didn't actually say he was being blackmailed by Jimmy the Fink and Chuck Costas. You just assumed he was because he said he was being blackmailed and he was looking for them."

Uncle Harry blinked. "Yes, I guess you're right. I never picked up on that."

"It's okay. It's what I figured."

"Are you all right, Gladie? You look out of sorts," said Lucy.

"I'm fine. I just have to go do something."

"Can I help?"

"Not this time."

Back at home, my car started on the second try. I gripped the steering wheel and willed my hands to stop shaking. It was hard to see the road through the fog, and it took me longer than I wanted to get to Cannes Center Park. I didn't know what I would do once I got there, but I had to get there fast, before it was too late.

I parked on the street. Even the crickets were silent. The whole town was at the ball. If Cannes Center Park was isolated to begin with, it was desolate in the fog at night. I took a deep breath and made my way to the gazebo. My heels dug into the soft earth with every step.

I almost missed the gazebo, but I found it after a few minutes of stumbling through the trees and brush. After decades of neglect, the gazebo was decrepit. The first step creaked loudly when I put my foot on it. I hesitated, waiting to be attacked or shot. When nothing happened, I ran up the rest of the way.

"Grandma. Grandma," I hissed, searching the spiderweb-infested corners. Nothing. No one. "What an evil joke," I said under my breath. "Scared me to death."

Behind the gazebo, there was the sound of a twig breaking underfoot. I froze, listening for more sounds.

"Who's there?" I called. "Betty, I know it's you. Just come out and stop this whole thing before it escalates out of control."

Nothing. Then another twig snapped.

"Betty, don't get to the point of no return. I know you're angry, but there are other ways of resolving your issues," I said.

"Then you don't know my mother." I jumped in surprise. Jane Terns appeared on the steps of the gazebo, a gun in her hand pointed directly at me.

"Jane? What are you doing here?"

"I begged you to figure it out," she said. "Didn't I? Didn't I ask you several times to figure it out?"

"Jane, I tried to look into your father's death, but—"

"You didn't look in the right place! I gave you hints. I practically steered you to where you were supposed to go."

"I can try again. Jane, please, where's my grandmother?"

"You can't try again. It's too late. You made my mother mad. Don't you see?" Jane's hair was wild. She spit when she spoke, and the gun shook with each syllable.

"I'll tell your mom I'm sorry," I said. "We'll go for tea and scones. She liked it when we did it last time."

"No, she's mad, and when she's mad, it never goes away. She's my mom, and I've always looked after her. I'm her good girl. She needs me. She's always needed me. That's why I did things for her."

I inched backward. "Like what? What have you done for her?"

"Lots of things. I wrote letters, terrible letters to a woman who made her mad."

"You wrote the letters to Lulu?"

"I tried to tell you. I tried to talk to you. You were always busy, always running around, and you went in the wrong direction. I went to talk to you, but you weren't there. I tried to get your attention, but it wasn't you. It was your grandma."

"You threw the knish," I said.

"I was trying to get you to listen to me," she yelled. "I told you to follow the trail to the end. It was like you didn't want to see. Just like Dad. He didn't want to see."

My head was swimming.

"What didn't your dad want to see?"

"My mother gets mad. It's not her fault. She's had a

very hard life, and she depends on me. I have to help her."

I couldn't help but wish for a straitjacket. Jane was the queen of loop-de-loo. Her potato was half baked. Her pancake had flipped. Her milk had turned, and her brownie was all nuts. In other words, Jane was crazy, and despite being in a life-threatening situation, I was hungry.

"Jane, we all want to please our parents," I said reasonably. "But a loving parent only wants her children to be happy." Except for my mom. The last time I spoke with her, she was living with a biker gang in Wichita, and she gave me a lecture about my life choices and how I would wind up pregnant, on welfare, singing old Loretta Lynn songs in bowling alley bars.

"Your mother doesn't need you to protect her," I continued. "She's a grown woman, and so are you. Live your own life, Jane. Live your own life."

I looked to see if my rational words had gotten through to her. Nope. The light of crazy still shined bright in her eyes.

"I tried. I tried to tell you, to stop her before it got too late. You don't understand anything," she said. "My mom needs me."

"Why, Jane? What did you do for her? What do you know about your father, Jimmy the Fink, and Chuck Costas?"

"What are you talking about? You've gone in the wrong direction again."

"No, Jane. I understand now. I'm sorry I didn't before. You were trying to warn me about your mother."

Jane smiled. Her face relaxed, but she didn't lower her gun. "Yes. What a relief. You understand. I tried to warn you before she got mad, before I needed to help her. Now it's too late."

"Jane, please tell me where my grandmother is. I

didn't bring anyone here with me, just like you told me in the note."

"That's good, because I would have killed your grandmother right away if you had. No police."

"I did just what you said," I said.

"It's a shame I have to kill you. I thought we could be friends."

Jane cocked the gun.

"Wait," I cried out. "You didn't tell me about your dad. You didn't tell me why you killed him." I felt around behind me for any loose wood, something to defend myself with.

"You're right. I killed him. It was my fault. Dad refused to pay. He wrote back to Lulu, telling her that he didn't care anymore if she spilled the beans about the affair. He didn't give a shit what my mom thought. He didn't care how mad he made her. I wrote another letter, but it still didn't work. He didn't care anymore. By then it was too late. He had to die. Just like now. Too late."

"But it's not too late, Jane. We can find help for you. We can be friends just like you wanted."

Jane stomped her foot hard on the step. "That's not true! It's too late. Now, come on. I've got to do this."

I clutched the rail.

"No, you can't make me go. You'll have to shoot me here," I said.

Jane tried to pry my fingers off the rail with her gun-free hand.

"I can't shoot you here. I have to make it look like an accident. You and your grandma are going for a swim in your car."

I gripped the rail for all I was worth. "No. You are going to have to shoot me here," I said. There was a method to my madness. I hoped that Jane would get tired and some shred of sanity would pop into her head and make her realize what she was doing.

"You're going to make my mom so mad," Jane complained.

Now that she was close enough, I grabbed for the gun, but Jane was quicker and meaner than I was. She pulled back and swung the gun into the side of my head. I slumped sideways and gulped air in an effort to stay conscious.

I was half aware of her shoving me across the gazebo, and then I was off-balance, trying to right myself as I was thrown down the stairs. I hit my arm with a crack, rolled over, and landed on my hip.

"Get up or I'll hit you again. You don't have to be in one piece when you drown in the lake." That was a good thing, because I wasn't in one piece. I was reasonably sure my left arm was broken, and blood was trickling down my face from the gash on my head. I saw stars floating in the fog. I fell a couple of times as I struggled to stand up. One of my shoes was missing, and my dress was torn completely up one side. Jane grabbed my purse and threw it over her shoulder.

I kicked off my other shoe. I willed myself not to go into shock, but I needed to see a doctor. Formulating a plan to overpower Jane and save my grandmother was hard in coming, especially since I couldn't seem to concentrate on anything at all.

Twigs and rocks scraped my feet as we made our way across the park, but the pain was nothing compared to my arm, which sent spikes of agony through my body with each movement. My head throbbed, too, like my brain was swelling and pushing against my broken skull. Maybe it was.

"Here," said Jane. We arrived at her car, a nice silver sedan. She opened one of the rear doors, and Grandma tumbled out. She wore her nightgown and slippers, and there was duct tape hanging from the corner of her mouth.

"I want to go home," she cried, her voice fragile, cracking.

"Grandma, it's going to be fine. I'll get you home," I said.

"No, you won't. Don't fib."

Jane pushed us forward, threatening us with the gun.

"Gladie, I'm not in my home," Grandma said to me, choking on her own tears.

"I'll get you home. I promise. I have a plan." It was a terrible lie, but I didn't want Grandma to panic any further.

"I picked a hell of a day to be blind," said Grandma. "But I did tell you they were all losers."

"Here," said Jane. We had arrived at my car.

"You're going to drown us in my own car?"

"You're going to go missing. Poor Zelda and Gladie Burger. Vanished."

"No one is going to believe we vanished," I said.

"You never stay in one place for more than a couple months," Jane explained to me. "You can't keep a job. Everyone knows that. So you got tired of matchmaking and Cannes. You moved on."

"My grandmother would never have moved on. She hasn't left her house in nearly twenty years," I said.

"She changed her mind. She wanted to go with you. She loves you. Who cares? Besides, they can find your bodies in the lake later. It won't matter by then. This is the way it's going to happen. We play it this way."

She opened the rear door and waved the gun at Grandma. "Get in."

I followed her, my feet fumbling over the plastic owl on the floor. Jane kept the gun pointed at us as she walked around the car to get in the driver's seat.

"When I tell you, get out of the car and run like the wind to Burger Boy," I whispered to Grandma.

"But—"

"Just do it. Don't look back. Get Spencer. Get ready to run."

Jane opened the driver's door and sat behind the wheel. "Go!" I screamed and picked up the owl and shoved it as hard as I could one-handed into the back of Jane's head, pushing her headlong into the dashboard. Grandma was already across the street. I rolled out of the car and ran for all I was worth.

"Dammit, Gladie," Jane yelled not far behind me. "I have to kill you!"

I ran for the trees. I doubted she could shoot accurately in the fog at night, but I wasn't taking any chances. I heard Jane running full out behind me, crashing over branches. Barefoot and broken, I was no match for her. My only chance was to hide. I made a quick left into a thick grove of trees and was hit by a familiar smell.

Someone was having a party with illicit drugs of the smoke variety. I followed my nose.

"Oh, dude, you so scared me. I'm buggin' now."

The skateboarders from Burger Boy were sitting in a circle on their skateboards, passing around a joint. They were dressed exactly as they'd been the first time I saw them, on Thursday.

"Help," I hissed. "Help, there's a woman with a gun. Help."

"Hey, it's the owl lady," said the guy with the beer bong T-shirt. "Did you stop by to partake in our friendly smoke? It's killer."

"No, a woman is trying to kill me," I whispered.

"Hey, dude, like, that owl flew away and never came back to Burger Boy," one of the skateboarders commented.

"Yes, I know. A gun. A gun," I said.

"What happened to your arm, man? It looks like a buffalo wing that's kind of broke."

"My arm is kind of broke. The bad woman with the gun kind of broke it." My desperation hit record levels.

"That shit is rough," said the beer bong guy, finally catching on.

"Why would she do that?" asked another.

"She's crazy, she has a gun, and she's coming this way. Will you help me?" I asked.

"Help you?"

"Like how?"

"Like karate and kung fu and all that?"

"Oh, man. It's *Matrix* cool, man. And we're like Keanu Reeves or something."

"Cool," said another.

"Get me out of here," I ordered. "Now."

"Sure, dude. We have a quick escape path for, like, when the cops or our moms are around. There's a bitchin' path right back here. You're gonna love it."

"Yeah, you're gonna love rollin' tonight. The fog makes it like riding on clouds."

"Yeah, dude, kinda like rollin' in heaven."

I was teetering on a skateboard with the beer bong guy pushing one-legged behind me when the first shot rang out.

"Was that thunder?" asked one of the skateboarders.

"That was a crazy woman trying to kill us," I said. Another shot tore off a piece of a tree next to us. "This is not going to work. Plan B." We stopped and hid behind trees. "I don't know why I didn't think of this before."

Jane came ripping down the path, waving her gun and screaming, "Come out, come out wherever you are, Gladie. Hurry up! I have to kill you."

I signaled to the beer bong guy just as Jane made it to

our tree. He held his skateboard like a baseball bat, and just like Babe Ruth, hit a home run against Jane's head.

"Dude, I think you killed her," said one of the skateboarders.

"This is like . . . ," said another, drifting off.

"Like wow."

"Yeah, wow."

"Is she really dead?"

"I hope so," I said. But Jane moaned and stirred, and I knew she was still alive. They carried her to my car and put her in the trunk just as police sirens approached.

"Oh, man, like they know," said the beer bong guy.

"Don't worry," I said. "They're coming for me. You did good, real good. You saved my life."

"Cool."

"Well, see ya," said the beer bong guy, and they were off, skating on a cloud through the fog into the deep recesses of the park to smoke another day.

I slumped against the car, sliding down until I landed on the sidewalk, my body leaning up against the back tire. The sirens meant that Grandma had gotten to Burger Boy all right, and that was what I wanted. With Jane in the trunk and Grandma safe and sound, I could rest, I reasoned. I was so cold. I couldn't understand why it was so cold in August. My eyes drooped closed.

Chapter 20

Happy endings are never guaranteed, bubeleh. Sometimes they're in the cards. Sometimes they're not. We try our best to go down the happy endings road, but maybe we're on the wrong road and we didn't know it. Maybe somebody changed the sign. You can't know until you follow the road until the end. If you're lucky, there isn't an end. The road just keeps going.

Lesson 72,
Matchmaking Advice from Your Grandma Zelda

I WAS dancing with Spencer. He had one hand on the small of my back and the other caressed my cheek. "I'm so tired, Spencer," I told him. "I want to stop dancing now."

"Not now, honey," he said, his voice deep, reassuring, and full of caring. It was out of character, and it made me nervous.

"Why are you worried about me?"

"Because you're dying. But I'm here now. If you open your eyes, I'll save you."

I yawned. "I'd like you to save me. I'm tired of saving myself."

"Sure, Pinkie. Now open your eyes. Open your eyes. Open your eyes."

* * *

"PINKIE, OPEN your goddamned eyes. You're a royal pain in the ass. You know that? Son of a bitch, if you don't even try to open your eyes, I'm going to fuckin' kill you."

My eyes fluttered open, almost against my will. Spencer was standing over me and yelling obscenities while paramedics stuck tubes in me and wrapped things around my neck and head.

"Geez, you swear a lot," I said to Spencer.

He smiled from ear to ear. Not a smirk but a true, happy smile. "It's my second language, Pinkie. I'm bilingual."

GRANDMA, IT turned out, didn't have a scratch on her. After calling the police, she had the Burger Boy manager drive her home, and that's where she stayed. She refused medical care from the paramedics, insisting that only her doctor, old Dr. Goldberg, attend to her. He made a house call, gave her a Xanax, and told her to call him in the morning.

Jane Terns was spending the night and probably the rest of her life in the loony bin. Spencer found her in the trunk around the time I was put in the ambulance. "I did it. I did everything," she said when he opened the trunk, and she repeated it to whoever would listen.

Betty Terns was questioned, and she revealed that Jane had severe mental problems; she provided medical records to prove it. Jane's gun was found in the park, and initial tests showed that it was the gun that had been used to kill Chuck Costas. The Ternses' house was searched, and more letters were found. One letter contained a photo of Lulu's head Photoshopped onto the body of a young naked woman, with a death threat written underneath in Jane's handwriting. Apparently, Jane was a good forger. It was clear she had killed them all: her father, Chuck Costas, and probably Jimmy the Fink, which would be most likely proven as murder after the toxicology report came back.

My disappearance from the ball had been noticed pretty quickly. Bridget told me there'd been a scuffle between Holden and Spencer on my account, but it had been Ruth Fletcher who stopped it and alerted them to the mysterious blond woman who'd given Julie a letter for me. When questioned, Julie had explained that maybe the "old blond woman" she described was around forty years old.

I had a myriad of injuries, but I didn't need surgery. They shaved a patch of my head in order to give me stitches, and I doubted Bird could do anything to repair the damage to my hairstyle until it grew back. My arm wasn't broken, but it was dislocated and secured in a sling, tied to me at an angle. I was stuck in my hospital bed for at least three days, according to a very young doctor with a suspect tan. I didn't care how long I stayed in bed. I could have slept forever, although the atmosphere in the room wasn't too relaxing. Long after Bridget and Lucy left, Spencer sat in one corner of the room, and Holden sat in another. It didn't look like either of them had any intention of leaving.

Even though Holden was exonerated, Spencer still treated him like he was going to steal the silver. Or worse. Spencer watched over me like a pit bull terrier, slouched in his chair but jumping with every beep of the machines pumping drugs into my body.

Holden gave me water when I was thirsty and adjusted my pillows when I was uncomfortable. He cooed sweet nothings to me, assured me that my shaved patch of hair wasn't noticeable, and promised to shave his head to match mine. But I still didn't know what he did for a living, and I had never been in his house.

"I've only known you since Thursday," I muttered

once while on morphine. Alone in the attic on Thursday, in a hospital room filled with suitors on Tuesday. A fledgling matchmaker consumed with self-doubt on Thursday, a serial-killer chaser with a cracked skull on Tuesday. What a week.

At seven the next morning, Wednesday, a team of doctors came in and spoke about me as if I wasn't there. Then two nurses kicked everyone out and took over, changing my bed and my bandages. They chatted about murder and showed me the paper. I was on the front page. I had captured a serial killer in Cannes. I had saved lives, risked my own. And I was single and a matchmaker.

"Good advertising," I mumbled to the nurses. And then, "Are you single?" because I felt I had to.

The nurses told me how reporters wanted to interview me and how Spencer had stopped them. They talked endlessly about the good looks of the men around me. Spencer had the dreamiest eyes. Holden had the sexiest smile. I couldn't argue.

But I felt diffuse, like someone had let the air out of me, and I couldn't get excited about anything. Besides, I had a worrisome doubt inside that threatened to worm its way out, a theory that I was pretty sure was right.

After the nurses left, Spencer came back in. Holden had gone to work or garden or some secret activity that I wasn't allowed to know about. Spencer hadn't gotten any sleep, but there wasn't a wrinkle on his suit or a hair out of place.

"How long are you going to babysit me?" I asked Spencer.

He shrugged. "How long are you going to run around investigating mysterious deaths?" he asked.

"I think my running days are over."

Spencer took off his jacket and stretched his legs out in front of him. His chest was wide, his arms large. He let his head rest on his hand, and his eyes closed. Asleep, he looked younger. I could picture him playing catch with his father, going to baseball games. Maybe he would want to do that with his own son. He would sit his son on his shoulders, hike, picnic, play catch. *Whoa.* I stopped myself. It was not healthy to imagine Spencer as parental material. He probably never wanted to reproduce, anyway.

I dozed for a while, too, until Spencer's cellphone rang.

"It's for you," he said, passing me the phone.

"Dolly, it's Grandma. I can see again," she said.

"That's great, Grandma. I'm glad you called."

"I know you are. I thought I would wake you so you wouldn't be late."

"Late? Oh, yeah, Randy Terns' memorial," I said. "I should go. I need to talk to someone." I had unfinished business that needed finishing. I had a theory that needed to be proven.

"You might want to get there thirty minutes early," she said. "If you have a problem with Spencer, tell him to call me."

Spencer was ornery, but he was no match for Grandma. An hour later, I was in Spencer's car. I had a three-hour pass from the hospital with strict instructions to stay in a wheelchair and have Spencer wait on me hand and foot.

"I don't think this is a good idea. Have I told you that?" Spencer said, driving away from the hospital.

"I lost count after the fifteenth time you said it."

"You have to be very careful with what you say at the memorial," he said. "In fact, don't say anything. Don't get yourself wound up."

"Spencer, I'm on so much happy juice, it would take a lot of winding to wind me up."

We arrived thirty minutes early. A hearse was parked

in front of the funeral home, along with a couple of other cars. Spencer sat me in the wheelchair and draped a blanket over my legs, even though it was August and a particularly hot morning. We stayed by Spencer's car for a moment, looking around and waiting for the sky to fall or missiles to land or whatever else was in store for us. We didn't have long to wait.

Betty Terns, in her pink polyester suit, stormed out of the funeral home and lit up a cigarette. After a few minutes she must have noticed our reflection in the windows of the hearse, because she flinched and turned slowly toward us. By the time she was facing us she'd regained her composure and her initial surprise had been replaced with a welcoming smile. She inhaled the last of her cigarette and lit a new one with the butt.

"Are you sure about this?" Spencer muttered to me.

I nodded, and he went back to his car. Betty watched him walk away. When he was securely behind the wheel, she turned her attention to me.

"Oh, Gladie. I'm so happy you're doing well. I can't tell you how touched I am that you came all the way out here to pay your respects," she said.

"Touched in the head," I said under my breath.

She pursed her lips. "I'm sorry about Jane. She's had trouble since she was a little girl. She used to cut the heads off Barbies, and there was this babysitting incident."

"But you and Jane have always been real close."

"She's my daughter. Of course we're close."

"But you were closer to Jane than to the rest of your kids. Peter told me how you and Jane would skulk off to a room and talk, how Jane was a kiss-ass, as Peter put it. Jane felt she needed to protect you. Jane felt responsible for your happiness."

"She was a responsible child," Betty said.

"That's what I thought to begin with," I said. "I

thought, Here is a crazy woman who has done terrible things in some misguided notion of doing you favors. But maybe it wasn't a misguided notion. Maybe the notion was given to her, fed to her over her whole life."

"Are you calling me a monster?"

Yes, I was. I was glad she had caught on to that.

"So you had Jane write the letters," I said.

"Letters? Why would I do that?"

"You had Jane write threatening letters to Lulu Finkelstein, your husband's mistress, and threatening letters to your husband."

Betty squinted, as if she was studying me.

"It's disrespectful of you to mention her name to me, Gladie. Especially today of all days."

"I'm sorry, Betty. But you had Jane write her letters."

She pointed her cigarette at me. "Maybe that whore deserved those letters. Did you ever think of that? Maybe it wasn't crazy or wrong to send them. Maybe the both of them deserved to be punished for the way they acted."

Betty's eyes rolled in their sockets like she was trying to capture thoughts as they swirled in her mind. Her crazy quotient was actively rising. I hoped Spencer was watching and had remembered to bring his gun.

"What Randy and Lulu did was wrong," I said.

"You bet your ass. So maybe it was right to send the letters, to make the whore run away from Randy as fast as she could and stay away, to make Randy focus on me, his wife, the one he should have been loyal to. So maybe those letters were a good thing."

"I guess you could see it that way," I said. "Or maybe you wanted to make your husband's life a living hell. When your husband died, Jane asked me for help. She wanted me to follow the path of infidelity because she knew it would lead to Lulu and eventually lead to you.

She wanted it to lead to you, Betty. She knew what you were capable of."

"Where are you going with this, Gladie?" Betty asked. "Are you talking about Randy?"

"I'm talking about Cindy," I said. "The night I first met you in your kitchen, Jane explained that Cindy had suffered brain damage in a playground accident. But later Rob let it slip that Cindy had had an accident in the kitchen with you. Jane knew all about that accident, didn't she, Betty? She knew it wasn't really an accident. You have a temper, and you were responsible for Cindy's injury, and Jane covered for you. From then on out, she did whatever she could to prevent you from getting angry. She tried to warn me, to stop you before you made her cover for you again. She didn't want you to hurt anyone else, and when you get angry, Betty, you like to hurt people."

"You've got a lot of nerve, talking to me like that, saying I'm a bad mother, a bad person. You've been a pain in my side, sticking your nose in where it doesn't belong."

"But you wanted me in your business," I said. "You wanted to talk to me about Randy and your kids."

"And you turned your back on me! You had the letters. You knew about the whore. But instead of tracking her down and indicting her for murder, you came back to me and attacked me."

"So it was you who slipped the letters in my purse. It wasn't Cindy," I said. "You wanted to frame Lulu, but it backfired."

"I told you not to mention her name."

"What did you do with the money?" I asked.

"What money?"

"The blackmail money," I said. "You blackmailed your husband in Lulu's name. What did you do with that and with the bank money, Randy's big heist?"

Betty choked out a loud cackling noise, which turned into a coughing fit. She lit another cigarette and took a long drag.

"There wasn't any big bank heist," she said, catching her breath. "Are you kidding me? That idiot never could bring in a good living. Did you hear about the time he dressed up as a tree? What an idiot. I had a good laugh when Peter broke through all the walls looking for money. The apple doesn't fall far from the tree, believe me."

"You sent Randy's blackmail money to his old gang," I said. "Jimmy the Fink and Chuck Costas thought the money was coming from him, that Randy was paying them every month from his stash of bank heist money." Betty's expression confirmed my theory. She was proud as punch.

"You sent them the money as revenge against Randy," I continued. "He was already strapped for cash and you forced him to give away the rest. You let them enjoy the money instead of him. As an added bonus, you could frame them for blackmail if you ever needed to. But when Randy died, you couldn't frame Jimmy and Chuck because he had already gone to them about the blackmail. He complained to them about Lulu blackmailing him, and Jimmy the Fink put two and two together.

"You were the architect of the whole thing. So you had to kill Jimmy and Chuck. You couldn't leave behind any loose ends," I said. I knew I was right. I was so right I expected fireworks, a parade, or a Corn Flakes Junior Detective Badge.

"What are you saying, Gladie?" she asked. "Are you saying I got angry at my husband because he no longer loved me, no longer cared if I found out about his affair? So, what? So I waited until he went downstairs for a midnight snack, and then I snuck up on him and hit him over the head with the egg pan?"

"Well, I could be saying that," I said.

"And then what? Jimmy the Fink had suspicions and tried to blackmail me, so maybe I slipped something in his beer to give him a stroke? Are you saying that?" I raised my hand. "Oh! Oh! I guessed that."

"And that phony priest," Betty went on, ignoring me. "Are you saying he tried to hide from me, but I managed to track him down and shoot him in the head?"

"Uh," I said, "I guess I'm saying that."

Betty stubbed out her cigarette under her shoe. Her eyes flicked to Spencer's car before she looked back at me and leaned in close. "Well, look at you. Little Miss Matchmaker thinks she's a big, important detective. You did a pretty good job, actually. Heck, you are cleverer than I thought."

The hair stood up on the back of my neck, and I had a pins-and-needles feeling in my arms and legs. I wondered if I was having an allergic reaction to whatever medication I was on. No, it was probably a reaction to crazy Betty. "Betty, are you being almost nice to me?" I asked.

"Smart Gladys Burger, playing the police chief and the new neighbor boy for fools," she said, lighting up another cigarette. "Not easy to play that police chief. I've seen him lurking around town, bedding every whore he could get his hands on. But you're his special whore. You snap your fingers, and off he runs toward you."

"I wouldn't say he runs," I said.

"I'm the victim in this whole thing, you know. When Randy got the first blackmail letter, that son of a bitch told me he got demoted at work, and that was the end of movies, restaurants, and clothes. I had to live hand to mouth. I had to make a roast last a week."

Her logic was dizzying. "Yeah, that sucks," I said. "A decent man would have gotten a second job to pay blackmail to his wife, who was making their daughter write letters to him supposedly from his former mistress."

Betty sneered. "I like you knowing I did it. It feels good. Hey, look at that. We're bonding. There's no way you can prove I did it, Miss Matchmaker. That will have to be our little secret, just between you and me."

"I don't know if I can keep that particular secret, Betty." Did I say that? Did that come out of my mouth? How fast could Spencer run? Could he get to me before Betty shot me or hit me with an egg pan?

"They think Jane did it all. She confessed. You were right. She always was my favorite child. You can't pin it on me. I'm a poor, downtrodden housewife. And as far as I'm concerned, you're either with me or against me. If you're against me, then you're responsible for the deaths. You're the guilty one. You have anything more to say?"

"Crazy serial killer says what?" I blurted out.

"This conversation is over," she said.

I heard Spencer walk up behind me. "Not quite," he said.

"She has a point about you lurking around town with the whores," I told him.

"Are you happy? Was that what you came for?" he asked.

"Yes. Jane didn't kill anyone. She wrote the letters, but she didn't know anything about Jimmy the Fink and Chuck Costas when I mentioned them to her. Betty's guilty. Are you happy? Did you get what you wanted?"

"Yes," he said, his voice thick and sultry. He leaned down and stared into my eyes. "You give me what I want." He slipped his hand under my shirt and let his fingers travel up. My breath hitched as he reached between my breasts and tugged. His hand popped out of my shirt, a tiny microphone between his fingers. "We got every word."

Betty gasped and threw her cigarette, hitting Spencer between the eyes. He swatted at his face as Betty ran for all she was worth toward the hearse. She jumped in, started it up, and burned rubber as she pulled away from the curb.

"She's getting away! She's getting away!" I shouted, waving my hands.

"She can't get far. I've got men all over this place," said Spencer, more concerned with his face than with Betty's escape.

I watched the hearse peel out. It was closing in on the exit fast. I was sure Betty was going to escape justice.

Before the hearse could reach the cemetery gates, a cement truck came out of nowhere at full speed and careened into the hearse near the back tire on the driver's side. Miraculously, the hearse remained intact, but it spun out of control, jumped the curb, and crashed into a tree. Spencer ran toward the scene, already calling the paramedics on his cellphone.

The funeral director appeared out of nowhere and ran toward the crash, understandably horrified by the sight of his totaled hearse. Betty's son Rob was on his heels, spurred into action. I had never seen him move so fast. The funeral director opened the driver's door of the hearse, stopped short, and then stumbled backward. "Help," he said. "Help. Coffin. Head."

Spencer and Rob stared in horrible silence. I couldn't take it another second. I threw the blanket off me, got out of the wheelchair, and walked to the hearse to see for myself.

Betty sat in her seat, slumped forward, her head knocked clean off her body. Deader than a doornail. The coffin had lurched forward during the crash and decapitated her.

"Holy crap," I said. "Randy got her."

"She's gone," Spencer told Rob. Talk about stating the obvious.

Rob sighed. "About time," he said.

I stumbled back to my wheelchair and took deep breaths through my nose in an effort not to faint. Cindy floated by, seemingly clueless about her mother's death. She noticed me, however, and ran toward me. She held a large bag, which she threw onto my lap. "Pennies," she announced with joy. She motioned to the bag, and I opened it.

"Pennies," I agreed.

There were more pennies than I had ever seen. Pennies in the form of hundred-dollar bills, that is. Cindy had found Randy's bank heist money.

Spencer made his way back to me, and I gave him the bag of money. I felt sick to my stomach. I was officially wound up. I took Spencer's hand and leaned against his arm. "Now I'm ready to leave," I said.

I BEGGED Spencer to stop off at Tea Time to get me a latte, and much to my surprise, he agreed. He parked right in front.

"Stay," he ordered. "I mean it, Pinkie. Stay."

He had to be kidding. I never wanted to move again.

After a couple of minutes, I heard a siren blaring, coming in my direction. A police car skidded to a halt, and Fred jumped out. At the same time, Julie ran out of Tea Time.

"He's over there," she screamed. She was panicked, and tears streamed down her face. "Where's the paramedics?"

"They're at the scene of an accident," said Fred. "Don't worry. I'm trained."

He ran two feet past her and dropped to the ground.

I craned my neck to see what on earth he was doing. And then I rubbed my eyes. Fred was poised over what looked like a dead possum. He took a deep breath and leaned down.

"Oh, God," I muttered.

Fred blew into the possum's mouth for all he was worth. CPR on roadkill. I needed more than coffee. I needed my morphine drip back.

After two breaths, the possum miraculously revived. It bit Fred on the nose and scampered off. Julie was rapturous. "My hero! My dreamboat!" And with that, she ran into Fred's arms.

Spencer came out with my latte. "What's going on there?" he asked.

"Love. Romance. The start of my career," I answered.

"Oh, good," Spencer said. "You're a success. I guess that means you're sticking around for a while."

Our eyes locked for a moment, and then I let my eyes slip to a spot on the car floor. "I guess. Grandma needs me."

Spencer sat in the driver's seat and turned on the ignition. "Sure she does. I'm glad you're an official matchmaker now. It will take your mind off trying to fight crime."

"I didn't do so bad with Betty Terns."

"Not so bad? Four dead bodies, a shot-up church, and a crashed hearse, not to mention some other obvious damage," he said, gesturing to my body.

"Well, Lulu Finkelstein doesn't have to hide anymore. Jane will get the psychiatric help she needs, and Betty has met with justice. That counts for something, doesn't it?" I said.

Spencer smiled and caressed my cheek. "Sure it does, Pinkie. You did good."

"And don't worry about my future crime fighting," I said. "You know nothing happens in Cannes."

"That's true. It's a very dull town, or it was until you got here."

"I don't know if that's a compliment or not. Give me my latte." I took a sip. Ruth made the best coffee. How could I ever leave her coffee? Spencer drove the car toward the hospital.

"By the way," I said, "Fred's going to need a rabies shot."

Acknowledgments

The author gratefully acknowledges the following people for their assistance: Junessa Viloria, editor extraordinaire and gorgeous, skinny bride; the editors of Ballantine and their superior knowledge of commas and Mallomars, among other things; Alex Glass, my favorite agent in the whole wide world, who I would fix up with my beautiful cousin if he was available; Trident Media, my favorite literary agency in the whole wide world; my friendly, loving, and extremely patient beta readers, Maria Sanminiatelli, Maureen Cavanaugh, and Kristen Reid; my beta readers/editors, Avery Aames and Janet Bolin, whose generosity I will never forget; all the women from RWA and Sisters in Crime; my sons, Max and Sam, who have to eat way too much takeout while I write; Lorenzo Canizales, who saved my life; Ruth Aguilar; and my mother, who made me believe in myself and told me to keep going. And a special acknowledgment to Stephanie Newton, who shared every step of the process with me. I called you first.

Read on for an exciting preview of the next book
in Elise Sax's Matchmaker Series

Citizen Pain

Available from Ballantine Books

Chapter 1

✦ ♥ ✦

Love is pain. Don't let anyone tell you different. You may be surprised that we're in the pain business. It's true. Love eats away at you like Murray's homemade horseradish eats away at your stomach. Eats away until you cry and wonder why you wanted love in the first place. Eats away until you beg for mercy. But there is no mercy where love is concerned. It does what it wants, and you are powerless to stop it. So you may have a couple of miserable clients, bubeleh. *A couple miserable clients in pain. They may even complain to you. Remind them this: pleasure and pain, they're not so far apart. Like pulling your hair. Sometimes, in the right context, having your hair pulled isn't all that bad. It may feel a little good, even. John Schlumberger pulled my hair once, and I kind of liked it. Get used to the pain and you can enjoy the love.*

Lesson 73,
Matchmaking Advice from Your Grandma Zelda

"NO!"

"Don't even think about going anywhere, Gladie. You can't get away. I've got you where I want you."

"Please. I'm scared," I whimpered. My ears grew hot, and I saw little silver spots in front of my eyes. Her voice came at me in a booming echo, as if in a cave. A cave with no exit. A cave with no exit and not enough air.

Great, now I was in fear for my life and I had suddenly become claustrophobic. I made a play for her sympathy. "Please. Let me go. Please, I want to go home," I said.

"No way." She was tall and muscular, in much better shape than I was. I hadn't exercised in months, not since I worked at the juice bar at the Phoenix Women's Gym for ten days. What was wrong with me? Would it have killed me to hop on a treadmill or at least try yoga? Yoga. Who was I kidding? One downward facing dog and I would dislocate something important, like my spine or gallbladder.

"Don't look at me that way, Gladie. There's no way you can take me."

I gulped air. "Don't hurt me. Don't hurt me," I said.

"Gladie, at worst it will sting a little. I need to do this. This is bigger than the both of us. Look at yourself."

She turned my chair to give me a good look at myself in the mirror. I looked how I always looked. My hair stood up in frizzy spikes around my head, mimicking my panicked mood. I shut my eyes tight.

"Fine," I said. "Fine, Bird. Just do it."

My hairdresser, Bird Gonzalez, clapped her hands together and hopped on her heels. "Oh, Gladie. Thank you, thank you. You won't be sorry. I've been wanting to do this for ages. You're going to be so happy. The Ecuadoran Erect will change your life. Straight hair, Gladie. You'll be a new woman."

Being a new woman wasn't entirely a bad idea. After years of moving around from one temporary job to another in one city or another, my Grandma Zelda had convinced me to settle down with her in the small mountain town of Cannes, California, and work in her matchmaking business. I wasn't a great success in my new career. So far I had made two matches, one on my own and the other with my grandma's help. Two matches in four months didn't set any records, but Grandma said I was cooking with gas.

My personal life was going at an even slower pace. There had been a burst of interest in me a few weeks before. My first client thought I was Angelina Jolie on a Ritz cracker, and the womanizing chief of police, Spencer Bolton, flirted with me nonstop, but I matched my client with a clumsy waitress, and Spencer moved on to dating half the town. My hunky new neighbor Arthur Holden took me out a couple times, even called me his girlfriend. Then he disappeared. Not totally disappeared, but he was busy every night and day and never offered me any explanations. I didn't know where he was going, didn't even know what he did for a living. And I didn't think I had the right to ask him.

I knew one thing for certain. I was a woman with wild, out-of-control, frizzy hair. Maybe change needed to start at the top. In my case, my head.

Bird squirted Ecuadoran Erect solution into a bowl, added water, and stirred. The salon was at once filled with a noxious smell.

"It doesn't cause cancer, does it?" I asked Bird.

"Gladie, you are going to look just like Kate Hudson with boobs."

"So it doesn't cause cancer?"

Bird painted the solution onto my hair. "I don't think that was ever proven," she said. I held my breath and thought healthy thoughts. It was too late to change my mind. Half my head was covered in stinky Ecuadoran Erect.

"It's starting to sting," I said.

"That's normal. It will go away in an hour or two."

Two hours later, my hair was straight as a board. Dark blond hair fell flat down past my shoulders. I was unrecognizable, unless I really was Kate Hudson with boobs. Bird was thrilled with her work.

"Uh," I said.

"You have twenty-year-old hair. You know what I mean?" she squealed. "It's soft and supple and luxurious just like you're twenty years old again."

"When I was twenty I was growing out a pixie cut. I looked like a cotton ball after it was plugged into a light socket."

"But it was soft, right?"

"I don't know. I was scared to touch it."

I ran my hair over my new hair. It was soft.

"You look bitchin'," Bird said. "Men are going to chase you down the street. Oh, speaking of that, I have something for you."

She handed me a box. "Chinese tea," she explained. "Special diet tea. Imported. Shh. Don't tell anyone I gave it to you. I've got a waiting list."

"Diet tea?" I sucked in my stomach.

"Don't give me that face, Gladie. You told me before you wanted to lose a couple pounds. I know what you're up against in that house with your grandma and her junk food habit. The tea works. Trust me."

She was right. I had turned a little soft in the four months I had been living with my french-fry-loving grandma.

My hair swished against my shoulders as I stuffed the tea in my purse. I paid Bird, emptying my bank account with the one check. Ecuadoran Erect and Chinese diet tea did not come cheap. I would have to make another match, quickly. Luckily I was on my way to see Belinda Womble. Belinda had curly hair and heaps of disposable income, and she wanted me to match her.

BLISS DENTAL was located in the old Cannes Small Animal Hospital building on Pear Lane just outside the historic district. Dr. Simon Dulur had bought the building about twenty years before and transformed it into a cutting-edge dental practice.

I had a phobia of all things medical. I couldn't even watch medical shows. So I never set foot in the Bliss Dental building. The idea of X-rays raised my blood pressure. The idea of a routine teeth cleaning made my gums bleed. No way was I getting near any possible root canals. But now I had no choice. Belinda Womble, the receptionist at Bliss Dental, was my new client. A job was a job, and Belinda had requested me as her matchmaker. It was my first request. Normally clients wanted my grandma, and why wouldn't they? *She* knew what she was doing.

I had to overcome my fears, overcome my sympathy pains every time I was near suffering or disease. Successful matchmakers didn't imagine they had tuberculosis every time someone near them coughed. Successful matchmakers didn't imagine they had leprosy every time their foot fell asleep.

Sure enough, two blocks away from the Bliss Dental building, a searing pain shot from my upper right bicuspid through my nerve endings and into my brain. I grimaced in agony and gripped the wheel, swerving into traffic.

I narrowly missed a Toyota Camry and a Chevy Malibu, driving my ancient Oldsmobile Cutlass Supreme up onto the sidewalk and coming to a screeching stop inches away from a fire hydrant and a group of backpackers, who were walking down the street wearing tin pyramid hats and T-shirts with ALIENS, TAKE ME FIRST! written in neon pink.

I stumbled out of my car and closed the rusty door with a creak. I gripped my face, willing the pain in my tooth to subside.

"You're breaking the chakras of the path."

The head backpacker tugged at my sleeve. He was tall

and good-looking, about fifty years old, and smelled of old money. His T-shirt was tucked into perfectly tailored slacks, cuffed over Prada loafers. He wagged his finger at me, his wrist wrapped in a gold Rolex watch.

"Excuse me?" I asked. The pain in my mouth cooled to a throb. The backpackers gathered in a group around us, the better to hear what their leader was saying.

"The chakras of the path. You're in the way. You're blocking the chakras and putting the arrival in jeopardy," he said.

"The arrival," echoed several of the backpackers.

"I'm sorry?" I said. "Did I hit you with my car?" I looked over at my Cutlass. The front bumper hung at a weird angle. That didn't mean anything. My car was built during Clinton's first term. It was a miracle it still had a bumper. I would have sworn I didn't hit anything. Besides, nobody was bleeding, as far as I could tell.

"The energies of tomorrow," shouted one of the backpackers.

"The arrival," the others said.

"The arrival?" I asked.

The hair on the back of my neck tingled, and my palms got sweaty. I took stock of the situation. I was surrounded. Strangers speaking in unison had me cornered between the fire hydrant and Andy Gilmore's closed hardware storefront. Cannes was a very small town. The only strangers were tourists who came up the mountain to hunt for antiques, sit in tea shops, and eat apple pie in the fall. We didn't get a lot of strangers wearing pyramid hats, shouting about chakras of the path and the energies of tomorrow.

"Did you hear?" the leader demanded. "You're blocking the chakras. Chakras. It's simple."

"The arrival!" the others announced a little more forcefully.

"Terribly sorry about your chakras," I said, sweeping the ground with the bottom of my shoe to clear away any bad chakras. "I'll just be on my way."

I enunciated each word slowly. I took two steps backward and smiled. *No sudden movements,* I thought, easing into the car. I waved goodbye, bounced off the sidewalk, and made my way toward Bliss Dental. In the rearview mirror, the backpackers were studying the spot where the Cutlass had run off the road. From their expressions, I must have flattened the path's chakras, and tomorrow's energies would come at least a few hours late.

THE BLISS Dental waiting room smelled like Lysol, dental putty impressions, and fear. Two women sat on plaid upholstered chairs, busy texting with their phones. Belinda Womble, my new client, manned the front desk, separated from the waiting room by a sliding window.

Belinda was busy reading through patient files. I caught her eye and gave her a wave. She scowled and stuck her index finger up in the air, the international symbol to wait, and then pointed toward one of the plaid chairs.

I checked the time. Ten o'clock. Right on time. I had two hours before I was supposed to bring Grandma back a bucket from Chik'n Lik'n for lunch. Grandma usually wanted fried chicken after her Tuesday morning Second Chancers singles meeting, which I was missing to meet with Belinda.

I picked up an old copy of *People* magazine to catch up on reality show gossip. Matchmakers in training don't have a lot of downtime, and my grandma didn't have cable. I was reading about a real housewife's new breasts when one of the women in the waiting room screeched.

"What a jerk. I mean, what a total jerk."

She flashed her phone at the other woman, who grabbed it to study it. Whatever was on the screen made the woman's eyes bug out.

"What a jerk," echoed the second woman.

"I have never seen anything like it. Not even at the zoo."

I craned my head, but I couldn't get a good look at the phone.

"Turns out he was screwing most of the town," the first woman said.

"And telling them all he was in love with them, no doubt."

"Well, obviously. Otherwise they wouldn't go around talking about him like marriage was on the horizon."

"Men are dogs," the second woman said. "He made eyes at me, too, you know."

The first woman looked doubtful. "Me too," she said after a moment. "But I saw through his charm and good looks right down to his little mercenary heart."

I craned my head a little more, but I was still getting nothing. I was about to change seats, when Belinda opened the sliding window. "Do you have an appointment?" she asked in my direction.

"Yes, ten o'clock," I said.

"With who? Dr. Dulur or Holly?"

I broke out in a sweat. I stumbled over to the sliding window. "No, Belinda. I don't want to see the dentist. My teeth are fine. No dental work needed," I said, flashing her my toothy smile.

"That's what they all say. It's called denial. I see it all the time. Whatever. It's your mouth. But there's a fifty-dollar fee for cancellations on such short notice."

I didn't have fifty dollars. All I had in my purse was three dollars, a maxed-out Visa card, a Hershey bar, two lipsticks, and a mascara wand. Besides, I didn't have a dentist appointment. What was Belinda talking about?

"Belinda, what are you talking about?" I asked. "I don't have a dentist appointment. Don't you remember? *We* have an appointment. You and me. You called me." Belinda squinted and leaned forward. "Gladie? Is that you?"

"Of course it's me. Who did you think it was?"

"I didn't recognize you. You don't look like yourself." She pointed at me. "Your head. It's your head. Your head is different."

"I had my hair straightened. Do I look that different?"

"You look like you got a new head. Not a Gladie head at all."

I pictured someone taking my Gladie head off my shoulders and replacing it with a non-Gladie head. Maybe having a non-Gladie head would be an improvement. I flicked my soft hair back. It swished against my shoulder, falling in a cascade before returning elegantly to its original position. Oh, nice. It was like a commercial for bouncing and behaving hair. My Gladie head would never have done that. It would have poofed out at some weird angle with renewed frizz, making me look like the bride of Frankenstein.

"Come on back, Gladie. We'll chat." Belinda pushed a button, and the door to the back buzzed open. Belinda sat behind an L-shaped desk that stretched along one wall. The other wall was covered from floor to ceiling in patient files.

It smelled wonderful, not like dentistry and torture at all, but like a botanical paradise. At least twenty flower-pots covered Belinda's desk.

"Beautiful," I said. "Someone must really like you."

"Oh, these weren't gifts. I grew them. I'm a flower enthusiast."

I was honestly impressed. "You grow all kinds of flowers," I noted. "My grandmother is proud of her roses, but she's never grown anything this varied and exotic."

At the mention of my grandmother, Belinda flinched and took a step back. "I'm glad you took my case, Gladie," she said. "I saw what you did for Ruth's niece, and it gave me hope for, you know, me."

I had fixed up Ruth's danger-prone niece, Julie, with my client, a danger-prone police sergeant. It was my one real case and a resounding success, if the cooing I heard from them in the back of the dollar movie theater last Friday was any proof.

I took a long hard look at Belinda. She and Julie had nothing in common. Julie looked like a prepubescent boy in slouchy clothes with her hair perennially in her eyes. Belinda's hair was curly but tamed in a tight bun. Her clothes were ironed and starched. Her no-nonsense size-eighteen tan slacks met her glittery gold and black sweater, which was emblazoned with a lavender appliqué flower that took up most of her ample abdomen and flat chest, at about mid-thigh. Two little gold flower earrings adorned her ears, and her face was painted with thick layers of foundation and blush, her eyes draped in lavender—to match her sweater, I guessed.

"Maybe you have a police sergeant for me, too," she said.

"At least a sergeant," I said, trying to sound positive.

"Do you have pictures to show me so, you know, I can choose?"

We took a seat at her desk. "I thought I would first get to know you better, see what you're interested in," I said, taking out a notepad and a pen.

"Well, I'm looking for a man. Someone who appreciates me. And I'm losing weight! I have been drinking Chinese diet tea, and I've lost four pounds. These pants were tight on me last week. Usually I have a metabolism like sludge."

I nodded. Maybe there was something to Bird's diet tea. I promised to brew myself a cup when I got home.

"Where the hell are the brownies? Did you eat all the brownies?"

Belinda's office was invaded by a woman in a tight miniskirt and camisole. There was something off about her face, as if I was seeing her through an altered Hollywood camera lens.

"I am on a diet, Holly. Of course I didn't eat the brownies," Belinda said, clearly upset by the woman.

"Yeah, right," she sneered. Her lips were unnaturally curved up like the Joker's, pulling at her taut skin. Everything about her was tight. Her body defied gravity like it was made of wax. I caught myself staring and looked away quickly, pretending to go over my notes about Belinda's desires in a mate.

"Here they are," Holly announced, pulling out a Tupperware container filled with brownies. She took a big bite of one and tossed the container on the desk, unconcerned about resealing it and unconcerned about apologizing to Belinda. I disliked her instantly.

"That was the hygienist," Belinda told me the moment Holly left the room. "She had fat from her ass put into her boobs, and she had Phil the plumber stick her with industrial Botox so her face never changes expression."

I realized my mouth was open, and I snapped it closed. "Her face has been that way for four years," Belinda continued. "When she won Sunday night bingo, her face stayed the same. Ditto the day a patient had a heart attack and died in her chair when she was flossing him. She's a class A whore, too. I don't want to tell tales, but she likes them young." She said "young" in a conspiratorial whisper that made me lean forward to hear more. But Belinda strayed from the topic. "She doesn't need Chinese tea, that's for sure. She's got a metabolism like a hummingbird. She must eat ten times her weight. Of course, that's only about ten pounds." She found this uproariously funny and burst into hysterics. I had to slap her on the back for her to catch her breath.

When she came around she described what she was looking for in a man, which sounded eerily similar to George Clooney. "How long do you think it will take?" she asked.

"Well, we can't rush these things. Love, I mean." It was the wrong thing to say. Belinda looked at me like I had told her Santa Claus didn't exist. "Give me a week to look through my files," I amended. "I'm sure Mr. Right is in there."

What was I saying? I didn't have files. I had Grandma's stacks of note cards I could pilfer and look through, but otherwise, I had no clue who to fix Belinda up with.

"Now, who do we have here? Hey, pretty lady, here for a checkup?"

I jumped three feet in the air. Dr. Simon Dulur stood in the doorway, a shiny dental instrument in his hand, pointing at me with it. The instrument was metal and long with a sharp hooked end. My eyes swirled in their sockets, and I saw stars.

"Whoa, we got a fainter! We got a fainter! Code six!" Dr. Dulur waved his hands around and moved his head from side to side as he shouted, like a quarterback at a football game calling the plays before the snap. He was moving the dental instrument around pretty good now, and it caught a glint of sun and shined in my eyes.

I wonder what codes one through five are, I thought just before I lost consciousness.

"THERE SHE is. She's coming around now."

"Where am I?" I asked, but I knew exactly where I

was. My body hung almost upside down in a Bliss Dental chair, a spit cloth draped on my chest. Dr. Dulur hung over me, his polyester shirt unbuttoned halfway to reveal a tuft of curly gray chest hair and three gold chains that seemed to float in midair as he leaned perilously close to my head. His hands were in my mouth, the scary dental instrument between his fingers, busily inspecting my teeth and gums. "Where am I?" came out muffled because my mouth was open and full of Dr. Dulur.

"Uh-oh. This is what I feared," he said.

"What are you doing?" I tried to say.

"Dr. Dulur likes to take advantage of a fainter." The voice came from somewhere to my left. "That didn't come out right," the voice said, and a head appeared behind Dr. Dulur. He was young, no more than twenty. I noticed he was prematurely balding and had perfectly straight white teeth. "What I meant to say is that he likes to do as much work on you while you're unconscious as possible so you're not scared," he explained.

"But I'm not here to see the dentist," I tried to say. Sweat had popped out on my forehead. I wanted to swat Dr. Dulur's hands from my mouth, but I was paralyzed with fear.

"That's what I tried to tell him." Belinda appeared above me, the third head to hang over my face. "He wouldn't listen."

"Well, I'm afraid the news isn't all that great, but it's fixable," said Dr. Dulur. "Lucky you came in when you did." He put the instrument down and smiled at me. "Seven cavities."

My hand flew to my mouth. "Seven what? No, I don't have cavities. I'm just neurotic. It's in my head."

"Yes, it's in your head all right," he said, still smiling. "All seven cavities are right there in your head. Somebody hasn't been brushing regularly."

"But that can't be. I brush and floss religiously."

I wasn't lying. I was a big brusher, and I changed toothbrushes every month. I did what I had to so I wouldn't need to see a dentist.

"Oh, then it's probably age. We're not as young as we were, you know." Dr. Dulur was still smiling. He must not have realized how close my fist was to his face.

"Age?" I echoed. "Age?" I was carded at the 7-Eleven only last year. Was it the generic face cream I was using?

Dr. Dulur flinched. "Maybe not age. You probably just need to do a rinse before bed. Keep your mouth moist during the night. Dry mouth can cause cavities. You must have your mouth open at night when you snore."

"Snore?" I said a little too loudly.

"Should we fill up those little holes right away? How about I get you numbed up and start drilling?" Dr. Dulur asked.

And then I was running. I made it out of the chair, through the office, and out the front door in a matter of seconds.

Once outside, I gulped fresh air. Matchmaking wasn't easy.

I started counting my teeth to make sure they were all still there. That's why I didn't see him until it was too late, until his strong arm caught mine in a viselike grip and pulled me around the side of the building.